The Macabre

Also by Kosoko Jackson

ADULT

I'm So (Not) Over You

A Dash of Salt and Pepper

YOUNG ADULT

Survive the Dome

Yesterday Is History

The Forest Demands Its Due

Out Now (anthology)

Night of the Living Queers (anthology)

The Macabre

A NOVEL

Kosoko Jackson

HARPER Voyager
An Imprint of HarperCollinsPublishers

This is a work of fiction. Names, characters, places, and incidents are products of the author's imagination or are used fictitiously and are not to be construed as real. Any resemblance to actual events, locales, organizations, or persons, living or dead, is entirely coincidental.

THE MACABRE. Copyright © 2025 by Kosoko Jackson. All rights reserved. Printed in Italy. No part of this book may be used or reproduced in any manner whatsoever without written permission except in the case of brief quotations embodied in critical articles and reviews. For information, address HarperCollins Publishers, 195 Broadway, New York, NY 10007.

HarperCollins books may be purchased for educational, business, or sales promotional use. For information, please email the Special Markets Department at SPsales@harpercollins.com.

Harper Voyager and design are trademarks of HarperCollins Publishers LLC.

FIRST EDITION

Designed by Alison Bloomer

Library of Congress Cataloging-in-Publication Data has been applied for.

ISBN 978-0-06-345086-8
ISBN 978-0-06-339446-9 (hardcover deluxe limited edition)

25 26 27 28 29 RTLO 10 9 8 7 6 5 4 3 2 1

For Sydney, The House of Shadows,
and, of course, Kat.
Thank you for inspiring my Turning.

The
Macabre

Prologue

"THE *GUARDIAN* DID IT BETTER."

Lewis Dixon didn't know how long he had been staring at the newspaper in his hand. Long enough that the words didn't read like actual words, just a mixture of black smudges on the paper. Long enough for the antiseptic smell of the hospital waiting area to turn his nostrils numb.

He looked up, following the voice to its owner. He drank in her visage, bathing in the starkness of her blond, short-cut hair. The tall, lanky frame and the high cheekbones and warm, bright-blue eyes burned into his mind. He would remember her.

As a painter, he enjoyed people. They were always his favorite thing to immortalize within his art. It was ironic, really, because he found himself born a few centuries too late to capitalize on that skill. No one in the twenty-first century was paying for elegantly done portraits. And yet, if he had found a way to cut in line before God, Buddha, or whoever had punted him onto earth, he would have made a killing.

Or, at least, probably far more than he made now.

He brought his thoughts back to this woman, and a new thought struck him:

She's not someone who seems like they should be in this hospital. Too privileged. Too perfect in the way she spoke.

"The article you're reading," she said, gesturing with a hand that held a coffee cup. "The oligarch and his family found dead in Russia? Frozen inside their home even though no doors or windows were open? The *Guardian* had a segment on it. Already interviewing Russian sources."

"That sounds dangerous. Russia is not a bastion of free speech," he replied. He didn't *want* to talk, and he knew his words sounded hollow. He might love the idea of people as an artistic concept, but this wasn't really the moment he wanted to explore that. And yet, responding was the respectful thing to do. His mother, who was in a hospital room halfway down the hall, would have wanted him to.

Besides, he would be lying if he didn't admit how interested he was in his row mate at MedStar Harbor Hospital, in downtown Baltimore. Elegant, refined, the type of person whose consonants were polished round from good breeding and the right type of education the wrong type of money could buy.

Those types didn't find their way to Baltimore. Definitely not this part of Baltimore. Washington, DC, sure. But never Charm City. That, in and of itself, meant there was a story here. And there wasn't an artist alive who didn't love a good story wrapped around a beautiful muse.

"Agreed. But isn't journalism supposed to report the truth, no matter the consequences?"

"I suppose," he said, sidestepping the earnestness her declaration tried to stab him with. "Who are you here for?" Maybe they could bond over that.

The problem was, again, that Lewis didn't particularly want to bond. More, Lewis knew what would happen next. She would tell him, he would sympathize, and then she would ask the same question in return. He would have to explain that his mother had tried to call his father, who hadn't answered because he was on a work trip, because she felt funny. How she passed out while dialing Lewis, after leaving a voicemail for his father, and when the ambulance came, blood was pouring out of her eyes, nose, mouth, and ears. An aneurysm, they said. Nothing like they had seen before, but it was the only logical explanation.

He would have to tell this stranger the doctors didn't seem confident about that.

But the answer the woman gave? That was a surprise.

"I'm a donor here," she said.

"Blood donor?" That would explain it. For a relative, of course. She wouldn't be caught dead in someplace like this otherwise.

She laughed, light, like a flint crackling. "It sometimes feels like blood, but no—money. We had a board meeting in the attached wing, and it ended early. I'm waiting for my Uber."

"You wait for your Ubers in hospital waiting rooms?"

"I like to see what my money is going toward." She smiled, a row of perfect pearly-white teeth shimmering back at him. "Whoever you're here for, I'm sorry."

Another unexpected reply. How much did he want to tell this woman? That he had missed his mother's call, her final attempt to reach out for help? That he only found out she was dead because his father called over and over and over? No. She didn't need to know that much. He would never see this woman again.

"My mother," he said after a moment, leaning back in his chair and pulling his black hoodie down from around his head. "She's dead."

No one had said it like that. Even the doctors danced around the crudeness and bluntness of the word, like if they waited until they could pick up some telltale sign he was ready, then when they actually said the word—*dead*—it wouldn't hit as hard.

It would always hit that hard. Because, in the littlest or biggest, the widest or thinnest of ways, her death was his fault.

If he hadn't been obsessed with that painting, maybe he wouldn't have missed her earlier call that afternoon and could have been there when the aneurysm burst.

Of course, it wasn't as if there was much he could have done. But at least he would have been there. At least she wouldn't have been alone.

Except that was never an option. Because it wasn't just any painting that kept him busy for the whole day, missing his mother's call by four hours, but one of his fugue paintings. That's what he called them. They always started with a tingle in the back of his head, then an itch he couldn't help but scratch that, if ignored for too long, turned into a headache—blinding, terrible, debilitating. But once he sat down and gave in, the euphoria of letting his fingers take the brush, mix the colors, and let go was . . . unmatched. Time moved quicker when he painted like that, and not in the way most artists described. In what felt like a second, he would have a painting.

And often that painting would come true.

Which was something he definitely didn't want to get into with this random person, let alone at this particular moment.

"Oh, Lewis," the woman said softly, reaching over to gently put her hand on the back of his. "I'm so sorry. Your mother was a wonderfully talented woman."

"Thanks. I should have been there, should have answered her call. I wanted to tell her in person that evening about—" Lewis blinked, suddenly yanking his hand from under the woman's touch. He wanted to finish his sentence with *the invitation from the British Museum*, but—"I never told you my name."

The woman blinked slowly. "I'm sorry?"

"You called me Lewis." Then his face scrunched up as he chewed on something else she'd said. "And you said my mother *was a wonderfully talented woman*."

"Yes?"

"I never told you anything about her. How could you know that?"

The woman's beautiful features, almost like polished porcelain, darkened as her wide doe eyes lidded slightly. Her open mouth closed into a tight line, making her cheeks more pronounced as she sighed and ran her right hand through her hair.

"I slipped up," she said. "Again. I really need to get better at remembering what you do and do not know."

Every cell in Lewis's body told him to move. In fact, he ordered himself—*screamed* inside his head—to get up, walk toward the nurse's desk, and warn them about the woman in the suit that probably cost more than his whole year's salary as a part-time art teacher.

But his body wouldn't move, as if the commands were lost somewhere in delivery.

The woman slowly turned her body toward Lewis and leaned in to press her lips against his right ear. To anyone watching, it would look like she was telling him a secret.

"I lied," she whispered, with soft hints of lilac wafting off her. "Your mother wasn't a talent; she was a worthless fraud. And if I could kill her again, I would. I'll just have to settle for you once you've done what your mother was unable to do for me."

Fear bubbled inside Lewis like a geyser. He wanted to scream, to fight, to do something in response to those words. He wanted to question her, punch her, demand she tell him she was lying, or telling the truth, or something in between. But something had a hold on him, keeping him glued to the seat, and every time he tried to move, it felt like barbed wire was tightening—not around his body, but his soul, hurting him so deeply he wasn't sure the pain would ever go away.

"But for now, mourn your mother," the woman said. "And pack your bag; you're heading to London soon. I've heard it's beautiful this time of year."

Lewis gasped as, with a snap of her fingers, the restriction and pain disappeared in a microsecond. It wasn't nothingness that replaced the empty feeling, though; it was something else, something like longing, something cavernous and missing.

What had he just been talking about with the stranger in the seat next to him?

"Sorry," Lewis said, flashing her a hesitant smile. "Have we met?" She was beautiful, after all. The tall, lanky frame and high cheekbones and warm, bright-blue eyes were burned into his mind. He would remember her.

The woman returned the smile. She had a kind face and seemed like the type of person his mother would have liked to have known.

"No, we haven't," she said, extending her hand. "I'm Cassandra. It's a pleasure to meet you."

PART I

"He was swimming in a sea of other people's expectations. Men had drowned in seas like that."

—Robert Jordan, *New Spring*

One

EIGHTEEN WEEKS LATER

"The entrance for artists is around the back."

Lewis blinked owlishly as a voice to his right broke him from his trance. It was his first time in London, or anywhere outside the United States, yet he couldn't stop staring at his phone, distracted by what was on his screen.

"Sorry?" Lewis asked, shifting his weight and pocketing the phone before the man, tall enough to discreetly—or not so discreetly—look over his shoulder, could see. Doing so meant letting go of the canvas leaning against him for a moment, not long enough for it to fall onto the people in line with him, but long enough for it to sway.

"You're here for the gala," the man said as he gestured to the canvas. "Lewis Dixon, correct?" This time, unlike the pointed accusation of his previous words, Lewis noticed smoothness in his voice, like polished marble. A sort of slickness to it that made Lewis stumble and feel off-balance. Like a trick taught in some *how to get ahead in a corporate environment* training the man had paid for.

Lewis looked down, as if he hadn't just lugged the canvas across the Atlantic, and then back at the other man. The canvas bag he had purchased, which had made him short on his rent this month, was unmistakable. The awkward width of the bag. The worn, used strap that frayed at the edges, appearing as if it might break at any moment. Lewis felt his cheeks burn under his dark skin. That's what he got for buying something like this secondhand.

Every inch of him was, well, passable for an event like this. Passable canvas bag. Passable clothes. Passable confidence. That couldn't be further from the other man, whose name tag read "Noah Rao, Museum Curator," and who was taller than him by about six inches, with dark hair pulled into a tight man-bun, a sharp, gaunt jaw, and a pressed suit. He looked unamused by Lewis's ignorance, like he had places to be—anywhere but here. It made Lewis feel small, much like when his father called about his mother's death. Funny how the strangest things in life could trigger a wave of grief.

"How do you know my name?"

Lewis mentally winced before Noah responded, knowing what would come next.

"I would hope I did know who was coming, considering I helped put together this exhibition. In fact, I oversaw your selection. And because if you weren't, it would be incredibly weird for you to be carrying a canvas around London."

"Weird indeed."

As Lewis said it, he couldn't help but wonder if the invitation he had received in the mail—handwritten, on the heaviest and crispest of papers—was sent by this man himself or one of his lackeys. He supposed, in the greater scheme of things, it didn't truly matter. The way Noah spoke would make some people's pulse rise, pupils dilate. The accent and razor-sharp edges would be responsible for that.

"Right," Noah said with a nod. "Now, come along, please, you're in the way of guests trying to get in. Wouldn't want you to be a burden to your guests." Being a burden was something Lewis was well acquainted with.

But instead of focusing on how many ways he was a burden to Noah—and already he could think of *at least six*—he recalled the invitation he had read at least, oh, a hundred times.

Distinguished Guest Lewis Dixon:

As you may know, England has a long, accomplished and storied history. But often at the expense of others, leaving a gash on our beautiful nation's relationship with previous and currently held colonies.

That is why we are honored to invite you to the British Museum exhibit, in partnership with Tate Britain, entitled: A Lesson in Deference. This exhibit will showcase one artist each from the 120 colonies held by Britain over the years.

And we have selected you to represent your nation: the United States of America.

We kindly request that you provide us with one piece that best represents your work to showcase during our gala. Your airfare, hotel, ground transportation and all related expenses are covered by the British Museum. Displaying your selected piece in our Rising Artists exhibit for a period not to exceed five years will be considered payment in kind.

We eagerly await your answer.
Evangeline Thompson
Director of Curation at the British Museum

"We should hurry," Noah said, pulling him out of his memory. "You're already late. Come along. I'll take you inside."

He turned swiftly on the heels of his polished shoes, walking briskly down the sidewalk without checking to see if Lewis was following. He *was* following, of course, though slipping out of the line with the awkwardly shaped canvas wasn't easy. It required a string of soft apologies under his breath as his canvas bumped against a woman's legs and jabbed at a man's portly stomach.

"Need help?" Noah asked.

A little bit too late, but Lewis assumed the ask wasn't really an ask, just British niceties in action. "I'm good."

"It's rather large," Noah continued. "Your piece."

Smoothly, Noah pulled the lapel of his dark jacket back, revealing where his ID badge was clipped, slightly hidden so it wouldn't be an eyesore—so Lewis assumed. Lewis studied how easily and quickly Noah flashed it. How it returned to its slightly hidden safe space. But more importantly, how the guard, with his sharp, angled jaw, dipped in deference when the ID was shown.

That wasn't the only thing Lewis noticed in that flash of a moment. He got a small glimpse of the pass and Noah's smile in his photo. He was younger in it, Lewis assumed from his quick look. There was optimism in his eyes, but also pain.

"You mean awkward?" Lewis said.

Noah didn't reply, but his lips pushed into a slightly thinner line. Was that because he was annoyed Lewis saw through his thinly veiled insult, or did he find Lewis's perceptiveness appealing and worth his respect? Probably the latter, Lewis decided.

"Large," Noah repeated. "If I meant awkward, Mr. Dixon, I would have said it. And correct me if I'm wrong—"

"Something tells me, Mr. Rao, you are never wrong," Lewis muttered.

"Excuse me?"

"Nothing—just a bit of a cough."

Rao clearly had heard him—but that British politeness once more showed its head. *"Correct me if I'm wrong,"* he repeated, "but I believe the instructions said for all honored guests to bring something no larger than twenty by sixty inches."

"And this is exactly that; no larger."

It was clear to Lewis that Noah wanted to say more, and after they had stepped through the expedited security, he did. "You are getting a spot in a once-in-a-lifetime exhibit at the British Museum, and your first thought was to push the requirements to their absolute limit?"

"The requirements," Lewis replied in a low voice, as if someone might hear him chastising the curator, which was the last thing he wanted, "were to bring a piece that represented the artist's best work. That showed their talent and their passion. A piece that represented their style."

"And this large piece does that better than a smaller piece could?"

That was a harder question to answer. The instructions gave a size limit of twenty by sixty inches—and he had followed those guidelines. On the other hand, the canvas had been the bane of Lewis's existence since he'd left his apartment in Baltimore. The museum had offered to pay to ship it before he arrived, but, one, Lewis felt self-conscious about the piece he had chosen to submit, and two, he had been a little worried they would open it before he got here and decide to turn him away.

He had other pieces. Better pieces to submit, if he was being objective. Ones that had come near to winning festivals. Ones that had gotten hundreds of likes on social media. Even some that his father, who hated art and barely said twenty words to him a year, had grunted at, a sign of at least something passing through that facade of his.

But this piece? This piece spoke to him. Clawed out to him in his dreams, screamed at him when he was in the same room. A metaphor and an honest-to-God statement all at once.

This was the only piece he had painted in the past five months or so. The piece he had made when his mother was in the hospital. He hadn't raised his fingers to touch charcoal, or paint, or a pencil since then.

But not only that: How do you explain to the British Museum that the piece you are immortalizing in their halls is not your typical style of art but rather more surreal? A painting of a painting, specifically a landscape with a lake in the center, water overflowing the frame and into the room. How could you explain that as you painted it, while your father was calling your phone over and over again, leaving message after message growing in urgency, you were having one of your moments—one of those times when reality melted away, starting from the corners, and time folded in on itself?

You don't. Because if you do, you sound crazy, as an ex-hookup of his had told him three years ago. You keep that shit to yourself. Especially around prim-and-proper Noah Rao.

"Exactly."

"Hm," Noah said, a rumble in the back of his throat. He pushed the side entrance door with his left hand, exposing a flash of his wrist and the raised echo of a tattoo. The artist in Lewis knew exactly what it was—or at least, what it had been: ravens. It must have meant something for Noah to stain his skin with the ink. And it must have been painful enough of a reminder too, for him to go through the process of removing it.

Either way, it looked like it had been detailed and expensive. Maybe if they smoothed out the bumpiness of their relationship, Noah would let Lewis get a photo of it for Ana, his roommate. She would love that.

Together, they stood in the entryway, and Noah made no movement to take a step forward. Lewis glanced over at him, tilting his gaze slightly up.

"We're blocking the entrance, Mr. Rao," he cheekily told him, a bit of lightness in his voice.

Noah didn't respond, not at first, his eyes focused forward, toward the flow of people moving like waterways as they made their way through the museum.

"Once you step through this alcove, Mr. Dixon, everything in your life will change," Noah said slowly and quietly. "You won't look at the world the same, and if we're correct, the world won't look at you the same. Not everyone wants that level of scrutiny. It's okay if this isn't for you, but you have to tell me that now. Otherwise, this is a chance few people have."

Lewis thought it over for a moment. There was subtext here Noah wasn't telling him.

"To do what exactly?" he asked slowly.

"Cement your legacy, Mr. Dixon. Isn't that, at its core, what every artist wants to do?"

Lewis could tell from the way Noah's voice dipped slightly that there was something else hidden behind the refined nature of his words, peeking around the corner of each letter, just out of reach whenever Lewis tried to look too hard. Honestly, it was infuriating, the way he was clearly speaking around something else.

This was all so weird. The way the letter just appeared. How everything seemed to be falling into place for him, *finally*. But the universe had a peculiar way of keeping itself balanced, and at the moment, it was tilting in his direction.

Yes, he wanted this—whatever it was.

"God took my mother from me, Mr. Rao."

"Gods," Noah muttered, at the direction Lewis had turned the conversation. "But continue."

Lewis's brow twitched. "Someone took my mother from me, and in return, it seems I have been given an opportunity that many artists would die for. I'm not going to pass that up, not at least without seeing what could come from it. That's what my mother would want."

Noah gave a slow nod, as if he was processing and accepting what Lewis said. With a gentle gesture of his hand, he gave Lewis permission to move.

"After you."

Noah said "after you" as if he was holding the door for Lewis at a supermarket, but at the same time, as if he was almost ashamed at Lewis's statement—a concern that left Lewis's focus the moment they stepped through the doorway. This would be the British Museum in all its glory. Lewis hadn't known what that meant, not exactly, until he stepped through the doors.

Lewis expected to step through the alcove and be greeted by the ornate entrance of the museum he had looked up on Google Maps. He already had pinpointed specific exhibits he wanted to see, for his own interest and for inspiration, and the fastest way from the entrance to reach them. But this wasn't the main entrance of the British Museum, and it was as if stepping over this particular threshold transported him from *there* to *here*.

Here being somewhere sterile and white, somewhere that made his eyes burn from a light source that came from nowhere and everywhere all at once.

Here was still, with the bustle and murmurs of street life—behind him just moments ago—suddenly absent.

Here was only him, Noah, and a woman.

She stood with her back to them, looking upward at a rectangular item draped in a white sheet, hovering in the center of the room about a foot and a half off the floor. In a room with no doorway or windows.

Here—

Suddenly, pain erupted from behind his eyes. Lewis hissed and pressed the heel of his free hand against them. Splashes like watercolor appeared in the darkness as he pressed harder, trying to push the pain away. He bent over until his elbows rested against his knees as his stomach began to unknot itself from dozens of complicated somersaults.

"The feeling will go away, Mr. Dixon," said the woman in a crisp voice laced with only the thinnest layer of concern. "Just give it a moment. Magic, for the uninitiated, tends to leave you dizzy."

Magic?

But he had no time to think more on that. Every hair on his body, every cell, every inch of bone felt like a low current of electricity had passed through it. There was nothing else but this feeling. It wasn't exactly painful, but it wasn't comfortable either. If he had to pick a description, it felt like his body was charged with caffeine and every function was executing its autonomous orders at 110 percent. Even if that feeling went away, Lewis figured he would be exhausted, sore, and in pain for the rest of the day.

But, slowly yet surely, the sensation subsided. Not completely, no. But enough that he could take a shuddering breath and stand. His vision returned to normal; the splotches of color coalesced into familiar shapes, sharpened, and took form. Shaking the feeling off, Lewis glanced over at Noah, who gave a nod forward.

"I'll take your piece for you," Noah said, gently yet firmly pulling it from Lewis's grasp. "You should go talk to her. Ms. Thompson has been excited to meet you for some time now."

"Evangeline Thompson?" Lewis asked.

"Director Thompson," Noah corrected.

Evangeline laughed, turning her head slightly to look at him. "Evangeline is fine."

Tall and sinewy, with a skin tone like Lewis's, dressed like Noah, head shaved bald, and with catlike makeup that made her sharp eyes look even sharper, she dripped with confidence. Her exceptionally tailored pantsuit helped with that. She didn't have a name tag; a power move, Lewis could only assume. But that didn't matter.

The word *magic* danced around his head, teasing his memory. The alcove he had stepped through, that transported him from one place to the next; this room with no doors or windows; the floating piece in the center of the room; and his own artwork . . . the piece he had just known he had to bring.

All this time, Lewis had wondered if he was crazy, if the

things he painted—which more often than not came true—were some twisted versions of déjà vu. Of course, he'd thought of the possibility of magic, but only for a moment. He wasn't *that* insane, after all.

But maybe there *was* magic. Maybe there were things in the world that defied the laws of physics and bent reality to their will.

Which led his mind down another path, one that always seemed to be lingering deep inside him:

Maybe there was a power that could bring his mother back.

"You said magic," Lewis muttered, his throat feeling tight, as if for a moment he had forgotten how to make words and his mind was, quickly, remembering how.

"That I did," Evangeline replied. "Don't tell me you haven't ever assumed it was real."

"We don't have time for this," Noah muttered.

Evangeline sighed. "Please excuse Noah. He forgets that not everyone is born knowing magic exists. Class jades how people see the world.

"But," she continued, "he isn't wrong. Not exactly. Tell me what you sense, Lewis. Tell me what you feel."

What he felt? Typically, being in the room with another Black person gave him comfort. An unspoken kinship that told him everything would be okay. But not *this* room. Magic or no, there was something necrotic in the air. It stank in such a way that he couldn't actually smell it but rather sensed it in the pit of his gut. It made his pulse flutter with each slow and cautious step closer to Evangeline and the floating object.

He felt . . . sorrow. Like a weight pressing against his chest, pulling him under the murky depths. Down down down he went, drowning in this feeling of cold dread.

Something was very, very wrong in the British Museum—if he was even still in the museum. But that didn't scare Lewis. Quite the opposite, actually. It excited him.

After all, Alice's greatest adventures came after she dove down the rabbit hole. And ever since he'd gotten the invitation to the museum, Lewis knew his greatest adventure lay before him. Even if it hadn't meant coming to this strange non-space, he would have thought that. But before Lewis could ask Evangeline about magic, or the room, or what hovered in front of them, she flicked a finger and the white sheet fell off, like a woman letting her slip slide down her shoulders, and it melted with the white floor to reveal an art piece.

The same painting he had brought with him today to the British Museum.

Two

INITIALLY, ON SEEING THE SAME PAINTING THAT HE HAD LUGGED ACROSS the Atlantic in such vibrant detail in front of him, Lewis felt like he was falling into a bottomless pit.

Nothing in the world was original, no. But artists didn't want to be accused of plagiarism. At least, no real artist. And Lewis was looking at a direct copy of his work. Or his work was a direct copy of this piece.

Sort of.

Even though the subject of the painting was the same as Lewis's, the details were ten, maybe even twenty times sharper. It was also much, much bigger: Lewis estimated it was roughly seven feet by nine feet. Any painter worth their salt could estimate the size of a canvas at first glance. It didn't make him impressive. But the piece?

That was impressive.

The vertical portrait depicted a bloodred lake surrounded by trees. Houses in the distance glowed faintly with lit windows. A sinewy, nude woman stood in the center of the lake, with a black tail slithering from her body and out into the land like a pathway. Ever since he'd painted it, he had pored over it. Deposited more time than he wanted to admit in understanding it. Not only was it darker than his usual works, it was, well, beautiful. Capturing something Lewis rarely was able to do when he was lucid. The painting that had stolen his time, time he would never get back, had taken and birthed something else too.

Authenticity.

Lewis had deduced the tail was a representation of her soul, whoever she was who had stolen his attention for what he inferred was roughly four and a half hours, tethering her to the ground. Perhaps she lived there? Wherever *there* was. It didn't look like anywhere he had been. Not that he could remember, anyway.

But as he looked closer, he noticed the woman in *this* painting, this painting with not only depth in its paint strokes but also depth in its well of emotion vomited onto the canvas, was . . . wrong. Her proportions were slightly off. Her arms were too long. Her legs too. And, well, her head was upside down, crowned by the place where her neck should have been. Her eyes rolled back, showing only whites, and her mouth opened wide in a scream that Lewis felt he could hear in his bones. It seemed as if her teeth chattered slightly when he looked for too long.

"Do you know of Edgar Dumont, Mr. Dixon?" Evangeline asked.

Lewis knew he should answer, or at least acknowledge what she was saying, but he found it impossible to tear his eyes away from the piece floating in front of him.

Logically, his first thought was that perhaps there were invisible strings. The finest of wires folded around each other with a tensile strength that would make the strongest of spiders jealous. But there were no wires connected to the ceiling, or none that he could see. The temptation to reach up and run his hand across the top of the painting to check was quite strong.

Lewis turned to look at Evangeline. "Answer my question first," he said, not waiting for her to accept or deny his stipulation. "Explain the magic to me."

"You're going to have to be more specific."

"All of it. How we got here, how this thing is floating, everything."

Evangeline paused, a small quirk forming on her lips. "You're not scared?"

"I'm terrified," he admitted. "But fear isn't a reason not to understand something."

Evangeline smiled in a way that reminded him of someone who heard something familiar and longed to hear it again. "Right answer. Magic, Mr. Dixon, exists all around us. Like electrons and protons, the air we inhale and the food we eat. It has existed since the dawn of time and will exist far after us."

"You know the Hadron Collider?" Noah asked. "The one that smashes atoms together?"

"Science was my worst subject in school, but I know of it, yes."

"Think of magicians like human colliders. We break the barrier between magic and reality, scoop the pulp out from the center of the magic well, and mold it to how we wish," Evangeline explained. "The magic that allowed Mr. Rao to take you from point A to point B? When you leave here, examine the alcove. You'll see runes etched into the wood. This room is layered on top of many different spells by magicians more talented than me or Mr. Rao to construct a room where things we don't want the rest of the world to know of can exist."

"You said *we*," Lewis noted. "Who is . . . ?"

Evangeline shook her head. "I answered your question on the expectation you would answer mine, Mr. Dixon. Your turn. Do you know of Edgar Dumont?"

She was right. He owed her an answer.

"I don't, no. Is he a featured artist here? A guest? Patron?"

"In a way," Evangeline said. "What can you tell me about this piece?"

I can tell you're being annoyingly cryptic, he thought. But the look Noah gave him, the slight narrowing of his eyes, made Lewis think maybe the man had heard him in his mind. That wouldn't be the weirdest part of today.

"It's from the Post-Impressionist era," he said, focusing back on Evangeline.

"How do you know?"

"The vivid colors and thick application of paint. It's characteristic of the time. But not just that . . ." Lewis stepped forward, each step feeling less like a command he was telling himself to execute and more like the piece was calling him toward it. He wasn't sure how, exactly—there was no sound pulsing off the work, no scent that tickled his senses. No, the summoning was something different. Something he couldn't place. He knew, even if he split his chest open and dug around his insides, he wouldn't find the source of the itch. No, this was something deeper. Something spiritual.

"The distinctive brushstrokes and real-life subject matter . . . It's a form of distorted expression. The colors, too, don't match what you'd imagine when you see a lake. You'd expect to see blues and greens, but this artist uses blacks and reds. Like . . ."

"Like he's trying to depict horror?"

"Exactly." Lewis turned. "You said a man's name. Edgar . . ."

"Dumont."

"Yes, is this one of his? Is . . ." He looked at the brass nameplate on the bottom center. "There's no name for the work here."

"And that is the reason why you are here," Evangeline said smoothly. "Well, one of the reasons."

"What if I told you the historians were wrong?" Evangeline asked. "Paul Cézanne is often regarded as the father of Post-Impressionism."

"The Bay of Marseille," he said without hesitation. "Sometime between 1883 and 1885."

"Correct. But we have reason to believe Edgar Dumont created it first. Never credited, as history tends to go. Born in the early 1850s, he painted this when he was just sixteen years old, in 1869."

"About fourteen years before Cézanne's piece."

"Which is why this is so interesting."

Without hesitation, Evangeline walked over to Lewis's wrapped piece and ripped the paper off unceremoniously. The strewn wrappings folded in on themselves once, then twice, then three times, growing smaller and smaller until a little brown square floated into the right pocket of Evangeline's jacket.

Lewis knew what they would see when they looked: the same painting as Dumont's, but slightly out of focus. Blurry, like he had tried to re-create it from a dream.

Evangeline studied it, unmoving, for a moment. "You have talent," she finally spoke. "Does it have a name?"

Lewis shook his head. "No piece that I paint through . . ." He paused, but Noah nodded, like he was encouraging him to keep going.

"Any painting you paint when you're in a trance?" he asked.

It felt odd to have someone else say it. Even odder considering he had never told Noah that. But as he'd already noted, it wasn't the weirdest thing that had happened since he arrived in London, and Lewis noticed his limit for exceptional things was rising. Very quickly.

And so, all Lewis did was nod.

"Are all your paintings like this?" Evangeline asked, the tips of her fingers brushing against the ridges of black oil.

"Blurry?"

"Prophetic. That's what you were going to say, correct? That they come true? Sometimes days ahead of an incident, or even months."

Lewis's breath hitched for a moment. No one else called his paintings prophetic because no one else knew. But considering all that he had seen—the magic, the floating painting, the room with no windows or doors—prophetic art wasn't weird for Evangeline and Noah. Perhaps artists throughout history were right; there is more than can be physically sensed.

Just knowing that could be true, that the limits and rules which had been beaten into him weren't as firm as one might think, made him itch. Not in a bad way. But in a way he knew Evangeline and Noah could scratch.

"Some of them do," he said quietly. "Some of them, just barely. And some of them are just fiction."

"And you have no control over how they happen?" Noah asked. "No trigger?"

Lewis shook his head. "Not really. Perhaps one or two have happened around stressful life experiences. But that's when the most beautiful and important art usually happens. Artists put their blood, soul, and pain into their work all the time."

"What my associate is getting at," Evangeline said, "is that your art is magic, Lewis. If you want, I could run some tests and help you figure out its origin, but I'm fairly certain it's connected to our painter here." She gestured to the larger piece. "We believe Edgar painted ten of these. None of them brought him any fame or success while he was alive. Each painting depicted a horror from his own life. He used art as a medium to channel his sadness. He called them the Macabre."

"Like I said, sounds like most artists," Lewis muttered. He took another step forward, now within arm's reach of the piece. Each brushstroke was exceptional. There were subtle details that one wouldn't see at first glance. For example, in that dark trail, Lewis could see faces. No, not faces, skulls. But they were all the same and, from his study of anatomy—a community college class he thought would make him a better painter—he could tell the faces were all the same too.

"Like most painters," Evangeline continued, "van Gogh, Cézanne, Gauguin, Toulouse-Lautrec—his work skyrocketed in value after his death. The exclusiveness of the Macabre has turned the collection into pieces that individually sell for tens of millions of dollars. It doesn't hurt that there are rumored to be ten paintings, but art scholars have only identified nine of them."

"Leaving a sort of scavenger hunt for the rich and those with too much time on their hands," Lewis concluded.

Evangeline chuckled. "You could say that, yes. But, additionally, like most things, the uncertainty and mystery surrounding the paintings is part of the wonder, and the value. Anyone who owns multiples could see a compounded investment. But we at the museum aren't interested in them for their profit."

"You want them for their historic value, right? If this is Post-Impressionist, then this piece is at least a hundred and twenty years old," he said, taking another step forward. "And if what you say is true about him being the founder of Post-Impressionism, its value can't be quantified." He shouldn't be this close, he knew. His breath could affect the paint. In fact, the floating piece shouldn't be this exposed. It should be at a distance from human contact. Shame on Evangeline; she had to know better. "And if you believe there are ten, generally sets tell secret stories when you have them all together."

Evangeline smiled widely. "Oh, he is good, isn't he?"

From the corner of Lewis's eye he saw Noah's jaw clench. Just slightly. Almost unseeable by someone who didn't know how to pay attention. It gave Lewis pause, for a moment, reminding him of annoyance . . . yet not quite.

However, something dawned on him that pulled his attention away. "Or do you want it for its magical value?"

"Right again," Evangeline said proudly. "Any descendant of Dumont would be, especially around their own ancestor's heirloom."

"I'm sorry, *what*?" Lewis said, snapping his gaze back to Evangeline. Before he could complete the full turn, Noah had moved next to him within a single blink, gripping his wrist firmly enough that Lewis was sure he could snap the bone clean in half with just the right twist.

"Hold your breath, Mr. Dixon. And if you could do one thing for me? Find the painting's name," Noah whispered.

Lewis didn't have time to ask what any of that meant before Noah's surprisingly strong grip moved his hand forward. Lewis tried to scream, to yank his hand away, as Noah forced his palm against the painting. But his concern for the integrity of the painting—which somehow outweighed his concern for being manhandled so violently—disappeared the moment his hand touched the canvas . . .

His mind flooded with thoughts and memories that were not his own. He tasted wine he had never drunk. He smelled cologne and perfume that seemed foreign to him. A warm, pulsating sting radiated from his cheek as images flashed. A woman, much like the one in the painting. A wedding, with the same woman dancing with a man, which caused hot, bile-like rage to boil in his stomach. An argument with the same woman. The man bursting in.

Pain.

So much pain.

And then, the pressure of his fingers against the painting disappeared, as if the artwork had been pulled out quickly from in front of him. Lewis stumbled forward, reaching out blindly to grab on to something, even though he knew nothing was there. The painting, after all, was hovering in midair. He braced himself for the sharp burn of his face colliding with the linoleum floor, tensing his body to steel himself for the fall.

But it never came. Instead of feeling a cool, hard floor, he felt . . . wet. Lukewarm, brackish water and the familiar warmth of humid summer air.

Hold your breath, Noah had said.

Too late. Lewis sputtered and flailed for a moment until his palms sank deep into mud. He hoisted himself up, panting heavily, wiping the salty mixture from his eyes. They burned horribly, but he blinked through the pain. There were more important things to be concerned about.

Just moments ago, he was standing in a room that should not exist in the British Museum of London, England, and now he was standing in a lake that *also* shouldn't exist. More precisely, he was standing in a lake like the one in the painting, drenched from head to toe, while a boy, no older than sixteen, blinked at him curiously from the shore.

Three

SO THIS IS WHAT IT WAS LIKE TO BE INSIDE A PAINTING.

Lakes were either cold to the touch or warmed from the sun. They smelled like algae. They were dark, or green, or clear, or sometimes brown. But this lake? This lake was too perfect. Too smooth, like silver painted on a surface and evened out with a brush into a facsimile of a lake to trick the senses.

It took a moment for Lewis to understand exactly what he was trying to say, and once it hit him, everything made sense. The lake was more like something in a painting than something that actually existed in real life. And the water didn't feel like water, but more . . . like . . . paint.

But that wasn't all. The sky wasn't the right color either. Because of how high the sun was in the limitless blue above and the balmy, skin-prickling heat, he guessed it was around one or maybe two in the afternoon, probably in the summertime. The sky should have been a shade of brighter cerulean, with toupees of white clouds lazily drifting through the endless blue seas. Instead, it was a vibrant explosion of purples, oranges, and reds. Colors that reminded him of sitting on the docks during summer camp in Virginia when he was in elementary school. The same docks where he had his first kiss with Aaron Mickelson, while campfire songs, bullfrogs, and childlike laughter drifted through the air—laughter from voices with no idea what life had in store for them.

As strange as it all was . . . it was beautiful here.

Yet everything was also perverted in some way, shape, or form. Like something had poisoned the landscape and tried to fix its mistakes, yet missed the mark.

"Hello?"

The voice came from a boy, who, Lewis realized, was staring at him, standing in front of something Lewis was intimately acquainted with: a canvas on an easel.

"Are you here for the funeral?" The boy gestured with his head to something in the distance. Men and women, roughly a dozen or so, stood on a hill like splotches or black thumbprints. Lewis could hear the soft wails of a woman whose body was slumped against an older gentleman doing his best to hold her up.

"I am," Lewis said, even though he wasn't. The words didn't feel sour on his tongue like lies usually did. He felt a twinge of guilt for lying to the boy, but what was he supposed to say? How do you talk your way out of falling from the skies?

There was a moment of silence between the two, the boy looking at him in that way children and teens do when posed with something their young minds can't quite process.

"I don't remember you," the boy finally said. He didn't seem angry or upset, nor did he seem concerned that Lewis's clothing was in stark contrast to his own. Just curious, as if he had discovered something he didn't understand and had to unravel it. "Did you know my sister from school?"

"I didn't, no," Lewis said, walking over to stand next to the boy. "But I bet she was a great person."

"She was an idiot."

There was a sharpness in his voice Lewis wasn't used to hearing from someone so young. The words burned. His tone, on the one hand, had a directness and clarity that felt, at first, like a knife slipping between tendons without him noticing, yet the pain grew. On the other hand, he noted a sense of regret.

"Marrying him," the boy whispered, viscous disgust dripping from his lips. "Mother and Father loved him. Said he was a man of money."

"Who?"

The boy jutted his head toward the hillside. "William. My sister's husband. Good family, my mother told her. Wealthy family, brilliant connections, my aunts said. And your brother, they said..."

His voice dropped, but Lewis didn't need him to finish. He knew, not from his mother or his father like this boy, but from other family members, exactly what *they* said.

"Your son's an artist?" his aunt had said in that upward inflection that showed confusion and disrespect. *"What sort of life does an artist have?"*

That was the common statement he heard. Or rather, often overheard, as most refused to dignify him by saying it to his face. It was his mother, an exception, not the norm, who came to his defense.

"I'm doing fine for myself, Elizabeth," she had reminded her sister.

"Yes, but not everyone has as much talent as you do, Jessica," Elizabeth said in reply. *"Very few do."*

There was no point in reliving that memory, Lewis thought, forcing his attention back to the boy. The way his brow knit, his jaw locked, like Noah's when Lewis came to the conclusion of magic in the clean room just moments ago. It looked... unsettling on the soft features of such a young boy. Like it was hastily painted on his pale face.

What had the world done to this boy to make him have to grow up so quickly? Where was his youth, his sense of wonder, his openness and belief that people were inherently good? The cutting coolness of his words didn't come from a boy who believed those things, but one who knew that the world was cold, cruel, and, frankly, shit to those who let it swallow them whole.

No kid should know that. Not at this age. Not yet. Not for a long while.

Unless something—or someone—in the world had pried open his jaw and forced that reality down the boy's throat.

"Your sister," Lewis said slowly, eyes focused on the painting the boy was so fixated on that looked just like the one he had fallen into. A lump appeared in Lewis's throat. Coincidences weren't something Lewis believed in. Magical happenings, luck, some sort of divine intervention, and such. But chance? The world was too magical for random events to just be random.

Besides, it made it so much more boring.

"Her surname was Dumont, right?" he continued slowly. Part of him hoping he was wrong.

The boy nodded. "Until she got married. Then she became Savoir. Amelia Savoir."

"Which means you're Edgar Dumont," he replied, and then thought, *and my ancestor, according to Evangeline*, but that wasn't something he was going to say now.

Edgar nodded again.

At least that was one thought out of the way. But it begged another: Edgar had made the painting that sucked Lewis in. Had he somehow summoned Lewis? Maybe through some connection of their blood?

Lewis swallowed thickly, taking a moment for himself to process the words he just said. Sure, the fact some of his paintings came true whispered of something ethereal, tickled something in the back of his mind. But it wasn't a thought he ever acknowledged or accepted.

Now, in the span of less than an hour, he had been not only shown magic, but stepped into a goddamn painting; some unseen world thrown directly in his face, splattering his skin with its stink he could never get rid of.

Magic existed, and the faster he came to terms with that, the faster he could adapt. And survive.

"How did she die, your sister?" He remembered Noah's request to find the painting's name. Somehow he knew that was buried somewhere in Edgar's truth.

Edgar was quiet, with large brown eyes fixated on the painting, eyes that looked like they had seen too much. It was the first time Lewis really noticed not only how perfect the boy's posture was, but also that he was wrong about the painting. The version of the painting he had first seen was great. But this? This one was perfect.

How perfect the brushstrokes were, how they told a rich and honest story of the lake Lewis had just come out of. One of beauty and vibrancy but also of sorrow that made Lewis's heart ache.

It was a sorrow he knew well, having felt it when he found out about his mother. A surge of emotion he would have done anything to channel into something of meaning. To fuel his art. To convert it into something so his bloodcurdling screams that came from the depths of his chest when he was alone and reality was crashing all around him meant more than anguish.

He knew what it felt like to be helpless. He knew the urge to grab on to something, anything, often a paintbrush, and create something that could be controlled. Even in the finite world of a canvas, being in control when the rest of the world was careening toward destruction, or at least it felt like it was, made everything a little easier.

He wondered, remembering the flashes he saw before entering the painting, if Edgar felt the same. He wondered . . .

"Did your brother-in-law kill your sister, Edgar?"

Edgar's paintbrush stopped moving. Slowly, his eyes turned to look upward, and in them Lewis didn't see innocence but quiet rage.

"Drowning," the boy said with a curtness that left much to be desired, turning back to the painting, continuing to add gray to the skies.

"Excuse me?"

Edgar nodded toward the hill where his family and the mourners were. "That's how my sister died. At least, that's what the report said." He paused. "But it seemed a little too convenient. We were always told not to go too close to the lake, my sister and me. She knew better. This was her ancestral home. She wouldn't have let that happen to herself. She was . . . too smart, too careful for that."

Lewis opened his mouth to say something, but Edgar continued, his eyes fixed on the painting; his brush, an extension of his right hand, moved with precision. Lewis watched additional details come into shape. It wasn't long before Lewis recognized who the figure was.

A woman. Coming out of the lake. Much like the painting he saw moments before.

"I want to kill him," Edgar continued. "I want to open my sister's casket, pull her out, and shove him in. Alive. I want to bury him, hearing his muffled screams turn softer and softer as more and more dirt piles on top of him. I want to sleep in my house and fondly look, every so often, to the patches of overturned grass and know he's there. Rotting. That the last thought he had was of panic and pain and regret."

There was no hesitation in his words, Lewis noticed. The boy spoke with conviction and determination, like he had been waiting for someone to let him say what was on his mind. Lewis slowly blinked, processing what he had just heard. They didn't sound like the words of the aggrieved. The words of someone out for justice.

They sounded like the words of a killer.

The sky had gotten darker in the last few passing seconds. Purples and oranges morphed into a dark navy hue. And just as the sky had darkened, so had the painting Edgar was creating. Or—perhaps—it was the painting that had changed the sky. The lake was more turbulent—not like it was before, a still and pristine moment in time. Now it looked violent. Chaotic. Alive.

A loud wail, like a woman shrieking at finding her child dead, pulled Lewis's attention away. He turned toward the funeral, just in time to see a woman collapse on top of the casket, practically straddling it. The man beside her gently but firmly attempted to pull her off—to no avail. Her wails continued, loud enough to gallop on the wind. Lewis frowned. If she kept that up, kept screaming like that, begging for someone—anyone—to help her with her sorrow, she would rip open her vocal cords. But he guessed she didn't care.

"I have a question for you now," Edgar said. "Are you going to tell my parents?"

"Should I?"

"I just told you I want to kill my sister's fiancé, in graphic detail. Most people would be terrified. But you . . . seem calm. Which makes me think you're either someone who has seen death or created it yourself."

Lewis's heart began to race as his gaze fixed on Edgar's. What would happen when he was considered a threat and not a curiosity? Lewis wondered. It was something he didn't want to find out and could only imagine, considering he still couldn't fully wrap his head around how he had gotten here. But he didn't need to understand; he just needed to get out, and if possible, fulfill Noah's request. A request that seemed increasingly reasonable and balanced, compared to what he'd been told moments ago.

"This painting of yours—what will you call it?"

The question came out of left field, Lewis admitted, but that was the point: to distract the boy and throw him off-balance.

"I ask," Lewis continued, nodding to the artwork, "because something that good deserves to have a name attached to it. When you're famous and rich, and people see this first piece, what do you want people to call it? Edgar Dumont and . . ." He gestured. "What rolls off the tongue? What is going to . . ."

"Cement my legacy?"

"Exactly. Cement your legacy."

There was that familiar phrase. The desire to be famous, to be known, to be seen. The hunger for it made him ravenous. He could only guess Edgar felt the same way. He was a creative; he knew the struggles of balancing the desire to make good art but also to be known and revered. After all, why put your heart onto a canvas if not to be validated?

"*The Drowning*," Edgar said without hesitation. "Edgar Dumont and his painting, *The Drowning*. A study of life, death, and love."

"I think that's a beautiful name."

Edgar's eyes burned bright, not with anger but with pride. Lewis couldn't help but smile back—something about the infectious grin of a kid soothed a dark fear in him. But, as Edgar opened his mouth to speak, nothing came out. His lips moved, but there was no sound, as if he had been muted.

Lewis started to ask him what was wrong, but from the corner of his eye, behind where the funeral was, he saw something far more terrifying than death.

He saw nothing.

The edges of reality were bleaching, like someone was rolling white paint over the landscape from all sides. It closed in on them, erasing everything. Within a blink, the funeral was gone. Another blink, and the whiteness was several feet closer. It wouldn't take long before the vibrant colors, the smells, and the sounds of whatever moment Lewis had stumbled into were gone.

Himself included.

His first instinct was to run. That disappeared quickly, the chilling effect of terror freezing him in place. His second was to take Edgar with him, to grab his hand and try somehow to escape. Yet as he reached out, his fingers passed through Edgar's flesh, smudging his skin, his bones, and his blood, as if he were a three-dimensional figure made of paint. Which, Lewis supposed, in some sense he was.

Edgar didn't even seem to notice the whiteness. His focus went back to the painting in front of him, as if the crawling whiteness didn't matter or didn't exist.

"It's just a memory," Lewis whispered to himself. "It's just a snapshot. A moment in time."

His voice was the only thing echoing in the vast blankness that was eating all the color from the painting. Reality seemed to bend within the vast, endless world. His simple sentence, a chant he repeated to ground himself, was loud, echoing off walls that he couldn't see or feel—but it was also quiet, like a reassuring feeling he held on to to keep himself sane.

However, that chant did little to keep at bay the dread of what might happen if he was stuck here, wherever here was. Or if, worse, he was simply erased. From all angles, the virus spread. There was no place to go, no direction to outrun it. There was only one thing that could possibly save him.

The lake.

It was in the center, Lewis realized, almost perfectly, as if it was the epicenter of everything. He had fallen into the lake, sprung out of it, and arrived here. Could the reverse be true?

It wasn't like he had much of a choice.

Lewis gave Edgar one last look. He willed himself to give him a sign, something to confirm he'd heard him or could come with him. But the boy just continued to paint, layering final strokes of green and brown to add dimension that wasn't there before. A simple yet profound action of art.

Despite the impending nullification, Lewis had to admit Edgar really was an impressive artist . . .

Not the time.

Lewis pushed off the ground, keeping his body low as he dashed toward the lake. He didn't think, simply acted, jumping into it headfirst as the whiteness nipped at his heels. He ignored the slipperiness of the water, pushing through and swimming downward, away from the endlessness he could still feel chasing him.

Lewis couldn't see the bottom, not really. It was blurry and out of reach, no matter how hard he swam. But it didn't stop him from kicking, from pushing his body until his muscles—even the ones he didn't know he had—burned. Even though he couldn't fully explain it, something inside him knew being erased was worse than dying.

Lewis swam deep into the darkest parts of the lake until only blackness surrounded him, dark enough to swallow the white that found its way into the water. He never stopped, even as his lungs burned and he grew dizzy; even as the blackness began to burn away and fluorescent lights slowly burst through. He didn't take a break until his head pushed through the surface of the water and he took a gasp of much-needed air.

That moment was the only pause he got.

He had burst out of murky, brown water that was filling the room where Noah and Evangeline were. He quickly turned his head, snapping his eyes toward the source of the gushing sound—the painting, where gallons upon gallons of water were spilling out of the frame and filling the room.

"Fuck!" Noah screamed.

Lewis twisted toward him, watching as what looked like dozens of hands clawed and yanked at Noah's body. That was startling enough, but equally unreal were the half-dozen ravens that fought against them, pecking and ripping flesh from the arms and exposing bones and cartilage. Some of the arms swiped, hitting the birds and knocking them into the water. Enough hands were taken down, however, to give Noah—his body covered in scratches—a moment to stand. It was then Lewis noticed they were the same ravens he'd seen in the hint of a tattoo on Noah's wrist; the tattoo that was now fully gone.

Evangeline, from what Lewis could tell, was faring better. She, at least, was standing, runic symbols made of white light circling around her like sentries. Each time an arm lunged forward, a rune would block its path—the arm entering one rune and exiting through another. It reminded Lewis of a magician's trick . . . which he realized was exactly what it was.

Evangeline's eyes landed on him, a flicker of a smile appearing, but only for a moment. "Did you get it?" she yelled.

Lewis nodded. "I—"

"Behind you!" Noah yelled.

Lewis turned to see a woman looming over him. She was waterlogged, her skin a light, translucent green. A white dress clung to her form like a second skin; her hair was thin and mostly gone. But what Lewis noticed most was the bruises on her neck, and he knew in that moment exactly who she was.

Noah started to speak a word in some beautiful lyrical language, but before he could enunciate every syllable, Edgar's sister—and by extension, Lewis's great-great-great-grandaunt—slapped Noah across the face. The force was stronger than Lewis expected, hard enough for Noah's body to slam against the far-right wall. He let out a pained cry before dropping like a heap of heavy sand into the lake, arms from the painting molesting him like vultures hungry for meat.

Lewis tried to turn, to speak and call out to Noah, but he barely had time to jump backward before Amelia lunged at him. Her hands wrapped around his neck, tighter than Lewis thought humanly possible, so tight he worried his neck might snap right then. He lost his footing, her body pushing him back into the water, submerging them both.

For a second, he thought he would sink like before, within the endless lake. But his back thumped against the white floor of the museum's special room moments later. That was no relief, as the half-dead woman, Edgar's sister, kept her grip on his throat, elbows locked and expression filled with rage, as if she thought killing Lewis would bring her comfort—or maybe even back to life.

Lewis wasn't a strong man; he knew this. His strength was never physical. On the best of days, he *might* have been able to fight this thing off. But after almost passing out from swimming, combined with his loss of balance? There was no real hope for him. No amount of clawing at the arms, kicking, or trying to get leverage would work. So he did the only thing he could possibly think to do.

He opened his mouth as wide as he could, letting the cold water fill his throat and lungs, and screamed the only words he could form, even as those words got swallowed by the water.

"The Drowning!"

Lewis wasn't sure what he hoped would happen. Possibly not anything. Maybe he just wanted to say it, to speak a name to the piece, as if Edgar would know that it wasn't forgotten in some cosmic sense. Death does weird things to people when it gets so close. He remembered his mother babbling in Latin in the hospital, a language he knew she knew almost nothing about.

But the words *did* do something. When he said them, everything stopped. The woman's grip on his body, the gushing sound of the water, even the way the waves ebbed and flowed. It was like time had paused for everything related to *The Drowning*.

And slowly, the world burned away.

Like flecks of paint fluttering in the wind, starting with the woman's fingers around his throat, his surroundings began to disappear. It took no more than ten seconds for the room to fill with paint chips, a maelstrom of particles sucked back into the painting. Each chip—thousands, millions of them—found their proper place in the painting as it returned to its original static form.

Lewis's whole body burned; every nerve was on fire. A mixture of fear, pain, and adrenaline—a cocktail he never wanted to drink again—made it nearly impossible for him to stand or even think straight.

Noah rushed over, fell to his knees, and grabbed Lewis's shoulders, gently pulling him upward so his back rested against Noah's suited chest. Lewis looked up over his shoulder at the other man. The side of Noah's face was red and bruised, claw marks dragging against his skin that looked like a beast had been gripping for dear life on a cliff. But, overall, he seemed fine. Lewis couldn't help but be envious of how brave and strong Noah must be to still be functioning.

"Keep calm," Noah whispered. "Don't move too much. You might have a fractured trachea."

"He almost certainly has one," Evangeline said, glancing at him. "How is your healing magic, Noah?"

"I . . . it's not the best." He quickly added, "I know the basics all agents should know."

"You should brush up on those, especially considering what Lewis just proved he can do. I imagine you'll find yourself in the field more often than not in the upcoming weeks," she chastised. "Iqbal's Chant of Stitching should be enough to patch up that wound. It's—"

"Arabic in origin," he said, nodding. "Thank you."

"While you do that . . ." Evangeline muttered, walking with purpose to stand in front of the painting. Lewis watched the string of hand movements and shapes she made. She whispered something in a language that sounded Slavic before thrusting her hand out . . . and doing the unthinkable.

She set the painting on fire.

Instantly, the canvas burst into white-hot flames. Twin colors of red and blue danced around each other as the painting screamed. Lewis didn't just hear it—he felt it deep inside, a feeling of anguish and pain. If personified, it was a cry for help. Noah and Evangeline felt it too; he could tell by the way they winced.

Like a real, living person being burned alive, the screams slowly subsided, going from feral, to a whimper, to nothing but a burning pyre. When it was done, and the voice of . . . whatever . . . had been stilled, the painting still floated in the same space in which it had before, the frame charred but the canvas itself untouched. But something had changed, been burned away within the holy fire of whatever was caused by speaking its true name.

"Stillness," Lewis whispered, his voice coming out broken and hoarse from the pain.

There was no more dread. No more sadness weighing down, pulsing from it. Just . . . an eerie stillness that felt like something had been ripped out forcefully, the space left hollow and crude.

Lewis had no other way to describe it, but it felt like someone had died right then and there. Their carcass cold, their body disregarded as expendable.

Evangeline turned swiftly on her heels and waved her hand. The seams of a door appeared against the rightmost wall, a soft hiss following as it opened slightly. Lewis saw the carpet from the lobby inside. Somehow, this other room, outside of time and space, led there.

"When you've composed yourself, Mr. Dixon, come find me. That is, if you're interested in what you just saw. Usually when people pull the veil back and see the world for what it really is, they either run toward it or away from it. I'm curious to see which type of person you are."

So am I, thought Lewis.

Four

IT HAD BEEN A FULL TEN MINUTES SINCE LEWIS SAW THE DUMONT BURST into flames, and he still couldn't process what he had been party to.

It was reasonable to say logic no longer applied. Or, at least, the rules of logic had changed. Other worlds existed. Magic existed and, somehow, there were people who could harness it. Himself included? Was that a fair assumption?

His vision was hyperacute, noticing every bruise on his body, every droplet of water still lingering on his skin. He saw how his chest rose and fell and heard the raggedness of his breath. But more importantly, one singular voice rang through: Noah's.

"Breathe, Lewis," he said.

Lewis hated flying. It was strange to think that in this moment, but it's what struck him in the here and now. It was one of the reasons he'd hesitated to take this trip across the pond. He'd even considered the seven-day boat journey instead of flying. His therapist had told him to ground himself, to feel the metal of the armrest when he was nervous, or count to twenty backward, or focus on the soft, relaxed expression of the flight attendant.

Now, to calm himself, he focused on the roughness of Noah's hand on his shoulder as it squeezed Lewis to remind him he was there. That he wasn't going through it alone.

"I can also help calm you down," Noah said, sounding like he was speaking through a layer of film. "If you want."

Lewis opened his mouth to respond, but nothing came out. So, instead, he simply nodded.

Noah's lips pushed into a thin line, and he nodded curtly. "Just . . . for the record," he said after a moment's pause, "you shouldn't give a magician control over your senses so easily. Giving over control is dangerous."

"Having my heart going at two hundred beats per minute is more dangerous," Lewis rasped back. "Do magicians not suffer from stress?"

"No, we do," Noah said, smoothing his hand from Lewis's shoulder onto the center of his chest. "We just know how to control it better."

Before Lewis could fire back another quip, Noah added pressure to his chest with the palm of his hand.

"Breathe," he said. Except the word wasn't heard by Lewis's ears but in his mind. The word felt heavy there, like the weight of it was pressing against his brain, causing him to feel dizzy. But the heaviness that affected his nerves quickly morphed into euphoria, and within a matter of seconds, Lewis's breathing had returned to normal.

"Better?" Noah asked, slowly pulling his hand back.

Lewis nodded gently, his eyes lidded in a dopey expression.

"It's a balm," Noah clarified. "Think of it like laughing gas. It'll trick you into thinking you're calm until, hopefully, you're actually calm."

Lewis flexed his fingers, looking at the palm of his hand. "Constellations," he whispered.

"I'm sorry?"

Lewis showed his palms to Noah. "My mom used to say my freckles were constellations. Are they glowing for you? Or is that just the magic talking?"

Noah's lips curled into a momentary smirk. "That's . . . absolutely the magic talking."

Lewis frowned. "Well, that's no fun," he whispered. His eyes trailed upward, looking at the door that Evangeline had walked through. It led to the center of the British Museum's gala halls. Through the portal, he could see nearly three, no, four dozen people, all in elegant attire, a variation of his own suit and tie but a few rungs higher in class and stature, going about their business. He couldn't hear the chatter; the space that separated the two rooms blocked out any sound.

Lewis pointed. "I can't hear them. They can't hear us either?"

Noah stood next to him and nodded.

"And they can't see us?"

He nodded again. "I imagine someone with strong magic could probably sense us. Maybe someone even stronger might be able to see ripples. But Evangeline's magic is powerful enough that she naturally veils things just by willing it to be so. We call it Inspiration. The ability to just . . . make things happen . . . within reason."

"Can you do that? Inspire?"

Noah shook his head. "Only some of the strongest magicians can. It's a bloodline ability, much like in your family." Noah dipped his chin as if to apologize. "I'm getting ahead of myself—and you, for that matter. Evangeline will explain it all—assuming you're going to see her?"

It was a question, but Lewis wasn't sure if he really needed to answer. It sounded like the decision was already made for him, and everyone was simply waiting for him to catch up. "There isn't a choice, is there?" he asked.

"There's always a choice. You could decide this isn't something for you."

"You're asking me to decide something while only having bits and pieces of the puzzle. That's not fair."

"You're right. It's not. One thing you should learn quickly—"

"Magicians aren't fair?"

Noah nodded. "I imagine Evangeline would try and convince you, and if you weren't movable, she would let you go. Wipe your memories of what you saw. Send an agent to tail you for a few months, making sure the spell stuck. But . . ."

Lewis arched his right brow. This conversation with Noah was like being doused in cold water when drunk. The spell was starting to wear off. But his anxiety was no longer a raging inferno, more a smoldering pile of coals, and he latched on to that, telling himself, *You're getting better, you're getting better* . . .

"You have prophetic magic," Noah explained. "Eventually, as fate would have it, you would paint something that would lead you back here. There are only so many prophecies someone can have in their lifetime, and somehow, for reasons beside your blood, you are tied to this story, Lewis. I imagine that most of your prophecies will be connected to these paintings."

With a wave of his hand, the image outside blurred and rotated, as though the room was a globe and they were looking through a peephole. Once the blurred image reappeared, there sat Evangeline at a large oak desk that was almost comically too big for her. But what was perhaps more interesting was the window behind her.

Lewis would have expected to see a London street, or perhaps the side of a building. But the window rippled and shifted. For a moment, it *was* a London street. Then it changed, became murky before emerging crystal clear and sharp, a view facing a bright-blue, crisp ocean. Another ripple, another view, like a magical slideshow.

While Noah talked, Lewis kept his gaze on the view.

"Right now, everything must seem very confusing. But I can promise you one thing, the next five minutes will change everything you have seen about the world and everything you can and will see moving forward. The choice is yours, to continue on with your life as is, or to be part of something greater, a current flowing under the surface. There is no right or wrong choice, only the choice you're willing to make."

"You're speaking around the issue," Lewis said, leaving out *and it's annoying.*

Even without all the pieces of information, though, Lewis knew that something terrifyingly important was happening here. Noah was delivering a sales pitch, and he was the right messenger. With his charm and swagger, his sharp dark features, baritone voice, and the way he carried himself without a wrinkle, Lewis *wanted* to trust him.

And Lewis was pretty confident that wasn't magic talking.

But what Noah conveniently left out was everything else involved with, well, *magic.* Lewis had seen the horrors within the painting. Seen how Noah and Evangeline—and he himself—had almost died from forces that didn't make sense to the average mind. Was that something he wanted to be involved with? When it was possible to just . . . forget?

Of course, it was something he wanted.

With that thought firmly in place, Lewis didn't hesitate any longer. He stepped forward, through the veil and into Evangeline's office. Freed of the queasiness that came from magic in the white room, he noticed how . . . weird it felt to be normal. It was like when you wear sunglasses and take them off, how rich and vibrant colors feel once again. That was how the simple scent of a burning lavender candle smelled, and the sound of a record player in the corner and its soft lulls of jazz. Simple things he hadn't realized how badly he'd missed.

And yet . . . he also somehow missed magic too.

Noah walked through the portal right behind him. As it closed, the wall returned to nothing but a wooden panel.

"Tell me," Evangeline said without looking up from the stack of papers she was signing, "in your own words, what you just saw."

When Noah didn't answer, Lewis assumed she was talking to him. "I saw the boy at a funeral. I saw the world melt away around me, and saw the lake, the same one in the painting, become some sort of entrance between one world and the next."

"And?"

"And I saw . . . I saw magic," he said. "I saw things that don't make sense, brought to life in front of my eyes."

Evangeline paused with the stack about three-quarters of the way done. Slowly, she leaned back in her chair, a soft creak filling the room as the metal strained. Her eyes lifted to him. "Right information, wrong conclusion," she said. "That world that Noah pushed you into? It wasn't a different reality. Not in the way we magicians define it."

"What do you mean?"

"It was a snippet," Noah said, walking into view, glancing out the window behind Evangeline. "A segment in time that has an end and a beginning, repeated over and over again."

"A memory," Lewis clarified.

"Yes, that's a simple way to put it," Evangeline added, and somehow it was clear she wasn't quite complimenting his succinctness. "A snippet, though, can be fictional or real—but yes, we can call it a memory. A fractured moment of a sorry man's life, thrust into a work of art."

"One created by Edgar Dumont?" Lewis reasoned. "Through . . . magic?"

"Not just any magic," Evangeline pushed. "The same magic you have. Edgar is what we call a Node. The first in a magical bloodline to show the ability to thread what makes magic *magic*. As such, his powers are uncontrollable. The most powerful they'll ever be in the family, without practice and the introduction of another bloodline and simple genetic flukes, of course. That's what made Edgar's paintings so dangerous. There are plenty of artists, I'm sure you know many of them, who pour their heart and soul into their works. But none of them create monstrosities like those."

"Like your Inspiration," Lewis added. "That's your gift."

For a moment, surprise washed over Evangeline's face, her sharp gaze shifting toward Noah, correctly deducing he must have told Lewis. As quickly as the look came, it passed. "Yes. Exactly. Just like your ability to create prophetic art. Not every magician comes from a family with a bloodline ability. Some, like Noah here, are just born with the power to see, sense, and mold the threads that control magic. But there can be dangerous consequences for those of us who *do*."

"Or it can be used for good," Noah added gently. "Like with you, Lewis."

"There are nine known Macabre," Evangeline explained as she stood up and walked to the right side of the desk while Noah walked around to the left side. "A trinity of a holy trinity. A magical number triplicated. You had the pleasure of meeting one of them and neutralizing it."

"You mentioned nine known paintings," Lewis noted. "You intentionally added 'known.'"

Evangeline nodded yet didn't quite respond to what he'd just said. "Each of the Macabre is dangerous, as you have seen," Evangeline explained, standing next to him. "Nine paintings with nine sinister origins. Each born from a moment in Edgar Dumont's history that was horrific enough to trigger his ability to enchant art into a curse. Magical enchantments aren't abnormal. Swords, talismans, crucifixes, runes. You can trace throughout history artifacts given magical properties and enhancements.

"But most die when the caster dies, unless they are upkept. These paintings defy that logic."

"Because Edgar was a . . ." Lewis paused. "You called him a Node, right?"

Noah nodded. "That's where you come in."

"The ask is simple, the task is not," Evangeline chimed in. "I believe, despite many in the field who disagree, these paintings are a trail. Each piece contains a small magical clue, like a coded signature, to find the Lost Dumont.

"The idea isn't unfounded. Those art historians who do find Edgar Dumont's work of interest believe it isn't unreasonable to conclude there was a tenth piece."

"Artists create work all the time that is lost," Lewis said. "Especially if he wasn't famous when he died. A lost work in a set is common."

"Exactly," Evangeline said, her voice crackling with excitement. "And if the other paintings have power, then can you imagine what sort of gifts this last painting would hold?"

"One would argue that power should be kept lost," Lewis replied. "If the other paintings can do anything like what *The Drowning* did, it's best no one has them."

"That's not how the world works," Noah said. "They will be found. They will be used, and they will be a weapon."

"It's better we have them," Evangeline reasoned. "To neutralize them. That's where you come in. I want you to help us neutralize the paintings that we find. Allow them to be simply works of beautiful art and nothing more."

Lewis didn't buy that for a second. Not solely, at least. Two things could be true. Evangeline could absolutely care about the preservation of art and the sanctity of life these paintings might erode. But neither the British Museum nor the British Empire were known for being . . . selfless.

"What else do you want?"

Lewis's tone was sharper than he wanted it to be, and the way Noah stood up just a hair taller told him his hackles were raised.

Evangeline noticed too, gently raising her hand to still her attack dog.

"It's all right. It's a fair question. There are dozens if not hundreds of artifacts here, just like the Macabre, that have cursed lineage. I want to use the last painting to find people like you, descendants who can use their connection to the works of art to purify them."

"So they can be seen?"

"And so I can get a promotion," she said plainly. "If I succeed at this, Lewis, I will be head of the Royal Arcane Intelligence Agency. A position that has only been held by a woman once, and a Black woman never. I want that. And a success like this guarantees it's mine."

Lewis could relate to that. Being passed over because of reasons out of your control wasn't something Black Americans had a monopoly on. Evangeline was a woman, a Black woman, in a high-powered position that Lewis could only assume had been run, dictated, and created by men. But a success like this . . . they wouldn't be able to overlook it.

In a single blink, Evangeline was right in front of him, his hands cupped in her soft ones. She met him directly in the eye, her warm brown ones looking at him, looking through him, deep inside. At least, that was what it felt like; like his soul was being unspooled and the soft, inner engine that every bit of his mind, body, and soul protected was exposed.

"The Dumonts are dangerous, Lewis. You've seen what they can do. We have been tracking them through history, but Edgar's gifts have made them nearly impossible to track."

"They hide themselves," Noah clarified, out of view. It was as if everything but Evangeline was softer, muted, muffled. While she was crystal clear. "Getting *The Drowning* cost us over a dozen agents. It's unsustainable."

"But you," Evangeline said, "as a descendant of Edgar, can not only help us find them, but help keep the death toll down and help us neutralize them."

But Lewis only cared about one thing. The one thing he had ever truly wished for, at least recently.

"If I help you," he finally said, "can I use the magic of the last painting to bring my mother back?"

Evangeline broke her eye contact with Lewis, and the world around him returned to feeling more balanced. She took a step back, rolling her shoulders, a wince passing over her features. As she did, the shoulder of her suit jacket shifted, revealing a pale line that looked like a jagged, healed cut that disappeared under her clothes.

"There are some rules that even paintings like the Macabre cannot violate." She paused. "Should not violate."

"So that's a no."

"That's a no. But," she said, then paused. Looking at him shrewdly, she continued. "Not because it can't, but because the ramifications would be far too great. I need you to trust me on this. Magic can do anything. Magic shouldn't be used for everything.

"But, at your core, you are an artist, Lewis, and we are the British Museum. I don't think it's unreasonable to say that, over the past quarter of a century, we have helped solidify and define what is greatest and who is remembered through history. So what I can offer you, in exchange, is the second-best thing: recognition."

How is that even close to having my mom back?

"You help us find these Dumonts, and we'll help you become more than just a painter. These paintings will be nothing but that: beautiful lost works of art now found. The British Museum will house them. Art historians will come from far and wide to research them. Lovers of art will travel across the globe to see them. Someone will have to be the premier expert on these paintings.

"That someone will be you."

Noah interjected, "Think of how that will elevate your status in a world that has been slamming the door in your face since you graduated from SCAD. It can only help your art. It can only make you . . ."

"Immortal," Lewis concluded. *And thus, in a way, my mother could still live on, through me. Through my work . . .*

The realization sent a shiver down Lewis's spine. At his core, he liked to consider himself a caring individual. He held the door for people. He firmly believed he was kind and nice. He cared about the world at large. But the idea of being one of those artists—and a Black and queer artist—whose work was solidified in the artistic canon? He wanted nothing less, even if he rarely let himself believe he was worthy of it.

"And all I have to do is help you? Like before?"

"We will be with you every step of the way," Evangeline promised. "Once we find the last painting, every tool the British Museum has—and, by extension, the Crown—will be yours. Within a year, you'll be all the buzz amongst some of the most influential art curators around the world. Within five, you'll be a household name. That, I promise you."

"I want my student loans paid off," he quickly added. Why not shoot for the moon? "Do that too, and I'll help you."

Evangeline smiled, extending her right hand with no hesitation. It was the first time Lewis noticed the nail polish on her fingernails—a soft plum. His favorite color.

"I think that's a very reasonable request for one willing to risk their life to help our cause."

Lewis shook her hand firmly. For one brief moment, Lewis thought he had made a horrible mistake. But, as far as he could tell, there was no turning back now. Evangeline didn't seem like the type of woman who allowed anyone to back out of an agreement with her. No matter their reason.

Down the rabbit hole we go, Alice, he thought to himself.

Five

CASSANDRA HATED FRANCE, SPECIFICALLY PARIS, WHICH WAS A BIT COM-ical considering she was French.

She hadn't always hated the City of Light. But travel helps change the mind and redefine the palate. From the farthest corners of the globe to the underworld right beneath her nose, she had seen the earth's most wondrous cities and backwater hovels through a new lens and learned that, frankly, her people were annoying as hell.

But the one thing Cassandra could appreciate about her brothers and sisters was their ability to drip themselves in opulence. It was a part of herself she could not shake, regardless of how many times she had reinvented herself, folding inside and outside over and over and over. It was why, for the past sixteen months, Hôtel Plaza Athénée had been her home, despite having an apartment in her name just twenty kilometers outside the city center.

A deluxe suite with a view of Avenue Montaigne? Nothing could beat that, she had to admit.

It was early evening when Cassandra finally found her way back to the hotel. Her skin had been itching all day in a way no moisturizer or bath could cleanse. She knew what that meant: the hunger and annoyance that came from failure. Not just failure, but repeated failure. Time and time again, over the past few months, her searches had come up empty. Her connections in the Parisian underground—ones that she had cultivated over the years—and the magical for-hire agents she had been able to morally bend had come up empty. That frustrated her. More than she was willing to admit. Not because Cassandra expected people to be useful in fulfilling her goals—she had learned at a young age to never trust another person—but because it was a reflection of her own ability.

In her mind, she was a failure, and shopping in the Champs-Elysées and the Golden Triangle was the only remedy for that.

"Busy day, mademoiselle?" Guillaume, the handsome doorman who had made her body quiver more than once, asked respectfully.

Looking through the bangs of blond hair that framed her angular face, Cassandra smiled, nodding a thank-you as he held the elevator door for her. "Always, Guillaume, always," she said.

"Will you be requesting food tonight from Épicure?"

"No, not tonight," she said, half under her breath, lost in thought. "I won't be here long. I'm simply dropping these off."

These being the half dozen bags in her hands.

Guillaume smiled. "Of course," he said, giving her one final nod before letting the door close.

The elevator ride up to her suite was smooth and easy. It gave Cassandra time to think, to chew on her bottom lip until she tasted copper; a bad habit she had yet to break. It was true that shopping was a good momentary relief from the storm of thoughts in her head. But just remembering the pain she felt in her chest earlier today—a familiar pang, like a stab in her heart, that could only mean one thing—made her sick. Not because she felt it, but because she had trusted someone, and this was the result.

A Dumont had been destroyed, and she had a feeling she knew which one it was.

The elevator opened, and Cassandra briskly walked down the hall. She didn't bother pulling out her key. The rune flashed for a brief moment as she approached the door, unlocking and slowly pushing it open. As soon as she crossed the threshold, the door closed, locked, and sealed, a wave of magic passing over her like a breeze, isolating perception by all senses from entering or exiting the room without her permission.

"You lied to me, Frank," Cassandra called out to the suite, dropping the bags unceremoniously on the ground. "You know how I feel about lies."

There was no one in the massive, beautiful room. At least, no one visible. Cursing under her breath, Cassandra angrily gestured with her right hand, twisting her middle and pointer fingers into a crooked shape and aiming the shape toward the farthest bare wall. A moment later, the air rippled and a man appeared. He was starfished—knives sunk deep into his wrists and ankles—and pinned to the wall, a runic shape drawn over his skin with his own blood.

Cassandra wasn't fazed. She simply crossed her arms over her chest, staring with a narrowed, annoyed gaze at Frank.

"Did you lie to me from the start? Or was this a last-minute change of heart?"

It wasn't fair to ask that question, especially when he couldn't answer. After all, Frank didn't have a mouth anymore. Barbed wire had been stitched with surgical precision through his top and bottom lips. Even attempting to speak probably made him burn with white-hot agony. Cassandra was genuinely curious about what hurt more: the barbed wire or the knives.

Maybe she could ask him now. But first . . .

At the whisper of a single syllable, the barbed wire pulled out of his mouth and dropped onto the ground. The British Special Forces soldier–turned–underground goods dealer let out an unmanly whimper.

"Answer me," Cassandra whispered, bridging half the space between the two of them. "What. Happened?"

Ragged, pained breath escaped the bald man's mouth. "I . . . didn't . . . lie."

"You didn't? Then how did the British Museum end up with a Dumont?"

"I don't know."

"You don't *know*? Then why did I pay you, Frank? Why have I put your daughter through college? Why have I done anything for you if you cannot get me what I ask of you?"

Frank had no answer. Of course he didn't have an answer. Cassandra growled, running her fingers through her hair. She kicked off her heels, a small relief in a moment of total annoyance. She quietly paced around the room, thinking.

"I had it," Frank gurgled, coughing up blood and spitting a crimson glob onto the carpet. "It was . . . in a warehouse. I set up the runes, like you told me."

"Well, clearly, they were not good enough," she hissed. "Which one was it?"

"My warehouse in Perth. They—"

"I don't care what warehouse!" she roared, whipping around to face him. "Which. Painting?"

Her mother always told her that yelling made her soft, pretty face turn into something grotesque. *A monster of unlovable proportions*, her mother had called her. Good. Let her be a monster. Let her rule. That was all she ever wanted, anyway.

"It . . . was of a lake, with a woman," Frank recited. "It was . . . morose."

"There's a reason they are called the Macabre," she muttered, bored. Sighing, Cassandra rolled her shoulders. It was bad that one was gone, but there were still many paintings in play. All wasn't lost. This was just a reminder there was no one she could trust.

"I can give you something else in return," he whispered. "I have . . . a grimoire, one from an agent from the British Museum. Took my men weeks to break the runes. It belonged to Ishita Rao."

"You say that name like I care," Cassandra replied. Of course she knew why Frank said it. Ishita was a well-known agent, a threat to most people like Frank. But she was not a threat to her. Not anymore. "I do not want a grimoire. I *wanted* the painting. But since you are unable to give me that . . ." Cassandra conceded, bridging the rest of the gap between the two of them, standing close to Frank. She tipped her head toward the right. He knew what to do.

Frank nodded slowly, his gaze following Cassandra's. His eyes shimmered, runic symbols on his irises glowing for a moment. The air rippled where his eyes fell. A small portal, only large enough to fit one's arm through, appeared; a portal into a safe where the grimoire sat.

"It's a shame you decided to be such a piss-poor dealer, Frank," Cassandra muttered, reaching through and taking the grimoire for herself. "You could have been something useful. I know the British Museum would have loved this bloodline trait of yours."

"I serve—"

Before he could continue, Cassandra sliced her right hand across his neck. A single thin line appeared there. Frank coughed, blood spilling like a red curtain out of his esophagus. Weak and wet coughs followed, and then gurgles and watery pleas as he squirmed against the knives pinning him in place.

"I do not care," Cassandra whispered, tossing the grimoire haphazardly onto the nearby couch. Only belatedly did she remember she hadn't asked which had hurt him more. *Oh, well.* As Frank bled out slowly, she descended to her knees. Cassandra closed her eyes, turned her palms up, and bowed her head.

"Our Father, Who art in heaven, hallowed be Thy name . . ." she whispered rapidly under her breath, with the sound of Frank's death drifting into the background. Cassandra's mind began to go white. The world around her—the beautiful, expensive, six-thousand-dollar-a-night hotel—disappeared under her knees.

Maybe this sacrifice would bring Him closer to her. Maybe this time He would hear her. Maybe this time she would know peace.

Or maybe she would have to continue down this path as she always intended—and remind herself that if she wanted something done right, she would have to do it herself.

Just as the case had been for the past one hundred and thirty years.

PART II

"Every word is like an unnecessary stain on silence and nothingness."

SAMUEL BECKETT

Six

SITTING IN THE BACK OF THE SLEEK BLACK CAR THAT NOAH HAD SUM-moned in a rush of hushed whispers as they walked out of Evangeline's office, Lewis couldn't help but think that perhaps he had made the wrong choice.

The feeling wasn't front and center in his mind; rather, it lingered behind pillars, half-submerged in the icky black shadows of his forbidden thoughts, rearing its head every so often before disappearing again. Lewis had struggled with anxiety since he was a young child, and everything that had happened in the past few hours—especially after the rush had settled—only stirred up that raging feeling inside him.

He rubbed gingerly at his throat. Noah's spell had calmed the noose of fire that had burned there, white-hot, but there was still a lingering discomfort, like that of a finger wearing a too-small ring for a bit too long.

"It'll pass," Noah said. "The pain."

"It doesn't hurt that much," Lewis said. Noah hadn't asked, but it felt right to offer up the information, especially given Evangeline's seeming skepticism of Noah's healing-magic abilities. From what Lewis could tell, Noah had stitched the tissues of Lewis's trachea back together; he felt fortunate to escape with a little soreness, so long as he could speak again.

"Hm," Noah said.

What did *that* mean? Lewis's eyes drifted from the passing view of London through his window to Noah in the seat beside him. Noah wasn't even looking directly at him—which he supposed he should have expected. He was instead focused on his iPad, his long, pianist-like fingers tapping in a rapid heartbeat on the screen. The display was black, though; at least, that was what Lewis saw.

"Magic?" he asked, nodding his head toward the iPad. A smooth change of subject to something that was firmly in Noah's domain, and perhaps a little more of interest to him.

At first, Noah didn't speak, but as the car cruised to a stop at a red light, his bright eyes glanced over at Lewis. A puzzled, confused look painted his handsome face before he looked back down and then back to Lewis.

"I forgot about that spell," Noah admitted, his calm, deliberate voice betraying the faintest hint of—was it embarrassment?

"Keeps prying eyes from seeing your screen, right? Like a privacy panel."

Noah nodded. "Precisely. Allows me to do museum work—"

"—and other work—"

"—and other work, in public."

Lewis arched his eyebrow. "Magicians use iPads, then? I would have thought all of you would be carrying, what are they called—"

"Grimoires?"

"I was going for spell book, but sure, grimoires, right. I thought they were big tomes that smelled like mothballs."

Noah looked at him unpleasantly. It made Lewis's heart sink; less because the sour expression spoiled Noah's looks than because it made him feel small. Like he had said something terribly asinine. Noah quickly composed himself, though, and tapped the top button on his iPad, turning it off. "There are some who still prefer the physicality of a book," he said.

"But not you."

"We exist, live, and breathe in the twenty-first century," Noah said. "Gone are the days when we could walk around with heavy, thick books without attracting curiosity and indignation. Casters have to adapt. Magic has to adapt. It always has. I'm not exactly sure why there is such hesitation to adapt this time, but alas." He waved his hand dismissively.

"I imagine they are unwieldy. Spell—grimoires," Lewis corrected.

"You're right. Most people aren't carrying around first editions of *Les Misérables*, no. Still, a grimoire was a spellcaster's lifeline back in the day. Eventually, casters opted to memorize a set of spells for whatever mission or need they had. Far easier to know six or seven utilitarian spells you can cast in a heartbeat rather than carry a clunky book you have to flip through."

"However," Noah said, shifting his weight, "some still do. They like the notion of having their whole magical knowledge at the ready."

"Like someone who prefers physical over audio or digital books."

"Correct. You've probably seen them, honestly."

Lewis arched a brow. Noah attempted to return to his iPad but caught the inquisitive look Lewis gave him.

"The type of mage who still uses a grimoire has a look about them. They look out of place. A little sketchy. I think Americans might call them hipsters," he informed Lewis. "They are usually carrying a large book or two, but the book is magicked. It might look like a copy of *Infinite Jest*, or Chaucer, or a collection of Emily Dickinson's works, but it's all an illusion."

"But nobody actually reads *Infinite Jest*."

"Exactly."

"What would it be for you? If you weren't so modern and evolved." Lewis grinned.

For a moment, the prim and proper facade that lay draped

over Noah's shoulders like an elegant shawl frayed. There was an owlishness to his eyes that made Lewis wonder if no one ever asked him such a personal question. The way Noah paused, tapping idly at the black screen, confirmed it.

"*Ramayana.*"

"I'm sorry?"

"It's an Indian epic. It follows Rama, the virtuous prince of Ayodhya, who is exiled to the forest for fourteen years along with his devoted wife, Sita, and loyal brother, Lakshmana." Noah paused. "My mother used to read it to me when I was young."

And then Noah glanced back at his iPad, ending the conversation. That was as much information about his past Noah was going to offer up at this time. Another question formed in Lewis's mind, but he held back—not because it wasn't worth asking, but because he had a feeling Noah wouldn't give any more information about himself for free.

"Ask me," Noah said, as if reading his thoughts. He crossed his legs, a hint of light purple sock peeking out from under the hem of his dark dress trousers. "It's going to eat away at you if you don't."

There was some truth in that, but it didn't make Lewis's words feel any more natural.

"I read somewhere that witches use grimoires. Are you all witches?"

Noah shifted in the seat, half-facing Lewis. "That's not a stupid question," he said coolly. "In fact it's only logical, considering everything you've seen today. But no, we aren't witches. Casters, that's what we prefer to call ourselves."

The car cruised to a stop, so smoothly that Lewis barely noticed until Noah unclipped his seatbelt and slipped out the door. Lewis followed, squinting slightly as he exited the dark interior of the car. His brown eyes scanned the street around them. It looked like any city back home in the States: people on their way to whatever and wherever, without much of a care about anyone around them. None of them seemed to notice him and Noah. This seemed odd to him; perhaps absurdly, he had assumed he would look different to passersby—dripping visibly with magic, or at least with the sticky effects of it from his experience with *The Drowning*. But, it seemed, he was just a normal, everyday boy once again. Nothing special, nothing different.

"Casters are a little different from witches," Noah continued, stepping along the sidewalk. "If you're really interested—"

"I am," Lewis said without hesitation. "Interested in learning more. Everything I can."

Noah's eyes fixed on him, as if looking for something Lewis could not even guess. "You should hold that thought until after you've gotten some rest," he said. "You're here for a task, remember. Once it's done, you might discover this world of which you thought you wanted to be a part is in fact nothing you want." He looked away. "In fact, I wouldn't blame you if you ran for the hills."

Noah walked on for a moment, Lewis following speechless in his wake; then he indicated the building in front of them. "First things first," he said. "Your new home."

There was, on first glance, nothing notable about it. Another building; an apartment complex, he guessed—a block of flats, they'd call it here—with a black door, six or so rows of windows, and rust-colored brick walls.

"This is the Contract House," Noah said, gesturing toward the door. "I think in America you would call it a safe house. Individuals from across the world who decide to partner with the museum are given a place here while they work with us."

"*With* you?" Lewis asked. "Not *for* you?"

Noah cut him a sharp glance, and Lewis knew he wasn't wrong. "With you" had an implication there was some mutually agreed-upon decision to work together. "For you" seemed more correct. The sun never set on the British Empire back in the day.

That didn't come from collaboration and camaraderie. That came from a refined boot on the back of a nation's throat.

He debated saying all of that to Noah, but they were in a good place now. And something told him Noah knew, anyway. Even if he consciously decided to turn the other cheek.

Noah didn't flinch; Lewis hadn't really expected him to. "With us," he said. "The choice wasn't forced upon you, Lewis. You were offered, and you accepted."

Lewis couldn't argue with that, but he wondered if he was a special case—or if, like the iPad, this was more a vestige of twenty-first-century thinking and hadn't always been the case. Either way, he nodded to Noah, who in turn gestured for Lewis to join him where he stood, an arm's length from the door. Lewis stepped up without hesitation. Noah flexed his right hand, stretching the fingers out so they curled slightly backward. "Put your palm against the door," he said.

Only then did Lewis consider he might not want to obey without question. But he trusted Noah enough to do this—at least, for now. Without a word, he pressed his palm against the black wood. He flicked his eyes up and down the sidewalk, expecting to see some passerby staring at these two men caressing a door; but again, no one seemed to notice or care. Perhaps this was why you put a safe house in the middle of one of the biggest cities in the world. There was privacy in anonymity.

Suddenly he felt warmth pooling around his hand. The heat matched his own body temperature within moments. It was soon impossible for him to distinguish the wood from his own flesh, as if he and the building were one. His senses blurred. He could feel the gaps in the wood, sense the age of the building. The rumbling of the Blitz that had rattled its bones. The great fire of 1666 that licked at its wood. Every moment this house had stood, all its experiences, passed through him in a matter of seconds. Filled him. Overwhelmed him. Fused with him.

As quickly as the sensation came, it passed. The wood was cooling again. His senses sharpened, and something felt hollow—as if a part of him had been surgically and stealthily removed, and he would never get it back.

"It'll pass," Noah said, again before Lewis could speak. "Congratulations. The house has accepted your contract."

The door unlatched by itself. A hiss of air, like pressure being released or a gasp being exhaled, puffed outward as the door slowly creaked open, revealing not a hallway, but a portal directly to the interior of a one-room apartment, modestly designed. Noah stepped inside; Lewis followed without having to be told. The moment he stepped over the threshold, the door sealed itself behind him with a hiss. He saw, under the gap of the door, the passing of shadows; the sounds of people and traffic drifted in

"A Contract House has an infinite number of rooms," Noah said.

"But only one front door?" Lewis asked. "How does that work?"

"The door is attuned to each guest," Noah said. "When *you* open it, it will lead only to your room. Any other guest here, under contract of the museum, will have access to their room and their room alone."

"You walked into my room easily enough."

"I'm not a guest," Noah said dryly. "As agents of the museum, Evangeline and I have access to any room in the house." He began to pace the perimeter of the room. His steps were measured and even. His fingers danced over the wood-grain bookshelf. Lewis followed with his eyes and was mildly surprised to recognize the books: favorites from his childhood, many of them, and a selection of art theory books. The flat had designed itself to make him feel at home, he thought.

"The whole point is to retain anonymity," Noah continued. "There's no chance of running into any of your fellow guests. No one will know you're here, and vice versa."

"What if I try to leave at the same time as another guest? Say I head out to get some fries." Lewis smiled. "Or chips, rather."

Noah was stone-faced. "That won't happen," he said. "The house will offset both your departures. You might stumble over the rug, the water faucet might turn on, or a sound distract you or the other guest. Small things. Inconsequential things."

He had completed his circuit of the flat and stood facing Lewis, only a foot or so in front of him. "Bathroom is to the right. The window looks out to the street. It doesn't open. You can look out, but no one can look in." He seemed to hesitate.

"There's more?"

"You are now connected to the Contract House," Noah said. "For as long as your employment with the museum lasts, the house and you will be intrinsically bound. You need only to think about returning here when passing through a door—any door, anywhere, no matter how far from home—and it will lead you back to this room."

"*Any* door?"

"Wherever you are in the world," Noah said. "The house will also provide you anything you need, within reason, simply by thinking it."

Lewis whistled low. This was powerful magic.

"The split second it takes to pass through a doorway might make the difference between life and death," Noah said. "If things get bad."

"Do you expect them to?"

Noah fell silent. Darkness, like the passing of a storm, washed over his handsome features. "Director Thompson is a powerful channeler. One of the best I've ever seen. And her skills navigating the bureaucratic red tape of the museum are even more impressive. I would never second-guess her decisions."

So . . . you're not going to answer my question? "I sense a *but* coming."

"*But*," Noah said with a sigh, "I'm worried she was a bit too hasty with you. She brought you on board without giving you the full story."

Lewis nodded. It was clear that Evangeline wanted something from him—that his position here, ordained by whatever powers, wasn't simply coincidence. He should have questioned her offer a bit more; but he had been taken in by the idea that he was *needed*. That he was *special*—even if he didn't see it in himself. It galled him to admit it, but in the moment he had been flattered. No one ever saw things in him. Not investors. Not lovers. Barely even friends.

And now it was too late. He had allowed himself to be dazzled by the promise of magic, without considering the dangers working for the museum might hold. Now the contract had been signed. And Evangeline didn't seem like someone with whom you went back on a deal.

He saw Noah looking at him. "I'll be fine," he said.

"I applaud your desire to be involved."

"I handled myself against *The Drowning*," he noted defensively.

"You got lucky," Noah replied. "And you almost drowned in the process. If I hadn't been there to heal you—"

"—but you were."

"That's not the point." Noah sighed again, pinching the bridge of his nose. "Magic was there—this time. I was there—this time. But what about next time? What if we get separated? What if the next painting is more powerful? It's reasonable to assume that each one will be stronger and more dangerous than the last. We barely survived this one."

"Then I guess we have to just make sure we survive the next one too."

Before Noah could respond, a thump to the right of them attracted both of their attention. A book had fallen off the shelf, landing right side up.

Lewis walked over, picking up a thick red book with black binding from where it had landed.

"*The Art of Magic*—Volume 3, Spiritual Edition, 1 of 3."

"It's a good book. Required reading for senior agents," Noah informed him. "Chapter 23, I believe, through Chapter 27 focuses on bloodline traits. You should read it. Might help you."

"Seems the house wants me to succeed." Lewis smiled. "And I reckon we should trust a sentient home, don't you think?"

Noah pursed his lips into a thin line. *Handsome*, Lewis thought yet again. Even angry. Before Lewis could gather the nerve to speak, Noah stepped past him and opened the door, the city street just a few steps away.

"I know better than most what fighting these things can cost you, Lewis. I wouldn't wish them on anyone. I have my duty. I took an oath when I joined the museum." He fell still for a moment. "You don't have that duty, not in the same way. You can leave at any time. Say the word, and I'll spirit you home."

"I don't think Evangeline would like that, considering how valuable and important she says I am to this."

"I'll deal with her. I won't have another unwilling participant's blood on my hands," Noah said. "Not if I can help it."

His voice felt heavy against Lewis's ears; as if Noah's words bound them both to some secret, some promise of mutually assured destruction if either of them mentioned this conversation to anyone else.

There was so much he wanted to dig into there, so much he wanted to know about what Noah knew and, perhaps as important, why Noah felt so keen on protecting Lewis. If nothing else, he liked that someone was concerned about him. Before he could continue, though, Noah spoke.

"Before I forget," Noah said, "your wallet, please."

Lewis was curious, but obeyed, fishing the worn billfold from his back pocket and placing it in Noah's outstretched palm. Noah made a sign with his index and forefinger, then traced a triangle on the leather while murmuring under his breath; Lewis couldn't quite make out the words, though he thought he heard snatches of French, German, and English. Noah bisected the triangle with a line, then repeated the gestures and the incantation twice more. The whole process took perhaps half a minute.

"Your wallet has been magicked to link to our coffers," Noah said. "Swiping your card will draw from a private fund, not from your bank account, and be untraceable to anyone watching."

Lewis had grown up relatively poor. When he reached adulthood, not much had exactly changed. It was why he'd been so adamant about having his student debt paid off. So the idea of not having to worry about money—for however long that lasted—was possibly even less comprehensible than the idea of magic itself.

Noah seemed to see all this pass along Lewis's face, and gave him an understanding smile. He handed the wallet back and stepped into the street. He turned one last time before pulling the door shut behind him. "Welcome to London Town, Lewis."

Seven

WHAT THE HELL DID I AGREE TO?

Soon after Noah left, the high of . . . well, everything that had happened over the past few hours subsided and found equilibrium with his own natural state of skepticism and concern. Here he was, in London, with no way of getting home—not easily, at least—and seemingly the inability to decide, on his own, if and when he wanted to leave.

He knew this because he tried.

The Contract House was a stubborn, and actually living, thing. When Lewis first tried to open the front door and exit, the house made the doorknob warm, like a canine putting its fangs on someone's hand but not clamping down. When Lewis wouldn't budge, the house shuddered, hissed, even.

"Okay, then," Lewis said, looking around. "So, you're going to be like that."

As the floorboards creaked and the house hissed, the expansion of air sounded like someone speaking in a single breath.

Not yet.

But Noah's facts about the house were correct. Anything he wanted did appear. Once he had decided that whatever tit-for-tat arguments he was going to have with the Contract House were going to end in him being sorely disappointed, Lewis settled for trying to make it his own.

Wandering into the small kitchen, which was more cramped than the kitchen in Lewis's Baltimore apartment, he found an empty fridge with a note on the small whiteboard clipped to it.

"Instruct Me," it read in big blocky black letters, reminding him of *drink me* from Alice's adventures.

That didn't end well for her, though, if he remembered correctly. But what did he have to lose?

"BLT on rye with a peach soda?"

The words on the board disappeared, as if someone was wiping them clean, before, without the use of the small marker attached to it, new words appeared.

Coming right up.

A moment later, the fridge door swung open, giving Lewis barely enough time to step back. Sitting in the middle of the rack was exactly what Lewis had ordered, including the soda. The sandwich had the crust cut off too.

Exactly how I like it.

"Thank you," Lewis said awkwardly, in a half whisper under his breath.

Taking the sandwich and drink, he made his way back into the main room. He debated between sitting on his twin-size bed, or at the desk, but opted for the latter—especially since there was a piece of paper that had not been there before.

Lewis put the plate and glass bottle down on the bedside table, half of the sandwich in one hand, reaching for the note. But before he could, it took flight, suspending itself above the desk. The note shot off like a rocket, spinning twice around Lewis before stopping a full 180 degrees away from its original position, forcing Lewis to turn around.

Spinning on his heels, he saw the paper fold on itself, then unfold, as if more of it was hidden beneath the folds. As the paper folded and unfolded, with each iteration it grew in size, quickly taking an origami-like form of a facsimile of a person.

A facsimile of Noah.

"Lewis," the paper version of Noah spoke, its voice raspy. "I have been called away on some important business. I expect I will return by the end of the week . . ."

Lewis pulled out his waterlogged phone. Frowning, he glanced over to the mirror.

"What day is it?" he asked the house.

The mirror rippled, a word appearing—*Wednesday*.

"Great."

Noah continued.

"Please use this time to familiarize yourself with the Contract House and with the beginnings of magic that will aid you in our journey to find the other Macabre. I do not expect you to be an agent, nor to start performing any kind of spells, but a basic understanding will be useful. I'll update you if my trip is extended. Remember, the Contract House is here to serve you."

With that, the paper version of his . . . bodyguard rolled its shoulders and exploded into flames.

"Jesus," Lewis muttered, taking a step back as the fire burned hot and white. The flames never left the borders of the carpet, the soot even sinking into the fabric as if it was being absorbed back into the earth from whence it came.

As Lewis slowly chewed on the first half of his meal, he couldn't help but wonder: *Wouldn't a phone call have been easier?* Perhaps something he'd understand if he started reading.

Munching on his food, carrying the plate with him, he walked over to the bookshelf, scanning it. His eyes flittered over to the book that had fallen, which he had placed on the upper right-hand corner of the table.

"Let's get started."

Lewis quickly learned the ins and outs of the Contract House. For one, "the Contract House," aside from being a mouthful, was not the name it preferred; that was "Abernathy," or "the Abernathy Estate," if he wanted to be formal.

"Nice to meet you, Abernathy."

The house seemed to settle around him, as if agreeing it was nice to meet it.

In less than a day, his life had sped up to one hundred miles per hour. It was a relief, this change of pace. Something else to think about, to focus on, besides magical paintings and danger and—he found himself thinking about this a bit more than he would have expected—where Noah was. He needed to turn off that part of his brain, if only for a moment, so that he could try to make sense of everything from a rational state of mind. And within the home—his home, for the time being—Lewis was safe and sound. That was enough for now.

On Lewis's second night in the flat, he wondered aloud about the building's history; when he awoke the next morning, a book had materialized on his chest while sleeping—a slim biography of the second director of the British Museum, George Abernathy. It was he who had ordered the creation of the Contract House in 1802, by fusing his soul with a home that had a storied history, roughly thirty years after the Cursed Antiquities Department was founded and nearly fifty years after the creation of the museum itself. Abernathy had served the shortest tenure of any of the museum's directors, only six months. What Lewis's little book made plain—what, apparently, the official biographies left out—was that working the magic that set the Contract House into being had killed him.

Lewis took an evening break to shower, get another meal from the kitchen—clam chowder this time—and picked up the book again.

"Does this mean your soul is Abernathy?" he asked the room. "Like you're possessed in some way?"

The house didn't answer, but it didn't contradict him either. No flicker of lights. No shudder of windows. Perhaps it didn't know, Lewis thought. How sad. He would ask Noah next time he saw him.

The good news was, once he had finished *The History of Contract Homes*, *A Beginner's Guide to Magical Properties*, and *A History of Magic: Western Edition*, the glass fogged up once more, a single note appearing.

You may leave as you wish and return as you wish.

Noah's spell on his wallet, as he learned from the books the house summoned on his behalf, was called Plutus's Mark. As promised, it had activated the moment he left. Swipe after swipe at Nando's, Primark, Baileys Fish and Chips, and Cinemark, and the card was never declined.

When Noah finally did knock on the fifth day, Lewis half expected a lecture about his extravagant shopping. He hesitated, scanning the room and grimacing at the mess he had left, a tornado of processed food containers in his wake. Abernathy hadn't cleaned up after him, though it was fully capable of doing so; perhaps it assumed that Lewis, as a creative, thrived in the mess.

Well, I do . . .

But that wasn't the point.

"Give me a second," he called, slipping on a pair of joggers and a loose-fit T-shirt. Lewis wasn't exactly sure when his clothes had appeared from his hotel room, but when he opened the closet after his first shower, everything was there. Laid out exactly how it was in his British hotel room.

He did his best to scrape everything into the modestly sized trash bin, then put the bin in the closet. He'd barely had time to shut the closet before the front door forced itself open and Noah swept in.

"I thought no one could enter this place but me?" Lewis said.

"I did mention before that as agents of the museum, Evangeline and I have access to any room in the Contract House," Noah corrected. "Good morning, by the way."

Lewis ignored him. "I get that, but you could have at least told me you were coming or something. What if I had been . . ."

"Been what?" Noah asked, arching his brow.

Lewis had many words he could fit in there. Walking around naked from showering, getting dressed . . . other, more intimate things.

That was the wrong thought, though. It made his gaze avert and his cheeks burn hard. The mirror fogged up again.

Lotion and tissues are in the bathroom, the mirror read.

Noah's eyes flickered over to it, paused, then turned back to Lewis. "Really?"

"I didn't tell it to say that!"

"It reads your mind." Noah scanned the room for a moment, his eyes landing on nothing in particular, but Lewis knew he was judging. He had the face of someone who judged. "But yes," he said, "all agents are bonded to their informants' rooms."

Lewis found it a bit odd Noah wasn't bound to *him* directly. If something happened to Lewis when Noah wasn't here, of what use was that to the museum? He searched for a way to ask the question that wouldn't sound needy. Finding none, he pushed the thought aside and took a good look at Noah, realizing that he had been a bit dazed the first time he met him—magical paintings and all—and then it had been nighttime. Here, now, Noah stood in his room in daylight, and Lewis had a chance to take him in.

He looked different, somehow. There was nothing particular that stood out; every strand of hair was in place, and his suit, the color of metal shavings, fit his sinewy body perfectly. But his aura, for lack of a better word, seemed off. His footsteps seemed heavier. He appeared tired, exhausted even. His voice, which usually carried an undercurrent of annoyance that Lewis had taken for cockiness, was curt and direct, as if speaking was a great effort.

"Long night? Or long few days, rather?"

At first, Noah didn't answer, only appraised the clutter strewn about the room; Lewis could only wonder what assumptions about him Noah was making in the moment. Then he shook his head as if to clear it. "Yes," he said distractedly. "It's why I'm here. You're needed at the museum. We're needed."

That meant whatever had him like this was connected to the Macabre. "Let me get my shoes," Lewis said. Sitting on the edge of the bed, he slipped his feet, sockless, into his worn sneakers, so worn that there was no need to tie or untie them.

"So, you found one?" he asked.

"Not me; one of our scouts. The museum has many eyes and ears. Junior agents, aspiring agents, people like you who work with us to scout anomalies across the world within their networks and professions. We take all of that into consideration when examining the weirdness in the world." He closed his eyes for a moment. "But yes, we found one."

A feeling like the crackling of a live wire flooded through Lewis's body. It felt like something wrapping tightly around his inner core, constricting him; a mix of excitement and terror all at once. A hot itch of pain bloomed again in his throat. That moment, when he had been on the edge of death, rose up in his memory. The painting—*The Drowning*—had caused that. Was still causing that, to some degree.

What would the next one cause?

"You don't have to come, you know," Noah said softly—more softly than Lewis had ever expected.

But Lewis shook his head. There was no turning back now. "Just let me grab my coat."

◆

"**DO YOU KNOW** how to make a real cup of tea, Lewis?"

It was an hour later, and they were at the museum, having been ushered into Evangeline's office. They had been sitting for fully half a minute, waiting for her to acknowledge their presence. Noah seemed unfazed by waiting; but Lewis felt wrong-footed. "Tea?" he said, puzzled. "Water, lemon, tea bag, I suppose? I'm more of a coffee drinker."

She gazed at him levelly, humming low in her throat. Her office felt different somehow from how it had a few days before—the sweet smell, the way Lewis's body felt almost weightless here. There had to be magic at play: barriers to keep watchful eyes away, sensors to detect the honesty of anyone who spoke in her presence, perhaps safeguards for her own life. Lewis flicked his eyes around the room, hoping to pick up *something*—a rune, a marker, some sign of magic. But there was nothing he could identify, and he found himself disappointed. He'd been studying those books for almost a week and wanted to put what he'd been learning to the test.

Evangeline rose, seeming taller, more imposing than before. She drifted over to a small table in the corner and gave a flick of her hand; a cupboard opened on its own, its items dancing lazily in the air in a coordinated routine.

"Boil the water, pour it over the tea bag, and let it steep," she said. "Always pour the water over the tea bag. Never add the bag to the water."

"Does it matter?"

"Does it matter?" she repeated with a chuckle. "Of course, it matters. Everything matters. The smallest of choices matter. They can be the difference between life and death. Your actions, or the lack thereof, have consequences for yourself and others, Lewis."

It struck him what magic the room held came from Evangeline's presence in it. Magic was woven into the bookcase, the fabric of the carpet—even the air—so perfectly most people would miss its presence. Perhaps even Noah.

"Take this tea, for example," she continued. "The way you prepare it determines whether the flavors burst out, or are muted, which can determine whether your guests have a good experience, or the time together is sullied. What if this meeting of minds would determine an allegiance?"

"I'm not sure I'd want to align myself with someone who would decide whether or not to work with me based on the quality of the beverage on offer."

"If you think people aren't making important decisions for trivial reasons, you don't understand how the world works," she said firmly. She shifted her glance, and a bubbling teakettle glided through the air to pour itself over three different cups rotating on a magical lazy susan. Wisps of steam rose like wishes cast hopefully to the sky.

"Take you, for example," she said. "I decided in a split second whether you would be an asset or a liability to us, simply by how you approached *The Drowning*. I made a decision today whether you should join us on the mission to deal with this new painting simply by how you conducted yourself in this room."

"And what have you decided?" With one eye, he watched the cups and saucers float effortlessly to the table on his right, arranging themselves in a pyramid while the tea steeped.

Evangeline sat down again behind her desk and opened a folder. "Have you ever been to Australia?"

The question was absurd. He was a kid from Baltimore; she may as well have been asking if he'd been to the moon. But he put on his best poker face. "Always wanted to go," he drawled, "but I never could find the money." He saw a tiny smile flicker over Noah's face and saw him tilt his head to prevent Evangeline from seeing it.

"Beautiful country," said Evangeline. "Mind you, Perth isn't the most welcoming place in the country, but the waters! That's something every person should see at one point in their life." She snapped the folder shut. "But this won't be your time, I'm afraid."

Lewis felt as if he'd been slapped. Beside him, Noah's face betrayed his surprise. "I'm sorry," Lewis said, leaning forward. "But didn't you just tell me a few days ago how you needed me?"

"That still stands," she said.

"And how useful I am in purifying these paintings?"

"Correct."

"Then why shouldn't I go with you?" He looked at Noah, who only stared helplessly, then back to Evangeline.

"It's for that exact reason you're not going," she said. "Do you know how long we've been searching for someone who can do what you can do? It's not just being a descendant of Dumont that matters, Lewis. Bloodline traits don't appear with every offspring. Not with enough concentration to be useful. A person needs to have the right disposition to wield magic. The right temperament to hear its call. Not everyone born with the spark ignites. The ingredients simply aren't enough.

"We can't risk losing that ability just because you want to go on a field trip." She laid her hands flat on the desk. "This work holds dangers even I cannot foresee, Lewis. The museum is a sanctuary, not a fortress. Our people have talent and are dedicated to our cause, yes—but we have to assume there are leaks. I imagine word has already spread that we have something, or rather someone, who can find the Macabre—and more importantly, destroy them. People will be interested in that. People who can hurt you. You're safer here."

"I think we threw safety out the window when you made me touch that painting," Lewis argued.

"I must agree, Director," Noah said; he spoke slowly, uncertainly. "Lewis proved himself with *The Drowning*."

"I'm not questioning that," she said with a sigh. "But that was in a controlled environment. There were protections in place—sigils and charms that kept the painting subdued and gave us an advantage. In the field, we'll have none of that. You, out of all of us, know how these paintings can surprise you. Anything can happen to turn the tide of battle in an instant."

Noah shifted uncomfortably in his chair but said nothing, and Lewis realized he would have to continue this argument alone. "Madam Director," he said, turning to Evangeline. "You asked me before if I wanted to help in the work. And I do. That's why I stayed. I never would have agreed if I'd known I was going to sit around in Abernathy House waiting for someone to need me."

"Think of it as a vacation," Evangeline said; she gestured toward the tea, indicating that it had finished steeping. "You can catch up on your art, see London. A paid artistic residency. Many people would—"

"I don't want a fucking residency," Lewis hissed, more sharply than he'd intended. Evangeline's sculpted eyebrow rose ever so slightly. He saw Noah's eyes cut over to him in silent warning: *Careful*. A warning that didn't stay silent for long.

Don't overextend your hand, Noah's voice whispered in his mind. Lewis knew better than to look over at him, to signal to Evangeline, if she didn't already know, that Noah was coaching him telepathically.

He did roll his shoulders, though, as if a chill had trickled down his spine. Would he ever get used to things like, well, *that*?

Evangeline values strength as much as logic. Show her why you're useful, not just in skill, but in fortitude. It is better to impress her but make an enemy than to be unmemorable.

Lewis rose and stepped toward the small table, picking up the teacup closest to him. He took a slow sip; it warmed him and more importantly gave him a moment to think. But he noticed it was missing something. If the British didn't use lemon, what *did* they add to the leaf juice?

"I did what you asked of me with *The Drowning*," he said, keeping his voice even. "And I did it without any backup or experience.

Now that I have one of these things under my belt, think of how useful I can be."

"You *are* useful." Evangeline sighed, a tinge of annoyance in her voice. "Alive. Safe. *Here.* Putting you in the field is a liability."

She cut her eyes toward Noah, as if in a command to speak.

"I was looking for this painting while you were in the Contract House," he explained to Lewis. "Took a lot of contacts and sway, but I found it. That wasn't easy. I had to go places, do things I couldn't have done with you with me."

"Because what? I don't know magic? I'll study up, then. Read."

I thought you were on my side, Lewis said.

Fight for what you want, Noah replied.

"Because it's too dangerous," Evangeline repeated. "We're talking in circles here. What you did last week was incredible," she said. "No one will doubt that. And if, when this is all done, you want to learn the ways of magic and become an agent, I will see to your training myself. But to get to that point, you have to stay alive. You are our greatest weapon thus far against the Macabre. I'm not going to risk losing that because you can't keep your ego in check."

"Just let me help put us on the right track," Lewis interjected. "Let me go, or I'm returning to Baltimore."

A chill draped itself over the room, in a way Lewis wasn't sure stemmed from his own nervousness or actual magic. Evangeline's face settled into something sharp and cold, unblinking, studying him.

"Excuse me?"

"You *need* me," Lewis said, his voice cracking before he cleared his throat and continued. "And I'm making my demands. You want me to help you, I want to be in the field."

"That wasn't what we agreed upon."

"And I didn't agree to just sit in a magical house eating sandwiches. Things change."

He wasn't sure how Evangeline would react to a threat, but he saw no other option. She was clearly a woman who responded to power and confidence. Lewis had neither in any great supply, but he could fake them when he needed to. Lewis firmly believed that any artist could.

But it was more than that. The need to be involved with something big, to change the world? This was what an artist dreamed of. Even if he had to shed his own blood, he'd be putting his mark on the world. Irrevocably changing the landscape to something better, like a painter using swatches of blues and blacks to change the mood of their masterpiece. This would be the greatest masterpiece of all time. Making the world better.

How could he pass that up?

Evangeline didn't speak for a moment, like she was deciding if she wanted to blast him with enough magic to send him flying through decades or was mulling over his words. Lewis wasn't sure which one, but the former seemed more likely than the latter.

"Do you know what business we're in, Lewis?" She didn't wait for him to answer. "The business of keeping people alive. The purpose of our work is to save human lives. Greater men and women have come before you, Lewis, full of confidence in their ability to handle the Macabre. Agents who had trained for months, years, decades even. Talented, intelligent casters—world-renowned, some of them." She took up a teacup. "And when they came face-to-face with the paintings, they died. Struck down in moments."

"I'm not saying I'm better than them—"

"But aren't you? In so many words. You think your . . . whatever this is," she said, gesturing at him in a vague, dismissive motion, "trumps my years of experience, the history of missions like this we have under our belt. Because of, what, a feeling you have, a desire to be someone more than you are? My decision is final and—"

I'll take over now, Noah whispered mentally.

"A test," Noah interrupted.

Evangeline paused, turning her head slowly to Noah. "Pardon?"

"That's how we can determine whether Lewis is ready for fieldwork. We set him a test and see how he fares against the next painting." He straightened his jacket. "I'll evaluate him myself. We do field tests for junior agents, and you just said yourself he has the talents to become one. We can simply accelerate the process."

Evangeline gazed at Noah, annoyance flashing like lightning across her face. "I cannot fathom why you two don't understand the importance of this. We have the opportunity to neutralize the Macabre for good. Noah, you of all people—"

"My sister would agree with me, Director," Noah said smoothly. "You know how she loved lost causes. After all, I was one."

Lewis took issue with being called a lost cause, but he pushed past it. "There's no unbreakable contract between us. You said yourself, I can change my mind whenever I want. Give me this chance to prove myself in Australia. I'll show you that I'm more useful on the front lines than holed up in some safe house at your beck and call. Give me a reason to stay. Make me feel useful. It's a win-win for you."

Noah joined the two of them at the table, taking the last cup and downing it in one long draft. "Having him with me makes more sense, Director. It's better for him to be there and neutralize the painting rather than us trying to contain it and then bringing it here. It'll be like *The Drowning* all over again."

"And we can't afford that much loss of life," Evangeline muttered.

"Exactly. After all, the Macabre aren't the only artifacts our agents are investigating."

"But they are the most important," she said.

"I know that better than anyone," Noah pushed. "Which is

why I have a personal stake in our success. I won't let anything happen to him."

Lewis could see Evangeline turning Noah's reasoning over in her head as she sipped her lemonless tea. Finally, she said, "One painting. One test. And know that you'll have Celsus's Spell of Vision placed upon you, Noah."

Noah nodded and dropped to one knee, like a knight swearing fealty to his queen. Evangeline put her hand beneath his chin, tilting his head back; then with her fingers she spread wide the top and bottom lids of his right eye till Lewis could see nearly the full sphere of his eyeball.

Evangeline began tracing symbols in the air a mere inch or so from Noah's eye. There was, however, apparently no incantation associated with the gestures, for as she worked she spoke to Lewis in a matter-of-fact tone. "Celsus's spell allows someone to see through the eyes of another and thus obtain information. It's usually used for spy craft, piggybacking on an unsuspecting person's vision to gather information without their knowledge." She completed her operation on Noah's right eye and paused speaking to pull back the lids of his left. "We also use it to evaluate missions without the filter of memory," she said, again cutting invisible figures in the air uncomfortably close to Noah's eye. Noah struggled to remain motionless; his fist clenched three times before stilling. "If you succeed in getting the painting back, I'll review what Noah saw and evaluate your field performance. Then we'll decide what happens next."

Lewis nodded, definitely more intrigued than concerned. Evangeline finished her gestures, and Noah rose to his feet, shaking his head like someone who had just put in contact lenses for the first time. Lewis could see a faint glow in the center of his pupils; they shone like a cat's eyes in the dark. The glow lasted only a moment before fading.

"I want to be clear," Evangeline said. "If I decide you are not fit for duty after this, you will remain in London, within Abernathy House, and only leave when I give you permission to do so."

"Because I'm so good at following orders," Lewis said facetiously.

Evangeline was unamused. "You wouldn't have a choice. You've been reading the books?"

"Yes..."

"Then you will know how we will keep you confined," she said. "First, Florence's Kaleidoscope, followed by a restricting spell bound to your very soul, and a tracking spell. Finally, the house will also be commanded to keep you inside. If you should somehow find a way to bypass the house's defenses, the additional spells will cause you a great deal of pain. And there would be no chance of you leaving—or getting far—without us knowing."

"Torture," Lewis concluded.

"Protecting our investment," Evangeline countered. "But you call it what you want, I do not care. That is the agreement. If you do not wish to abide by the rules, I'm more than happy to—"

"I get it," Lewis said. "I wouldn't dream of leaving. But it won't be necessary—I'm going to pass this test."

"Of course." Evangeline smiled, seeming to care little either way as she finished her tea and set down the cup. "Just know that if we *are* forced to take such measures, it's for your protection."

For my power's protection, he thought, but said nothing—he was going to Australia, and that's what mattered.

She then crossed to the door of her office, which stood firmly closed. With a counterclockwise twist of her hand, and a muttering of words that sounded like the crackle of dry kindling, the seams of the door glowed. Lewis could feel a burst of warmth from the gap at the bottom; there was a smell of salt water on the hot, dry air.

Noah looked at him and nodded. They walked to the door. Turning to Evangeline, Noah murmured, "Thank you," then reached out and opened the door.

Before them lay a green park, filled with people; the vibrant-colored skies indicated sunset. The whole scene glowed like the screensaver on a computer. Lewis would never get used to this aspect of magic.

"I hate Australia." Noah sighed. "Every animal there wants to kill you."

"That's just a joke, right?"

"Sure," Noah said, a smile flickering over his face. "We'll go with that."

"Lewis," Evangeline said, once Noah had stepped through.

He turned to face her.

"Milk," she said. "That's what you're supposed to add to tea. It'll taste better."

Eight

NOAH'S EYES WERE SO BLOODSHOT THAT LEWIS THOUGHT EVANGELINE might have done him permanent damage. "You look like you're high," he said matter-of-factly.

Together they sat, almost like two people on a date, in a coffee shop. If one looked at it only through a pinprick hole, a singular moment, that might be true. But, if the view expanded outward, one would see what the coffee shop was attached to: the Art Gallery of Western Australia. With memorabilia and overpriced key chains. But also, coffee. And a great vantage point for people watching.

Noah looked up from the menu. "I've never been high before."

"You're not missing out on much," Lewis said, and immediately regretted it, anticipating where the conversation might go from there; some crude assumption about Americans, an even cruder assumption about drugs and Black people, or some inane question about *The Wire* and was Baltimore really like that.

But when Noah finally spoke, it was none of that. "I'm sorry," he said.

That caught Lewis off guard. Apologies looked different on different people. On some, regret framed their faces well, highlighting their softer features. On others, it rested uncomfortably, like a shirt a size too small. He wasn't sure at first how it suited Noah; and before he had time to decide, a server appeared and a sort of mask came over the agent once more. Instantaneously he performed the role of a wide-eyed tourist, with a grin that lay on the surface of his face but no deeper. He pointed to the menu, asked questions with a lighter tone, engaged the server in a way that bordered on flirting . . . and caused something hot to flare in the center of Lewis's chest. By the time Noah was done and the woman was gone, the mood in the booth had shifted.

"For?" Lewis finally asked.

Noah resettled his weight a half an inch or so.

"Leaving you alone." He paused. "In Abernathy House. I should have given you more information. You're not a prisoner there, Lewis."

Lewis intended to throw a snide comment about how he was certainly starting to feel like one. But Noah was showing vulnerability Lewis wasn't sure he would see again if he took it as a joke. So instead, he gave him a small nod, and moved on.

"Well, seems we both have things to say. I was going to say thank you," Lewis stated flatly. "For standing up for me with Evangeline."

Noah shrugged. "I'm not in the habit of going against what my boss suggests, so do not assume that will happen again."

As he spoke, Noah tapped the side of his face, bringing Lewis's focus back to the faint white ring in his iris—reminding him that Evangeline, as if looking through a crystal ball, could see everything Noah saw, including the movement of Lewis's lips when they talked. Their conversations would not be private; not when they were face-to-face, at least. Lewis almost nodded to show he understood, but instead stilled himself, letting his eyes drift toward the ocean.

Really, what that told Lewis was that he would have to be careful. Was it security theater, her breathing over Noah's shoulder, or was Evangeline actually watching and recording every interaction they had?

Either way, the spell accomplished its goal. And then some.

"Does that usually happen?" Lewis asked slowly, thanking the server when she returned. This time, instead of letting her get a word in edgewise, he cut off the expected next question before she could say it.

"We're good, thanks."

Noah's gaze cut to the server for a moment, then back to Lewis, a smirk twitching against his lips. When she was gone, he replied, sipping his drink.

"Be more specific."

"The spell, the oversight," Lewis said. "Does she not trust you to accomplish your mission without oversight?"

Lewis wasn't surprised when Noah paused before answering. There was subtext there. That in some way Lewis was saying Noah couldn't do his job properly, or at least, was assuming that Evangeline didn't think he could do his job properly. It was a shot across the bow. One he hadn't intended. But there was something not so altruistic about Evangeline that tickled at the back of his head when she cast that spell without even *asking* Noah if he was okay with it.

"Oversight is a common requirement for agents who are going into the field," Noah muttered nonchalantly. "Trust isn't a factor we take into consideration."

"Doesn't that bother you?"

"No, it doesn't. The only thing that matters to me is the success of the mission. But your opinion on the matter doesn't surprise me. You're American."

Lewis frowned. "What does *that* mean?"

"You view the world differently than we do. More of a self-determination point of view. Individualism over the whole. It's what led to you all seeking independence. It's a level of selfishness that guides you." Noah looked upward from the rim of his cup. "Not that that's a bad thing."

His tone made something inside Lewis twitch. "It sure as hell *sounds* like you think it's a bad thing."

"It's an observation, neither good nor bad."

"No, but it's in your tone. I'm the first to admit America isn't great, but—"

"That's an understatement," Noah muttered.

"*But* we're not going to pretend that you're that much better. I'm not even talking about England as a whole. You work at the *British Museum*."

"How astute of you," Noah teased.

"Which is exclusive enough without adding on the fact that you work in a department no one knows exists. You don't get that kind of job without connections.

"Besides"—Lewis shrugged—"you carry yourself like someone who comes from money."

"That's not a crime."

"I never said it was. But you're awfully flippant throwing out there, 'Oh, Americans are all about themselves and not about others. They don't care about the collective. They only care about themselves.'"

"First, that's a terrible impression of me. Second, is anything I said wrong?"

"No," Lewis admitted, "but you threw it like it's a negative. A mark against us."

"Is it not?" Noah sighed, took a moment, and continued. "That level of individuality is what you are known for. The choice to make your own destiny. Americans flaunt it like a badge of honor."

"Again, not sure I understand the negative aspect of choosing your own destiny. This isn't the eighteen hundreds. You can do the same."

"It's not that easy."

"I know where this is going," Lewis muttered. Noah arched his brow, gesturing widely with his arm in a "please continue" motion. So he did.

"You left me alone in the Contract House. I had a lot of time. I used it to read up on the books you suggested—"

"Gold star for you."

"—but I also researched you and Evangeline."

Noah's eyebrow quirked up just a touch.

"That's right. As much information as I could get. You and your sister aren't just two people with magical talents. The Raos are a powerful family in India. Magical lineage that goes back several decades. Not only that, your parents are wealthy. Major players in the telecoms space."

"What's your point?"

"My point is that you're not some 'woe is me' individual like you're making it sound. You might have had expectations and demands, like everyone does, but you're not someone who has ever been forced into a situation. If magic doesn't pan out, if Evangeline fires you, you can always go back to India. Work for the—what's it called—IMGC?"

Noah didn't answer, simply set his jaw tightly.

"Again, I'm not saying you haven't had it hard. Everyone has hardship in their life. A varying degree, sure, but no one's life is perfect. But I'm not going to sit here and pretend, from what I've seen, that working for Evangeline is some walk in the park.

"But I'm also not going to let you sit across from me and slap across my face these preconceived ideas that I have it better than you based on your ideas about Americans. I'm still Black and gay in America. And I don't expect you to understand that, but it fucking sucks."

Noah hummed, barely audible over the rumble of the café. Lewis braced himself for what might come next. A snide comment about how Lewis didn't know better, how ignorant he was, or something. He had heard it time and time again on his home soil.

But instead, Noah turned his head toward a loud-speaking woman with a man who walked by their table. His eyes followed them, and so did Lewis's, watching how they approached the doorway and had their tickets scanned.

"Daniel and Amy Harte," Noah said quietly.

"What?"

"Those two," Noah said, gesturing with a small motion of his head. "Art collectors. When Amy got a cancer diagnosis ten years ago, they made it their mission to see as much of the world as they could in the time they had left together and ended up falling in love with this place. Two things happened in succession: Daniel's grandmother died, leaving him a large inheritance, and Amy went into remission. With their new wealth, they settled in Australia and began a new life, surrounding themselves with art."

So, they were just going to glide right past their discussion, huh? As if it never happened? Back to work, then, Lewis thought. "And they got a Macabre, I'm guessing?"

Noah nodded. "And Amy's cancer is back."

Lewis swallowed thickly. Memories flooded his mind: the way his father called him, the panicked voicemails, seeing his mother lying in the hospital bed . . . how quickly it had all come. In some ways, Lewis thought in the back of his mind, that was a kindness. It was swift for his mother.

But the idea of it lingering? A painting causing this to last, pulling life from a person, feeding off it? It was cruel.

"How do you know the cancer is back?"

"Medical records aren't that hard to get," Noah said. "Publicly, England and Australia's bureaucratic ties are no more than historical . . ."

"But under the surface, there are some magical bonds that keep the two nations connected?"

Noah nodded. "Any agent can get anything they need from the government of a previous commonwealth or current one. It is how it was so easy for Evangeline and me to find you."

"And here we thought London was the most surveilled city in the world simply because of the cameras."

Noah nodded.

"How long does she have?" Lewis asked.

"Our guess is one, maybe two years," Noah said, then hesitated. "But—and this is going to sound cruel, and I do apologize—it doesn't matter."

"Because you're hoping that if we destroy the Macabre, her symptoms will stop?"

"No." He shook his head.

"What do you mean?"

"I mean we don't care about that."

Lewis was taken aback. "Wait, sorry—*what?*"

Noah sighed. He raised two fingers—the universal gesture for the check—and the bubbly server made her way to their booth. Lewis looked at her; here was someone who knew nothing of the dark underbelly of the world. She was too happy. Too pure, too welcoming. You could always tell by their eyes.

"Our priority is the painting, Lewis. You know this. We have to ensure, no matter what, we neutralize that Macabre."

"And then after that we can help her?"

Noah shook his head.

"Don't. Don't give me that. You're magicians. You can do anything."

"Not *anything*. If you read—"

"I know about fucking semantics," he hissed. "You know what I meant, Noah. Helping one woman not have cancer. Her life is worth saving, no matter the cost."

"Where does it stop, Lewis? Who do we not help or who do we help next? Ending the Macabre will help protect more people in the long run. Millions over one single life. We neutralize this one, and then we move on to the next. We keep focused on the goal, and we don't get distracted."

"People's lives aren't a *distraction*."

"When the lives of millions are at risk, they are. We cannot tell her anything or change the plan. Because if she finds out, and they uproot their lives like before, the painting might be lost. Again."

Lewis's jaw set tightly. How could Noah weigh one life over another? It seemed unforgivably callous. With each blink he flashed back to his mother in the hospital. Seeing his father openly cry for the first time. If someone could have saved her, told them what was coming . . . they could have handled it differently. Spent their time together differently. Noah had the power to change that.

"I know you don't agree," Noah said, quickly signing the receipt. "But you wanted to be involved."

"I thought fieldwork meant solving problems, not just letting them fester while you observe."

"Sometimes." Noah sighed. "Sometimes it means fighting cursed objects with magic you learned and never thought you'd use. Or it means convincing someone to invite you to their home. That's the only path we can take, sometimes."

Nine

AMY HARTE REMINDED LEWIS OF HIS MOTHER. HER MANNERISMS, THE way she laughed, the smile and the warmth that radiated from her youthful features gave him flashbacks to the photo albums his grandmother had showed him during the last family reunion. There had been a goodness and a warmth in his mother when she was young, burning under her skin like a concealed sun.

She lost that fire sometime after she married Lewis's father. He always meant to ask what had stolen it. He always meant to try and get it back.

That was his justification when following Amy and her husband into the boutique after leaving the café and surveilling them as they browsed the racks. He couldn't save his mother—but maybe there was a way he could save Amy. A metaphorical strike through on a growing ledger of mistakes, his own and others', that he would do anything to go back in time and fix.

You could gather a lot about a person from people watching. Great artists of many disciplines did it; and though Lewis rarely admitted he deserved to be in the same breath as the greats, this was a skill he had that reminded him, even at his lowest of lowest points, that he was a good artist. But there was a sort of honesty that came from watching another person when they had no idea they were being surveilled. They loved each other, the Hartes.

There was no question about it. It pulsed out of them like a beacon, reminding anyone on that frequency that love was possible. It made it hard to swallow, knowing what would happen to Amy—and by extension, Daniel—if Lewis and Noah didn't find some way to change her fate.

It *was* possible. He knew it was. Magic could, as Noah reminded him, bend the fabric of time and space, make gravity and the laws of physics fall to their knees. Could they not find a way to save one woman? If Evangeline was right, and they couldn't save his mother, at least he could save Amy.

Lewis circled Amy and Daniel, studying them from about seven feet away. Close enough he could hear their conversation, but not so close that he was noticeable. He followed them through each room of the AGWA, ignoring the art—which burned at his soul—and stalked his prey. Waiting for the right moment.

Eventually, as the woman showed her husband a blank space on her forearm, tapping it, then pointing to the Frederick McCubbin painting in front of them, and then pointing to the tattoos that stained her flesh, Lewis had an in.

Lewis took a deep breath and bridged the space between them, holding his breath as he approached and letting it out along with the planned sentence.

"Excuse me," he quickly said. "I couldn't help but hear your accents. Are you American?"

"Yes," the man replied warily.

"Me too. Here on vacation."

"Who comes to Perth on vacation?"

"A fellow art lover."

Smooth.

At first, Amy and Daniel didn't speak, only blinked owlishly at Lewis. *Fair*, he thought. He would be put off if someone hijacked his private conversation. He probably would have acted the same if he was in their shoes.

Quick on his feet, Lewis continued. "I've always wanted to see the AGWA. Can't see that in Sydney."

This was to be his first test, Noah had said: finding an in. He had made it sound so simple, like Lewis just had to flick his fingers, say the right words, and secure a written invitation to the Hartes' home. But if there was some magical spell for that purpose, Lewis didn't know it. He would have to rely on the one thing no one had ever accused him of having: charm.

"Any particular piece?" Amy asked, curious.

"I love the whole collection, but I've always wanted to see Rowan's *Floral Study*."

"That's a favorite of mine," she said, eyes softening. "Daniel too."

"It's an incredible piece," Daniel admitted.

"Well, if you can point me in the right direction, I'll get out of your hair—"

"We'll show you," Amy said. "Won't we, Daniel?"

"Of course," Daniel said, and Lewis could see this man would do anything for her even as he sighed.

"I'm Lewis," he introduced himself.

"I'm Amy. This is Daniel."

Lewis held out his hand, and they both shook it. They started to walk together to another part of the gallery.

"As I said, I couldn't help but overhear your accents and what you were discussing. You were talking about adding a tattoo to your forearm, yes?"

Amy nodded, already eager to engage. That was something Lewis had noted a long time ago—most people *want* to interact, as long as it's on *their* level and on *their* interest. To tell their story. And for him, that was all art was: someone's story. Knowing that, and seeing how much Amy was interested—anyone who went to art museums to pick out their next tattoo was his kind of people, Lewis thought—he knew Daniel was sure to follow.

Lewis tilted his head back toward the piece they had been looking at. "*Down On His Luck* is a good piece, but it won't look good on your forearm. The detail will be lost, and considering it's one of Australia's most valued paintings, if you're going to get it, I'd suggest it as a print, or if you're serious, a back piece."

Amy shuddered. Lewis smiled. "Pain, right?"

She nodded. "So much pain!"

"But . . . maybe the one we're about to see might work better?"

And he could see Amy's mind clicking away, letting itself be persuaded. Letting it weigh the negatives he'd just laid out for her against the positives he was suggesting. It helped that he'd always been a fan of the artist they were about to look at, and it didn't hurt that he could tick it off his proverbial artistic checklist of pieces he wanted to see before he died.

"I think you might be right," Amy said as she and Daniel took him to another gallery. When they got there, Lewis smiled. It was exactly as he hoped it would be, and no matter what happened, at least he got to see it in person.

In front of them, no bigger than roughly 11 inches by 8 inches, was a singular watercolor and gouache on paper. Muted backgrounds with fiery reds and warm blues took shape like plant stalks.

"*Floral Study*," Lewis said. "Incredible."

"So was the artist," Amy said. "Marian Ellis Rowan."

"Oh, you don't have to tell me! Rowan, known for her meticulous attention to detail and vivid use of color, presents each bloom with lifelike precision," Lewis expounded. "She was known for showing a different version of a plant's life with her work, showing not only the vitality of a plant but also the beauty of it."

"A representation of life itself."

"Exactly," Lewis continued. "I see you already have a sleeve going on this arm—some Morris, Ruskin, and Mucha—so my thought was expanding on that. You could perhaps combine some of her motifs in a wraparound fashion, showing different facets of life through the language of plants . . ."

"Giving an homage to the human life cycle . . ."

"And to her."

Amy glanced at the piece again, then back at her husband, whose hesitation morphed into an approving handsome smile. It reminded Lewis a bit of Noah's smile. The width of it, the warmth, and how it made him feel tingly inside.

"You have a good eye," Daniel said.

"I'm a trained artist."

God, Lewis hated saying that. It was true enough but felt oxymoronic. *A trained artist.* As if art could be taught. Of course, skills could be sharpened and honed; but art, at its core, was emotional, it was visceral. You could train to get better, but that would only take you so far. Calling himself "a trained artist" seemed to diminish his gift, even more than failing to create any sellable art did.

"I *am* impressed!" Amy's voice was light with glee. "This is perfect. Just what I'd want."

"It wasn't when we walked in," Daniel muttered, but good-naturedly.

She hit him on the shoulder. "I *changed* my mind. Or rather, this young man did." She looked back at Lewis. "And you clocked it by just looking at me? That's talent!"

"I guess my student loans were worth something." He chuckled and relaxed into the conversation. "I'm surprised you two know Rowan. Floral art isn't the hottest topic anymore. Hasn't been since the eighteen hundreds, really."

"We're collectors," Daniel said. "Of course, we know Rowan."

Amy's face clouded over slightly. "My husband speaks too quickly."

Daniel shrugged. "Well, we are."

"Yes, but that isn't what he meant."

It was clear Amy understood art in a way Daniel didn't. They both had a passion for it, but there was space between them, detectable only by those who understood art, but as wide as the universe itself.

Lewis turned his eyes to Amy. She, not Daniel, had established herself as his in, and he wasn't going to lose that. "I think I understand," he said. "It's the beauty of the world, isn't it? The vastness of it? How all of this was just created thanks to a collision of molecules, and everything just so happened to fall into line so perfectly and so beautifully. The way it's random but at the same time preordained—and no one understands it, or can even really try."

"And yet, there's so much natural beauty," Amy said, nodding. "How can the world be so beautiful and so random all at the same time?"

"I think the beauty comes from the randomness," he said. "Anything too structured lacks that sort of—"

"Animalistic rawness?"

"Exactly!" Lewis composed himself. "I'm sorry, I'm making a scene."

A smile slowly spread over Amy's face, further softening her already-soft features. She reached out, squeezing his arm. "There is no reason to be ashamed for falling in love with the world. Life is too short for us to not take at least a few moments to appreciate what's around us."

Lewis's breath hitched a bit. Her touch was surprisingly welcome. How long had it been since someone had touched him? Not carnally; how long since he had let someone in, let someone push through his walls and let their energies crackle against his own? Since before the funeral, at least. And somehow, so easily, Amy had known just what he needed. Again, he couldn't help but compare her to his mother, who had been like that, a brilliant empath. Perhaps that was what he had picked up on before.

An uglier thought occurred: Perhaps that's what had attracted the specific Macabre painting to her, as well. Maybe, in some way that no living human could understand, it had picked up on her empathy and kindness, and that had piqued its hunger, driving it to devour her until not a morsel remained.

There was a part of him that even admitted that, perhaps, this was too easy. Yes, the British Museum helped get him to London. And yes, magic was the reason they were in the right place at the right time.

But this museum, this room, this painting? The ease with which Lewis was able to converse and connect with Amy and Daniel? Had their proximity to the painting, which was connected to Lewis by blood and ancestry, somehow made this all easier? It sounded foolish, but the true limit of magic, Lewis didn't even know. And if that was the case, shouldn't they approach this with more caution and concern?

A thought worth running by Noah next time they connected, Lewis decided, filing it away in the back of his mind, turning his focus back to Amy. Because: At its core? Even if he was right? Lewis had no intention of letting the worst happen.

Amy's eyes flickered to her husband and then back to Lewis. "You say you're on vacation?"

Lewis nodded.

"How long are you staying?"

For as long as needed, he thought. Was that even right? Was there a time limit for dealing with the Macabre? The only limit he could think of was how much time Amy had. Cancer was cruel. Cancer was unkind: Even if it was the Macabre that had brought it back, after some point no modern medicine could stop the train from colliding with its destination. If he was to have any chance of saving her, they would have to move soon. "I leave in a week," he said.

"Oh, excellent," Amy said. She looked at Daniel with her large, almost childlike eyes. An exchange of understanding passed between them, like signals in a relay. It took only seconds. Scholars, Lewis thought, could write volumes about the way the two looked into each other's eyes. No, not scholars: poets.

". . . This might seem a bit forward," Amy finally said. Did he detect a . . . suggestive note in her voice?

Wait . . .

". . . And, please, if it's too weird, feel free to tell me . . ."

Were they about to . . .

". . . My husband and I are having a small gathering of friends tomorrow evening. We run an arts appreciation group for a small group of people—"

"Lost souls," Daniel corrected, with a hint of amusement.

This was really happening, wasn't it? Lewis's eyes flickered between the two of them. Was there a vibe that swingers had? And if so, did Amy and Daniel fit it? Was *swingers* even the right word?

"—who see the world like we do. I'd love for you to stop by. I mean, anyone who is a fan of Marian Ellis Rowan is someone worth getting to know better."

Lewis blinked. "This is an art party?"

Amy nodded. "A celebration of it. Daniel and I got some new pieces we want to show off to people who would appreciate the work. And you seem like just that type of person."

Oh. That made sense. And made better sense.

He gave his warmest smile. "You've been forward with me," he said, taking her hand. "So allow me to return the favor. I'd be delighted to come—and I'm hoping I could bring my boyfriend as a plus-one."

Ten

AMY'S HOUSE REMINDED LEWIS OF WHAT HOME COULD BE.

He felt bad thinking that as he stood next to Noah—close enough to maintain their cover, but not so close that he ran the risk of forgetting it *was* a cover and embarrassing himself—but the obvious love and warmth on display actually made him a little angry.

It was the way that Amy and Daniel flitted around the rooms, two butterflies who had found each other despite all odds. What were the chances of two people so perfectly matched meeting on a planet of over eight billion souls? But find each other they had. An American woman and an Australian man—people from opposite ends of the world—had come together to make this home the center of their universe.

Lewis wondered if he would ever have something like that. And with his mother gone, and his father most likely never going to remarry, he would never know. And he had no role models to show him what real love was.

So now, in the moment, listening to a joke whose ending he had guessed thirty seconds previously, he imagined that Noah's fake laughter was real; and that on the way home, before they tussled and turned in bed together, they might reminisce about this night and compare their relationship to Amy and Daniel's, all the ways they were similar or dissimilar, and be happy for those reasons. After all, that's what married couples did, right? That's what couples in love did. At least he supposed so.

"So, tell me," Amy finally said, flicking her fingers in a shooing motion as Daniel teed up another in what Lewis assumed was a carefully curated routine of jokes, "how did you two meet?"

Before Lewis could even think, Noah broke into a warm grin. "It's actually pretty funny," he said, making his British accent a touch thicker than usual. "We met at uni."

Noah placed his hand on the small of Lewis's back, making him shiver. The touch wasn't expected, but it should have been. Such a simple action, especially when Noah rubbed his thumb over the space—it was such a boyfriend notion. Lewis could even tell in the way Amy looked at them how cute she thought they were.

And he was starting to think that maybe he liked it.

It was dangerous, a risk, to fall into the lull of his own illusion. Which was what this was. Nothing more than a ploy to get closer to Amy, her husband, and the painting. It wasn't real; they weren't going to go home after this, get a late-night snack, and fuck.

Noah Rao *wasn't* his boyfriend. Despite how easy, in the moment, it was for him to imagine that to be so.

Yet it was also easy for Lewis to piggyback off this charade, like doubles partners setting each other up, or dancers playing off each other in a well-rehearsed routine. And though he was surprised how easily their lies just worked, he wasn't going to look a gift horse in the mouth. A win was a win.

"We met at SCAD."

Daniel's face furrowed. At first, Lewis thought it was a look of displeasure, like he looked down upon the institution. But the way Amy placed a soft hand on his chest, her light blue cornflower-colored nails glistening in the light, cleared that up. "It's in Georgia."

"Ah," Daniel said. "I don't quite hear a southern twang, though, Noah. How does an Indian Brit end up in Georgia?"

Amy smiled brightly. "Yes, tell us. Now I'm even more curious. I love hearing lovers' origin stories."

Noah smiled, not missing a beat or taking any offense. "Well, I guess 'at uni' wasn't exactly right. Lewis here always loves to take the path of least resistance, even if it's a lie."

Noah leaned down and pressed his forehead against the top of Lewis's head, like it was a thing they did to show connection. Lewis didn't hesitate to lean into it, evoking a wistful sigh from Amy.

Got her.

Noah straightened, turning his attention back to the two. "But while we were both in school is more accurate. My parents were visiting London from Mumbai, and I took them to the British Museum. I made a comment about a piece of art, and Lewis—who was studying abroad—was there to correct me."

"So technically, we did meet through university," Lewis added, hip checking Noah. "Not exactly a lie."

"It's still a lie, love," Noah purred. "A lie of omission."

"Oh, you two are adorable," Amy said, her doe-like eyes even wider than usual.

Noah chuckled sheepishly. "My mother was smitten right away."

"And you?" Amy asked, clearly quite smitten herself.

Noah turned his gaze to Lewis, beaming with apparent admiration—even adoration. Lewis worried he might be piling it on a bit too thick; but at the same time, dopey as it was, it was wonderful to see Noah's face, usually sharp with crevices and angles that caught and held the darkness, so flooded with light. He was carrying something heavy—Lewis had known it the first time they met—but joy looked nice on him, even if it was feigned. He wore it well, better than any suit. Had anyone ever told him that? Had anyone ever stopped and called him beautiful?

"There was no way I couldn't fall in love with him after that," Noah finished.

Amy let out an "Aaawww" straight out of a romantic comedy. Even Daniel chuckled, raising his glass in accord.

"To be fair," Lewis chimed in, "he accused Jan Vermeer of painting by numbers. As a lover of art, Amy, I'm sure you understand—I could not let him get away with that."

She gasped. "Noah! And to think I was just beginning to like you! Lewis, we can find you someone better. Someone who appreciates art the way it's supposed to be appreciated. What's your type?"

"Let's see." Lewis smirked. "Tall, British, Indian. A bit too posh for his own good."

"I think I know someone like that," Noah said.

"Really? Think you can introduce me?"

"Fucker," Noah growled, leaning down and kissing his cheek. Lewis might have been projecting, but he felt that Noah let his lips linger a moment longer than was strictly necessary.

Another cooing sound came from Amy. Lewis appreciated it, but he was ready to segue into the matter at hand. They had been at the party for nearly an hour and had been dancing around the topic of art for the last twenty minutes. They had made the rounds, making sure to be seen by the rest of the guests but also on the lookout for *the* painting. Most of them, like Amy and Daniel, were obsessed with art but not directly involved in the process of creating it. They were voyeurs, looking to art to give them a taste of emotions that they had not experienced. Lewis knew the type: Someone who would look at a piece steeped in longing or sorrow, the type of art that was like sharp black nails dragging against flesh, ripping open the most vulnerable parts of the artist for view, and rather than see in it what he saw—life, beauty, truth—all they could think to say was *How tragic* or *How depressing.*

Lewis didn't mind. Artists understood one another's work in a different way from many of those who bought it, talked about it, or found political and social capital in exchanging it. If he wanted to be an artist worth being talked about, he knew he would have to figure out a way to relate to those people. Maybe this arrangement with the British Museum would work in his favor.

"Speaking of which," Lewis said smoothly, "I was walking down your hallway looking for the bathroom, and I noticed a room that was closed off. Is that your bedroom, or—?"

"Babe," Noah said with a hiss, "you can't ask about their bedroom. Jesus! We just met these people."

Amy shook her head and raised a finger, signaling them to wait while she walked to the sideboard and fetched four glasses of champagne. Lewis hadn't even finished his first; but he understood this as a silent test of sorts. He drained the glass quickly before taking a new one from Amy's hand.

"No, it's not our bedroom," she said. Her eyes shifted left and right conspiratorially. Lewis knew then he had struck gold. "You said something before, when we met in the shop, that I've been thinking about," she said. "That art is about the natural beauty of the world."

Lewis smiled. "I think actually we both said that, but I'll take the credit."

"You're right. So, my question is: What do you do when art scares you?"

"I stare right back at it," he said without hesitation. "It's rare for an artist to articulate true fear in a piece of art. They had to put a piece of themself into that canvas for it to truly resonate with you. And if they did, then I think it's worth staring at. I think they deserve to tell us their story, because maybe it will help us to process, just a little bit, what scares us the most right now. And maybe we'll take that pain, understand fear a little bit more, the very way that we try to process the world and make it a better place. Help a next generation understand fear a little bit more."

The look in Amy's eyes told him he had her—hook, line, and sinker.

He felt bad about manipulating her. And that regret had manifested in a dull ache in the back of his head, like he'd been crying. But there was nothing for it.

"I was hoping you would say that," Amy said, taking his hand. "Come. I want to show you something. You too, Noah."

Daniel gestured grandly, bowing as they formed a little procession, Amy in the lead and Lewis bringing up the rear. They walked down the hallway; the sounds of chatter and music faded into white noise.

Daniel pulled out a key when they were halfway down the hallway; Lewis saw him hesitate before turning it in the lock. Half a second, or a second perhaps. But he hesitated. Lewis wasn't sure Amy had even noticed. His headache was growing worse, thundering downhill like an avalanche gaining speed and power with each passing moment. It had snuck up on him; usually he would notice these sorts of things building ahead of time. He pinched his nose for a moment, then realized there was blood in his mouth.

He swallowed twice and shook his head, focusing his thoughts. When he opened his eyes, Amy and Daniel had entered the room without them. Light spilled out into the hallway as fluorescents crackled to life. Noah moved to stand next to him.

"I feel it too," he said under his breath, glancing down at Lewis without moving his head. "Are you sure you want to do this?"

"We have to." *For Amy.*

Noah nodded.

They walked forward in unison. There was a warmth in that, in knowing that he and Noah were facing this together. But the moment they entered, that spark of confidence flickered out.

The room was filled with paintings. Lewis clocked at least a dozen different artists, the works ranging from inexpensive reproductions to priceless originals. He understood suddenly that Amy and Daniel were far, far wealthier even than he had imagined—the kind of wealth that comes either from old money or criminal activity. But that revelation didn't matter now. The only thing that mattered was the painting in front of him—the Macabre that dominated the west wall of the gallery.

While *The Drowning* focused on its bloodred lake and trail of skulls, this one was only four colors and a few simple figurative elements; a stark black background that seemed to represent endlessness; a bed with a single sheet thrown over what Lewis quickly understood was a human body; a brown table with a white case on it; and rose petals, stark red rose petals, scattered across the monochrome fields. Some were still on the stems of wilted roses, while others had fallen onto the bed linen, showing the passage of time. Those had left blood-hued streaks on the white sheets as they drifted into the endless darkness of the painting, a darkness so empty it was as if it were incomplete. But Lewis knew the way the black swallowed up the red was intentional. It showed the finality of death.

Amy was turning to face him, mouth open to speak, when she stopped. Truly just stopped, her body balanced on one foot as if she had been frozen in place. At first, he might have thought she was just holding very, very still; but there was a faint blur around her form, like she was a figure in a paused video. Daniel, too, was unnaturally motionless, and the same blurry halo was on him.

Both stuck in time.

"You did this," Lewis said, turning to Noah.

"What did I do?" Noah spoke in the manner of a professor employing the Socratic method—asking a question to which Lewis knew the answer, teaching him how to think. How to understand magic better.

"You pulled time out of the air," Lewis said slowly. "To effectively pause them."

Noah shrugged. "That's crudely put, but yes. I isolated this room, specifically this moment, and pulled them out of the timestream—rather like snipping a sentence from a paragraph by highlighting and cutting it—draining magic to rewind time while pushing more magic in to move it forward an equal amount."

"Pausing time in the gallery."

"Pausing time for them," Noah corrected. "I've only done it for a few seconds, but that's all we need. We're leaving."

"What? No. Absolutely not. The Macabre is right there. This is what we've been looking for."

Noah turned to face Lewis, and in that moment Lewis felt the force of his physical presence as never before. Somehow, his shoulders right then looked even were broader. He could make himself imposing if he wanted to.

"Look at it," he said, his voice a sharp hiss. "Each Macabre gives a clue to what it does. *The Drowning* was a lake. This one is a dead body. Whatever that painting can do has something to do with health. That headache you're feeling, and which is getting worse by the moment—it's linked to that. Everything that's been happening to *them* is linked to it."

"Even more of a reason for us to stop it now. There are people out there! We don't know what this painting could do to them."

"Exactly. Think, Lewis. When you touch it, that painting—like *The Drowning*—will activate. How are we going to stop what is dictated in that painting from happening to everyone here?"

Noah took a deep, shaking breath. A droplet of dark red blood trickled from his nose. Before Lewis could comment on it, he raised his hand to silence him. "I'm fine. It's the effort of keeping time frozen, not the painting."

"Are you sure?"

"No, I'm not sure," he snapped. "I have no idea what this painting is doing or might be doing to them, to the guests—hell, even to us. Another reason we have to go. We're going to leave, wipe their memories of us being here, and come back later. Tomorrow, after they've left for the day. When the house is empty, we'll deal with the Macabre."

"Wipe the memories of a dozen people?" Lewis said. "I thought you just said we're supposed to hide our magic in public. This seems the opposite of that."

"Not unless it's necessary," Noah said. "This is necessary."

Lewis understood why Noah believed what he did. In another life, with another history, Lewis might feel the same. But right now, he only saw his mother lying in a hospital bed. He only heard the sounds of her coding, smelled the sharp antiseptic. If he had the chance or the power to change that, wouldn't he do it? Shouldn't he?

"If we come back tomorrow and her cancer is worse, what will you do?"

Noah frowned. "What?"

"If we come back tomorrow and she's worse, but we get the painting out, will you use your magic to fix her?"

"I told you before, that's not why we're here," Noah said after a pause.

"Answer my question," Lewis interrupted. "Will you use your magic to help her?"

Noah didn't even hesitate. "That's not why we're here."

A cold fury descended upon Lewis. "Then answer me one more question," he said. "What you're doing with time right now, how much energy does that take? Because I'm guessing that if I touch that painting right now, you won't have the energy to stop me."

Before Noah could answer, Lewis strode across the room to the western wall. He could hear Noah's voice, of course—demanding he stop, warning him, threatening him; that he would burn his soul to ash right there, make him feel every ounce of pain he had ever felt in his life ten times over in an instant, if he didn't stop.

But Lewis also knew he was right. And there was freedom in that. Freedom to act.

"Lewis," Noah said. "Don't you dare. Evangeline is watching us, remember? We made an agreement."

"I don't care," Lewis muttered. He didn't look back at Noah, his partner, his fake boyfriend of the moment. Because if he did, he might actually fall victim to his warm brown eyes, his beautiful features, and his commanding presence. He might second-guess what he was doing and believe in whatever drivel the British Museum had sold to Noah about duty, country, and the value of human life—or lack thereof.

But maybe, Lewis thought as he pressed his hand to the painting, feeling the coolness of the oil paint and the ridges of the brushstrokes, maybe this would prove to Noah that helping people was more important than following orders.

Maybe.

Eleven

LEWIS KNEW SOMETHING WAS WRONG THE MOMENT HE STEPPED INTO the painting—something beyond the fact that he'd stepped into a malevolent piece of art.

It didn't feel like it did with *The Drowning*. Yes, there was the same weightlessness, the same feeling of nothingness, the same sense that his mind and body and soul, for a fraction of a second, disappeared from the mortal plane and reappeared, reassembled, a moment later.

And there was the same feeling as if he was watching in real time while a painter in the sky created a world with him at the center. Uneven bricks formed at his feet where he stepped. Large archways of cold stone rose up and loomed overhead. Sounds, murmurs of voices echoing off said arches, emerged in the distance, softly at first but growing in intensity as the world assembled around him.

But there was also something darker. Something looming, heavy, and weighted. Something that was a familiar damp blanket thrown over Lewis's shoulders.

Guilt. And a heavy thickness like pushing through something semisolid.

He knew exactly where he was. Anyone who spends time in a hospital never forgets that feeling of dread, that heavy hook in the center of your chest. There was death here. There had been, there was, and there would be for years to come.

Lewis flexed his fingers, examining his hands. He seemed every inch his normal human self, just as he had in *The Drowning*. He was in a corridor. He looked to his left, and a nurse and doctor hurried by, discussing a medical treatment in rapid tones. Their voices were purely British, sharper, clearer, more stereotypical than Noah's. It helped him place the era. He assumed it was the late Victorian. Their dress seemed to confirm it.

Knowing his location was a good thing. Knowing where the painting had dropped him in time would help him find Edgar as quickly as possible; for if this painting was anything like *The Drowning*, it would eventually collapse. Lewis remembered how he had escaped the swallowing world of the previous painting with mere seconds to spare; something told him if it happened again, he wouldn't be as lucky.

With urgency, Lewis walked quickly down the hallway, keeping his distance from the doctor and the nurse. He wasn't sure if the people in the background could see him. They weren't part of the painting in Amy and Daniel's home. These people who moved toward him and by him, on a loop created by a memory, weren't evident in the painting's physical manifestation in the mundane world. This seemed like useful information; he would tell Noah the moment he got out. The more they knew about the Macabre, the better.

He followed the doctor and nurse up a set of winding brick-laid stairs; they turned left down a hallway and vanished into what he assumed was a patient's room. A chorus of wails and screams erupted—a woman's voice. A mother, a sister, a daughter, perhaps the patient herself. It made no difference. All that mattered was her pain; unadulterated, raw-nerve-exposed-to-the-air pain that would never heal. It might lessen with time, but never disappear. He knew that sound, because it was the same exact sound he had made when the doctors told him his mother had died at 3:42 p.m., on a day that was warm and brisk all at the same time; the type of day she would have loved to spend outdoors.

It was then that he spotted Edgar, sitting in a crumpled heap on the floor some distance down the hallway, and was almost grateful to have something beside the memories to occupy his mind.

Edgar looked different. Not just older, though that was part of it. His body had settled into itself; bones and musculature had found equilibrium. His face was a little sharper, his hair a little wilder than before. He seemed to be about twenty years old now; old enough to know now that the bitter, caustic attitude he had when younger was an accurate reflection of life, but still too young to find a way to harness it into something meaningful. It was a cruel age, your early twenties.

Even at a glance, Lewis saw on him the telltale signs of an artist: smudges on his fingertips, flecks of paint on the hem of his ill-fitting shirt. And something else: soot. Not charcoal, which had a different look, but soot, in places that maybe it wouldn't be if he used it as an art medium: on his cheeks, on the cuffs of his trousers, on his shirt collar.

And more: Dried blood stained his shirtfront. Lewis wasn't sure how he had missed it at first, and the closer he approached, the more likely it seemed the blood wasn't Edgar's.

At first, Edgar didn't look at him or even seem to register Lewis's presence. His eyes were glassy, looking forward, not at a stained-glass window that gave a warped and colorful view of London, but through it. Lewis wondered if he wasn't just looking through the glass, but seeing the particles of space and time, and wondering if he could manipulate them, twist time and thwart whatever ill fate had led him to this hospital. Lewis knew that feeling well; the fixed stare, that feeling of having vacated your body, that came from the realization something horrific had happened on your watch. Trauma, he thought, was the thing that bound all generations together.

After a moment, Edgar's eyes seemed to focus. Lewis attempted a reassuring smile, and failed. He wasn't even sure if Edgar could see him—*really* see him. His facial expression remained fixed.

Then he spoke. "I haven't seen you in a while." His voice was flat and even.

Lewis sat down next to him. What did he say to that? He couldn't tell the truth, even if Edgar already was starting to put the pieces together; their last encounter had been less than half a decade ago, from Edgar's perspective. "What happened to you?" he asked.

Edgar's eyes drifted down to his hands. He turned them over, revealing his palms and his knuckles covered in small cuts and bruises; nothing that would impede his motor functions, but there was a slight tremor in both hands. His knuckles were red and bruised like he'd been punching someone. No, not punching; his nails were cracked, too, split and bleeding, the cuticles torn in some places, pads bruised in others. As if he had been digging through rubble.

Lewis frowned. "Did you do something?" he asked. *Did you hurt someone?* was what he really wanted to ask.

Edgar let out a thin chuckle. "You haven't looked outside, have you?"

Lewis stood and went to the stained-glass window, all pale yellows, pinks, and soft blues, in the form of a butterfly. Gazing out, he saw the London streets, fire and smoke in the distance. There were muffled bells of fire engines roaring toward the flames. He turned back to Edgar.

"I have his blood on me," Edgar said, looking down at his hands. "I didn't know blood was this warm, but then so cold. Did you?"

Lewis understood that Edgar wasn't really present. Whatever had happened outside had broken him. Lewis squatted down, grasping Edgar by the shoulders, but Edgar only stared at his fingers, at the smudges of blood like red chalk. Those stains, Lewis knew, would never truly disappear, however Edgar might scrub at them.

There was so much he wanted to ask—not only about Edgar, but about the painting. But before he could draw breath, the double doors down the hallway burst open and three gurneys came careening down, a gaggle of doctors and nurses following behind. One of the bodies was draped in a sheet. The other two were uncovered; their faces were mangled, fragments of shrapnel protruding like stalactites had grown from their flesh. One—a young girl—had lost a leg, and her arm was nearly severed, dangling by a few strands of tendon and ligament.

Lewis felt sick, more from the smell than the sight, but before he had the chance to react, two more figures entered the scene, trailing behind the doctors and the nurses and the dead, or the undead, or the soon-to-be dead. An older man and woman, expensively dressed. Parents of the victims; Lewis knew without question by the looks of devastation and grief on their faces—grief that turned to anger when the father caught sight of Edgar.

"*You!*" he roared.

Lewis moved out of the way just in time. Again, he wasn't sure if the older man could see or touch him, but he didn't want to risk it; not with the way the man lifted Edgar from the floor and slammed his back against the wall. Lewis knew that had to hurt, but Edgar didn't wince. He did cry out, but from a different sort of anguish. "I'm sorry," he choked. "I didn't mean—"

"I don't give a damn about what you *meant*," the man snarled; even his anger could not disguise the cut-glass accent. "My boy is dead because of you!"

Lewis watched Edgar struggle. Watched as his nails dug

through fabric deep into the man's arm, tearing small lines that revealed dark red sinews. No one else passing or standing nearby even attempted to stop him, not even the man's wife. He supposed they all agreed with him that Edgar deserved to have the life thrashed out of him. And if it ended with a soul being snuffed out that day, *another* soul, then so be it.

"It wasn't—our—intention," Edgar gurgled, a foam of spittle dripping from the corners of his mouth. The mourning father's hands were around his throat, his grip powerful enough to lift Edgar's feet off the ground, preventing his scuffed-up shoes, a size too small, from finding any purchase.

"Do you imagine I give a damn about your intentions, Edgar?" growled the father. "You're a stain, a parasite feeding off my family and the pity of my beautiful boy. I thought it might be a lesson to him—to teach him that kindness was a liability—when you betrayed him, as I knew you surely would. But by God, I never thought you would be the death of him." His face was purple with rage. He brought it within inches of Edgar's. "If I had known it would come to this, I would have killed you the first time I caught you in his bed."

If it were within Lewis's power, he would have pried those hands from Edgar's throat. It pained him to watch without intervening; but this was just a memory, a fixed pocket of time. He could only bear witness.

At least, that was what he thought—until a sharp pain tore through him, flinging him out of the world of the painting and back into his physical body. Back to the Hartes' gallery.

He stood for a moment, unable even to breathe. Pain howled through him; his eyes blurred with tears. He became aware of an unpleasant acrid smell, and looking down he saw to his horror that the flesh of his hand where it rested on the surface of the painting had rotted away, leaving his fingertips nothing but bone.

Twelve

LEWIS HAD NEVER FELT SUCH AGONY IN HIS ENTIRE LIFE.
The moment he came out of the Dumont, the feeling in his hand was like cold water against the tips of his fingers, as if they had been dipped in an ice-cold bath against his will. But quickly, the initial shock gave way to fire, as if he had dug foolishly past the surface, past the enamel, and into the white-hot molten core of pain, a place no human should ever find or experience.

His vision went white. Every nerve in his body tried to compensate for the initial fiery pain that started from the tips of his fingers. He couldn't think, couldn't process what was happening. He only knew that he would do anything to make it stop.

Perhaps this was what happened when humanity pulled back the curtain and touched the live-wire current that made the universe what it was. What had Noah called it? Resonance? A power no man should try to harness.

Or maybe, that *he* shouldn't try to harness. Perhaps this was his punishment for thinking he could be something special.

Almost as if some God had taken pity on him, the pain instantly subsided. It didn't go away, simply lessened; it was as if a knife was only plunged an inch or so into his flesh now instead of carving into his marrow. It was only barely tolerable, but it was weak enough that he could function.

With the waves of full-body pain receding, he became aware

of individual polyps of suffering across his body. His lungs burned; he tasted copper in his mouth. Every inch of him throbbed. But there was one specific feeling that was strangely familiar, a prickling sensation on his back; focusing on that sensation helped ground him.

It took him a moment to pinpoint it, then he remembered: In his freshman year at SCAD, he had been drunk and gotten a tattoo—a cartoon character on his left biceps. He'd done it to impress a boy, who was now a happily married man—to a woman—with beautiful twin girls. He remembered the feeling of the needle tracing over the lines, over and over and over again, a feeling like hot glass on the surface of his skin. That's what he felt against his shoulder blades and spine. If he followed the lines of pain, they made the shape of a star.

"Lewis," said a familiar voice. "Lewis, can you hear me?"

Noah was calling to him—but the voice was inside his head. Noah, he realized, was no longer standing in the room. He was alone.

Well, not alone. Where Amy and Daniel had been were piles of warped, rotting flesh, barely recognizable as human. Amy—a woman he barely knew, but whose warmth and passion he could feel every time she spoke—was slowly decomposing before his eyes. Shreds of salmon-pink flesh clung to the naked skull, pulsing and twitching with the misfiring of the few remaining nerves. Daniel had been luckier, in the loosest sense of the word. His body had been torn apart as if by an explosion. The remaining bits, scattered around the gallery, hissed like meat against a hot skillet.

That was the smell lingering in the air that Lewis couldn't place at first. Something like pork, roasting on a spit.

"They're dead," he whispered. "They're fucking dead."

"Yes," Noah's mind-voice said, the firmness of it palpable. "But you are not. I need you to calm down, control your breathing, or what killed them is going to do the same to you."

"Calm down?" he sputtered.

"You wanted to be an agent. You wanted to be in the field. I'm going to make sure this isn't your last lesson. But you need to work with me. Do you understand?"

No, he didn't understand. He didn't understand how they were dead. He didn't understand why he *wasn't* dead. He didn't understand why Noah was no longer standing beside him. And he fucking didn't understand why his hand, when he dared to look at it, was eroding more and more with each passing second.

But it didn't matter. Only surviving mattered. "What do you need me to do?"

"The air has become caustic," Noah's voice said inside his skull. "The moment you touched the Dumont, the smell of roses filled the room. The Hartes started coughing, drowning in their own blood."

Lewis's eyes turned back to Amy's and Daniel's remains, and he swallowed hard to hold back vomit.

"It gets worse, I'm afraid," Noah continued. "Every rose in the house started emitting a toxic perfume. The guests—"

"They're *all* dead?"

"We need to focus on you right now." And that answered that.

"Where are you?"

"I got out of there as quickly as I could when I realized I couldn't pull you from the painting. It was like you were glued to it."

"Which is what happened to my hand." Lewis was calmer than he thought he should be, considering, well, everything. The bone was exposed, and his flesh was being eaten away as he watched the creeping corrosion spread. "Did you do something for the pain?"

"Whatever this painting is doing, it destroys organic matter. The only thing I could do was place a protective rune on your back, keeping you from experiencing the brunt of the Dumont. But it won't last forever."

"So, what do we do now?"

"My priority has to be keeping this caustic gas from leaving the house. I have to maintain this barrier holding the gas inside and keeping the glamour up on the house, no matter what."

The subtext was clear. "Even if it means sacrificing me."

"It won't come to that."

"But it might."

"Not if you listen, it won't." The voice was sharp, almost painful in Lewis's head. Then, more gently: "I'm not going to leave you, no matter what. But I need you to fight through the pain. Walk to the front door. It's unlocked. Once I see you, I'll let the barrier down enough to yank you out."

And for once, for a moment, the way Noah said it, made Lewis feel like Noah was actually speaking the truth.

A wave of relief passed over Lewis, knowing an exit plan was in place; but the dark painting still loomed in front of him. How beautiful it was, and how morose. How lonely and passionate each thick brushstroke. It made sense—the painting and its effects. Death was a bottomless pit that could never be filled. Edgar must have had endless reserves of sorrow from which to draw. And that sorrow became something corrosive.

They couldn't let this spread.

"What about the painting?" he said.

"Fuck the painting, Lewis," Noah said. "We'll come back for it later. I can place a seal on the house that'll hold for that long."

"We can't leave this here, Noah."

"And we can't fight it either. Not this one. We came here to fix a problem, and it got ahead of us." Noah's voice was urgent. "This is not the time to argue. I have to keep my focus, and you need to get out of there."

"Noah, we—"

"You're not stupid, Lewis. You might not be an agent, but you understood resonance better than most agents do. It's only my magic and your connection to Edgar keeping that painting from devouring your arm. But that won't hold forever. The air you're breathing is going to start corroding your organs from the inside out. It won't matter if your arm is still your arm if you haven't any lungs to use."

"Your healing magic—"

"I can't reverse those effects," Noah hissed. "Or anything this Dumont does. If you don't get out of there, you are going to die, and it is going to hurt. And then who will help us with the other paintings? Who will help us save more people?"

"I haven't done such a great job of that so far, have I? If I hadn't stuck my nose into this, Amy and Daniel and all the others would still be alive." Lewis didn't know whether to laugh or puke. "They didn't even know. Their only crime was ignorance. A dozen souls, because I wanted to do the right thing. Because I had to touch the goddamn painting."

"Lewis," Noah said, "I need you to focus. There will be time for regret later. Right now, there's one more thing you need to do before you leave."

Lewis let go a long, shaky breath. "Go ahead."

"You have to cut off your hand."

"*What?*"

"I said it before. The effects can't be reversed, only contained. If that corruption keeps spreading, it'll consume you altogether. The only thing you can do—"

"Is separate it from my body," Lewis said.

"Exactly. If I was there . . . if we had more time . . ."

Just then, a sharp jolt of pain electrified every nerve of his body. Lewis whimpered, almost losing his footing.

Noah cursed under his breath. "I'm having trouble keeping everything balanced. I used too much resonance when I froze time before. Coupled with the barrier and the spell on you—I don't have much left in me."

"I can't leave."

"Yes, you can. I know you're scared, but—"

"No. I mean I can't leave this room. Not until I deal with this painting," Lewis said. "You're pushing yourself to the limit. You can't contain this forever. The only way to stop it is to seal the painting. To *end* this."

Lewis and Noah weren't face-to-face, but he could tell Noah was frowning. Maybe some type of feedback from their connection. After a moment, Noah said, "Did you even gather the name?"

"No. The connection broke before I had the chance."

"We don't have time to argue this. I have maybe three more minutes before the shield comes crashing down."

"That should give me time to—" Lewis was interrupted by a bout of coughing. Blood spattered on the floor—not just a few specks, but a brimming mouthful of thick, red liquid.

"We're running out of time," Noah said.

"Then shut up and let me do this."

Lewis had thought being so close to death would feel different. Maybe it was Noah's magic, but all he could focus on was the chance to do good. There was real and present danger here—a danger to everyone in Perth, maybe to everyone in the world. He had a chance, however slim, to avert that danger. And if he had to die to do it, well, what better way to go out?

He looked at the painting, studying it for any sort of clue. If this painting was anything like *The Drowning*, with its endless flood of water, there was no guarantee that the noxious gas would ever stop or could ever be contained unless it was destroyed. He swallowed thickly, tasting iron, and began to think. *Name the magic*, he thought. *Name it, and you can tame it.*

Lewis steadied himself and spoke the first title that came to mind.

"*The Blood.*"

There was no response; only pain, as if the painting was laughing at him, pulsing out magic in retribution for his failed attempt to name it. Lewis coughed again, stumbling backward.

"Whatever you just did—" Noah began.

Lewis ignored him. *"The Pain,"* he wheezed.

Another pulse of agony brought Lewis to his knees. Instinctively, he reached out with his right hand to break his fall. But the bone connecting with the floor sent a searing jolt of pain through him; he fell on his side, collapsing into the pile of smoldering flesh that had once been Amy Harte. He groaned. The floor was slick with blood and human filth, but he forced himself up into a kneeling position using his good hand.

"Lewis, fucking stop," Noah cried. "You're not going to—"

Lewis pulled every memory he could from inside the painting. They flashed rapidly in front of him. The pain in Edgar's eyes. The scent of death noxious in the air. The way the boy's father slammed Edgar against the wall. The blood on Edgar's shirt. The glimpse Lewis saw of the boy's mangled, broken body.

And the words spoken to Edgar before the memory broke.

"The Stain," he whispered.

Lewis braced himself, but no pain came, no feeling of life or dread; just weightlessness, much like when he had entered the painting for the first time.

And that was how he knew he had found its name.

Knowing what was to come, he shielded his eyes moments before the Dumont burst into white-hot flame. The blinding white shifted to red, like the light of a rising moon, a vibrant rosy color that reminded him of the petals in the painting. As he had with *The Drowning*, he heard a scream emerge from the painting's depths. Images flashed in his brain like the reels of a movie spinning at a thousand miles an hour: images of Edgar and the boy, of the family he had seen in the hospital, the fight he witnessed.

Here was Edgar on a bench in London, his arms wrapped around the boy; their love, and their growing political radicalism.

The labor protests in the heart of London; their dreams of bringing down the exploitative system; the dank cellar where, together, they had constructed the chemical bomb. Edgar's second thoughts, and his argument with the boy, trying in vain to convince him not to go through with the sabotage. Trying again, after the bomb had been planted, to convince him to disarm it. All useless. And the bomb, exploding ahead of schedule, leaving Edgar alive but claiming the boy among its victims, the caustic fumes of the ruptured gas main igniting in the flames, sending out a lethal plume that annihilated the entire neighborhood. None of it was Edgar's fault, but that didn't matter. The outcome was still the same. And the pain that Edgar felt, physically and emotionally, scarred him forever.

And then the flame subsided; the painting was reduced to a charred frame.

Lewis sighed. "It's done," he said. He spat again; it was more saliva than blood. He could no longer smell the cloying fragrance of the poison anymore.

But his hand was still a ruin, and the corruption was still creeping perceptibly up his fingers. Noah was right; once that ball had started rolling downhill, the magical momentum could not be undone.

"One problem solved," Lewis said, inspecting his hand. The corruption had spread to the second knuckle. The flesh was turning black. It reminded him of frostbite. "I figure I'm going to lose all the fingers on this hand," he said. "And I'm feeling weirdly calm about it. Are you doing this?"

"I told you, the rune on your back was to make your pain less—not just physical pain, but emotional trauma too," Noah said softly. "We're in this together, till the very end. I can make it so you won't feel it when you cut your hand off, but I can't do anything about what happens next. You'll have to make the cut yourself. I can't break my concentration or I risk being exposed to the necrosis too."

Lewis understood all this—logically, at least. He couldn't linger here forever; and the longer he waited, the worse the eventual severing of his hand would be. Lewis sighed, giving one last look at Amy and her husband—or what was left of them. "I'm so sorry," he whispered.

Quickly, he walked out of the room, swallowing back his nausea. He made his way through the house toward the living room; heaps of corrupted flesh, toppled sprays of withered roses, and clothing lay in his path. The house seemed like some necropolis surrounding the final resting chamber of a sinister god.

He passed through the kitchen. There was a body close to the front door, a woman's body, only partially decomposed. Lewis thought he heard breathing, and his stomach lurched. But even if she was somehow clinging to life, there was nothing Lewis could do for her. He recognized the woman; he had seen her when he had walked into the party with Noah. She had a bright, infectious laugh, he remembered that, and the man she was with had been embarrassed. *You deserved better than him*, he thought. And maybe if he had told her so, she would've left before everything went to hell.

A sound broke Lewis's thoughts: a crackle of wood and shifting groan of the house as if it was settling in its foundation. A spiderweb of cracks spread across the wall.

"Noah," he said quietly.

"I know," Noah whispered. "The house frame is collapsing. The poison affects everything organic, including wood. I'll get you out of there. Don't worry. You just have to—"

"I'm looking," Lewis said. He could feel a shift in his body, as if the chemicals were being redistributed. Warm elation flooded over him as his fingers moved among the drawers, searching for anything sharp. The feeling reminded him of the laughing gas he used to get at the dentist. He assumed Noah was shifting the magic to help him stay clear and make the choice he needed to make.

Within a drawer full of various knives, he saw an enormous butcher's cleaver, its edge keen and bright. "Found it," he said.

Even with the magic calming his body, Lewis's injured hand trembled. He took up the cleaver, watching as the light flickered along the blade, causing his vision to blur. He wasn't much of a cook, but he knew how to cut meat. He knew to put his hand on the chopping block and take a wide enough stance to center himself.

"One chop," Noah said, his voice soft. "One chop. Walk to the door and I will yank you out of there. We'll see what we can do about your hand when we get back to London."

"One chop and my painting hand is gone," Lewis whispered.

He felt like laughing; a morose response, sure. But then he heard the creaking and snapping of the timber frame. He couldn't hear Noah in his head; Lewis supposed he had enough to do holding the house together. He drew a deep breath and raised the cleaver, brought it down to within an inch of his wrist. Raised it again. Another false start. Another shaking of the house, another grumble of the timbers. It was almost as if the house itself was warning him, trying its best to keep itself together for him. Now Noah was speaking again, but he couldn't make out the words. All he could hear was his own pulse, the shaking of his breath. His vision was growing black at the corners, not because he was about to die or his mind was short-circuiting, but because he was staring down a tunnel at the only choice left to him.

He swung down his arm with all his strength. There was a moment of pain, a fracture of disassociation as his one hand chopped off his other, making itself an orphan.

That fleeting instant of white-hot pain, and then the magic of Noah's rune kicked in like a generator and he felt only a dull throb, like splinters in every single finger. Lewis didn't have to be told what to do. He grabbed a towel, not caring if it was clean, and wrapped it around his wrist. He wouldn't have to hold the bleeding back for long, he knew; Noah would have some spell to help him as soon as he walked out the door. He gave one last look to his ruined hand, lying there alone on the butcher block, and stumbled to the door.

From the doorway under the overhanging veranda, he saw Noah standing on the lawn, concern painted over his handsome, dark features. Concern for him. He had never thought he would see that on Noah's face.

Relief washed over him, more of a balm than the magic Noah had used to calm him. He had done it. Whatever the casualties along the way, he had survived and beaten another Dumont.

That relief was short-lived. He heard the final anguished grumble of the house, a cry of sorrow that gave way to the sounds of cracking timber, like a mighty tree falling in the forest.

There were only moments left.

Part of Lewis wanted to give in. To accept his fate and find warm peace within it. There wasn't enough time for Noah and him to connect, no. But there was time to try one more thing to save his life.

Lewis had read somewhere that the human mind produced a thought in as little as 150 milliseconds. If you stacked those on top of one another, with the time he had left, he could write a sonnet.

But instead, he focused on a single thought.

Abernathy, he flung out. *Help me.*

And with a leap of faith, Lewis threw himself forward, toward Noah, toward the doorway, and braced for either death or safety.

He felt his feet leave the ground as the magical pull tugged him forward. Not enough. All at once, the house collapsed around him. Pain tore through him—different from the pain that originated within the Dumont. He was being skewered in a thousand places by splinters and rods of timber and rebar steel; crumbling shards of drywall and cement crushed him under their weight, and everything went dark.

The last thing he saw before he was buried alive was Noah's look of absolute despair.

Thirteen

CASSANDRA HAD LEARNED VERY EARLY ON THAT THERE WERE TWO TYPES of people in the world, reactive and proactive.

Reactive people didn't survive long and found ways to blame the world for every bad thing that came their way. They were sufferers, victims, passive individuals who never sought or reached their full potential. They were the ones that people sighed about during their funerals, mentioned that they were going to be such a missed soul because they had so much to live for . . . mostly because they hadn't done anything.

Proactive people, on the other hand, were lions. They ripped and shredded, pulled apart and violated every piece of the world to get their due. They didn't say, *I'm sorry.* They didn't feel regret for seizing what was their birthright.

At one point, Cassandra had seen herself as a reactive person, and she had been fine with that. The world needed a yin-and-yang-like balance to keep it functioning. But quickly, she discovered: If she was going to drench this world in blood and atone for her own sins to claw through the mud and find that piece of her soul that had been lost so many years ago, she would have to become proactive.

She was as yet unsure of her feelings about Australia—Perth, specifically. Deep down, though, she wished the Macabre had been in some gallery in Sydney or some penthouse apartment, not this suburban vibe of a street with the cookie-cutter homes. The nearly two dozen of them along the two blocks that comprised the subdivision made her stomach boil. It was so simplistic, so resigned. Each one of these individuals had potential, and they were willing to just be complacent and plain.

It made her sick.

And honestly, for the first time in many years, her fingers twitched, a burn and a desire to rid the world of those who didn't see or value their own potential. Magic and arcana were an energy-based engine that could neither be destroyed nor created. If they weren't going to use their magic, at least giving it back to the world would mean that there was a chance that someone could use it for something more impressive.

But as she arrived on the street in question, she realized she was too late. Too late to hit the reset button for these people, and too late for her own immediate access to the painting. Amy and David Harte's home reeked of magic, smelled like deviled eggs left out too long, and made a feeling deep within her soul prickle and spike. It was the sense of something nefarious and evil that pulsed from that home, a familiar sense that she had grown to love because it meant she was one step closer to absolution. A step closer if she'd been a bit faster.

After the incident in Paris, she had reached a dead end for the location of the next Macabre. The grimoire she had acquired wasn't as useful as she thought it would be at first. Layers upon layers of magical spells, inked in the blood of the previous owner, kept the enchantments working that prevented prying eyes from looking within it. It took her days to unlock them. And there was still one she needed to break, a cipher that made the words illegible.

The bone in her right hand twitched and hummed. The magic she'd had to pull from deep within the marrow of her body to overcome the magic that protected the contents of the grimoire hadn't fully healed yet. Her right hand, each time she flexed, flinched in sharp, electric pain. Eventually, it would pass. And having a distraction was a good way to forget her temporary setback.

The British Museum weren't the only ones who had feelers across the world. Except, unlike them, Cassandra offered money instead of platitudes and goodwill to get their service. Which meant she got information surprisingly fast. So, when one of her informants had called her just moments ago to say that a British agent and an American had whisked themselves across the world using magic, she knew it was something worth following.

And so, after she finished her microdermabrasion and her full-body massage in the Swiss Alps, she made her way there, disappearing in a blink from among the white, powdery peaks, appearing in a temperate climate that was the complete opposite of where she was before, wondering if she should have skipped the facial and the extra time it took until after this.

At least I look good.

Not that anyone would see her—not here. With a twist of her left hand, her nondominant hand, and a muttering of a word with origins in Aztec linguistics, a language that she never fully grasped but was passable in, her image rippled and disappeared, as if a swirl of color was disappearing in psychonic reverse. A cloaking spell was all she needed to stand watch.

Across the street from the home in question and one abode down, she saw them both enter, Noah and Lewis. She watched through the windows as the party engaged, seeing the two follow the host and her husband into the back.

Cassandra licked her plump lips, tasting the lingering aroma of apples and brie that she had eaten an hour ago. It was tempting to barge inside, to explode out of her body every bit of magic that she had in order to take what was hers.

She could overpower them both, there was no question. The American would be a liability for the British agent, and he wouldn't be able to protect him, himself, and all the residents. She could use that to her advantage. But as the darkness seeping from the back room oozed and drifted around the walls, she knew she could just wait it out.

And just like that of a person who described themselves as proactive, her plan shifted and changed, adapted to the situation at hand. And whatever Macabre painting they had found, it was clear to Cassandra it had some sort of corrosive properties, able to burn through magic, flesh, wood, carbon, everything that existed natural and true. That was good for her. At worse, containing the Macabre's magic would occupy Noah and his little friend for a considerable amount of time, drain and waste their energy so she could step in and pilfer what she needed for herself. At worst, they would all be dead, and she could step over their bones and once again pilfer what she wanted for herself.

But—and Cassandra didn't feel this often—she was impatient.

How many years had she waited for a perfect moment like this? Now three birds could be destroyed with one stone: weakening the British Museum, that American, *and* getting a painting for her own. Years of planning—decades of trial and error—had brought her here, lurking in the shadows, just waiting for the right person to come along to lead her unknowingly to the Macabre. Not this painting, necessarily, but the final Dumont—the one she knew existed somewhere, if only she could find the key. She knew impatience would be the death of her, as it tended to rear its ugly head at the most inopportune moments. She wasn't dead yet, though.

And as she watched the Indian British man make his way out of the building and speak through a connection she only guessed was magic to the American still inside, she knew this was her time.

Cassandra threw her right hand out, ignoring the throbbing pain as magic unspooled itself from her chest and rode the currents of her veins and muscles to the tips of her fingers. She didn't need words to summon this spell, one that she had used time and time again. It was, in fact, one of the first spells she ever learned.

Expanding her fingertips as far as they could stretch, pushing her body to the limit as if she was dislocating each of her joints, she quickly brought her hand together in a crunching fist. Magic could not be destroyed or created, but it *could* be manipulated. And that manipulation of the natural properties of anything in the world was attainable just as long as the mage was willing to pay the price and had the reservoir of magic to do it. She was willing. She had the magic.

And so she manipulated one of nature's most powerful constants: gravity.

Within a merciless instant, the supporting beams of the house snapped all at once. The remaining beams couldn't keep the diseased house afloat, and it collapsed right in front of them. The American inside wasn't a concern of hers, as long as she could go in, get what she needed, and leave.

But before she could make a conclusion about whether or not she was going to have an American zombie to play with, she saw something interesting. The Indian man stepped back and screamed a guttural cry.

"Fuck!" he yelled, voice echoing in the night.

She could tell his magic was still wrapped around the building. Anyone on the streets wouldn't have seen the aftermath yet. She imagined the party was still going on to anyone with prying eyes, and noted he must be a talented magician to be able to hold that illusion together, contain the crawling necrosis, and help out his friend. He was someone she should watch and perhaps fear, a deduction she concluded was true when he stood up from his crouched position and slowly turned 180 degrees to look behind him.

Cassandra was fairly confident he couldn't see her, but the way that his eyes bored through her did cause her breath to catch at the back of her throat. His warm, brown eyes had become sharp and almost hawklike, the iris rings glowing white. It wasn't natural, not an expression of magic of his own volition, but a clear sign that someone was piggybacking on his senses. And Cassandra was fairly certain she knew who it was.

And that *someone* she did actually fear, and she hadn't been afraid of anyone in a long time.

"I know you're there," Noah said, his voice calm and even, "or at least watching from somewhere far from here. And I doubt you're going to lower your guard and make yourself known."

He was right. She had no intention, but she would hear him out.

Noah took a step forward. "I don't know who you are or what you want with these paintings or even Lewis, but if you don't leave, now, I will rip the veil of magic apart and pull you from whatever hiding spot you're in and wring your neck myself with my bare hands. The Macabre are of interest to the British Museum. They are under the jurisdiction of His Majesty's Crown and Royal Arcane Intelligence Agency. And the American is under my charge. I've sensed your presence before, in Baltimore some weeks ago. If I detect you again, I will not hesitate to act."

Noah lingered for several seconds as if he was waiting for Cassandra to quiver in her boots and make herself known. He wasn't without his justification: The threat was real. She could feel the icy hotness against her neck. But she also wasn't stupid, and neither was he.

She watched as he turned, heading briskly toward the door of a neighboring home. With a wave of his hand, the wood shimmered, revealing the Contract House. And to her surprise, not only did she see Lewis in a heap on the floor, body broken and with a large piece of wood protruding out of his chest—a consequence of her crude spell, she imagined—she also saw a familiar woman, Evangeline, standing right there looking directly at her.

And with Noah's back to her and a desire to be just a little bit messy, she lowered her illusion for a fraction of a second, blew the woman a kiss, and disappeared into the air.

PART III

"More than ghosts,
I believe in
guardian angels."
MANINI MISHRA

Fourteen

THE NEXT FEW DAYS LEWIS SPENT DRIFTING IN AND OUT OF CONSCIOUS- ness, like floating in a saltwater bath.

Lewis remembered what happened in Perth. He remembered jumping through the doorway and calling upon the Contract House's assistance. He remembered landing on the floor of his apartment, hearing the collapse of the home behind him, still smelling the lingering scent of death.

He almost remembered the stake of wood that pierced his chest and hitched a ride with him after the collapse.

A moment later, the door to the Contract House opened, Evangeline looking at him with horror, eyes flicking through the doorway he passed through. Lewis's consciousness wasn't in a place for him to follow her gaze, but he could only assume, for a moment, she saw Perth too.

But her face? Her face told him she saw something else. Something that passed as horrific recognition . . .

"I've got you, Lewis," she whispered at last, the light scents of lavender and vanilla rolling off her body. "Noah will be okay too. You rest."

Evangeline's voice shined through. It was softer than it had ever been, than he had assumed it could be—laced with kindness and a gentleness that he wasn't sure was natural to her. The lightness and the way her voice stitched his soul back to his body made him assume there was magic involved.

But that was his last conscious thought.

Sleep suffocated him in the nicest of ways, and when he awoke, it was raining. Lewis wasn't sure how magic was involved, but he knew that more time had passed than just a few hours, maybe even a day. Or more. He guessed he'd been out two days from how his body felt a lingering level of soreness, like he had overexerted himself at the gym.

It wasn't long enough, though, for him to forget what had happened.

He supposed that was a kindness. The jarring fact of his hand being gone, cut off by his own choice and sacrifice, might have been too much of a mental shock to experience suddenly on awakening. The memory in the forefront of his mind's eye helped soften that blow, anchor him to the reality he had signed his soul over to.

He was, indirectly, an agent of the British Museum—at least for now. But the consequences of his choice to fight the Dumonts would live on forever. Let it be so.

The skin had healed over nicely—a confirmation that more time had passed than he assumed. The flap of flesh had been pulled tightly over the wound, and the stitch line was thin, barely noticeable. That didn't stop the wave of anguish crashing against his chest, making him feel tight, as if every nerve was hypersensitive.

So he focused on other things. At first, he thought he was in a hospital. And in truth, in many ways, it was. Soft grays and peach-colored walls gave a muted, calm tone to the room. The sheets, albeit soft and of the highest quality, itched. The air, at the perfect temperature, felt moist, and his heart pumped in such a way that made the world seem like it was twisting upside down.

But the walls flickered every so often, showing him what was under the surface—his apartment. As if the hospital facade was a layer placed over it to make him feel more comfortable. After all, as Noah had said, the Contract House could provide him anything and everything he needed. Including changing its shape.

The door to the right opened slowly. With a twist of his sore neck that caused him to wince, Lewis came face-to-face with Noah. He looked better than in his last memory. His hair was still disheveled, and a tiredness lay heavy on his bones, making his skin look sullen and gaunt.

Noah studied him. "You're awake," he said softly. "That's good. Means Chelsea is doing her job. Not that she wouldn't. She's great at healing."

"You're rambling," Lewis muttered.

Noah let out a low, thin chuckle, closing the door softly behind him. He walked slowly over, and from the corner of his eye, Lewis noticed he had a slight limp, favoring his left leg. Lewis wondered if that was a by-product of the magic he had extended or something Lewis had never noticed before. He seemed fine, all things considered. Chelsea, the woman Noah had mentioned, might have been responsible for that too.

"That I am."

Lewis looked down at his hands or, rather, his hand.

"I'm not sure I want to be awake."

"The pain will go away. The physical, at least." Noah gestured to the bedside chair, not waiting for a confirmation but taking the fact Lewis didn't say no as an invitation to sit. "The emotional, well, that's a little harder, but judging from what I've seen from you, you'll get through that."

Lewis didn't have enough time to let the kindness of Noah's words sink in before Noah spoke again.

"What do you remember?"

At first, Lewis didn't answer, trying to parse on his own what was reality and what was fiction, but maybe Noah could help. They were, after all, in the loosest of terms, partners. And partners helped each other, right?

"I remember Australia," he said slowly. "I remember people dying because of the Dumont. Thank you, by the way."

"When I took the job as agent of the British Museum, I swore an oath to protect as many people as I could. That includes you. But," he said, cutting Lewis off before he could counter him, "let me add some clarification for you. Yes, people died, but you saved more people than ended up dead, Lewis. You stayed behind and risked yourself to stop that painting. You purified it. I didn't do that. You did."

"Amy and her husband and all of her guests are still dead because of us."

"Yes, but also, maybe not. What's one-hundred percent true is that there are millions of people alive because of us. Because of you," he emphasized. "I'm going to let you in on a little secret all agents learn within their first year of fieldwork. Being an agent isn't about saving as many lives as possible. I wish that was so, but it's about keeping the casualties as low as we can. Cursed antiquities do not care who they hurt. They were born from some of the darkest points of a person's life, imbued with resonance and on a loop that cannot be fixed, only eliminated.

"Our job is not retribution or rehabilitation or any of those words that you might hear in other careers. We are simply here to stop evil in its tracks and to ensure it doesn't hurt any more people by whatever means necessary. And that often means destruction. People will die because of that."

Lewis frowned. It was what Noah had said at the café, too, and he'd hated hearing it from him and certainly disliked it being reinforced now, after all he'd seen. "I refuse to believe that. We were able to stop *The Drowning*. No one was hurt there. Why can't that be true for the other paintings?"

"Because *The Drowning* was a specific, unusual circumstance. We were able to isolate that in a room where no one except us might get hurt. Nine times out of ten, we are not given that luxury. I know that firsthand. *You* know that firsthand."

Lewis studied Noah, concentrating on the words he said, feeling the emotion and the raw pulp of the truth behind them. He knew what this was about; at least, he assumed he did.

"There were people who were hurt in bringing *The Drowning* to you," Lewis reminded Noah. "You told me before, to remind me how important and dangerous the painting was."

Noah paused, and Lewis could tell he was deciding how to navigate the answer.

"They signed up for this," Noah said, his voice half an octave lower, almost as if he didn't believe it. "When I say no one, I mean no one innocent."

"Do you not consider yourself innocent, then? By that logic, anyone who works for the British Museum isn't."

"You're right, and so, no, I don't," Noah said without hesitation. Lewis didn't push it any further. Not because he wasn't curious, but because something else, in the way Noah spoke about responsibility and guilt, caught his attention.

"You know," Lewis said quietly, "every person who has lost someone, when they speak about death, speaks about it with a heaviness that you can't understand unless you've also experienced that loss."

It was the point of no return, like he was stepping off a ledge between Noah and himself. Lewis wouldn't say they were friends, but perhaps approaching it. This conversation, moving too quickly, could shatter that.

Oh well.

"Your sister. She died because of one of these paintings, didn't she?"

Noah let out a hitched sigh that Lewis knew he wouldn't have heard if Noah hadn't been too exhausted to hide it. It was evident on his face—in his mannerisms—a solemn heaviness weighed on him. Lewis could paint a picture of it, a representation of Noah's exhaustion, easily. Of a man who had done so much in so little time that he was fraying at the edges like a piece of leather exposed to the weather for millennia.

Maybe Noah had protected himself, shielded himself with every imaginable resource—magic, therapy, probably even drugs, alcohol, sex, and of course, the age-old compartmentalization and justification that what he was doing was worth more than his life or his sanity. But that only lasted for so long. That shell would keep the darkness inside for only so many batterings.

Noah's expression stayed wounded only for a moment, as if he hadn't expected Lewis to put the pieces together or he hadn't had someone ask him so directly about her. He shifted uncomfortably in his seat, picking at the ends of his shirtsleeves.

"I'm sure you gathered already, but she was an agent," he said. "One of the best, actually—significantly better than me. She's why I'm involved with the Macabre at all."

"Because one of them took her?"

"Yes. No. Both." Noah clarified, "She was the one responsible for them, assigned the task of looking for the paintings. Looking for you, actually. In fact, she was the one who found you about six months ago."

Noah continued, resting his elbows on his knees. "She was the one charged with finding *The Drowning*."

Lewis frowned, remembering something Noah had said earlier. "You told me you lost more than a dozen agents getting that painting."

Noah nodded curtly. "I never told you who those dozen were.

My sister was one of them. My sister was a driven person. She never stopped once she decided to do something. This was an asset, but also a liability. Because she was headstrong, angry at the world—angry at our parents, really. I see a lot of her in you."

"Thank you."

"That wasn't a compliment. It is what got her killed."

Lewis paused, noticing, like the beginning of a storm, a shift in the air between them. Quietly, though, he said, "I think it is."

Noah looked up, a bit startled by Lewis's words, but Lewis didn't back down. Instead he held the other man's gaze, hoping to convey only compassion and empathy and the idea that *I'm right here. You don't have to push me away.*

Swallowing, Noah continued. "Evangeline was nice enough to expend every resource to keep her safe, but I . . ."

Noah's voice trailed off as he closed his eyes. Lewis watched as he took in a slow and shuddering breath, holding it for three seconds and letting it out again.

"That doesn't matter," Noah said, standing. "It's in the past."

"It clearly isn't, though," Lewis murmured, sitting up, making sure to straighten his back. "You can say it."

"It doesn't matter," he repeated.

"How can you keep saying that?"

"Because that's the problem here." Noah sighed. "There are systems and rules, Lewis. Not just doing things on a whim because we want to."

Lewis was confused. Was Noah talking about his sister, or . . .

"This is about me touching the painting."

"It's about everything. I told you we were here to handle the Dumont, nothing else. And yet you jeopardized the whole mission instead of following orders." Now people are dead, you almost died, you lost your hand . . ."

"You are *not* going to blame me for—"

"Who else is there to blame?" Noah asked pointedly. "All those actions came from *your* choices, your desire to go off on your own, to rebuke orders. No one else but you."

Me, he thought. *But again, this isn't just about me. It's about Ishita too.*

"It was the right thing, to help," Lewis said, steeling his voice.

"And now we have a house of a dozen people dead and a wounded asset."

Asset. That word rang true stronger than he thought it would. Lewis swallowed thickly, narrowing his eyes.

"Is that all I am to you?"

Noah didn't answer, not at first. He stood, smoothing his fingers over his pants and his shirt. Lewis supposed Noah wasn't sure what to say or whether he should apologize. Neither of those came, only the soft thump of his shoes against the floor and the hissing sound of the door opening once more.

"Let me know if you need anything," Noah finally said. "When you're feeling better, Evangeline would like to speak with you some more."

But Lewis didn't care about that. He cared about talking to the hurt young man that was walking out of the door, a lyric from an Otis Redding song looping in his head:

And this loneliness won't leave me alone.

That was Noah. And, once more, it was Lewis too.

Fifteen

FOR THE PAST THREE AND A HALF DAYS IN THE "HOSPITAL," LEWIS HAD had a lot of time to do the one thing he never liked to do—think.

He was an artist, and self-reflection was part of his job, one of those skills that came highly recommended. Folding in and looking in on himself, exposing the pinkish inner, weakest, and most sensitive parts of himself to the world, was a natural expectation for how great art was made.

But he could control that. He could decide how much of himself he wanted to reveal and in what manner he wanted to do it, manipulate his art to reflect parts of himself that he wanted and obscure other parts he didn't.

Clever artists knew how to do this well, to evoke the strongest of emotions while revealing the most hidden parts of themselves. Of course, Lewis suspected this was what held him back. Many of his mentors had told him that to create the greatest art, he'd have to feel it, to hurt.

Lewis now had the opportunity to see what that meant, both mentally and physically, through his own experiences and others'. He wasn't sure if that was what his professors meant, but if there was something Lewis now understood, it was pain.

The agony from his missing right hand had mostly subsided. The healers at the British Museum were exceptional, to say the least, most of them using the highest caliber of magic and medical science to make the stitch look nearly invisible. The pain was good. It had a purpose.

But the memory still lingered. Phantom pain, he supposed it was called. Amputees had it all the time, sometimes for years, sometimes forever. But this, Lewis imagined, was different. Whenever he thought about Perth, about Amy, about *The Stain*, his hand ached. In the back of his mind, like it was happening across a crowded room, he could still hear the crumbling of the house. Sweat prickled on his brow, as if he was back in Australia all over again.

Chelsea, a woman with fire-engine-red hair cut short, who reminded him of what Anne of Green Gables might look like if she were older and had grown up in the twenty-first century, had become his favorite healer. She was the one who spent the most time with him. She explained to him what she was doing, unlike the nurses and doctors—who were cordial, yes, but treated him more like an inconvenience, a mistake rather than a person—which he really appreciated, as it seemed to ground the thoughts that were threatening to untether him.

She was the one who came up with the idea for the runes on his stump.

"I'm sorry, what?"

Chelsea had spent her time helping him understand how resonance was used to heal. It was a unique type of magic that literally created new cells from a mixture of the healer's resonance and the recipient's resonance and acted in a constant loop—a version of dark magic made light, she had summarized.

But this, this was different.

"I got approval from the director," she said, as if that justified her choice to essentially do experimental magic on him. Soft fingers grazed over where his hand should have been. He twitched, steeling himself from pulling away. Her fingers weren't touching the barely evident scar but the faint runes that glowed along the midline of said scar. Lewis squirmed just slightly at the faint feeling like a tickle through fabric.

"We can't give you your hand back, but these should allow you to function as if you have one."

Lewis was sure his face was conveying all Chelsea needed to know about how puzzled he was.

Chelsea sighed, pulling her wild curls into a messy bun. "All right, let me show you. Work with me here?" she asked, walking to the small table across the room. She took the clipboard with Lewis's biological data on it, showed it to him, and held it out an arm's length away.

"Grab it."

Lewis arched his brow, seeing he was going to get no further explanation. When he swung his legs over the bed, she shook her head.

"With your mind."

It took him a moment to understand what she meant, but—in her very Chelsea way—she gave no more information. So, he tried it. He focused on the clipboard. His eyes narrowed slightly, and he imagined grabbing it, feeling the wood, willing the item to come to him and be in his hand.

At first nothing happened, only the awkward silence of him acting like, frankly, an idiot. But then, with no discernible reason why the shift occurred, the clipboard twitched before yanking itself from Chelsea's grasp. Lewis barely had enough time to shield himself with his good arm before the clipboard slammed into his wrist, sending a hiss of pain pulsing through his arm.

"We'll work on that," Chelsea said, picking up the clipboard from the floor where it lay rattling. If she was impressed, she didn't show it. But when he started beaming like—again—an idiot, she shook her head. "Those runes allow you to do just that—

lift things in relation to the weight your hand could carry before you lost it. As long as the item is in your line of sight, it can be lifted, willed, thrown—you name it."

Lewis wasn't completely sure he understood. Yes, he understood the basic principles of it: His thoughts had been extended beyond the normal reach of his arm. Simple. But what he wasn't sure of was *why* this gift had been given to him.

Chelsea must again have read his question on his face.

"It was Noah's idea, if that helps," she said, smoothing the edges of the bedsheets. "Well, not only Noah—I came up with the idea, technically, and he got the buy-in. He used his collateral to convince the director. Said if you get yourself in a situation like before, you should have some way to defend yourself. This allows that."

For which he felt incredible gratitude.

And yet, he couldn't help but also feel confused. Because he still wasn't sure where he stood with Noah. All he did know was that if he and Noah discussed the failings of that mission and the magic that dripped from the Dumont paintings, they would eventually find their way back to talking about his mother.

And he saw no point in rehashing that.

Then Lewis had to admit something that lurked in the corner of his mind that he refused to see fully, that blurred and disappeared when he focused too closely: He didn't know Noah that well.

He only knew him as an agent of the British Museum, someone who had lost greatly and was willing to sacrifice greatly to right that wrong. But those weren't facts about a person. Those were the facts about someone who was barely living, who would crumble into nothingness once the mission was over and their purpose fulfilled, who didn't let anyone in because letting people in got them, and you, hurt.

Of course, he was sure that Noah did that on purpose, and he debated whether fighting through that rocky facade was worth it. It was something he had thought about far more than he wanted to admit, and he was tired of lying in this bed, rehashing those thoughts over and over. So, instead, he tried to stand once more, only for the room to reel. Chelsea rushed to his side.

"Careful," Chelsea said softly, grabbing his left hand with hers, holding him tightly. She was stronger than she looked, a skinny little thing much like the models he saw on TV. She looked naturally thin, almost birdlike, with sharp features and wide eyes. But in no way was she delicate. Too, she was warm, warm in a way that Lewis didn't know was possible. At first, he thought it was magic, some type of aura that she placed on the room or an effect that the hospital created to make him feel better.

Perhaps more logically, however, Lewis just needed company. He needed somebody in his corner who wasn't wanting anything from him, who wanted only the best for him. He hadn't felt that in a while.

"Look at you," Chelsea said. "I have to admit I'm pretty proud of my work here."

"You should be. Stitched me back together."

Chelsea let out a dismissive scoff and waved her hand. "You did the hardest part. Sure, getting rid of a curse is one thing, but you wanted to get better. And look," she said, raising his right arm where his right hand should be. "It looks good."

"It's going to take a bit of getting used to," Lewis said, "not having a hand."

Once again, Chelsea's eyes softened.

"I did my best," she said, "but the way that you lost it—it was magic I had never seen before."

"Me neither," he said with a wry smile, and she *almost* looked amused.

At least it was something.

Lewis raised his remaining hand and shook his head. It was

strange, but he had already come to terms with what he had lost, at least for now. He was sure the guilt of what happened in Perth would come crashing over him like a tsunami every now and then. Of course, the feeling of loss, eventually, would subside. Chelsea had found a way to give him something else in the meantime. The spell that made his arm an extension of his mind would be useful; there was no doubt about it. If this was the price he had to pay for one less Dumont on the planet? So be it.

The Stain was purified—one more on the list—and that meant the world was now a little bit better. People were saved because of him. Moreover, for the first time, he felt as if his life had meaning. That he had done something good. For now, that was enough.

"Okay. This time I want to see if you can stand up on your own," she said gently, placing her hands under his armpits to assist. Once he was stable, she took a step back, holding her thumb and pointer finger of each hand in an L-shaped pattern, connecting them to make a rectangle. With one eye open, she looked through the space, her eye a vibrant color shifting from green to blue, as if filters had been put in front of it.

Slowly, she moved her hand down and then up.

"There's nothing wrong with you," she finally said. "Your wounds are healed, at least the physical ones, and I think you're good to go. I can let Evangeline know, and you should be back in the field in a few days, assuming you still want to be back in the field."

It was a good question, a question he was sure Noah would be asking him. One he should probably be asking himself. He supposed, though, it wasn't the right question. Whether he wanted to or not, it didn't matter if the woman on high decided what he had done was too reckless. So, the question was whether *Evangeline* would let him back in the field.

But it brought up an even more reasonable thought, one Lewis chastised himself for not considering earlier. Perhaps Evangeline didn't care about his well-being; she only cared about the success of finding and neutralizing the Dumonts, which would make such a question moot. She would do whatever it took, strip the flesh and bone away of any living person, including himself, if it meant that the paintings were found. Nothing mattered, not who she had to rend along the way, what secrets she had to keep or lies she had to tell.

But that didn't sit right either.

Evangeline had said that there was no way to bring his mother back, at least not with the Dumonts, and he accepted that. But perhaps there was some way else. Perhaps there was magic here or *somewhere* in the world that could do it.

Why couldn't he invoke that power, then? And if the Dumonts were strong enough to be a threat to a great empire, perhaps, together, the collective magic in them would be powerful enough to bring his mother back.

And, perhaps, Evangeline didn't want him to know that.

Yes, that felt right. Something about that conclusion clicked and locked into place, some perception and intuition. Slowly, his eyes refocused, seeing Chelsea looking at him with a worried expression.

"Would you go back in the field if you were me?"

Chelsea bit her bottom lip. The balance between the spilling of blood and not was a fine line, one Lewis assumed she balanced often. The nervous tic seemed reflexive for her.

"I joined the British Museum because Ireland doesn't have an organization as powerful or as effective as England's. Trinity College has a department that focuses on the preservation of resonance, researching how to keep it balanced and creating documents about how our use of magic is tearing the carefully balanced fabric apart."

"Like climate change and the ozone layer."

"Precisely," she said. "But that's not the same as being in the action."

"But—and apologies for saying this—you're a healer. You're not in the action like Noah and other agents."

"You're right. But I *do* keep the agents alive. I make sure agents like you can go back into the field. That's enough action for me. After all, I'm doing something even more important than those stuffy agents."

"Learning how to defy death?"

"To be someone who can help those who are fighting the good fight a little longer. That's my calling. Yours is the field. But, before you can go off, and return, you need your rest."

Lewis was flattered by Chelsea's confidence, even if it wasn't fully earned. Noah had been very clear, just days before, that he had messed up. And like most things in life, time provided clarity. Perhaps he had acted out of turn, too brazen and cocky in believing that he could make a difference greater than the British Museum had. Despite what he was sure others would say, he felt like he'd failed. He couldn't do that again. He couldn't accept, like Noah had, that some number of lives lost were okay. There had to be a way to prevent that, to stay one step ahead.

And then it clicked.

"Chelsea," he said, "do you have a pen?" Lewis raised his hand. "I want to draw something. That's always calmed me."

She patted herself down comically before pulling out a ballpoint. "Will this do?"

Lewis nodded. As Chelsea took a step forward, he shook his head and focused on the pen in her hand. It took a moment for it to twitch before it hovered, shakily, pulling itself slowly toward Lewis. Each second, it seemed like the grip he had on it was going to break, but the pen continued to move by itself before settling in his lap.

Chelsea grinned, proud. "See? I told you."

"I'll get better at it," Lewis said.

"I have no doubt." Chelsea closed the door behind her as she left.

But right now, Lewis didn't care about getting better. He only cared about one thing: knowledge.

The logic he was using to get from point A to point B might be faulty, but he had to try. He remembered what he read in one of the books days before in the Contract House. Blood was the purest form of resonance, a way to tap into the richest vein of it.

If he was connected to Edgar through bloodlines, maybe he could use his blood as a stronger conduit to find the next painting. Force a fugue state and get one step ahead of Evangeline.

Lewis knew what was coming in the next few days. The ominous *Evangeline would like to speak with you* could mean he was being dismissed. Like when a principal wants to pull you into their office, or a boss puts a nine a.m. meeting with HR on the calendar on a Friday.

But unlike those situations, there was a sliver through the closing walls he could navigate to salvation. If he was smart and cunning enough. If he proved his usefulness, if he had something they couldn't get, then that might change. That *would* change. It would have to.

Will it work? he questioned as he reached over, grabbing a set of napkins to use as his canvas. He had no idea, but from what he'd read and understood about resonance and magic, it would. Focus on the idea of the painting, using his blood, mixed with the ink, and paint.

Lewis grabbed the pen with his left hand, wrapping his fingers around it like claws. It took a few tries, much like chopping off his hand, but eventually, the sharp, warm feeling of the tip of the pen stabbing into his right forearm flooded his body.

He hissed, digging the pen into his vein like into an inkwell, saturating the tip in his blood as much as he could. Pulling his shaking hand back, he studied the pen: how his blood and the ink mixed to make it a darker red hue, almost like rust, how the mixture dripped onto the napkins. Drop after drop, the ink and blood splattered, like a flower blooming and its petals yawning open.

Before he could stab himself again, Lewis felt his mind begin to drift away; comfort and ambivalence fell over him as whatever magic inside him that allowed him to paint the future took over.

And then there was silence.

Lewis couldn't be certain how long the silence and stillness lasted until he opened his eyes and noticed the warm purples, yellows, and oranges of the sunset were shining through the window. His body felt sore, his right forearm peppered with over a dozen small holes, his blanket stained with sprinkles of blood.

But the images on the napkins, five of them laid out like a puzzle, were done. An ornate house with rolling hills. The perspective was clearly from inside of a home looking outward. And it took Lewis a moment to realize he recognized exactly what it was. "Abernathy," he spoke to the home. "Call Evangeline and Noah. Tell them I know where the next painting is."

Sixteen

WHEN EVANGELINE AND NOAH ARRIVED—WITH A FLURRY AND FLUSTER as if they had been summoned with time not on their side—Lewis realized he wasn't exactly sure how he was going to handle this conversation.

Noah was, for lack of a better word, pissed at him, according to the scowl on his face. Which was fair, considering all he had done. And Evangeline wasn't exactly interested in supporting him. But Lewis knew the truth: There was a limited amount of time on his side. Noah had said that much between the lines. The way he'd acted in Perth had used up all their goodwill, and now he had to find a way to balance the scales.

As Evangeline entered ahead of Noah, her eyes scanned the room, noticing the bloodstains on the blanket, her eyes drifting back to Lewis.

"You shouldn't have done that," she said, her voice chastising and sharp.

"Touch the painting or stab myself? Because I agree."

"Don't be glib," she snapped, voice icy and cold. "Magic isn't a toy for you to play house with."

He opened his mouth to retort, to justify his choices, but Evangeline raised her hand. From the corner of his eye, he saw that Chelsea had reappeared, fiddling with the IV attached to his right arm within his biceps, flowing into his vein. Evangeline waited in silence until Chelsea left the room.

"What you two did was beyond stupid," Evangeline said firmly.

"He did what he had to do to protect me," Lewis replied, his voice careful.

"He almost alerted a whole city block, and a whole country, to magic and put unnecessary eyes on us," Evangeline sharply concluded.

"Be that as it may," she continued, gesturing a wide dismissal with a wave of her hand, "what's done is done. You called us here for—"

"I know where the next Dumont is," Lewis said firmly.

Noah frowned, a momentary sign of emotion that Evangeline didn't share. The stillness on her face was unnerving, but Lewis didn't falter.

"So the Contract House told us. What makes you think we don't know already?"

"Do you?"

Evangeline didn't answer, but simply gestured with her hand once more. "Humor me."

Lewis shook his head. "No. Not this time. Because if you knew where the next painting was, you wouldn't have come. I know I'm not on your good side right now . . ."

"You caused the deaths of a dozen people and the collapse of a home."

Lewis continued, swallowing past that. "Which means you need me to tell you where the next one is so that doesn't happen again. Am I warm?"

Evangeline fell silent. That was all he needed to confirm it.

"So, it's simple," Lewis said. "I'll guide you to where the painting is."

"Or I could just pull the information out of you," Evangeline reminded him, taking a step forward. "Your mind is fragile, more so than most, it wouldn't be that hard . . ."

"Except you might risk damaging my gift while you're in there, helping no one. When all you have to do instead is agree to this exchange and you'll get what you want."

Lewis, just for a moment, looked at Noah. He didn't expect his support, not now, and the way his jaw was set, steely and firm, confirmed Lewis was on his own. But Noah didn't speak out against him. That was something.

"Fine," Evangeline finally said. "Share."

Lewis hesitated, studying her. "How do I know—"

"I'm a woman of my word, Lewis," she said, frustrated. "And lying to you isn't worth my time when there are paintings out there that can do what was just done in Perth. Lying to you helps me not."

That was enough for Lewis, for now. Reaching under the blanket he pulled the five napkins out and laid them in a pattern, showing the expansive countryside landscape and the home.

"I didn't recognize it at first, but I took an art history class that focused on non-Western paintings." He explained, "The architecture and the landscape aren't exact, but they are reminiscent of Hiroshi Yoshida, a nineteenth-century painter known for his work in Japan. But specifically in Osaka."

"Shit," she muttered.

"Isn't that good news?" Lewis asked. "Now we know where the next painting is. I mean, Osaka's big, but it's a start."

"*Big* doesn't quite cover it," Noah replied. "Three million people live there, give or take a couple of hundred thousand, but even that's not the point," he said, looking at Lewis. "*Shit* is because Japan is not part of the connected countries." He fell silent there, pausing as if he wasn't supposed to continue with what he was saying.

Evangeline shrugged. "We're this far anyway. We might as well give him the rest."

Noah nodded, turning his gaze to Lewis. "More . . . we don't have the best relationship with Japan."

"That's an understatement," Evangeline said.

"I'm sure that you, despite your American education, understand that England has a terse relationship with some other countries historically."

Terse was a choice word, Lewis thought. He knew the way England had raped and pillaged nations throughout the world, throughout history. He wasn't here to cast judgment about that, especially considering he was American, but he understood Japan's stance. In fact, he applauded any country that was willing to puff out their chest against England.

Except, right now, that sense of justice was a hindrance to everything he, Noah, and Evangeline wanted to accomplish.

"Let me guess," Lewis said. "You're not allowed there."

"Not allowed there is . . ." Evangeline paused. "No, that's about right. We don't have a good relationship with Japan for many reasons going back hundreds of years. Japanese agents in their own magical division and our agents for the British Museum don't see eye to eye. We are an extension of the royal court here. So even though we function as an independent agency, we still take advisement and follow the edicts of the Crown, which don't always agree with what the rest of the world believes we should do when it comes to magical artifacts or magic in general."

That was an interesting way to answer the question, Lewis thought. But reading between the lines, the elegant ridges, and the pomp and circumstance, what Evangeline was basically saying was that England and Japan differed on something key and integral to their souls: how to use magic.

"So, what you're saying is if we go into Japan to try and get this piece, there's a chance it could cause an international incident."

It wasn't a question. It was a statement, one that neither Noah nor Evangeline countered.

"Well, we certainly can't go in there weapons blazing," Evangeline said. The way that she said those words made it sound as if she thought that's what the American would think they should do, as if some cowboy jingoism was his only MO.

Lewis didn't waste his breath dispelling the notion.

"It's much more delicate than that, particularly because we don't know if the Japanese already have it in their possession," Noah replied. "As you said, Osaka's a big city, and if the Japanese already have it, it's going to be even harder to get. They're not going to hand it over willingly, even if we do explain our rationale, which begs the question of whether they're using it. Unfortunately, too, your little blood painting doesn't tell us what that Dumont could do."

Lewis conceded that. But did it matter? All he could think about was what *The Stain* did to Amy, her husband, and their friends. To *him*.

If this painting was anywhere as powerful as that one . . . A shiver of disgust went down his spine. It wasn't that he thought the Japanese would use it for nefarious reasons, no more than any other country would, but he understood power, and he understood how it corrupted. The rot started from the top, and depending on who owned the painting, at best it could be corrupting only them.

At worst, it could lead to global corruption.

"There's something else to consider," Lewis said slowly, thinking through his own words. "When I touched *The Stain* . . ."

"When you acted against orders," Evangeline muttered.

"Sure. Let's go with that. I . . . felt something. Something . . ." Lewis held his remaining hand up, looking at the palm and clenching it. "Like resistance. Like the painting was pushing back against me."

"I felt it too," Noah added. "There was a malignant force in the house. A sourness in the air. It made Lewis's nose bleed. It was magic."

"Obviously," she said.

"No—this was different. Like . . . reactive." He turned to Lewis. "You're saying you felt it in the painting too."

Lewis nodded. "When I dove in, it felt thicker. Like it was fighting me." Lewis paused. "It might sound crazy, but—"

"Nothing is crazy when it comes to magic, Lewis," Evangeline said. He couldn't tell if there was a sense of compassion or annoyance in her voice.

"It felt like the painting knew I was there. Like, when we neutralized *The Drowning*, we tripped an alarm or something. It feels as if the Macabre know we're hunting them. That they know we're trying to destroy them and are fighting back."

Yes, these paintings were a blight, and the only answer—to him, at least—was to eradicate that contagion from the face of the earth.

Of course, if someone had told him months, even weeks, ago that one item could shift the axis of the world, especially one piece of art, he would've laughed at them. But knowing what a Dumont could do now, all he could think about was that there had to be a way for them to get the painting.

To destroy it.

"If you're correct, that would be reason to break the treaty," Noah said, tilting his gaze to Evangeline, asking for silent permission.

"Your actions would have global ramifications that neither of you, nor frankly, I, could understand," Evangeline said, shaking her head. "We're not going to ruin an already tightly wound relationship for an opinion or a conjecture."

"Except you're forgetting what *isn't* conjecture," Lewis said a moment later.

"And that is?"

"That I'm not British."

Both Evangeline and Noah glanced at him. There was a gap, an opening he could slip through and plead his case, and he was damn well going to take it.

"Sure, I'm working on behalf of you two, but I'm not part of the British Museum. I don't belong to your country. There are no issues with me going and at least talking to them."

"You still belong to a superpower," she reminded him. "You think that the British are the only ones that the Japanese have a problem with? In the field of magic, in the most mundane sense, America is still a corrupt capitalist nation. Fold in your magical history, not only inside of your country but outside, and the poison runs deeper than the surface. Not to mention certain nuclear incidents." How she was able to make an offhand reference out of Hiroshima and Nagasaki, Lewis wasn't sure, but he wondered if that sort of attitude had anything to do with why the Japanese hated the British as well. "They're not going to be any happier to see you than they are us. One could argue less happy."

"But I'm not working on behalf of my government either. I'm just a guy from Baltimore. I'm thinking—"

Noah interrupted. "You're thinking that if you lay all our cards out on the table, you might be able to convince them to hand it over. That you're just . . . a 'guy from Baltimore.'"

"No," Lewis said, gritting his teeth. "I'm not thinking that. I don't think it's going to be that easy, but if we put our heads together, I'm sure we can find common ground to offer them."

"The Japanese have an agency like the British do, as do the Americans—as part of your CIA," Evangeline said as if that was some slight against him personally.

Lewis said, "Which means they know of the Dumonts like you do. They understand the danger, and I'm sure over the years they might have crossed paths with one. *This* one, if we're lucky.

If they can understand, like you, how dangerous these items are and can understand that I can help destroy them, we can at least put aside our differences for that."

Noah sighed. "Your egalitarian view of the world is admirable, but we don't have the time to explain hundreds of years of geopolitical tension to you."

"Please—condescend to me more," Lewis said.

But Noah wasn't fazed by Lewis's anger. "On the surface that would work, but the intersections and the Cold War of magic are far different than anything you've learned about in your history classes. It's more complicated and intricate than surface-level warfare. Magic is a whole other beast . . . and our departments are not allies."

"And whose fault is that?" Lewis said. He knew he probably shouldn't, but he continued anyway. "No matter what you think of my knowledge of history, politics, *or* magic, they *are* interconnected. What you call surface-level geopolitics of the mundane world and the magical world are not two separate entities. They're not oil and water. Both play off each other, even if I don't know the specifics. And just as I might not know the specifics of why you all don't play nice together, it's obvious you are as much to blame if not more than the Japanese."

He knew he was wading into dangerous territory, but he had nothing to lose. At worst, he assumed that they would decide he wasn't a good enough pseudo-agent for this mission, but he did understand that he had something that they needed, and from that there was power in his voice.

"If you see another option, I'm open to it." *I'm not.* "But I am an independent agent here. I'm our best chance that the Japanese will see that I am not a threat to them, and we can neutralize this painting and get out of there." *Based on absolutely no knowledge of the Japanese and their thoughts on the matter.* "It helps everyone."

It helps me, *by making me feel useful and special again.*

"And what if the Japanese want to use you and the gift that the Dumont provides for their own nefarious reasons?" Evangeline asked.

"Why do you assume that will be their first idea?" Lewis countered.

Evangeline pursed her lips into a thin line. "Because I've been playing the geopolitical game longer than you've been alive, young man?"

Lewis could tell they were approaching a stalemate.

"I'm just saying, let me go on my own, and we can—"

"Absolutely not," she interrupted. "I saw what happened in Australia. Even if I didn't—" She gestured to his arm. "A missing hand. A dozen people dead. A house collapsed."

"That wasn't his fault," Noah said.

"No, it wasn't. It was mine for letting you two go. Lewis, you have a unique gift that we can use, yes. But it's not useful in the field."

"You can't be serious," he said. "I purified the painting—"

"Oh, no, I'm very serious. You purified it, yes, but without considering the consequences. So, once you are better, Noah will ensure you stay here until you are needed. We will bring you to the Dumont, supervised—or bring it here if possible—and you will do what has to be done and then wait until we find the next one."

"I'm—"

"This isn't a debate. This is what is happening," Evangeline said, turning toward the door. "It is my responsibility to find these paintings. It is also my job to keep you safe. Keeping you here helps with both."

"I'm not just going to sit here, twiddling my thumbs, waiting for you to call on me."

"Considering you have only one hand, I don't think that will be possible anyway," she said without hesitation, heading to the door. "We will call on you as we need you. Noah, come with me, please. We need to debrief with the others about how best to handle Japan. You know someone there, do you not?"

Noah's eyes locked onto Lewis. Lewis did his best, silently, to plead for him to say something, anything. But he knew where Noah's loyalty lay. He had made that clear.

"I do, I'll get on that right away," he muttered, turning on his heels and closing the door, leaving Lewis to his thoughts, the throbbing wound of his stump, which he was sure Chelsea would be in within moments to heal, and the heavy feeling of failure weighing on his chest.

Seventeen

AFTER EVANGELINE'S EDICT, NOAH HAD STAYED BACK, WAITING UNTIL HIS supervisor had left to speak his own order.

"You need fresh air," he said, opening the closet, examining the clothes in there. "Staying inside all day isn't good. Magic can't replace vitamin D."

Lewis stood there, hesitant about whether he could or even should trust him. Noah had made it very clear early on where his loyalties lay, especially after Lewis's choice to go against his authority in Perth.

But if Noah knew, recognized, or remembered, he didn't convey any of that in his actions. Picking out a yellow T-shirt and a pair of jeans, he placed them on the bed next to Lewis. "These would look good on you."

If anything, it reminded Lewis of someone who didn't know how to form an apology doing their best to do so. He could push back, and perhaps he should, but honestly? He was tired. And his mother always said, you got more with honey than with vinegar. And in this uncertain world, Lewis needed an ally; he knew that much.

"I'll wait outside," Noah muttered, leaving before Lewis could reply. Sighing, standing by himself, Lewis took a moment to slip on the clothes.

"Should I trust him?" he asked the house. He expected no reply, but the walls shuddered, the bookcase trembling as, once again, a book fell—Lewis, this time, reacting quickly, extending his right arm and willing the book to stop before it hit the ground.

It halted six or so inches before it collided with the floor, before, trepidatiously, it floated toward him. Lewis smiled, taking the book in his left hand, turning it over.

"*Magic, The Mind, The Body: How Mentality and Fortitude Are Half the Battle in Spellcasting*," he said out loud. "So, you have a sense of humor. Good to know."

But he made a mental note, placed it on the counter, and stepped outside. Sure enough, leaning against the wall, was Noah, sole of his boot pressed against the wall.

"Ready?"

Lewis nodded, following him down the street as they walked.

"I'm glad you're feeling better," Noah said moments later, about a block down the street.

"Is that because you don't want to lose anyone on your watch?" It was an unfair accusation, and Lewis knew it before the words left his mouth. "Sorry."

Noah raised his hand in a dismissing way. "No, I deserved that," he said.

Although Noah didn't explain why he deserved such a jab, Lewis had a few ideas. To start, one thing he'd learned about Noah thus far was that he cared a lot about other people. Even if he didn't want to admit it, he felt responsible, like their fates were intertwined. Lewis wasn't a psychologist, but he assumed this tendency had something to do with the death of Noah's sister.

But then again, agents of the British Museum were like law enforcement officers, except they were magical. There was a certain type of person who took a job like that. And though he hadn't seen that side of Noah yet that would cause Lewis to take a step back and protect himself, he knew it existed.

"I didn't expect you to say anything," Lewis said as they got into Noah's car. "In front of Evangeline."

"I should have." A beat. "You were right, you know. About Japan."

Well, that was a turn Lewis didn't expect. From the left-hand side of the car, he glanced over at Noah. He looked straight ahead as if he were afraid that if he turned to look at Lewis, he would have to admit something that he didn't want to admit to himself. But that didn't stop Noah from talking.

"We should go," he said. "Try and figure this mess out. Assuming the Japanese won't help us is projecting on our part, holding on to some age-old grudge and keeping us from even attempting to collaborate. It's keeping us siloed. Limiting us."

Lewis's shoulders relaxed half an inch. He had been thinking about what Evangeline had said, and it hadn't sat well with him, not simply because the view was, as Noah said, so limiting, but because it was a great insight into how the British Museum viewed other people around them. It was binary; there was no room for gray, which surprised him, considering that magic itself was not a black-and-white thing. It wasn't just zeros and ones. It was creativity, it was emotion, it was hope, it was dreams, all manifested into a physical force.

How could someone who used something like that, something so powerful, not see that the world, which was made up of magic, was just as complex as the spells they cast?

Simple. They chose not to because it didn't suit their goals. And that was a dangerous thing.

"You know you'd be going against your boss, correct?" Lewis asked. "If you and I go to Japan. I want to make sure you've fully processed what that means."

Noah shrugged. No words followed.

"That's not encouraging," Lewis muttered.

"The director is going to find another way to get to this

Dumont you found. And I have every confidence she will find it and obtain it. But it will take time. And that's not something we have."

Lewis quirked his brow. "You're not telling me everything."

Noah nodded. "We've been tracking movement. Of artifacts, of hedge groups of magicians. The knowledge of the Macabre to some is a legend, to others a myth not worth spending mental energy on . . ."

"And to others a reality."

"Exactly. And to many of those, those who look too closely, they've noticed the pattern. In London. In Perth . . ." Noah fell silent for a moment. "There was someone there, with us. Outside the house when it collapsed. I believe they were one of those hedge magicians."

"I didn't see anyone on the street."

"Neither did I. But I felt them. For a moment when the house collapsed. I thought it was the foundation breaking, but I think . . . I think they did it. Collapsed the house on us. I'm not sure for what purpose, but it stands to reason if they were there, they knew about the Macabre too, and if one person does, more people do."

"Did you bring it up with Evangeline?"

"I did, and she told me not to worry about it. Which, as I'm sure you can guess, made me worried."

Lewis silently agreed. Noah had reason to be worried, and it only prickled his senses about Evangeline even more. She should care about something like that. Be concerned with the situation at large. Shouldn't she be interested in collecting as much information as she could muster about her opponents, let alone amassing as strong a force against them as possible?

As they crossed the street, Lewis, turning his body to the right to avoid a group of tourists chattering rapidly and oblivious to those around them, smiled. They were finishing one another's sentences, giggling as they did so. A connection like that, especially among a group of four people, like-minded and in sync, was rare. He himself never had that with a person. Never was so much sync with another that . . .

Lewis paused, stopping in the middle of the street. It took Noah half a dozen steps to realize he was no longer beside him. Lewis saw confusion on Noah's face, then curiosity, as he walked back to gently grab Lewis's shoulder and pull him out of the street.

"Where did you go?"

"You mentioned you felt the person's presence, right?"

Noah nodded. "Pretty easy. Cloaking yourself is a basic technique, but it's harder to cloak yourself while using other magic."

"And everything has a signature, right? Even people without magic?"

"That's true. What are you getting at?"

Lewis smiled. "I have an idea," he said, extending his hand to Noah. "Trust me?"

Noah didn't hesitate long enough for Lewis to read into it. A playful, almost boyish smile spread over his features. As if this was the first time in a long while he had been excited.

"The Contract House can take us any way through any door, right?"

"Yes, that's right."

"Or anything that resembles a door?" Lewis asked, walking quickly down the street.

"Correct again, but the more questions you ask, the more hesitant I am to—"

Lewis didn't let him finish, pausing for half a moment in front of a coffee shop's door. He looked left and right, waiting for the street to be relatively empty before using his magicked hand to turn the knob.

He closed his eyes. "Abernathy, take us to the hospital."

His words weren't an order but a request spoken lightly and evenly. At first, nothing happened—no sounds, no shifting of stone, no recognition that the Contract House had even acknowledged what he'd said. But a moment later, the world around him spun and a gust of wind blew. As Lewis opened his eyes to acknowledge the house's response, he heard a whisper, so faint he almost mistook it for a trick of his mind from a whistling breeze.

As you wish.

Lewis knew that when he opened the door, the house would take him exactly where he wanted to be. He inhaled deeply and exhaled, his breath surprisingly shakier than he thought it would be.

"You know," Noah said, "in the past fortnight, you've dispelled two paintings, used magic twice, and survived an attack on your life. You're shaping up to be a talented agent."

I've also broken protocol by entering The Stain, *lost a hand, had an encounter with a strange magician, and am now breaking my confinement.*

Not exactly agent material, Lewis thought.

Lewis took in the space around them, the hospital from Edgar's painting, completely abandoned and cold, like forgotten stone.

"This place hasn't been used in years," Noah muttered, glancing around, letting his fingers drag against the walls of peeling paint and rust. With a flick of his fingers and a counterclockwise pattern with his left hand, and a clockwise one with his right, Noah closed his eyes and inhaled. He continued the opposing motion with each hand slowly, reminding Lewis of two clock hands moving in opposite directions.

"It was last occupied forty-five years ago," Noah continued, eyes still closed. "Shut down because of a scandal. Hasn't been used since. Which is strange. England wouldn't usually let a building like this stay abandoned. It's prime real estate."

"Unless something is keeping others from seeing it, or acting against it," Lewis suggested.

Noah smiled. "Exactly. It's keeping a secret, and the magic is protecting it. From the outside, I imagine someone might comment on why this abandoned building is still standing here but forget about it a moment later. I might have even passed it several dozen times..."

"So, I doubt we'll find any records here. That would be too easy," Lewis concluded, walking down the hallway. His steps felt familiar, and it took him only about a dozen to realize the Contract House had dropped him off exactly in the same hallway that the painting had taken him. He supposed that made sense. The house had no idea how to extrapolate the layout of the rest of the hospital given that Lewis never saw it. From the window halfway down the hall, he could see London like he had before. New skyscrapers and buildings had been erected over the past 150 years, but the view was otherwise still the same.

"No, we won't," Noah said, opening his eyes. "But that doesn't mean the trip is a waste."

Lewis turned to face Noah, and what he saw puzzled him. Noah's brow was scrunched, not from frustration and anger. It was the look of someone trying to put together a puzzle that was missing a piece.

"Do you sense it?" Noah asked.

"I smell mold and iron."

Noah shook his head. "No, focus. *Feel* it."

Lewis pulled at the threads of resonance Noah was hoping he would be able to detect. But it had become clear to him over the past few days that besides his own unique magic ability that had come from his ancestor, pulling at the strings of resonance to manipulate the world at large didn't come naturally to him. It made him wonder if it would come to him at all. Was manipulation of resonance something someone could learn? Or did there have to be a drop of innate talent to cultivate into something impressive?

Thankfully, Noah didn't push the subject.

"You know what a paradox is, correct?"

"Two things existing in the same space that shouldn't," Lewis said without hesitation. "The cornerstone of a lot of science fiction movies, TV shows, and books."

"Someone once said that magic is science that hasn't been understood yet. I'm sure you're seeing that scientific principles help us understand resonance. They're one and the same, two different sides of the same coin." He looked to Lewis, who urged him on, unable to dismiss how the excitement in Noah's eyes made *him* excited.

"Paradoxes do exist," Noah said. "Two things can't and shouldn't exist in the same space. It's not that the world will collapse on itself, as TV shows like you to think. It's as if they're like two same magnetic poles."

"Unable to touch no matter how hard they try."

Noah nodded. "It's nearly impossible for something to exist in the same space as something else. Not impossible in that you can't be there, but the universe will rewrite itself to prevent that from happening again. It's not that we can't use resonance to travel back in time and interfere with ourselves. It's that no matter how hard we try, the universe will make it so we never get there in time. Our spell backfires, or something comes up that will prevent us from being there by a second or two. The universe is itself a living, thinking, breathing entity, and it reacts accordingly."

"Which is all fascinating, Noah," Lewis said. "But what does that have to do with this?"

"It has *everything* to do with this," Noah replied quickly, bridging the gap between them, excitement crackling in his voice.

"Originally, we thought that when you went into a painting, you went into a pocket universe. You relived a memory. But I can feel the crackle of your previous self here. Every person has a signature, Lewis. I feel that same signature here. Twice."

"That's impossible, I've never been to this hospital before."

"But you *have*," Noah argued. "When you went into *The Stain*. I don't think you're going into a memory when you travel into a painting. I think you're actually going back in time."

It must have been clear on Lewis's face that he didn't completely understand what Noah was talking about. Noah was quick to explain further.

"Pocket universes exist because of memories; they're common. We can create them by taking memories out of someone's mind and housing them in something. It's the same principle of a Dumont, except the Dumonts are made of negative emotions, not memories. It's why we assumed the former.

"But I believe your connection with Edgar is allowing you to use these paintings, conduits of his soul that he put into these paintings when he created them, to travel to the inciting incident that created the painting."

Lewis hesitated. "It feels more like being inside a painting but . . ."

Noah shook his head. "The painting is the tunnel that takes you to the moment. It connects the here to the then. A moment in time captured from emotion and a thruway to that incident."

"In a sense it's the same principle as the Contract House latching on to a memory and using it as an express lane to a specific location?"

"Exactly," Noah replied, proud. "Except you're traveling through time because you and Edgar share a bloodline."

"That doesn't change—"

"It changes *everything*. If you can travel into the past via the paintings, it's reasonable to assume that you can edit the past, perhaps leave a marker for yourself to help us find a Dumont or change the past in other ways. It means things are more complicated. If everyone with an interest in the Dumonts who knows of you, is operating off the principle of you and a pocket memory,

I'm positive they would be far more interested in finding you if they knew you could travel into the past."

"Do you think this would make Evangeline more receptive to me helping out?"

Noah nodded. "And also put more of a target on your back. Both are good. Means you're more of a liability and an asset. And Evangeline loves those."

"It means we have to find the other paintings, even if that means bending the rules a bit."

Noah turned toward the door from which they had come, taking long, hurried strides.

A complex string of hand motions laced through his fingers, motions that Lewis recognized from Evangeline's office.

"So, we're really doing this?" Lewis asked, keeping up with him.

"Unless you don't want to and want to wait for Evangeline to call upon you?"

Lewis shook his head, placing his hand on Noah's shoulder. "You might get fired for this."

"My mother would love that." He smiled. "I don't come home nearly enough."

Eighteen

IN THE SHORT SPAN OF LESS THAN TWO WEEKS, LEWIS HAD TRAVELED farther than he ever thought he would—both figuratively and, now, literally.

From London to Perth and now Osaka—he wondered if this was what it meant to be an agent of the British Museum.

He could understand why Noah did this job.

The city was far more bustling than Perth was or even London. Lewis noticed that when they passed from the hospital into the Japanese city, for a flicker of a moment, they stepped through the Contract House. It apparently acted like an in-between space, a piece of fabric that stitched two other pieces together. It disoriented him enough that when he stepped down thousands of miles away, he was surprised and thrown off-balance.

Noah was kind enough to gently take his arm and steady him. An older Japanese woman glanced at him, although he didn't see disdain in her eyes, only curiosity. That feeling was confirmed when her eyes flickered down to his missing hand and back up to his gaze before she quickly shuffled away.

Lewis knew that look well. It was the look of someone who hadn't seen a Black person before but was too polite to say it directly to his face.

It was also the look of someone who tried to avoid looking like they were staring at his missing hand.

To her, Lewis was a passing moment, perhaps something that she would talk about with her friends or something that she would completely forget.

As Lewis scanned the streets of Osaka, listening to the bustle of new words and expressions he couldn't understand, all he could wonder was which one of these people had a connection to the Dumont.

For a brief moment, the weight of his own choices pressed down on him. What if he was wrong? What if his drawings weren't as accurate as he thought they would be and he led Noah on a wild-goose chase? Evangeline wouldn't take kindly to that, and the fragile alliance Noah and he had would shatter.

Lewis sighed, attempting for a moment to use his remaining hand to scratch at an itch on his cheek. Another harsh reminder of something he would have to get used to.

"I don't suppose you have a spell that will translate everyone for us?" Lewis asked, looking at Noah.

At first, there was no response. It was as if Noah didn't hear him, his eyes narrowed as he gazed slowly around the busy street. Noah's head moved like a scanner taking in every inch of the city block and processing it, like he was looking for something and wanted to make sure he didn't miss it, as if whatever glamour or sleight of hand used to hide it wouldn't escape his gaze.

"Noah?" Lewis repeated.

"The director is going to send people after us, you know," he muttered, shoving his hands into his pockets. "The moment she realizes we're not in London anymore."

"I assumed so." Lewis paused, clarifying, "I assumed you had prepared for that."

"Yes. No." Noah sighed. "Not really. This isn't . . ."

The words fell silent, but Lewis knew what he was trying to say.

"Isn't you?"

"Isn't me," Noah concluded. "But I do know one thing: There is a more pressing problem at hand than not having a plan."

Lewis quirked his brow.

"I imagine we have one, maybe two minutes before they find us," Noah said. "Every country, America, England, and Japan included, has casters whose sole job it is to watch and monitor who enters and leaves the country, especially those with magical signatures. They are experts at deciphering how refined and sharp a person's resonance is and can accurately pinpoint not only their location but skill level. I expect you had no idea you were being followed the moment you arrived in London."

Lewis thought he should feel a certain way about that, like a pinprick against his soul that touched a nerve, causing his temper to flare. But he understood why the British Museum did what they needed to do. He was quickly understanding that most choices, even if Noah was the one to execute them, didn't directly come from him. Would Noah have made the same choice if he was in charge? That was a hypothetical Lewis didn't want to think about. But for now, he could imagine a world where Noah would stand up against Evangeline if the situation was right and the stars aligned.

After all, Noah was here with him now.

"British agents work under the British Museum. American agents work under your CIA and FBI in a cross-departmental organization that has what you all would consider unilateral jurisdiction in America and beyond. And Japanese agents—"

"Japanese agents work for the Naikaku Jōhō Chōsashitsu," a voice said to the right of them.

Both Noah and Lewis turned quickly toward the unexpected voice. Neither had noticed the woman, about a few inches shorter than Lewis, suddenly standing there. She was dressed in a sharp red-and-black uniform, as crisp as Noah's suit. It resembled a pantsuit with a skirtlike covering on top of it and an emblem on the center of her right breast pocket reminiscent of the Japanese flag but with a kanji on it.

Her hair was black, pulled into a tight, sleek ponytail; she had molten-brown eyes that seemed to Lewis to be the most expressive part of her. Eyes were always, for everyone, a window to the soul. But Lewis could also tell that this woman's eyes would betray her without her knowing it.

Right now, though, they were sharp, as if she were focused on the kill.

"It translates to Cabinet Intelligence and Research Office," she said. "Unlike you and your British counterparts, our goals are simply to understand resonance, not weaponize it."

"I wouldn't say that's fully true, Akana," Noah replied. "You want to understand it *so* you can weaponize it."

"Defending one's own borders isn't an act of aggression, Noah. However, coming here on British business, and not gaining permission from us, is."

"How do you know we're not here to enjoy the wonderful sights of Osaka?"

"Are you?"

And this was the crux of it. For all their talk about being open with the Japanese, Lewis still wasn't sure how Noah was going to navigate the situation. In his estimation, there were two roads ahead of them: To the left, they could tell the truth and hope that this woman would support them—or at least stand out of their way—allowing them to do what they needed to do, and leave Japan as quickly and quietly as they had entered, like a whisper of smoke dancing on the breeze. And to the right . . . they could lie. Try to talk their way out of this and keep their distance from Akana and her organization, somehow sidestepping their surveillance and staying one step ahead.

Lewis was pretty sure he knew which Noah would prefer, and he wasn't entirely opposed to it either. Because the left road meant that their mission would be exposed to more people. More people meant more complications, and Lewis couldn't help but remember the heaps of flesh that were Amy and her husband.

He wouldn't let that happen again. No matter what Evangeline or Noah said.

Lewis made a motion to move forward and explain to Akana why they were here. But Noah put the palm of his hand against Lewis's chest, gently pushing him back. A gesture half telling him to back off, and half shielding Lewis from the person in front of him.

Noah Rao—the third time he had put his safety on the line for Lewis.

"We shouldn't talk about this here," Noah said quietly.

"That's not an answer, and it seems your friend wants to say something," Akana replied, looking past Noah toward Lewis.

"Talk to me, not him, Akana," Noah said firmly. "Agent to agent."

Akana sighed, running her fingers slowly through her hair. "You still haven't changed."

"I wouldn't say that. I'm being honest with you. That's more than either of us could say before."

Whatever the history was between Akana and Noah, Lewis could tell now that the threads that bound them together were thicker and stronger than steel. The tit for tat that they shot across each other's bows was playful, almost flirtatious, though Lewis wouldn't go that far. If anything, it reminded him of two professional rivals.

"No matter how honest you are, or how much you want me to think you've changed, Noah, the rules are simple: If you are here on magical business, you must announce yourself and gain permission. To the best of my knowledge, you didn't do that, correct? Which is an act of espionage and, I believe, enough for you to get your title revoked, correct?"

"You know I wouldn't break international rules if it wasn't—"

Akana raised her right hand, specifically her pointer and middle finger, the other three curled in on themselves. The way Noah shifted his right foot to steady his stance was a warning; Lewis's eyes followed Noah's, down to the ground, and saw Akana's shadow.

It was larger than any human shadow, and it was moving, expanding like a pool of ink spreading against a gray sheet of paper. Before Lewis or Noah could step out of the way, the pool of shadows formed a perfect circle and engulfed the three of them.

"I'm giving you till midnight to leave. Promise me."

"Akana," Noah said slowly.

"*Promise. Me.* I'm only giving you this warning because of your sister, Noah. She would want me to give you every chance to leave. Promise me."

Lewis looked at Noah, his own breath caught in his throat. If she knew about Noah's sister, she would know how she died. And if she knew how she died, perhaps she knew about the paintings? He assumed that was Noah's line of thinking, that Akana could be an ally because of this shared connection.

But Akana didn't seem interested in being an ally, and neither did Noah. He simply nodded curtly and bowed his head.

The shadow retreated obediently behind her. Akana took a step back. Lewis, for the first time since she approached, noticed from the corner of his eye a flicker of movement. He couldn't make it out, but it seemed like barely seen people, blurs that came in and out of focus for only a fraction of a second, long enough for his mind to register but not long enough for him to fully see.

"Midnight, Noah. That's when my kindness runs dry."

Nineteen

ACCORDING TO EVERY APP LEWIS COULD FIND, MIDNIGHT IN OSAKA would arrive in roughly five or so hours, giving them less than a quarter of a day to solve the mystery of this specific painting and get out of Japan. Never before had Lewis hated time zones more than now. Even more than he hated daylight savings time.

The ultimatum seemed impossible, and something in the depths of Lewis's soul pulled tightly like a wire, told him that they should return to London. The idea of failing wasn't something he liked to concede, but being listed as an enemy to a superpower wasn't on his list either.

After their meeting with Akana, Noah had stood in the middle of the sidewalk for a solid ten seconds watching her retreating form as she blended in with the crowd. Lewis's eyes followed too, uncertain if the way that she disappeared, slowly at first and then all at once, was a matter of distance between them or actually magic. He looked left and right before spotting a small izakaya across the street.

"Come on," he said to Noah. "Let's regroup."

Grabbing Noah's shoulder and tugging him firmly, he made his way across the street into the izakaya. After Lewis gave the universal symbol for two of holding up two fingers, the owner offered them a table, an inquisitive look on his face. Lewis wondered how often in this part of Osaka they got tourists, let alone tourists that looked like them, but he didn't dwell on it. Instead, he filled the awkward pregnant silence with words.

"The good news is at least we got to travel to a new city," he said, forcing a smile onto his lips. "Have you ever been to Japan before?"

Noah didn't answer, his eyes glued to the menu in front of him; but to Lewis, he was boring a hole through the table, past it and into the depths of the earth. Lewis sighed and leaned back.

"We knew it wasn't going to be easy," he said.

"Evangeline is going to have my head." Noah's voice was quiet, dropping to nothing more than a whisper. But even with the crackling live wire of voices that came from the other patrons, Lewis heard him clearly. "We shouldn't have come."

Lewis wasn't going to push back against that, not because he agreed or disagreed, but because it just didn't seem the time or the place. It was very clear that Akana was someone Noah didn't feel like he could overpower. Even the small display of her magic was clearly impressive. What hope did Lewis have to convince Noah, who had already resigned himself to losing, that winning was possible?

Then again, Lewis thought, fighting Akana brought up more problems than solutions. If they were trying to stay under the radar, engaging in combat in public, let alone with an agent in Japan, didn't seem like the way to do it. And so instead he shrugged. Lewis understood how hypocritical it was to be judging Noah, but time was not on their side.

Not only because Akana had given them an edict, but he imagined Evangeline wouldn't be very patient with them once she realized where they had gone. But something that Akana had said interested him, and as Lewis had quickly learned from the past two paintings, many questions could be answered by unspooling history.

"Akana and your sister knew each other." Lewis ended it as a statement rather than a question but added an open ending to it. "You never told me that."

"I never told you on purpose," Noah said, his voice cold and direct.

Even though there was a sharpness to it, Lewis wasn't offended. Sighing, he glanced up when a waitress came over to them, and with broken Japanese, he ordered Kirin Ichiban for both of them. Noah's eyes rose as he arched one brow inquisitively. Lewis shrugged in response.

"I watched a lot of anime when I was younger," he said almost sheepishly. "I'm sure they're used to it from American tourists."

A flicker of a smile for only a moment, like the initial spark of a flint, passed over Noah's face. He sighed quietly. Lewis allowed him the space to speak as much or as little as he wanted.

"Akana and my sister Ishita were junior agents together," he explained. "When my sister left India and came to England, one of her first missions sent her to Singapore."

Noah paused, pinching the bridge of his nose. "You have to understand, Lewis, my sister always wanted more. She believed she was destined for more. That her magic shouldn't be used for petty, simple squabbles that only reinforced India but could instead be used to make the world a better place."

"And," Lewis interrupted, keeping his words slow and cautious, as if saying the wrong thing might scare Noah away, "Evangeline jumped on that, right?"

Noah nodded, rubbing both sides of his face with his hands.

"I would never speak ill about my boss, and I wouldn't ask you to, but yes, Evangeline has a talent for finding those whose dreams are all-consuming and turning those dreams into nightmares. There's an argument to be had that manipulating those who believe in a higher cause is the way to create some of the best, strongest individuals. If you believe in something greater than yourself, if you believe that you are destined for something greater than yourself, then you will do everything in your power to achieve it—and someone who inspires you to achieve that greatness, you'll follow them to the ends of the earth."

Lewis knew the feeling well, when he thought about it; the way that Evangeline played on his desire to be well-known, to be someone of import, had gone amiss before, but it was very clear that dangling that carrot in front of him was a ploy. Even if she did intend to follow through with it, two things could be true at once.

"And so, I'm guessing she told your sister that she could help her achieve this goal, make the world a better place?"

Noah nodded, smiling and thanking the waitress in near-perfect Japanese when she brought the beer to them. Lewis frowned, and Noah winked.

"I never said I couldn't speak Japanese," he said before continuing. "Akana and Ishita met in Singapore. The British Museum had her investigating a cursed artifact, very similar to what we're doing now. It was a scythe that had the ability to extract the bloodline traits of the individuals whose lives it took and pass them along to the person who held it. Of course, naturally, as I'm sure you can guess, that could be a very dangerous power. Consider what might happen if the blade slashed and killed you, or Akana.

"That manipulation of shadow that she did, that you saw?" Noah said. "It allows her to create space within our world where the rules of logic bend to her own, including the rules of magic. Imagine what someone could do if they could amass more and more bloodline traits like that."

"So why did Evangeline send your sister after it?" Lewis asked. "It seems like that should go to a more senior agent."

"Normally it would," Noah confirmed, "but it was a test. For all Evangeline's flaws, if she believes in you, she's willing to push you until you break and then mend you back together into something stronger. It's how agents under her purview become some of the best agents in the arcane service. And my sister loved that.

"The thing was, England didn't know exactly where the item was. Japan did. Evangeline had originally tried to reach out to her counterpart in Akana's organization, but they were having nothing of it. But Ishita, who had yet to be in the field outside England, posed as someone antagonizing to the English government. Akana back then was more critical of her nation, and they bonded over that."

"And your sister manipulated her into showing the location of the item and then double-crossed her," Lewis guessed. Noah took a sip and nodded.

"They lost contact after that. I asked Ishita about it, but she would never talk about it. I can understand why Akana doesn't trust me or England, and by extension you."

Lewis remained silent for a moment, knitting his brow over his next question.

"You might as well ask it," Noah said.

"If you knew we were going to Osaka, you knew that you would probably cross paths with Akana again."

Noah nodded. "That's correct."

"And if you knew that, then you knew this would come up. Why didn't you bring this up earlier?"

"There was a part of me," Noah said, without hesitating to think over his answer, "that hoped Akana might have put it in the past." He shook his head. "I like to think that when Ishita passed, she was a different agent than she was when she was young. Not as brazen, not as confident."

"But you know that's not true," Lewis said quietly, gently. "It sounds like she was Evangeline's protégé, and Evangeline wouldn't think twice about double-crossing someone if it helped England."

Noah leaned back in his chair, studying Lewis. There was no feeling of a mind crawling over his psyche, but he could tell that Noah was trying to pull as much information as he could from Lewis's body language.

"Is that what you think of me?" he asked. "That I'm just Evangeline's pawn?"

Lewis didn't know how to answer the question. Truthfully, there was no easy answer. There was a part of him that understood that Noah was simply doing his job, but at the same time, Noah had made it very clear where his allegiances lay. At least moments ago he had.

But then he did a complete about-face and was willing to risk it all for this one mission.

Perhaps, Lewis thought, the reason why wasn't because Noah truly believed that Lewis was on the right path, but because when he realized the painting was in Osaka, there was a way to make amends for what his sister had done to Akana—and in some way, that brought him closer to his sister.

But before Lewis could even broach the subject, freezing cold liquid splashed against his chest. He stood up with a yelp, the front of his shirt stained light brown from the spilled beer bottle thanks to the clumsiness of a passing waitress. The girl immediately and fervently apologized in Japanese; at least that was what Lewis assumed she was saying.

"It's fine, it's fine," he quickly replied. Noah stood up, grabbing a handful of napkins and beginning to blot at his shirt. "I'm just going to wash up," Lewis said. "Give me a moment." Noah smiled slightly, a look of concern still on his face.

Walking briskly through the bar, dozens of eyes on him, and hearing the continuing apologies of the waitress, Lewis slid into one of the ten single restrooms and locked the door. Leaning against the wall, he sighed, closing his eyes. This wasn't going according to plan, but then again, how foolish of him to think that it would. Nothing about the Macabre was easy.

They had just learned that somehow, some way, Edgar Dumont had attached his psyche to a hospital and cloaked it from anyone's prying eyes. A magical sheen that lasted over 150 years. Did they really understand anything about these paintings, or were they swinging blindly? How could they—

Lewis's thoughts were cut off by a voice, a familiar voice, speaking in front of him.

"I'm not a big fan of manipulating the minds of our own people," Akana said, her voice clear as day as if she was only a few inches in front of him. "In fact, I'm going to get an earful from my boss about it tomorrow morning, if not tonight when he finds out. But I wasn't sure how to get you alone, and sometimes one has to be messy."

Lewis's eyes snapped open. Akana, from the waist up, was visible through the mirror in the bathroom. She stood in an office, arms crossed over her chest, studying Lewis, looking at the stain on his shirt. "I hope that wasn't too hot," she said.

"Do you really care?" Lewis asked back.

"If I wanted you hurt, I could have had her kill you," Akana reminded him. "I made sure not to scald you. For now, that's the extent of my kindness."

"So why did you do it?" Lewis questioned.

"There's something different about you. Noah wouldn't have brought you here if it wasn't for a very specific reason. You're not a British agent. You don't carry yourself like one. You're very clearly American, yet you don't have the bravado or overconfidence of an American agent, which means you're willingly helping him in some way, not based on some edict from a superior. And if you're helping him in some way that required him to come here, risking everything, that is of interest to me. So I'm giving you—not him, you—the option to explain why."

Lewis hesitated to give her any piece of information after how she had not only treated them out in public, but manipulated others to get him alone. Akana was playing three-dimensional chess while he was playing checkers, having just learned how to play the game. But if finding the Macabre was his goal, this was the most direct path there.

Taking a few steps forward to the mirror, Lewis sighed. He fished the napkins out of his pocket, holding the corners together as best he could to make the full image.

"We're looking for this location," he said. "There's something here that we need. I don't know if you've heard of them, the Macabre, but—"

Before Lewis could even finish his sentence, her gaze snapped up to him, a burning aura in her eyes. Every nerve in his body told him to step back from the mirror.

He only made it half a step before her hand reached out through the glass, grabbed his throat, and yanked him through it. A feeling of nothingness passed over him, weightlessness, as every bit of his essence disappeared and reappeared in another location within a second.

As his senses returned, Lewis yelped. He stumbled, his feet barely having time to find purchase before Akana spun him around and slammed him against the wall beside her mirror.

"Start talking now," she said coldly. "And explain to me as quickly and succinctly as you can why you have a drawing of my family home."

Twenty

EMOTIONS PASSED OVER AKANA'S FACE LIKE A STRING OF WAVES CRASHing against rocks. First there was confusion, then there was anger, then sadness, before settling on frustration.

Her brown eyes, sharp and focused, slowly lifted from Lewis's crumpled napkins to lock her gaze on him. It was the first time since the house collapsing on him that he actually felt fear.

"Is this some type of joke?" she asked, her voice venomous.

Lewis frowned. "I don't understand what you're talking about."

"Bullshit," Akana said, leaning forward. "So, you and Noah come here into my country to pull this shit and expect what? Everything to be fine?"

Lewis took a step to the side, attempting to put some distance between them, but failed. "Akana, I don't have any idea what you're talking about."

She snatched the napkins from him, holding them up in his line of sight, the tip of his nose brushing against them.

"No? You somehow happen to have a drawing of my family home, and you think that's a coincidence?"

Lewis, as gently as possible, lowered her hand. "Wait, go back. You're telling me that this—"

"You *know* this is my home," she said, interrupting him, giving him no chance to explain himself. "I don't know what type of magic you have, Lewis, or what game you think you're playing, or what Noah signed you up for, but this cross-cultural agreement between the British and the Americans that you two think is enough to best the Japanese isn't going to stand."

He opened his mouth, attempting to deliver some type of reason, but a chill filled the air, a familiar one that caused him to glance down and see that his shadow was no longer in the lumpy shape of a human but a perfect circle about five feet in diameter, encompassing both him and Akana.

Shit, he thought. Before Lewis could process anything else, he sank to his knees, and not of his own volition. It felt like gravity had been changed, forcing him down, and only the tip of Akana's fingers under his chin kept his head up, forcing him to look at her in supplication.

"I could *kill* you," she said.

He didn't doubt it, but, again, he was in no position to say anything. Second by second, the pressure in the space became heavier and heavier against his body. At first, it felt like a hard massage, but five seconds later, it felt like his bones were being pressed under too much weight, more weight than he could bear.

"I could snap you in half right now. Change the atmosphere in this space to dissolve your body so Noah would have no idea where to find you, and I would be perfectly within my rights."

Again, Lewis wanted to say something, to do something. He tried to will his mind to use the runes on the stump of his right arm to pull something, a book off the table to hit her in the head and break her focus. But even as he tried, Noah's warning rang true: Inside this black circle, Akana's will was law. He couldn't focus on anything but her, as if all his thoughts were centered on the woman who literally held his soul in her hand.

Yet he saw again the roller coaster of emotions on her face. There was still anger, yes, but there was also sadness, as if killing wasn't something she was accustomed to, which seemed at odds with how fearful Noah was of her retaliation. *No*, Lewis thought. There was something more. There was recognition . . .

And then it clicked.

"You've seen it," he forced out, his voice like a gurgle. "The painting, not your home—you know what I'm talking about."

Akana's face twitched only half an inch, but it was enough for Lewis to assume that he was right. As if in confirmation, the pressure lightened slightly, enough so his lungs no longer burned and he didn't feel a throbbing soreness over every inch of his body.

Akana was quiet, clearly processing how she was going to respond.

Lewis continued. "Help me," he said. The small opening had given him a little more energy, and the pressure wasn't nearly as crushing. "If I'm right, we can neutralize the painting and help save the world together. If I'm wrong—"

"I *know* you're wrong," she said. But then, immediately seeming to contradict herself, she said, "If you are wrong, I will be putting you in jail. You and Noah. Do you understand?"

Lewis nodded as best as he could with the pressure on him. He knew he wasn't wrong. At least he hoped he wasn't wrong. It seemed apparent Akana wasn't sure he was wrong, and that seemed like a good sign. Yet in the back of his mind, he couldn't help but worry about how he had overstepped once again. This could cause a deeper rift and tension between two powerful countries. This was bigger than what happened in Perth.

Except . . . also, it wasn't. People died there. People hadn't yet died here. That was the difference, and that was why he was doing this.

He wasn't so naive, however, as to think anyone at the highest echelons of either nation cared about such trivial matters as individual lives. Even Evangeline only seemed to care about the greater good when it helped accomplish her end goal.

Would Evangeline ever accept his apology? Did he think he

needed to apologize? He almost laughed at that—might have, actually, if he had enough control over his body. It didn't matter what he thought—Evangeline had made that abundantly clear. And if magic could do what Akana could do, create temporary bubbles of isolation where the laws of physics were broken, he wondered what Evangeline could do to his mind if she truly wanted to. Well, he didn't really wonder. He had an idea, and none of it sat well with him.

Suddenly, the feeling of resistance against his body was lifted. He let out a gasp as his hand fell to the ground; bent over on his knees, he gasped for air.

Akana took a step back, smoothing her fingers over her uniform. She studied Lewis, but it wasn't with a look of compassion or care, more with idle curiosity.

"You decided to come here alone, didn't you?" she said.

"You're the one who dragged me in here," he replied.

"I mean, you chose to come to Japan without Noah's consent."

"I planned it without Noah's awareness until the very end. He came along with me willingly."

She nodded, and Lewis was surprised when she extended her hand to him. At first, he didn't take it, thinking touching it would create some sort of cursed bond between them that he would regret having. But she didn't move her hand back. She didn't take no for an answer, and slowly he accepted her assistance.

Hoisted up to stand, he nodded. "I knew that Noah would say it was a bad idea."

"Because it is," she said. "I could have killed you right there, and I'm still not sure that I shouldn't have. Assuming this painting is what you say it is, that it is so important and dangerous, why do you think I won't take it for myself? Japan could do wondrous things with a painting with as much power as you seem to say it has."

"I know," Lewis said. "I would expect the same thing from the Americans or the British."

"So, I'll ask you directly: What makes you think I'll be different?"

Lewis *wasn't* sure. That was always the flaw—or, one of the main flaws—in his plan. But if she saw what these paintings could do, he liked to think that Akana would do the right thing. Not because she trusted him, per se, but because she'd become an agent to protect Japan. Like Noah had said, it had always been her priority. He just needed to remind her of that.

He decided to take a gamble. "You're a good agent. Noah told me about how you were one of the best that he or his sister ever knew," he lied.

"Still *the* best," she informed him, her voice sharp, a careful warning that he might be crossing boundaries.

"Still the best," he corrected himself. "And the best understands that sometimes some things don't deserve to exist. Their existence causes more harm than good."

Akana nodded in acceptance. Her eyes shifted toward the door on the opposite end of her office, and she paused as if she was debating something.

"I can help you," he said, interrupting her thoughts before she could decide. "You're not going to be able to deal with that painting on your own."

Akana arched her brow.

"It's not that you're not powerful enough," he said. "I just—" Again, he thought about what Noah had said, how keeping your magic close to your vest was your strongest advantage in a duel against magicians. But this wasn't a duel. This was a trust fall. He was holding out his arms, and if he expected Akana to fall back, she needed to know that he was going to catch her. "I'm the only who can stop them," he said after a pause. "I know that sounds egocentric, but I need you to believe me. It's possible for others to destroy them, but from what I gather, the amount of energy and damage that would cause would be catastrophic. Bringing me with you allows us to save as many people as possible."

Then, just because he thought it couldn't hurt: "If nothing else, if the painting is purified, you won't have to worry about the British or Americans or any crazy magical rando coming after it. Because unless you're going to spend the rest of your days protecting it, do you think Japan has enough agents to keep this safe forever?"

She narrowed her eyes, taking the compliment at her prowess along with the slight at her nation. But he could see her thinking, and Lewis knew he had struck home. He'd barely gotten a taste of fieldwork, but the moment Evangeline had tried to keep him chained to a stake in the yard, he had been ready to bolt. For someone as powerful as Akana, the idea of being the only one powerful enough to keep others from coming after such an artifact meant that would be her fate too.

Do the right thing and *be a little self-serving*, he thought, as if he could will her to agree to what was in his mind. If it didn't work, he'd then try another angle. Because all he knew was that he wouldn't let Perth happen again.

Akana still didn't seem fully convinced, but she shrugged. "You're not an agent under my control," she said. "If you die, that's up to you. I'm not going to bat an eye, and Japan's not going to care. You came here of your own volition. You die of your own volition."

He understood why she said it, but he also wondered if she didn't quite realize the danger she herself would be getting into. How the peculiar quirk of his bloodline made him necessary. He wasn't powerful enough as a mage in the everyday sense, but the skill he had made him the key to this particular mission. She might be trying to scare him off, might laugh at the idea that he was going to protect *her*, but either way, he was going with her.

"Thank you," he said.

"There's no reason to thank me," she told him, walking toward the door.

You didn't kill me, he almost pointed out, but she already knew that.

Akana pulled from her pocket a small pen, drawing a runic symbol on the door, tracing a pattern she had probably done many, many times before.

She continued to speak to him while illustrating.

"As you said, I'm a very good agent," she told him. "So, if I believe that this painting belongs in Japan's care, then I'm going to do everything in my power to keep it, even if that means killing you. If the painting is dangerous enough that it has to be destroyed, and your life is caught in the crossfire, then so be it. You and I are not working together, Lewis. We are two individuals who have a similar goal and who are allied for now. That's it."

Lewis nodded, keeping a decent distance from her. "I can live with that," he said.

"Just as long as you realize there might be a time when you won't live with that at all."

When she stepped back, the circular symbol had many different kanji characters inside of it, with more than a dozen along the periphery. Akana pressed her right hand against the center, muttering in Japanese under her breath. The black ink slowly glowed white before the symbols outside the circle rotated counterclockwise, while the symbol in the center rotated clockwise. Faster and faster they spun until they didn't look like individual symbols but one complete white line spinning on the outside and a white circle in the center.

The spinning lasted for several seconds before the white

pulsed out, taking over the entire door, giving it a pale glow. Then a pale mist retreated inward, like the process was going in reverse, and the door was no longer there. Instead, he saw a place in the same design as the sketch he had made in his fugue state.

Akana looked over her shoulder. "You make one wrong move, you do one thing that makes me think that you are lying to me, and I will end you," she said.

Lewis nodded again. "I understand."

He wished he could tell Noah. Let his partner know that he was going to Akana's home. Let him know that he was still alive. But he was positive Akana was not going to ask questions before obliterating him if he took out his phone, and the way she was charging ahead, he didn't want to be left behind.

Akana had already walked through the portal, looking at him impatiently from the other side. Lewis took a deep breath, rolled his shoulders, and tried to get rid of the soreness from the forces that she had pressed on him.

Lewis remembered reading *Through the Looking Glass*, and how impossible things were deemed everyday occurrences in Wonderland. Talking animals. Cakes that made you bigger. Drinks that made you smaller. And danger that lurked around every corner, disguising itself as quirky cats with wide grins, or powerful women with a confident demeanor. But one thing jumped out at him more than any other. Something the Cheshire Cat said to Alice, that *if you don't much care where you are going, any road can take you there if only you walk long enough*. Perhaps this road would take him where he needed to go. To ending all of this. It might not be the most direct path. But with Akana leading the way, he would get there, eventually.

Despite all that, he would do well, he thought, to be careful.

I would also do well to realize it's probably too late, he thought as he stepped through, following Akana inside.

Twenty-One

"SOMETHING'S NOT RIGHT."

Those were the words Akana said the moment they stepped forth into her home. Lewis glanced behind, watching the door they had stepped through ripple and dissolve, revealing the true nature of the room they inhabited now: nothing more than a closet with knickknacks, blankets, and towels.

He scanned the room around him. Compared to the office where they had been, he could tell that this place was ornate and beautiful, well-kept, and polished with everything in its right place.

But now that they were in it, he felt something wasn't quite right.

To the left there was an opening, the room's concept wide and sparse. There were no doors or windows on that side, only the expansive sense of a field. The floor under them was polished wood, slippery under his feet. There was a soft smell of juniper and lavender in the air, and he could hear wind chimes in the distance.

To his right there were windows with shades pulled down, made of some type of thin parchment that allowed him to see the outlines of houses in the distance. He reasoned that they were somewhere in the countryside, far away from the hustle and bustle of a city.

The home reminded him of the traditional buildings that

people assumed were the primary architectural style of Japan, almost as much a movie set as a real place. The home could have been in Akana's family for years, if not generations, and someone had done a meticulous job of keeping the house the way it had always been. It struck Lewis how much this idea affected him, because he didn't own anything like that, and neither did his family, and possibly they never would. Like many African Americans, ownership and history went back only so far. With this idea came a twinge of envy, coursing through his body. But also, a wave of adoration. The home was truly beautiful, and he was about to say so when he fully clocked what Akana had said. Looking at her now, he could tell that something was off.

"What's wrong?" he asked.

Akana didn't speak, but she did walk forward, her steps slow and careful. Lewis followed, making sure to stay right behind her in her footsteps.

"It's too quiet," she said. "Too still."

From behind he couldn't see her gaze, but her head moved side to side, sweeping like a scanner, looking for anything.

"Maybe your family's out?" he suggested. "Or asleep?"

"It's not that," she said. She fell silent again as if she wasn't sure what words to use. Moving to the exact center of the room, she stopped suddenly enough for Lewis to almost bump into her back.

"Stay close to me."

He didn't bother telling her he was literally as close to her as someone could be without touching, because Lewis knew that tone. It was the one Noah had used before with him. He knew what it was like when someone was so focused that talking expended too much energy. Akana was preparing for something, something magical, something that she felt needed all of her focus to deal with.

Something that, especially because he had no idea what it was, scared the shit out of him.

Akana was quiet for a minute. One minute turned into two, two into five, and Lewis wasn't sure she knew what she was doing at first, a thought he was embarrassed to think. He wouldn't have thought the same if Noah was quiet; he would've assumed that he was deep in thought, preparing. He should give her the same grace, but the tension coupled with knowing what these paintings could do had him on edge.

A moment later, Akana suddenly sank to one knee, pressing both palms of her hands flat against the ground. Her shadow twitched and spun, swirling to create the same circle that it had before.

She took a deep breath and exhaled, speaking a single word in Japanese. "Hagu."

The shadow rippled and pulsed like it was exhaling the same as Akana, spreading to the farthest corners of the room. It snaked up the walls, crawling and scratching, moving to the ceiling, engulfing the whole room in darkness.

That was not to say it was simply hard to see now. There was *no* light, no way to determine up from down, left from right. The darkness seemed endless and suffocating. As Lewis tried to find the seams, to find where the light had been, the separation between rooms, he realized the shadow had spread throughout the whole house, and there was nothing but blackness.

There was no way of telling time. The only thing he could focus on was his own heartbeat, which he did to keep from panicking. He had once been brought by friends to the woods on a camping trip while at college in Georgia, and it had been a cloudy, moonless night. So far from the lights of the city, he had thought it was the darkest he had ever witnessed. And yet, there was always still *something*, some hint that let shapes have definition.

Here, now, it was as if everything had turned two-dimensional, or four-dimensional, or some dimension that didn't represent reality. Stillness took over and made him feel like he was floating. He couldn't even feel the floor under his feet anymore. It was an odd, unsettling sensation until, from the farthest corners, the shadow retreated, in complete reverse of what had just happened.

A moment later, Akana's shadow was back inside her, and there was a palpable sense of relief. Until she spoke.

"There's foreign magic here. And I can't pull it off. It's like it's tied integrally to the house."

"Have you ever seen something like that before?"

"Our house is magically protected. We are a magical family. This house has been engraved inside our family lineage for centuries."

She paused, as if deciding to say something before giving in.

"In Japan, members of high-born magical families are buried under the house. The magic that resides inside the soul isn't wasted; it goes back into the home to keep it safe. Our house is our strongest magical point. I am at my strongest in my home, like my father. To put it bluntly, there should be nothing I cannot do. If there is magic here, it should be able to be stripped.

"But this? I can see it. I can feel it. I can even taste it; it tastes like copper. But I can't pull it off. It's not stronger than me," she said. "It's just different."

Lewis had an idea of what that difference might be—well, not an idea. He *knew*.

"Where is the painting in the house?"

She pointed, nodding for him to follow. Akana walked with confidence, but Lewis was warier, knowing that if this was the painting's doing, if somehow it had created a way to drape Akana's house in dark shadows and magic, it might even have a way to twist their perception of the house itself. Rooms might disappear or move—he didn't put it above the magic that this painting had—but moments later they were down the hallway, and a door was opened.

At first, neither of them made any movement, but Akana finally stepped forward, no fear evident in her body as she moved just inside the entryway. Lewis, to her right, could see the profile of her face and saw the flicker of surprise that passed over her before it morphed and evolved into something more sinister.

"Who the fuck are you?"

The strange woman in the room barely gave them any regard and for a moment didn't seem to notice that Akana was there at all, before her eyes drifted up to her and flickered over to Lewis in recognition.

"I was wondering how long it would take you to find this one," she said, pushing off the desk where she perched, behind which sat a man of middle age—a man he assumed to be Akana's father, which seemed confirmed by how she tensed when she saw him.

Akana's father reminded Lewis of every single other man in power. He was dressed well, even inside his own house, and he had the look of someone who'd had every advantage financially to keep himself young. But there was something looming over him. Lewis couldn't exactly see it, but he could feel it, like a dark malaise draped over his shoulders, like a flirtatious woman caressing his skin or a thinly veiled shawl, sucking the life from him.

Was it this woman? Or the painting?

Or both?

He was sure Akana could feel the same thing, but he imagined the sensation was new to her. It wasn't to him. There was a painting here, and it took him only a moment to scan the room and see it propped up in all its glory against the right-hand side of the office.

Unlike the other Macabre paintings, this one was warm. There was a house with a beautiful landscape, hills that reminded him of someplace in the Alps. The colors were bright, far brighter than those of the other Dumonts, and it looked almost as if it were painted by somebody different, someone happy, someone who enjoyed painting visions of life and vibrant emotions.

"You see it too, don't you?" the woman said. "This is a different version of Edgar than before. A metamorphosis of art styles. Beautiful, really."

"I don't give a fuck about the painting," Akana said. "What are you doing in my house?"

You should give a fuck, though, Lewis thought. But there was no point in warning Akana. She was too focused on getting her father's attention, a task that seemed fruitless. It was as if his soul and mind were tied to the kanji on the paper.

"Oh, I wouldn't try to disturb him, darling," the woman said flippantly. "Your father is a little distracted right now."

She moved then, standing in front of Akana's father, blocking their view.

"What did you do to my father?" Akana asked, taking a step forward. Magic sizzled and crackled in the air, smelling like burned plastic. The ends of Akana's black hair stood as if she had touched something electric, magic coursing through her veins, ready to be expelled.

But the woman raised a single finger and Akana let out a soft gasp as the magic sizzled into nothingness.

"*I* didn't do anything," the woman said, not at all fazed by the surprised and confused look on Akana's face. "But I do have a question for you." The question wasn't directed to Akana but to Lewis. "How much do you know about these paintings you're trying to purify?"

Lewis knew the question was loaded, in that the woman had information she was keeping close to her vest, possibly even fishing to figure out what the British knew that she didn't. So in perhaps the smartest move he'd made in a while, Lewis kept his mouth shut.

The woman continued, "I'll go first, then. Did you know that these paintings are actually alive?" she asked. "Each one of them is a representation of a moment in time when Edgar Dumont imbued them with his emotions. A piece of his soul went inside them."

"Emotions. Spirit. Intent. The basic tenets of magic," Akana gritted out. "Every magician knows that."

"True, but these are slightly different. You, Lewis, have seen their effects firsthand. The painting in Australia and the one that the British Museum had that they forced you to purify."

"They didn't force me to do anything," Lewis informed her.

The woman snapped her fingers, like a professor who'd latched on to a kernel of curiosity in a student's question they could mold into the right answer.

"But that's interesting, isn't it. Because if they didn't force you, then you are far more enigmatic than I ever thought."

The woman paused, as if expecting some response, but Lewis just looked at her, confused. A puzzled expression took over her own face, but only for a moment. It sat awkwardly on her, as if this woman was rarely ever confused.

"They didn't tell you, did they?" She chuckled. "Of course they didn't. That would be too noble, and when have the British ever truly been noble?"

Again she paused, this time, though, as if waiting for some applause or confirmation. Lewis gave her neither.

"Each one of these paintings has a soul. They're living. Breathing. They're not only charged with emotional and spiritual energy operating on a loop stuck in a moment, but they react to two different things. Individuals in the here and now who have the same energy as them . . ."

The woman walked to the painting, trailing the middle finger on her left hand over the gold frame.

"And you.

"See, these paintings remember who made them. They remember the pain and the emotion that went into them, and they are stuck in an endless cycle of feeling the sorrow and trauma from that moment. And you, being Edgar's descendant, remind them of that. When they find somebody who matches the same emotional pain as them, they activate. A shared symbiosis of suffering, that's what's happening here."

"I told you, I don't give a fuck about the paintings," Akana said.

"And I don't care about you," the woman said. "But if you listen to me, you'll get the answers to your question about your father, and maybe about what we can potentially do about it."

Akana didn't try to move again, not in a way that was threatening, but Lewis could tell she wanted to pounce at the woman with every muscle she had. The woman's magic was strong, though. She had nullified Akana's magical abilities with barely a flick of her hand.

The Japanese agent was smart enough to know that she couldn't win straight on, so she let the woman talk, her eyes flickering between the woman and her father, who was still frozen in space.

"Miss Ayako. You and your father suffered a terrible loss some years ago. No person should lose their parent like you did. That accident while she was traveling abroad was inexcusable."

"You don't get to talk about my mother," Akana said, her voice a venomous threat.

The woman raised her hands in a defensive, apologetic motion. "I'm sorry. That was ill spoken of me. But that emotion, that sorrow your father feels, it hasn't gone away. This painting he bought, I believe around that time—retail therapy, you called it when you found it for him—latched on to that because it has the same origin of creation."

Lewis finally decided to really study the painting then—not the brushstrokes, not the colors, not the way that Edgar Dumont was changing his artistic style over the years, but the painting itself. He saw from the distance, through the space between them, speckled spots that resembled humans without much detail. He saw the lake that reminded him of the one from the first painting, and he saw three people standing in a doorway: one clearly a woman, one Edgar, and one a man, nondescript, at his side.

"Knowing its name won't help you this time," the woman said to him, somehow anticipating what he would attempt with Edgar's painting. He didn't have time to question how she knew about that because she was already saying, "Anyone who knows much about Edgar Dumont, which are few, considering the lack of a legacy he left, knows of this one. *The Lingering*," she went on, "created when Edgar Dumont left England, fled to the Swiss Alps to restart his life, and fell in love with a woman who almost made him feel whole again.

"That's why this painting looks so idyllic, so beautiful, so still. She was the first person in his life to make him feel like he was someone other than the pain of his past. It's a beautiful painting, honestly. It's a beautiful painting that reflects the possibility of what could be when we open our hearts and forget about the sorrow that weighs on our shoulders."

"How is it doing this?" he asked

The woman smiled. "Do you think understanding the *how* will, what, help you cleanse them?"

"It's a good start."

She shook her head. "You're asking the wrong question. We'll get to the *how*. Right now, I think the *why* is more important. What's the subtext?"

Lewis didn't like the way she spoke down to him. But she was right. The more he thought, the more he focused. Every painting could do something that was reflected in the image. He let out a gasp.

A gasp that made the woman smirk.

"Exactly."

Before anyone could move, the woman took her right hand and pushed it forward against the painting, much like Lewis would to enter it. But instead, magic surged outward in response, a pulse of it rippling through the air and causing Lewis's bones to tingle.

The woman paused, confused, and tried again, and again, and again, but each time the painting refused her entry.

"Fine," she muttered. "We can do this the hard way."

"Like hell," Akana interjected. Her image flickered out of existence, for only a fraction of a moment, appearing a second later behind the woman.

But before Akana could act, the woman turned and threw her left hand out, colliding with Akana's chest.

Lewis heard the rushing of wind roar like a gale around her fingers and launch forward, slamming into Akana's body and throwing her against the far wall, where she landed in a crumpled heap.

He could hear her breathing, and he also heard the shifting of the wood beneath her as she crawled toward the center of the room.

"You didn't have to do that."

But the woman didn't respond, ignoring Lewis's concern.

"This painting, *The Lingering*, has the power to create idealism," the woman said, "to make the world seem like what it could be. Akana's father, when his daughter suggested that he take it, had no idea that when he touched the painting, it would have the same sorrow as him, and so it created this beautiful image of idealism. Not for him, no. For *her*."

With her attention back on the painting, the woman reached forward, grabbing the golden frame with both hands. As she yanked it off the wall, Lewis expected to see a hanger, or some sticky residue of what was used to connect the piece to the wall.

But instead he saw veins. Tendrils of dark, bloodred vines, dozens of them connecting the painting to the wall.

And with one hard pull, they snapped, and everything shuddered with a roar.

It sounded like a woman howling in pain, unrestricted, animalistic. It brought him to his knees, clutching his head—Akana the same. The only person unaffected was Akana's father, still looking glassy-eyed at the paper in front of him. In the space of a blink, the room around them changed.

It happened in a second—the beautiful, pristine house Akana had grown up in was replaced by something derelict and broken. The house reminded him of what the house in Perth would've looked like if it had been abandoned after its destruction for months, if not years.

The wood was rotting, the paintings that adorned the wall had been warped by time and water. Everything was layered and woven with death. This place had been destroyed and left to rot, to sit in its own filth over time. That included Akana's father, no longer a man but a desiccated skeleton.

"You see, Miss Ayako, your father only wanted one thing. To make you feel better. To help take the pain away from you losing your mother. He was a proud man, like you are a proud woman. He raised you to be such, and I believe he would be honored to see how you fought for him. But that pride was his downfall. The painting identified with it and seeped the life out of him to create this beautiful illusion. To the painting, helping you deal with the loss of your mother by making you think your father was fine, and helping your father give you some peace, was a kindness. And everyone who might threaten that peace was put under the same spell.

"There was no time that you ever came to visit your father or called him that he wasn't suffering, but you never saw it. You saw this beautiful home still erect and taken care of because that's what he wanted you to see. He wanted you to see peace, not to see how his heart was blackening and corroding on the inside. The painting gave him that, it gave you that, in exchange for his life."

"The painting fed off his resonance," Lewis said. "The house's too. It bled it dry."

"Exactly," she said, nodding in approval. "It was the price your father paid for you, Miss Ayako."

The woman twisted her hand, and Akana's body slowly rose, hovering in the air. She was limp, with cuts and bruises all over, but she would survive. With the woman's beckoning motion, Akana's body floated toward the woman, hovering face-to-face, unable to move, unable to do anything.

"Your father was a valiant man and a smart one too. Your family is one of the most powerful in Japan. He knew what he was getting himself into; he knew what he was giving you. I imagine that this world would have continued until there was nothing left of him, nothing to anchor this illusion of the home. He did that for you," she said once again, and Lewis couldn't help but think there was both a mixture of sympathy *and* scorn in these repetitions. "You should be honored to know that."

Once again, the woman's gaze shifted toward Lewis.

"The museum has you looking for each individual painting and trying to uncover the connections to find the next one. Have you asked them why they're so willing to sacrifice their agents for it? What should be so valuable that they throw away human bodies like scraps of paper? You should probably ask them before you continue forward, Lewis. I'd be curious to see how your opinion of them changes.

"Do you want to be part of a movement that is willing to affect the course of history in such a way? You don't seem like someone who would, but nonetheless." With a casual and callous flick of her hand, she tossed Akana's body toward Lewis.

He reacted in time, grabbing her so that she didn't land on the ground. He cushioned the blow, his back slamming against the wall, which cratered from his impact, making him stumble. But he was able mostly to hold his ground. The woman seemed impressed, giving a small nod of appreciation.

"Ask her," she said. "Ask Evangeline why she cares so much about these paintings. Ask about your mother. There are only seven left, Lewis. You're running out of time to decide your own destiny. Do not let her determine it for you."

"Wait!" he cried out. "Who are you?"

"No one."

And then she disappeared.

Twenty-Two

CASSANDRA HAD GOTTEN SLOPPY, LETTING HUBRIS GET THE BEST OF HER.
That was a mistake she could not afford. She knew better than to expect any Japanese agent to go on a mission on their own. Sure, having Lewis by Akana's side was some level of support, but it wasn't the support she should have been afraid of. The kages always accompanied a high-level agent, even if the agent didn't request their presence; they lingered in the corner out of view. Akana probably didn't even notice them. They were as second nature as a layer of skin or breathing.

But Cassandra knew better. At least, she should have.

She knew that the moment the girl stepped through the portal and brought herself to her childhood home on the outskirts of Osaka, they would have noticed her disappearance. They would've mobilized some of their most-skilled agents who worked in the shadows, watching, waiting, finding the perfect moment to strike—understanding the balance between letting an agent do their task on their own and ensuring their agent's success.

Cassandra had prepared for this; she'd studied and watched Akana from the periphery for the past six months. She had known the painting was in Japan and knew that eventually the British Museum would lead her to it. But she had let the sweet taste of success, the dripping gold of confidence, get the best of her.

Looking back on the interaction, she considered herself lucky. She had moved a fraction of a second before one of the kages had struck with their short blades, barely missing her skin. Cassandra was a skilled magician in her own right. She'd learned much over the one hundred thirty years of training. It was the only reason she could hold her own against three of the Akana's guards.

If the fight had gone on any longer, she would've lost. There was no doubt about it. But considering the fact that their goal was to protect Akana—and she wasn't in the best state at the moment—their priorities were split. And that was the advantage she had used.

Cassandra had wrapped herself in the cool embrace of shadows, her eyes locking with Lewis as she melted into the in-between space of reality. It was where the Gods lived, a place of magic and arcana that she hated to travel in. The Gods tended not to look favorably on those who upset the balance of nature itself, and Cassandra's existence did just that. She didn't like to spend much time here, but this time she didn't have a choice. Transportation spells took time to prepare: an exact location, an endpoint, an A and a B, a through line.

Knives coming at her throat weren't exactly conducive to putting the spell together, though. So, traveling through the stream of arcana, the magical source that so many called resonance, the sea in which the Gods lived, was the fastest way.

Cassandra hated the silky feeling, the stickiness of magic that clung to her when she stepped out of thin air. Unlike a transportation spell that needed some type of entryway, door, puddle, or shadow, she simply blinked out of existence and blinked into it again, almost bumping into a poor girl who was rushing on her way to class.

"Sorry," Cassandra said, poised and composed as ever—on the outside at least, while on the inside, she could still feel the hot, yearnful gaze of a God who looked down upon her as she rode the ripples of the magical stream. She knew that was a price she would have to pay later. She'd spent too much time in the in-between lately, and the Gods were taking notice.

But for now, she was safe, far away from Japan, with what she needed. The painting. Now she just had to decide what she was going to do with it. It was a bit of a Hail Mary, her actions in Osaka. And looking back on it, she felt a little . . . ashamed of her reaction. How brash. How foolish of her to try and destroy it then and there. But she was, for a moment, desperate. Hungry to solve just one problem out of the myriad of problems that had piled up over the years.

But for now, the painting was in France, back home. She would deal with that tomorrow. Or the day after. She needed a break.

Compartmentalization was one of Cassandra's best skills. It always had been. Being able to lump specific tasks into chests, lock them up tight, and then kick them into the endless black sea of her consciousness, letting them settle at the bottom of the ocean until they were needed, allowed her to do feats that many men claimed they could do but never truly accomplished. She had lived many lives in the past hundred-plus years, stayed one step ahead of the curve and always survived. That was something she was proud of, something she would always be proud of.

And despite hubris almost laying her low in Osaka, she wasn't one to cast off a skill because it reeked of pride. She would just take a bit of extra care in not letting it go to her head.

One hundred thirty years, and still much to learn. Then, *There— that should pause the karma police for at least a little bit.*

Dusting off her jacket, she rolled her shoulders. As she did, her outfit changed, shifting from the gray pantsuit she had worn in Osaka to a more casual outfit, a jean jacket covering a band T-shirt with a pair of matching jeans and stilettos. Her blond hair, cut short in a bob before, was now a high ponytail pulled tight, and she fished out of her pocket something that moments ago didn't exist but now felt heavy in her hand, a pair of black glasses.

The illusion wasn't needed, and in fact, it wasn't truly an illusion. She was wearing these clothes, simply changing the matter of the fabric into something different. The once-before, and the now-was. But the appearance was more what her great-nephew was used to. And considering he was the only living relative Cassandra bothered to keep in contact with, she was willing to bend herself slightly to make him comfortable. That was what family did, correct?

After all, she did owe him a visit, and subconsciously, she knew when she left Osaka, this was the only place she wanted to be. He was the only family she had left still breathing, besides Charles's child. Cassandra waved to the doorman, flashing a smile. They knew each other well enough. She didn't have to magic her way into the apartment complex, a high-rise that overlooked the Golden Gate Bridge.

"Good evening, Duncan," she said. "I hope you've been well."

"Yes, ma'am," he said, nodding in approval. "Very well. My daughter got into Columbia, actually."

Cassandra flashed a smile. It wasn't a fake one. She enjoyed talking to Duncan, a handsome man with strong features, the type of man she would bed in another life and perhaps still might. She could see herself spending the next few days in San Francisco lying low.

She might as well have some fun.

"I told you before. You don't need to call me ma'am. Cassandra is fine. Cassie, even—we're friends."

Duncan smiled. "I would prefer to call you ma'am, ma'am."

Cassandra sighed, signing into the log system. "If you must. Well, congratulations on your daughter. If she needs any contacts while she's there, let me know. I know many people in New York."

Duncan nodded in appreciation and pressed a few buttons on the phone on his desk.

"I have your aunt for you."

Cassandra knew who was on the other end, her nephew (she had long ago dropped all the "greats" that would accurately describe their true relation), Charles, and a moment later, she was in the elevator, riding smoothly to the thirtieth floor. Before the apartment door could open, halfway down the hallway, she heard the squeal of a young child. She flinched slightly, but far less than she did when the child was first born and his shrill screams filled the hospital room.

Funny, she thought, considering how she used to be a nurse. Life and death were in equal balance in her life, her past life.

How things changed over the years.

Cassandra wasn't sure if she had ever wanted kids, and that option had been taken from her long ago. She could have children, of course, but the idea of bringing them into the world, knowing the curse that she had and not knowing if it would pass on to them, felt particularly cruel. And so she hadn't.

Perhaps because of this, for many years, she resented the presence of children, the sound of their joy, the echoes of their voices, simply a reminder of what she could not have.

But the same curse that affected her did not affect her brother, and through him, through his lifeline, his lineage, she observed. For the past hundred and thirty odd years, she had watched, closer to some of the children than others. Some didn't even know she existed, but, because of her, they all had good lives.

For what was the point of long life and magic if you couldn't at least reward your family? Cassandra had been smart, cultivating financial success, manipulating the stocks in small ways here or there. Knowledge from the past led to foresight; no one saw her chess moves blatantly on display, and her money had grown exponentially. With coin spread across the world in different banks, Cassandra was one of the richest women alive, and as such, that money had gone toward ensuring the people who shared her blood were taken care of. Her great-nephew was no different.

"Hello there, sweetie," she said, her voice cooing as the little boy wobbled over to her.

For a moment, she was concerned—truly, actually, full-heartedly concerned. Had Charles let this child wander alone down the hallway? But that fear was appeased when her great-nephew, roughly thirty years old, leaned against the doorframe and smiled at her. Of those who happened to share her blood scattered across the world, Cassandra was partial to him, due in large part to this toddling ball of germs coming for her.

She looked up from the baby at Charles. He looked most like her brother, with features that had been repeated genetically: the same sharp jaw, the premature salt-and-pepper hair, the bright-blue eyes that sparkled with wonderment.

She remembered growing up with that face, and in her great-great nephew she felt in some way, shape, or form that her brother was still alive—a man whom she had last seen when she pledged her soul to the convent to become a nun. And then, when he had died after the curse had been placed upon her, Cassandra closed herself off to the world. He was dead by the time she decided to open herself back up, one of her biggest regrets. Perhaps that was why she cared so much for Charles.

Perhaps it was because she was lonely.

"He was wondering about you," Charles said, taking the baby from her. "Even said 'Auntie Cassie' a couple of days ago."

Cassandra rolled her eyes. "I highly doubt that," she retorted, but kissed him on the cheek. "Where's your wife?" she asked, closing the door as she entered the sprawling, two-bedroom apartment.

Charles ran a pharmaceutical startup in which she was a silent partner. Charles didn't know she was one of the investors, but her money had helped to ensure that he, his wife, and their child were taken care of. And that was all that she cared about.

"She's out. You actually just missed her. I'm surprised you didn't pass her outside. She'll be back soon."

Cassandra had known that, but it was polite to ask. In fact, she had been waiting outside for Amanda to leave.

For as much as she had an affinity for Charles, there was something about that woman she didn't like. She couldn't pinpoint it. Of course, it was Charles's life and his choice, but something about her felt predatory. Perhaps that was the right word, or perhaps she was overthinking. One thing was certain: The girl had magic, magic that she didn't understand. Her parents had not taught her how to use it, but it was magic that sparkled and crackled in conflict with Cassandra's own.

And that was never a good thing in Cassandra's hidden world.

Of course, Amanda wouldn't know what that feeling was. She would only know the discomfort. But eventually, that discomfort might morph into something more tangible. And while Cassandra and Charles were close, they were not as close as aunt and nephew could be. If Charles were forced to choose between Amanda or her, he would pick Amanda, as was his right and as he should.

The problem was that Cassandra would not let such a choice stand, which she knew would cause even bigger issues. So to prevent anything that she would regret, to prevent hurting her great-nephew and leaving her great-great-nephew without a mother, she kept her distance from Amanda as best as she could, like today.

"I'm surprised you came by," Charles said, offering her water.

Cassandra raised her hand, a silent refusal, and moved into the kitchen, reaching into the refrigerator to pull out a bottle of white wine. She scanned it and frowned, a frown she wasn't sure that Charles saw. It was no name brand, nothing to be proud of, especially considering their French heritage.

But Charles was as American as they came. The French lineage that she and her brother were so proud of had been diluted through the generations. Charles didn't even know French. He didn't have a French passport—a reminder, she thought, of something she needed to change.

"Surprise visit," she said. But they both knew what that meant. Charles was smart, smart enough, cunning enough, witty enough that some bit of magic he understood. It was ironic, really, considering the situation. Amanda had magic, but she knew nothing of it, and Charles had none and knew more than most people did. He knew enough to know that his aunt's business endeavors, her successes, and even her immortality came from magic, and he knew that it had its hooks dug into her flesh and heart, bleeding her dry constantly, without mercy, without remorse, without release.

When she had explained to him what she was doing and why, she could tell that he didn't fully understand it, and she didn't expect him to. But he never questioned it. He never tried to change her, never tried to make her see the world in its brightness, in beautiful colors. It would have been a waste, anyway. Many men over the years had told her that she was worth more than this vendetta. If anything, Charles tried to help, like he did now in his own, silent way. It was adorable how he was balancing his own wants with her needs, but the way that he stared was irritating.

"You can ask it," she said, sipping the wine slowly. It was too sweet, too sharp, but for now, it would do.

"This has something to do with those paintings you're looking for, doesn't it?" he asked quietly, as if his son would hear their words and understand. "That's why you're here?"

She shook her head. "No, not at all. I truly did come to visit. But where I was before did," she said.

Charles nodded, sipping his own water slowly. "Did you find it?"

Cassandra nodded again. "It was in Osaka, like I thought it was."

"Were you able to destroy it, like you wanted?"

Cassandra shifted, leaning against the silver refrigerator, her eyes flicking outside. It was a beautiful day, completely bright—cerulean skies with puffy, white clouds, a perfect day, a day that normally she would've spent in her past in the courtyard of her convent, but instead, she was here in a future that glowed with electricity, in a world where power didn't come from magic or faith but from technology and capitalism. She supposed, in some ways, the world wasn't that different now, only in the manner in which power was distributed.

"No." And that was that. A problem for the future.

"Do you have any idea where the next one is?" Charles asked. "I can always ask my college roommate again if you want, the one who works for the NSA. He helped you before."

"I know where the next one is, and it's not one I'm going to be able to get."

Charles was puzzled. "You are turning one down?" he asked. "I've never known you to do that. You've at least always tried."

Cassandra flashed him a smile, walking to her great-great-nephew, picking him up, and kissing his cheek.

"That's true," she said, speaking in a high-pitched tone as she looked at the child, a bright smile on his face, one that she couldn't help but match. "But this next one is going to kill them all. Physically. Emotionally. And once it does that, I will swoop in and pick through their carcasses for the remains," she gleefully said, her voice an octave higher than it needed to be.

She placed the baby on her hip, resting him comfortably against her body. "Now, shall we go out to lunch? It's on me, of course. I want to hear everything about my sweet, sweet great-great-nephew."

PART IV

"No act of kindness, no matter how small, is ever wasted."
—Aesop

Twenty-Three

LEWIS KNEW THE MOMENT THE WOMAN DISAPPEARED FROM AKANA'S family home that everything was about to change. It only took a fraction of a second for the shadows in his periphery to ripple.

From the inky blackness, out crawled men dressed in tight, black, sharp-cut suits. Lewis quickly put his hands up in a defensive innocent position. The men's cold eyes glanced over at Akana and then back at him.

"I didn't do it," he said.

There were half a dozen of these men, their fingers twitching to grab whatever was concealed inside the seemingly endless folds of their clothes. The rest happened quickly. Evangeline rippled into appearance with Noah standing by her side. Another Japanese man with frazzled gray-and-white hair and a slight hunchback appeared with them.

With a wave of his hand, the men turned their attention away from Lewis and headed to handle Akana.

"Stay quiet," Evangeline whispered, and for once Lewis didn't fight her.

They stayed in Japan for another six hours or so, Lewis, Noah, and Evangeline all separated from one another. Lewis didn't see Evangeline for the totality of that time until she exited a room across the hall from where he had been kept isolated and gestured with her head for him to follow. Peeling out of another room as they walked down the hall, surveyed by men in black lining the hallways, Noah also appeared, joining their duo.

With a turn once, twice, and then three times and a casual twist of her right hand, in a blink they were back within the Contract House, and Evangeline did not waste a moment to drill into him.

"I don't understand if you're stupid, ignorant, brazen, or some combination of all three," she said, her voice cold and even. "Both of you. I can accept what you did, Lewis. Ignorance will be your saving grace. But Mr. Rao, in what universe did you think this was a good idea?"

Noah didn't say anything, his head bowed slightly forward.

Instead, Lewis perked up. "It wasn't his idea," he said defensively. "I convinced him."

"I don't care whose idea it was," she cut him off, her eyes sharp and narrowed. "Because even if you are correct, Lewis, the fact that Noah was so easily manipulated by you and your whims is a bigger concern. You are an agent who serves the Crown, Noah. You understand the mission and the parameters of your responsibilities."

Noah kept silent, his head dipping lower and lower until his gaze was focused completely on his shoes. Lewis chewed on his bottom lip, not happy with how Evangeline continued to drill into Noah, but he knew better than to speak up. Noah was taking the blame to lessen whatever punishment might come Lewis's way. At least that's what he assumed.

They were, after all, partners, and partners helped each other.

"Not only have you caused an international incident in Australia"—Evangeline sighed—"but now we have one in Japan. Australia we could at least deal with. They are indebted to us, but Japan is just looking for a reason . . ." Her voice trailed off.

"Looking for a reason to what?" Lewis asked.

"There are accords," Noah spoke quietly. "Those accords are

only as strong as the trust that we have in one another, and one of them says that we will not enter another country's sovereign area and commit acts of magical origin without their permission."

Evangeline chimed in. "Of course, we break those laws all the time. It's common knowledge that we sneak into other countries, but doing something as big as this, destroying an agent's home, this will not be ignored," she said, crossing her arms. "I don't even know what type of ramifications this is going to lead to, and all because you two couldn't keep your nose out of other people's business.

"And yet my bigger and more rightful concern," Evangeline said slowly, her voice dripping with venom, "is how we let this happen. There's no universe where you should have been alone."

Both Noah and Lewis spoke at the same time, causing Evangeline to arch her brow. Their eyes cut to each other, with Noah giving him a look. It told him to stand down.

Without hesitation, Noah conceded.

"I was supposed to be watching him, yes," he said.

"And you shouldn't have been in Japan in the first place!" Evangeline reminded him. "You were supposed to stay in England, but that's another discussion. Continue."

"When we arrived in Japan," Noah continued after a hesitant pause, "we were approached by Akana. She made it very clear we needed to be out by midnight, and that was our intention until, while we were waiting in a bar, she must have hijacked someone's mind to isolate Lewis."

Lewis nodded. "Beer was spilled on me. I went to the bathroom to clean it up, and she used a mirror to lure me to her office."

Evangeline pinched the bridge of her nose. "It was so simple; it's embarrassing that you two fell for it."

This time Lewis spoke up. "I showed her the drawing. It was her family home. Of course, she was curious about it. I used that hoping I could get to the painting and handle it. For all intents and purposes, I thought she was on my side."

"She may very well have been," Evangeline agreed. "For then, at that moment, your interests aligned. I'm more interested in how she ended up like she had," she said, referring to Akana's wounded body. "You didn't do that, and we didn't detect any other individual in the room."

Lewis's brow furrowed, and he realized in that moment he probably shouldn't have let it, because it caught Evangeline's attention. "But that seems to be false," she said slowly. "Who else was there with you?"

At first, Lewis didn't answer. Weighing the options he had in front of him, he could withhold the information like he did with the illustration, hoping to make a bargain. But Evangeline was one step ahead of him, literally stepping forward to be within his personal space in the blink of an eye.

"If I have to pull the memory from your brain directly, I will," she whispered, the smell of her vanilla perfume countering the sickeningly dark nature of her words. "And I promise you, yanking the memories from your unwilling mind is one of the most painful experiences you will ever go through."

"Evangeline," Noah said, his voice a heavy whisper.

Lewis had never heard Noah use his boss's first name like that. And the way he did sent chills down his spine. Evangeline didn't even move to recognize her subordinate.

"This is no longer a little game, Lewis. International powers are at play that will not ignore what happened. This puts me and England in a very precarious situation, one that is your fault, which indirectly means that America is now involved. This could get a lot worse a lot quicker. And so, I need every bit of knowledge that I can get to prevent what could happen from happening. And if the only thing keeping me from having that is your . . ." She paused, looking him up and down. ". . . desire to feel like this is an even playing field, I will remind you of the different levels of our stature very, very quickly."

There was no part of Evangeline's words that Lewis didn't believe, but the last thing that woman had told him before she disappeared with the painting had been gnawing at the back of his mind. And each second he stared at Evangeline, that poisonous fruit's seed had taken root and spread its tendrils throughout his body. Small things about Evangeline, the way that she carried herself, how her lip curled when she was frustrated, even how the smell of vanilla had turned into something noxious and poisonous, something that days ago in the same light he found appealing, something worth admiring—which is why he blurted it out.

"You knew my mother, didn't you?"

It was the first time, and Lewis guessed the only time, he would see surprise on Evangeline's face. With her on her back foot, he didn't let up the pressure.

"You were right. There was someone there," he said, "a woman. She told me to ask about you and my mother."

"And you trust her?"

"I'm not sure yet. Why would she bring my mother up out of the blue if there wasn't something important there, something that you're not telling me? So, I'm going to ask you again."

"And that's where your mistake lies," Evangeline snapped. "There is no question that you get to ask me. Not with all the destruction and damage you have wrought."

Evangeline turned her back, gesturing with a flick of her hand for Noah to follow. They headed toward the door to the left. Pausing, Evangeline looked over her shoulder at him.

"As of now, Lewis Dixon, you—for your own safety and the safety of the reputation of the great country of England—are remanded to this room."

"Excuse me?" Lewis asked. "Remanded? You mean imprisoned."

"Whatever semantics let you sleep at night." She shrugged. "You are property of the Crown until we see fit to let you go—for your own protection, of course. We have no idea what forces are going to be looking for you now, especially after the spectacle you've made in Japan. You should be thanking me."

"There's no world where I'm going to thank someone for making me a prisoner. Maybe you're not aware, but Black people in America aren't too fond of being called property."

"You are not enslaved—"

"No. I'm just a museum piece, stolen from another culture, and now not even going to be displayed. Just stuck in a dusty room where no one can play with me until *the Crown*"—he said this last with a sneer—"says it's okay."

The house seemed to shake when he said "dusty," and Lewis muttered a quiet apology to Abernathy, even as he stared at Evangeline.

Noah spoke up quietly, interjecting like a mediator. "Ma'am, we should reconsider this," he said. "Lewis's gift is—"

"Lewis's gift will be useful when *we* say it is useful. It is very clear that he and, by extension, *you* do not understand when to show your hand and when to hold it close to your chest. I will not put you at risk, any of my agents at risk, or the reputation of my great country at risk any longer so that you two may gallivant around the world living your best adventures."

"Put me at risk? Or my power?"

Her eyes settled on Lewis once more.

"It amounts to the same thing in my eyes," she said coldly. "I am making this as clear as possible for you, Lewis: If you leave this house again without my permission, the consequences will be dire, and you will be treated as an enemy of the Crown. And I promise you, being a possession is a far better state than being an enemy."

With that, Evangeline opened the door. A burst of warm wind

from the outside invaded the Contract House, and the bustling street sounds of honking cars and a giddy group of college-age girls discussing their classes floated into the room. Evangeline's body disappeared as she stepped outside.

Noah stood in the doorway for a moment longer, his eyes locked on Lewis.

"I'm sorry," Lewis said. He knew Noah would understand why.

Glancing toward the streets to see if Evangeline was there and then glancing back at Lewis, Noah gave a momentary smile.

"Don't be," Noah replied quietly. "You were marvelous."

The door closed behind him, and Lewis felt like he could hear the magic knitting, with its locks clicking and thumping into place. He let out a deep, shaky breath, wanting for the first time since his mother died to cry, to just let out some sort of emotion, frustration for everything that had happened over the past twelve hours.

But before he could let himself fold in on himself, a thump to the left, a familiar sound, alerted him. Another book had fallen off the bookshelf, landing three feet to the left of him. Curiously, he walked over, picked the book up, expecting another volume about magical principles or history.

This book was different, however.

It was a diary, and Lewis knew almost immediately as he opened the first page who this book belonged to, because the handwriting—flowy in some instances, chicken scratch in others when time was clearly of the essence—was one he knew so well.

For it was the writing of his mother, dated on the first page exactly six months before he was born.

Twenty-Four

SEEING HIS MOTHER'S HANDWRITING SENT A SURGE OF EMOTION FLOOD-ing through Lewis's body like the dam holding back his heartache had just broken. The levees of self-defense had held strong for many weeks, but the familiar scrawl was the final straw, reminding him of what he'd lost.

He remembered his mother's handwriting so clearly, the notes peppered throughout his home on every possible surface; some of them were reminders, others half-written grocery lists, and some of them partially written inspirations for songs his mother wanted to compose. As Lewis had gotten older, he realized that each note was a kernel of truth about who his mother was, and this was no different.

"How long have you had this?" he asked the house.

There was no answer, so he flipped through the pages, finding writing in a language he couldn't pinpoint. It wasn't English; some of the symbols didn't even look like a language he had seen before. As he studied the pages, Lewis saw some of them had symbols that reminded him of Chinese, even Japanese. Others used the Latin alphabet for parts of words, mixed with symbols he couldn't even begin to decipher.

"This is some sort of code," he muttered. He looked up. "What was she keeping from who?"

If she did not want you to know, he imagined the house saying, or perhaps it did say, in a whisper in the back of his mind, *then it is not my place to tell you.*

Except for on one page, almost perfectly in the middle of the book, written halfway through the page, where there was a single, methodically written sentence in perfect English. The ink was thick, each stroke a bold expression of his mother's conviction and resolve as she wrote the sentence, taking time to underline it three times.

"*Sometimes,*" Lewis read slowly, "*I've believed as many as six impossible things before breakfast.*"

He knew where the quote came from, but that didn't matter. Because as he spoke it, a new sentence appeared in his mother's handwriting, as if she was writing it in real time.

"*But sometimes,*" he read along with the words as they appeared, "*all you need is one to turn your world mad.*"

The moment he said the last word, his mind became sharp, like the sensation when one stands up too quickly, and everything goes lighter, brighter, and clearer. A rush of feelings took over his senses, overloading them, and for a moment, it felt like his mind was being overrun.

But quickly, the feelings subsided, washing over him instead of through him, and he realized they were memories, each as rich as if they were his own. He could smell the perfume his mother used to wear, taste the chocolate cake that she indulged in; he could feel her skin, feel each scar that she had and had never told him the origin of go through its life cycle in a matter of seconds. These were his mother's memories, remembered with his own mind, blinding his vision, taking over every sense. And for a moment, he had never felt more connected with her.

But as his own senses came rushing back, the room looked different. The walls were no longer adorned with things that made the Contract House's room look like his: There were posters of Tina Turner, sheet music, and a piano taking up the western wall instead of books in a bookshelf. This was his mother's Contract House room. He could feel her presence here.

And as he turned a quarter to the left, he saw her: a younger version of herself, roughly about his age now, sitting cross-legged on the bed, her dreads thrown over her right shoulder, a sundress with flats adorning her strong but demure body. Her eyes focused on what was in her lap, her pen moving quickly over the paper.

From his position, he could see her drawing different shapes, stanzas, and musical notes. He couldn't read music, unlike his mother, but as she tapped her right finger against her knee, he could tell whatever it was brought her joy. And upside down, on the top of the page, he read the letters, *A song for Lewis*. Lewis swallowed thickly, forcing down whatever emotions threatened to erode his composure.

If there was one thing Lewis had learned, it was that memories had power and that history was steeped in magic. Somehow his mother's memories had been bound to that book and to the Contract House. He assumed the space they shared, even though it wasn't the same exact room, allowed the house to be a bridge between their two existences in this same space. This was something he was meant to see, something he imagined only he could see, and it was best that he listened.

Lewis jumped as the door slammed open. Evangeline, a younger, softer version of herself, came bursting in. Softer was the wrong word. She still had that sharp, angry scowl on her face. But time and belittlement from men with half her intelligence and accomplishments hadn't worn their grooves into her yet.

He stepped back, preventing himself from being in her line of sight. He assumed she couldn't see him. This was just a video he was watching.

His mother didn't react, continuing to tap her finger against her knee.

"What did you do?" Evangeline snarled, an expression Lewis had come to know far too well.

At first, his mother didn't answer, until Evangeline repeated herself.

"Jessica, what did you do?"

His mother looked up at her lazily, finishing a note before putting the paper to her side.

"I told you, if you ever lied to me, this relationship would be over," she replied, standing up slowly. "And that's exactly what you did. Perhaps it was because you were calling my bluff, or you thought that you could be one step ahead of me, but the lie was done, Evangeline, and that's all that matters."

Evangeline's jaw tightened, but she didn't counter what his mother said. Perhaps she knew she was caught in the lie, or she respected her too much. Probably both.

"She told me everything," his mother continued. "But I have known you longer, so I will give you a chance—one time to redeem yourself. But if you lie to me again, I'm walking out that door, and you'll never see me again."

When she stood, Lewis noticed something that wasn't as clear from her sitting position: the slight roundness of her belly. About three months pregnant, he would guess. Pregnant with him.

Evangeline swallowed, flexing her fingers by her side. "You can't trust her," she whispered.

"I can't trust you either. At least Cassandra was truthful to me, direct, very clear about her intentions, even if it set my favor against her. You, on the other hand, manipulated me, using this idea of helping people like me with ancestral bloodline traits to make the world a safer place, when all you ever wanted to do is have control."

Lewis frowned, looking sternly at his mother as though if he bored a hole into her face she would look at him to tell him what she meant.

Evangeline's shoulders rolled; she stood up a few inches straighter, at least appearing like she did. "I was always honest about my service to the Crown."

"Yes, you were, but you weren't honest about what the end result would be. You knew that I would never help you if your intention was to use that last painting to change history."

Lewis snapped his gaze over to Evangeline. Her face didn't show any amount of regret or desire for retaliation. "I was tasked with a single job, to help bring England back into power, so the sun never sets on the Empire again. That was always my responsibility."

"You just lied about how you were going to get there," his mother said. "Because you knew I would've never helped you."

Evangeline sighed, pinching her nose like she did in his timeline, putting space between the two of them. "Placing England back in power, having one superpower, is better than what exists now."

"In what universe does that make sense, Evangeline?" his mother asked hurriedly, as though, if she spoke with enough honesty and truth, it might break through Evangeline's insane thought process.

"One person in power means one funnel for information. 'Too many cooks in the kitchen,' isn't that what you Americans say?"

"Never in history has having one ruler been a good thing. That's a dictatorship."

"And where our world is now, with individualism, is better? Safer? Healthier? People don't know what is best for them. We cannot expect everyone to act for the good of the common man. England will. We can, and have, made the hard decisions."

"And that's the mistake right there," his mother said. "Edict, authoritarianism, dictatorship. You really think England wants to be empowered because it believes its rule will be better for everybody? It will only be better for the haves, and England will choose who they are. That is no different than how it is now."

Evangeline replied, "At least we can try this way; try to make the world better."

"Conflicts can be linked to two things: too many people having power or the wrong person having power. We've seen what happens when the wrong person has power, Evangeline. And too many people with power leads to bloodshed, leads to the reduction of resources, and leads to the world that we have today. We are failing ourselves, failing our offspring, and failing Mother Nature."

"At least this is a chance to start anew," Evangeline said, trying a different tack.

"With England being the one who determines the rules and laws," his mother said. "Of course. How convenient that is."

Evangeline and his mother stood at a standstill, the silence between them filling the room like the water of *The Drowning*, threatening to swallow him whole.

Eventually his mother spoke again. "Answer me this, Evangeline: With England back in power, we go back to colonies all under English rule, yes? What happens to those nations that have been flourishing without British colonialism? What happens to the nations that, with England back in power, never became colonized but are now British colonies?"

Evangeline sighed. "You are looking at it from such a microcosmic point of view. You do not understand that sacrifices in liberties should be made to help the largest group of people."

"And that is where we will always disagree," his mother said. "I'm just going to go out on a limb here and assume that those who help you have been promised some sort of position in this new rule under the Global Queen of England?"

Evangeline narrowed her eyes. "You shouldn't speak so glibly about the Queen, Jessica."

"And you shouldn't think that if you raise your hand to me, Evangeline, I won't remind you exactly who I am. I've been working with you for the past four months. I've spent a lot of time in this Contract House and around the world, and I've learned a lot of magic. I currently have inside of me a descendant of Edgar Dumont, just like me, which means two magical reservoirs exist inside of me. It would be foolish for you to think that you could strike against me and come out unscathed."

Evangeline seemed to acknowledge that, taking half a step back, tilting her gaze down slightly—a version of submission he never thought he would see from her.

"We can still make this right," Evangeline whispered, almost a plea in her voice. "There's still a possibility that we can change the world together, and I can ensure that your concerns are heard, that your family will be safe in this rewriting."

"You still don't get it." Jessica sighed, grabbing the papers and hastily placing them into her canvas bag. She hurried to the closet, shoving two or three shirts and pairs of pants inside her bag and a handful of underwear. "It's not just about me. It's not just about my future. It's about the future of those who you are choosing to rewrite who have no say. That is where I draw the line."

Jessica walked quickly by Evangeline, who turned her shoulder away so they didn't connect. "Do not follow me, Evangeline. And if I get a whiff of you or any of your agents around me, I will ensure they never see out of their eyes or are able to cast magic again. Find the rest of the Dumonts on your own. I will not be a part of this."

"Jessica," Evangeline spoke loudly. "At least tell me you're not going to help her."

Jessica didn't hesitate. "Cassandra does not have my loyalty any more than you do. She is your problem, and this war between the two of you has nothing to do with me."

"You do know eventually I will have to come for your child," Evangeline said. "The Queen will not allow this to just go unfinished. Not only do you know too much, but if the solution to her problems is only an ocean away, our friendship, your threats, are not going to keep me from him."

"I would expect nothing less," Jessica replied. "But I will remind you that, throughout history, unexplainable magic has always been linked to those trying to protect the ones they love. And I will not hold back to ensure that my boy stays as far away from you and the clutches of the Crown as possible."

As Lewis's mother slammed the door, the ripple of magic caused him to blink, and instantaneously he was back inside his room. He took a deep breath, realizing that he had been holding it throughout nearly the whole vision, coughing as he collapsed to the floor, breathing deeply and shakily.

He'd just learned his three truths. One, Evangeline had firmly lied to him; two, she knew his mother; and three, Cassandra was most likely the woman he'd met in Osaka.

"Thank you," he said to the house, standing up quickly. "Will you let me leave?"

There was no reason to believe the house would. It served Evangeline and the Crown, after all. But as the door creaked open, Lewis smiled, running out quickly, half expecting to appear inside the British Museum.

It definitely was *not* the museum.

As he stumbled out, the differences of his location from before to now caused his mind to feel jumbled. It was hotter, brighter, louder. The air smelled sharper. Not only was he not in the museum, he was positive he wasn't in downtown London anymore. Rather, he was standing in a hospital very different from the one in London.

Very different because the hallway was filled with darker-skinned people like him, hurriedly rushing to their loved ones, to rooms, addressing codes, or leaving from long medical shifts, all speaking fluent Hindi.

Twenty-Five

LEWIS PINCHED HIS ARM BY BRINGING HIS FOREARM TO HIS LIPS AND BIT-
ing it, gentle enough to not draw blood but firm enough to make him wince.

He had seen somewhere on a TV show he watched when he was a teenager a character trapped inside of an illusion who used pain to break themselves out of it. It seemed worth a try.

But the shock of electricity that coursed through his body confirmed to him that this was real. He was in fact somewhere in South Asia—almost certainly India—delivered here by the Contract House for some purpose.

The first and most chilling thought that came to mind was that there was a painting here. But that thought walked out the window when at the end of the hall, through a sea of people, Lewis saw a familiar face speaking with a short woman wearing the most elegant dress Lewis had ever seen, a dress that made her shimmer like diamonds.

The house had taken him to where Noah was.

Noah didn't see him, focused too much on the words of the woman and bringing her close to his chest, rubbing his hand over the back of her midnight, silky hair. The expression on Noah's face seemed pained, swallowing whatever it was that threatened to bring tears to his eyes. It was a side of Noah Lewis hadn't seen before. Not that Noah was a person who couldn't experience compassion, but this looked like a shared pain; one—Lewis realized—that he shouldn't have been privy to.

He thought about exiting back into London using the still-open door of the Contract House to give Noah privacy. Technically, he was breaking Evangeline's rules and, in coming here, putting more of a target on Noah's back.

But before he could turn a full 180 degrees and walk back into his makeshift prison, Noah's eyes caught his. They locked for a moment of stillness as if the world around them stopped. No words were exchanged, but paragraphs passed between the two of them.

Lewis knew that Noah was equally as confused, but he tried his best to keep his face neutral. He watched as Noah pulled his body away from the woman, kissing her on the top of her head and gently gesturing her down the hallway. Noah watched as she retreated out of view, long enough to make sure she made it to wherever she was going before turning to him and walking swiftly over. His steps were ones with purpose, but not with anger.

When they met halfway, Lewis spoke first, before Noah could say anything.

"I want you to know that I'm not following you," he said quickly. "Well, not really. I guess technically I am but . . ."

Noah smiled, very faintly. "I missed this."

Lewis arched his brow.

"Your . . . aura." Noah gestured. "The slight awkwardness you carry, like you're still learning the steps to a dance you secretly, deep down, already know how to do, even if you don't remember it yourself."

Lewis felt his cheeks burn slightly but pushed it down to focus on the topic at hand. "The Contract House just opened here. Like it thought you . . . needed me?" Lewis paused. "Do you need me?"

Noah's face registered confusion but relaxed a moment later. "I got a call when Evangeline and I left . . . a call from my mother.

I came here right away. I don't know why the house brought you to me, though. There's no painting here."

"I was wondering the same thing..." Lewis let his words trail off, an open invitation for Noah to explain further if he wanted to. "If there's no painting here, why did the Contract House bring me to you?"

And then, it all clicked.

Sighing and running his fingers through his unkempt dark hair, Noah took the bait. "My father is dying," he said, the words coming out quickly, almost like one single word, not an individual sentence. "I don't know how long he's been sick, but..."

The Contract House knew Noah was important to Lewis and vice versa. Noah had been the agent who had made the bond possible. Perhaps the house knew that Noah needed him and was attempting in some way to help.

"I'm so sorry, Noah," Lewis said, reaching up and squeezing his shoulder. He didn't need to say he knew how it felt to lose a parent. Noah knew, and he didn't seem like the type of person who wanted that level of compassion. "How long does he have?"

Noah sighed, shrugging. "I'm not sure. The doctors don't exactly know what's wrong with him. A week or so ago he was fine, and then he just started coughing, getting weak, his muscle and bone mass drastically decreasing."

"Is it a curse?" Lewis asked, though he assumed Noah had already considered that.

"I asked my mother, but she wasn't sure." Noah paused to explain: "My sister and I are more magically talented than my parents, but they know their way around a spell or two. My mother would've noticed if there was something cursed attached to her husband."

Lewis swallowed, stepping aside along with Noah as two doctors rushed with a patient on a gurney down the hallway. A thought bubbled from the back of Lewis's mind to the forefront. "Have you considered this is something else?"

Noah didn't turn his gaze away from the window directly in front of them. "Do you mean like an attack?" he asked. "I thought about it. Considered that someone might be trying to strike my family to get to me."

"Or to get to *me*," Lewis added.

This time Noah did glance over at him, turning his full body to face him. "What do you mean?"

Lewis thought, for a moment, about how to answer that. Perhaps he was overthinking it; he did that often enough. Or perhaps he was reading too much into it, seeing patterns that didn't exist.

But, like his mother said, one truth can change the world.

"Perhaps," he said slowly, "whoever is coming for your father knows that coming for you means they can get to me because you're important to me," he said in a whisper. "They know . . ."

"They know you'll do anything to protect me," Noah finished for him, his voice an octave lower. "It makes logical sense. If they wanted to get to me, targeting *your* father is one way they could bend *my* will."

To say Lewis was surprised to hear that was an understatement, and he knew his face showed it. Noah caught his gaze, with a soft chuckle like an afterthought.

"Don't act so surprised, Lewis. And besides, that doesn't matter. I am an agent of the British Museum. I understood the risk of taking the job, and so did my family. So did you when you joined us. Many agents have had their loved ones used as collateral against them. This would not be the first time, and it will not be the last. My responsibility is to the Crown." Noah swallowed. "And if that means that I have to lose my father in the process . . ."

He didn't finish his sentence, and Lewis allowed him that grace. It wasn't fair to make him vocalize that thought, but at the same time, Lewis truly wondered, if push came to shove, if that choice was put in front of him, if Noah would make it. He'd already lost his sister. Would he be willing to sacrifice his father too?

"This isn't the best time," Lewis said quietly, "and I'm sorry to bring it up. But there's something I need to tell you. Something I saw in the Contract House."

Instead of telling him, Lewis took Noah's right hand, feeling the softness of the pads of his long fingers as he pressed them against his temple.

"Look," he said.

At first Noah was puzzled, but quickly understood. He closed his eyes and whispered a Greek word under his breath. Lewis felt warmth pass through their connected skin. A shiver ran down his spine at what he could only describe as his memories being fanned through, making him roll his shoulder and squirm.

He saw, as if he was experiencing the memory for the first time, the moment inside the Contract House he'd experienced just moments before, now viewed by Noah. Roughly a minute later, Noah pulled his hand back silently.

"Did you know?" Lewis whispered, desperation in his voice. If Noah had known all this time and he was siding with Evangeline, Lewis would understand it, but the trust between them would be broken.

"No," Noah said, "I promise you I did not. Would've never brought you here if I knew."

Lewis frowned. "You didn't bring me here." He paused. "You mean into all this. How long had you been watching me?"

"My sister started it," Noah said, without hesitating or even trying to mask the truth. "She was your original handler. She's the one who got *The Drowning* to the museum. I picked up afterward. She left off after she made an attempt—" He swallowed. "An attempt to use the magic she had gathered over the years traveling the world to try and find a way to neutralize the painting without you."

Lewis hesitated. "Why would she want that?" he asked.

"My sister cared about power and recognition and fame. She cared about being someone of import. But at the same time, she took this job to protect people. Same reason you took the offer, and she knew, even as Evangeline masked the truth behind flowery language and empty promises, what would happen to you throughout this, the risk that you would be put in. And she wanted to prevent that, and it killed her."

"So," Noah said, after a pause, "when the opportunity arose for someone to take up the case . . ."

"You took it up for her," Lewis finished, "bringing you closer to your sister and assuring that I could make sure that you stayed alive."

"My sister died doing that, protecting you, ensuring that you, an innocent bystander, would not become prey to whatever megalomaniac desire of the Crown. And I'll be damned if I let my sister down."

Lewis wasn't sure what to say or if he should thank Noah, call him foolish for risking himself for a man he didn't even know months ago, or something else.

But before he could, the same short woman from before came walking quickly down the hallway. Her eyes settled on Lewis for a moment, a puzzled expression over her beautiful dark brown features before her warm gaze shifted to Noah. "Beta," she said, "who is this?"

There was no accusation or anger in her voice. Instead, there was pure curiosity and the light warmth that was an unmistakable tone of a mother.

"This is Lewis, Ma," Noah said, introducing him to his mother. "We work together at the British Museum."

"So nice to meet you, Ms. Rao," Lewis said, extending his hand.

Noah's mother glanced at his fingers before making a tsking sound, shaking her head and pulling him into a warm embrace.

"I hug," she said, "especially anyone who is a friend of my son's."

The way Lewis's knees buckled when Noah's mother hugged him was almost embarrassing. The honeylike sweetness that passed over his body made him resign himself to a feeling he hadn't felt in months. There was nothing like the hug of a mother to tell you that everything would be okay, to remind you that the world wasn't as scary as it liked to think it was.

He might have been embarrassed by how quickly he wrapped his arms around her body and held her close, the sigh that he let out, and the feeling of relaxation from his tired joints. But all she did was rub his back. She said nothing. She didn't comment on it. She just held him until he was ready to pull away.

Slowly Lewis did. And when he had, Noah's mother squeezed his right forearm.

"Come, I want to show you both something," she said. "Someone is here to see you. They came as soon as they heard that you were here."

Noah sighed, walking along with his mother and Lewis, each of them flanking one of her sides.

"Please don't tell me this is one of your friends trying to set me up with one of their daughters."

As Noah spoke, Lewis did wonder for a moment if his mother knew her son was gay. Which brought up a question he never thought to check—*was* Noah gay? Bi? Questioning? Did any of it really matter in the moment?

The answer, he found deep inside him, was yes . . .

The thought was pushed down as Noah's mother scoffed. "Even if it was, you will indulge me," she said. "I deserve to have grandchildren. At the very least, I deserve to have somebody to dote over, to show all your boring and embarrassing baby pictures to."

She glanced over at Lewis, looking him up and down once more. "You would look cute with my son. Are you seeing anyone?"

Noah cursed under his breath in Hindi, looking over his mother's head at Lewis. "I'm sorry for her," he mouthed, but Lewis smiled.

"I'm not," he said down to her. "And your son is very handsome."

"See." She beamed proudly. "He thinks you're handsome. Don't worry about all that red tape of bureaucracy. Ask him out, beta."

Noah grumbled, a faint redness spreading over his cheeks. But he said nothing. And as Lewis noted, that wasn't a no.

But as they rounded the corner and slowed their pace to the first door on the left, the warmth and lightness of the moment changed. Not, as Lewis had originally thought, because they were entering a room where death had claimed its domain.

Rather, it was because of a girl sitting by the side of the bed in a chair singing the most beautiful tune, a lullaby Lewis had never heard, one with an undertone of sadness but also of hope intertwined in the notes—a girl who caused Noah's warm, vibrant skin to turn ashen as if he had seen a ghost come back to life.

One who had a striking resemblance to Noah and his mother.

Twenty-Six

LEWIS HAD NO IDEA HOW TO PROCESS THE IMAGE IN FRONT OF HIM.
He didn't need to be told the woman sitting by Noah's father's side was Ishita Rao. The way his mother glided into the room and kissed the younger woman's cheek, wrapping her arms from behind around her daughter's shoulders, resting her cheek against her daughter's—and the way Noah looked at her, with panic and despair—told Lewis everything he needed to know. But Ishita was dead. There was no way, no logical reason, for her to be sitting here right in front of them.

Lewis, of course, recognized he knew very little about what magic could and could not do. But, with his limited knowledge, he had produced three options: One, Ishita had lied about her death, kept it from Noah this whole time, a conspiracy his family had cosigned, leaving the younger brother to pity and mourn his sister, changing his whole life trajectory based on the idea of absolution.

Two, someone had engaged in a forbidden act of necromancy, defiled Ishita's body, and brought her back to life. But that begged the question, who would do that? One of Noah's family members, who had missed her so much they were willing to break the law? Or possibly someone who was playing a cruel joke on the wealthy and well-connected Indian family?

And then there was three.

Perhaps, in some way, shape, or form, a Macabre painting was involved. Maybe that was far-fetched, but in just three encounters with the Macabre, he knew what it was capable of—and how it was growing stronger, its tendrils reaching out farther and farther. So that option was the most terrifying of all, because every person who touched or was in the vicinity of a painting, one way or another, was touched by death.

And as Lewis had learned early on, death wasn't something any mortal should be playing with.

"Isn't it great, beta?" Noah's mother said, turning to him with a smile. "Your sister has been here with your father for the past several days."

"Several days?" Noah choked out, his eyes slowly shifting over to his father in the bed. Lewis's gaze followed, seeing the gaunt man whose body looked almost comically small, like a poorly done CGI version of a person.

His cheekbones were sharp, his hands were too thin. Lewis could clearly see the outline of bone where his skin draped over it as if it was painted on—flesh and muscle and sinew drained from his body, leaving only a husk, as if his body had declared everything else but the bare essentials a luxury in keeping itself alive.

Noah's mother nodded. "She knocked on the door about a week ago. I was meaning to call you, but things have just been so . . ." His mother's voice trailed off. "Busy."

Lewis swallowed thickly, noticing how Ishita's eyes never left him. She kept her gaze focused, unblinking, almost terrifyingly so. She crossed her hands in her lap, her posture perfectly poised.

"We should step out," Lewis said, his voice cracking, betraying his facade of confidence.

Noah didn't respond. Ishita's eyes were focused on Lewis, and Noah's eyes were focused on his sister.

Finally, as Lewis reached over and squeezed Noah's arm, he snapped out of it.

"Yeah . . ." he muttered, voice light, almost a whisper. Louder, to his mother and "sister," he said, "I'll be right back."

But before Noah could turn and leave, Ishita spoke. "Brother," she said, her voice light, airy, inviting. Everything about it sounded so human. Like the type of voice Lewis would want to listen to. A voice he would ask questions of just to hear it speak, even if he didn't care what the answer was.

"You *will* come back, won't you?" she asked, when Noah didn't respond. "We have so much catching up to do."

"I'll be back," Noah said, no emotion—just a stone-cold response that was syllables somehow blended together into a sentence. He stepped out, Lewis following, flashing a smile to Noah's mom—a reassuring one, even though he wasn't sure she knew why she'd need it.

As Lewis closed the door, Noah snapped both of his fingers on both hands in perfect unison and then clapped his hands together, boldly saying a word in Spanish before rotating his fingers ninety degrees toward the door and fanning his connected hands outward, like shutters being opened. The door behind them glowed a faint yellow before the color seeped also into the wood and glass.

"They can't see or hear us," Noah said. "According to them and what their senses allow them to see, we did exactly what we said and walked away." He took a deep breath, then looked into Lewis's eyes. "Be my sounding board and voice of reason here. I cannot analyze this objectively."

"Your sister's dead," he said. "Sorry," he added quickly.

Noah brushed by that apology. "I *know*. But she is *there*, very much not dead. So, I'm assuming you've already come to the same conclusion I have, yes?"

"That it's probably a painting."

"Exactly. And that's the reason you're here. The reason the Contract House brought me here as well. The fact she wouldn't stop looking at me . . ." He shook his head. "I don't know how my parents got hold of a Macabre, though," Noah muttered. "They like art, but my parents are very specific. Picky, one would say. The type of art the Macabre paintings express wouldn't be something they would buy."

"Unless it was gifted to them?" Lewis supplied. "It's reasonable to assume, if someone gave your parents the painting, they did it intentionally. Currently, there are only a select group of people we know of who are actively looking for them. And there's only one person who I could reasonably assume would use your parents as collateral damage to accomplish their goal."

Noah gave a soft sound of agreement as Lewis continued.

"If the woman I saw in Osaka, Cassandra, and who was mentioned in my mother's memory has been hunting the Macabre since my mother worked for the British Museum, then it's reasonable to say she might hold a grudge, or she might be using us as a way to get back at Evangeline for one reason or another."

Noah considered Lewis's words. "If, like you said, this mission of hers has been going on for thirty-plus years, I doubt she'd have a problem with bringing in outsiders to achieve her goal. I also doubt she'd be willing to give a painting away just to get back at you."

"Perhaps," Lewis muttered. "But there's also the possibility she values hurting me, us, more than achieving her goal." Lewis looked back into the room through the foamy yellow barrier Noah had erected. He watched Noah's mother braiding Ishita's hair from behind. Ishita reached back and swatted gently at her mother's hand, though not aggressively enough to actually tell her to stop. As if this was something the two of them had always done.

As if she was truly her daughter.

"And besides," Lewis continued, "people will go to any length to succeed at their goals. This woman probably doesn't view hurting you or your family as much of a price to pay if it gets her what she wants."

Noah arched his brow, waiting for Lewis to explain.

"To weaken us. Think about it. Your parents saw your sister die. Something brought her back. What parent wouldn't want that? Wouldn't want to cling to whatever could do that? And then their son threatens to take that away?"

Lewis could tell Noah was thinking, imagining what would happen if he did rip the Macabre from his parents. What his relationship with his parents would become.

After a long silence, Noah said, "I think you may be right; given what's happening here, it makes the most sense. No matter how it ended up here, I don't think how it got to them is important. A Macabre has attached itself to my parents."

"To be fair," Lewis said, with little conviction, "we aren't even sure there *is* a Dumont here."

"No, but if something somehow brought a loved one back, or a facsimile of them, that sounds like something a Macabre could do. You've noticed it, too, I'm sure—the paintings are more . . . active. Or perhaps proactive is the better word. Either way, I don't know anyone this skilled in necromancy. Word of that would have reached the British Museum."

"Ipso facto . . ."

"Exactly. And if it's like the others, it's probably latched on to someone—my father—feeding off his life force," Noah concluded.

"The Macabre paintings don't provide anything without some sort of sacrifice in exchange. It's the law of equivalency and magic," Lewis said, faintly smiling, though he wasn't sure it was the time to boast, but Noah looked at him quizzically. "I've done a lot of reading in the Contract House."

Noah chuckled hollowly.

"You're working up to becoming a good agent," he said, his voice quieting. "So then, I have a question for you, agent."

Lewis wasn't even sure he wanted to be an agent, let alone if Evangeline would recommend him. But there were still problems at hand, just a doorway away. Evangeline with her goal of rewriting history was a major, looming threat, but, right now, according to Lewis and his priorities, it might be possible to save one person. And, for now, that was enough.

He also liked the way Noah called him "agent," so there was that too . . .

Noah continued, "If the painting has bonded itself to my father, getting rid of it means most likely a negative effect on him, possibly death. But our goal here is to find and neutralize all the Macabre. It doesn't matter who's killed in the process . . ."

"You don't mean that, though," Lewis said. "Because it does matter. It's always mattered, even when it wasn't your father. But it is now, and that makes it even more crucial."

Noah looked at him with a start, and Lewis just nodded, encouraging him to ask what he clearly wanted to.

"What would you do? Because I cannot be objective in this situation. And any choice I make will be heavily scrutinized by the Crown. I'm asking you, Lewis, friend to friend, partner to partner, what would you have me do? Bring us one step closer to saving the world? Or let my father and mother have this one piece, this one moment of joy, for now?"

"I think you already know my answer," Lewis said, reaching forward and squeezing his forearm. "This is a choice about possibly killing your father. And to me, that's not a choice at all."

"Yes, but if it saved the world? We've all made sacrifices, Lewis. You more than others." Noah's eyes couldn't help but flicker down to his missing hand. "Maybe it's my turn to make one."

"That's bullshit!" Again, Noah stared at Lewis, wide-eyed.

Quieter, Lewis pointed into the room. "Isn't *that* part of your sacrifice?" he asked, indicating Noah's sister.

He hated this. It was an unfair situation Noah was in. Even if his sister was a facsimile of her real self. Noah should have the time and space to process his grief. How many people got another chance to say their sorrys or goodbyes? To finish knotting those unfinished loops and tapestries of a family relationship because one thread was cut short? Perhaps this painting was giving them something, a kindness in a way that no other person would usually get. And perhaps they should take advantage of that.

"Listen, I don't think . . ." Lewis started, swallowing and starting again. "There's no easy answer here. You've been trained to believe the whole is greater than the individual. But you've also seen what that has meant, and it certainly hasn't been the neutralization of the Macabre. They're still out there, and so maybe Evangeline's way isn't the only way. Consider this: Your family has already lost a daughter once. Evangeline will come for the painting eventually. With me here and you here, it won't take her long to put two and two together. We can always make a plan then. For now, go and be with your family."

"But when she comes, it will be to do whatever it takes to get this painting out."

"Then we face that bridge when we get there. Together."

Lewis noticed a wave of relaxation pass over Noah's body. He let out a sigh, tilting his head up toward the ceiling.

"Thank you," Noah whispered. He reached over and gave Lewis's hand a single squeeze. "Would you like that?" he asked.

Lewis's face twisted in a look of confusion.

"What my mother said," he whispered. "If, when this is all said and done, could I maybe take you out for coffee or something?"

Lewis wasn't sure how to answer, and it was very clear, by the way Noah smiled, that the surprise on his face must have been comical.

"You don't have to answer now."

"It's not that," Lewis said quickly. "Trust me."

"It's okay."

"No, seriously. It's not that."

Noah turned to Lewis to face him, gripping his shoulder with both hands, locking their gazes together. "It's okay," he repeated. "You can answer me whenever you want. The offer will stand until the offer cannot stand."

Lewis wasn't sure why he didn't just answer him then and there. But something held him back, something he knew intrinsically, yet couldn't articulate. It pained him, how much he wanted to just say, *Of course!*

How much he just wanted to grab Noah's hand and go right now.

It just wasn't right—not now. Not yet.

Lewis's eyes were filled with hope and apology, and Noah seemed to see all that. He nodded.

And with that, Noah pulled back and snapped his fingers again. The yellow hue of the door shattered like petals falling toward the ground and burning before they touched soil.

"Will you join me?" he asked.

"Of course," Lewis said, without hesitation. After all, what was a partner for?

Twenty-Seven

"WE NEED TO TALK. ALONE," NOAH SAID, DIRECTLY TO ISHITA. HIS EYES were dark and focused on his sister. His mother's expression was puzzled, a frown creasing her well-taken-care-of skin.

"Beta," she said in a warning tone. "That's not how we talk to people. That's not how we talk to your sister."

Noah didn't seem to care. Completely ignoring his mother, Noah had eyes only for his sister, and Ishita's were similarly locked on his. She had the same soft smile as before, plastered almost permanently on her lips, as if she couldn't form anything else but a grin.

And Lewis realized that he hadn't, in the past ten minutes, seen her let that smile falter even once—almost like it was a mask.

"It's fine, Mom," said Ishita.

Their mother turned her frown toward her daughter. "You spent too much time with the British," she said, sighing. Realizing it was a losing battle with her two children, Noah's mother stood, her gaze settling on Lewis. "Would you like to get something to eat with me?" she asked.

Lewis said, grinning apologetically, "I should stay." Quickly recovering, he tried to give a more logical explanation. "There's some things I want to ask your daughter too. You know, to get to know the family better."

Noah's eyes glanced over for a fraction of a second. Lewis glanced back and offered a very slight shrug.

This was his silent way of saying, *Might as well try*. Sure enough, Noah's mother fell for the ruse.

"See?" she said, smirking at her male child. "A mother always knows best."

She kissed the top of Ishita's head before doing the same to Noah, except on his cheek. She squeezed Lewis's arm and then left the three and her husband alone.

Ishita stood, smoothing her fingers over the light purple blouse that complemented her own light brown skin. She opened her mouth to speak, but Noah interrupted her.

"We're not going to play this game," he said. "You and I both know exactly what you are. You can try and lie and pull the wool over my mother and father, but it's just going to waste our time."

"*Your* mother? No—*our* mother," she corrected softly.

Noah stilled. Repeated slowly, threateningly, "*My* mother will not be gone for long. So let's cut to the chase. You're a painting, correct?"

Ishita shook her head. "I'm a representation of one of the paintings."

"Then I'm guessing," Lewis chimed in, "whatever the painting does allows you to take a form that most suits the . . ." He trailed off.

Ishita's gaze slowly drifted over to him, looking him up and down. "You look like him," she said softly.

Lewis frowned.

"Like Edgar," she clarified.

Noah took half a step to his left, standing just slightly in front of Lewis. Noah's go-to move, Lewis realized—putting himself between whatever the threat was and his charge.

"What do you mean, 'I look like Edgar'?" Lewis asked, moving to the left himself to keep the line of sight between him and

Ishita clear, a silent way of telling Noah he didn't need his protection. "How could you possibly know that?"

Ishita walked around the foot of the bed.

Noah and Lewis both took a step back as she moved over to the counter and poured herself a glass of water from a pitcher. Lewis watched carefully as she drank it slowly, slightly surprised that whatever she was needed to eat and drink.

"I'll answer my own question. Then you tell me if I'm wrong," Lewis said. "Each one of these paintings is a microcosmic representation of the emotions and feelings Edgar had when he painted them."

Ishita nodded thoughtfully.

"Each painting, then," Lewis continued, "holds in it those emotions on a loop. The dark magic that comes from my family's bloodline trait is what gives them life, imbuing them, enchanting them to be what they are."

Ishita crossed her arms. "Correct again. Two for two."

"So," he said slowly, "if your curse allows you to attach yourself to a specific person, then the same would be true for Edgar. Following that logic, the moment you materialized and took form, then the same would be true for Edgar Dumont. You are as much him as you are Ishita. If you can access her memories, you can access his."

"Exactly," Ishita said, cracking her hands. Her eyes shot over to Noah. "He's a smart one. I can see why he's your partner." There was a warm overtone in the use of *partner* that made Lewis think about what Noah had asked him out in the hallway.

"Shut up," Noah warned coldly. "A facsimile of my sister or not, a harbinger of Edgar Dumont's magic or whatever you are, it doesn't matter. You don't belong here."

Without hesitation, Noah brought his right hand up to his mouth and bit down hard on the fleshy, pulpy skin of his palm right under his thumb. Lewis winced, even if Noah didn't, and watched as he smeared his blood over his eyes from right to left.

As he did so, his irises changed, as if a drop of the same red hue was placed in them, shifting his beautiful dark eyes into something horrific in maroon.

"I can see them," he whispered. "Threads of magic that connect you to my father. You took the form you did through some type of contract that was made between the two of you."

Much like the painting in Osaka. Similar in origins. That might be of use, he thought.

Ishita didn't seem fazed. "My memories are linked to your father's memories of your sister, and also those of the man who created me. But what you forgot is that every single individual who has laid their eyes on me, poured their hopes and souls and feelings into me, I remember.

"Over the past hundred-plus years, many people have looked upon me. And do you know what they all say? That in my painting, if they look close enough, they can see the one they love the most. Lovers, brothers, sisters, other family—or someone they happened to see in the street—I give them that solace. And it was no different with your father. He looked upon it."

"And you took the form of his lost daughter," Lewis finished. "Did he even know what type of pact he was initiating?"

"He didn't need to," Ishita said. "His heart and the request were pure. And so I granted it."

"In exchange for what?" Noah growled. "His life force? My father wouldn't have agreed to that."

"He can cut it off anytime," Ishita replied, lowering her right hand to touch the older man's shoulder as he lay in the bed. "Unlike my sibling you met in Osaka, I'm not as malevolent. If he tells me he wants this to end, I'll end it. But he hasn't. And I suspect you know he won't."

"Careful," Noah warned. The screens of the machines hooked up to his father flickered, turning static for a moment as the lights flashed in the room.

Ishita didn't seem fazed. "Your father made this contract with me. That contract can only be broken by him—"

"Or someone willing to replace him," Noah finished. Lewis glanced over at him curiously. And, without asking, Noah provided the explanation. "Contract magic can only be broken by the individuals involved in it. But the contract can be shifted over if a willing participant comes forward."

"That's correct." Ishita nodded. "If someone was willing to take your father's place, he'd be set free from it."

Now it was Lewis's turn to stand between Ishita and Noah, his back facing the Macabre representation. "You're not seriously thinking about this? Attaching yourself to that painting will cause exactly what happened to your father to happen to you."

"Faster," she chimed in. "I can taste the energy coming off you, Noah. Pure. Rawer than your father ever had. I will feast on that. Gorge myself on it."

"I don't need the details from you," Noah remarked, focusing his gaze on Lewis. "It will save my father and also bind me to the painting. Perhaps I can figure out something through it. That connection isn't just a one-way street."

"Are you guessing that? Or do you know it?" Lewis asked.

Noah paused. "It's a solution that helps everyone . . . except for you," he said, smiling and gripping Lewis's shoulder. "I serve at the pleasure of the Crown, and my duty is also protecting you. This does that. Perhaps I can get some information that will put you in good favor with Evangeline—or use it as collateral to put some distance between the two of you. This works for everyone."

"As you said, it doesn't work for me," Lewis replied.

"For now, it will have to. I'll make the contract, and you go back to Evangeline. Tell her what happened. Say you came here to convince me otherwise. Use me as a scapegoat to win her favor."

Lewis opened his mouth to retort, but Noah held up his hand.

"If what you saw is true, and I believe it is, we need to get as much information about Evangeline and her motives as possible, and staying as close to her as possible will do that. She'll appreciate you ratting me out."

"And what if she comes for you and your family?"

"As you said before, I'll handle that when it happens."

"Except what I said is that we'd do it *together*."

Noah smiled, leaning forward, pressing his lips against Lewis's forehead for only a moment.

"Plans change. Agents must adapt."

"I'm not an agent."

"Maybe not in title, but certainly in spirit. Now, please, go," Noah said, nodding to the bathroom door. "Use Abernathy to go back to London. I'll see you again, I promise."

Lewis pulled back and looked over at Ishita. "If you lay a finger on him . . ."

Ishita smiled sweetly. "He's my brother, Lewis. I'd never do anything intentionally to hurt him."

There was no part of Lewis that believed that, but he wasn't sure he had much of a choice. So he focused his gaze back on Noah. "Promise I'll see you again."

Noah nodded. "I promise."

But as Lewis walked to the bathroom door, whispering the command to Abernathy to take him back to London, he wondered how good at the art of subterfuge agents of the Arcane Crown were, and if that lie was told for his benefit or Noah's.

Twenty-Eight

LEWIS WAS HOPING TO BE SENT DIRECTLY TO EVANGELINE'S OFFICE. HE didn't expect the Contract House to drop him off in the center of the British Museum. Maybe he should have. As he had told it before, Abernathy did seem to have a strange sense of humor.

He stumbled out of the bathroom—he had appeared in the same type of room he'd entered, one of the men's restrooms—surprising a man who tried to enter the stall at the exact same time.

"Sorry," Lewis said, quickly nodding his apologies.

He stepped away, walking in reverse as he gave the man a quick wave before exiting the restroom and weaving his way through the crowd. It was the middle of the week; the British Museum wasn't as full of guests as on a weekend, but the building was still big enough that it took him several minutes to reach guest services.

A woman with a short frizzy bob didn't even get a chance to finish asking him what he needed before he gave his order. "Please let Evangeline Thompson know I'm looking to speak with her."

The woman with the name tag that read *Siobhan* frowned. "Evangeline Thompson is a very busy person," she said, clearly a bit annoyed at being unable to finish her sentence.

"And I'm not?" And that threw off Siobhan just a bit, because she clearly had no idea if he was important or not... but he could see she was starting to wonder how much trouble she'd be in with Evangeline if she was wrong.

Something Lewis knew very few people were probably willing to risk.

More gently he said, "Please just tell her Lewis Dixon has some information for her that she'll find interesting."

A standoff took place between the two of them before she finally sighed, conceded, and called Evangeline's number. A moment later, she hung up, nodded, and gestured for him to wait to the side.

Less than thirty seconds later, Evangeline appeared through a side door. "Lewis," she said slowly, apprehension and confusion in her voice.

Lewis nodded toward the door from which she came. "You can be angry at me for leaving the Contract House, wondering how it let me out, or even why, but, first, I think we should talk—privately."

Evangeline studied him, deciding his fate before nodding and gesturing with a wide horizontal movement of her hand for him to walk in first. Stepping over the threshold, he appeared in her office. The door to the cluttered and crowded lobby closed behind her.

"Noah's in India," he said.

"Mumbai, I know," she replied, almost bored. "You don't think I keep track of my agents?"

"Then you probably knew I was there too."

"I was curious," she said, walking over to her desk with long strides, twirling her middle finger, causing a pot of tea to pour a new cup for her, but none for Lewis.

Lewis frowned. "You're not at all curious or concerned why Noah was there?" he asked.

"Not really," Evangeline replied. "I'm assuming it has something to do with his family. And, with you being there, it probably had something to do with a painting. There's no point in me rushing in, guns ablaze. That's such an American thing to do. As long as Noah is there, and I have eyes on him, the painting won't move. You, on the other hand," she said after a slow sip, nodding her head gently toward him, "saved me a trip downtown.

"I've been thinking about your indiscretions, and your insubordination, and wondering if part of the reason might be because you don't have a strong enough hand guiding you. I'm wondering whether, if I gave you an opportunity to redeem yourself, how different it would be if you and I went on a mission together."

That wasn't what Lewis was expecting, but he kept his composure as much as he could. "I didn't know you went into the field."

"When it suits me," she replied. "Are you interested? It's better than staying in that dusty house, don't you think?"

Lewis wondered if he really had a choice. And, much like before, when he felt her skimming against the top of his mind, he felt the same itching feeling again.

"At worst you get a little bit of time to see a new country that I imagine you've never seen before. At best, you gain my favor."

Lewis knew there was something else here, a deeper meaning under the waves in the inky blackness of her subterfuge that he had yet to navigate. He had no way of knowing what she might be thinking, though.

And that was a concern to him. But he had nothing to lose and everything to gain.

After all, Noah had said he should do his best to stay close to her. What better way to accomplish that than winning her favor? And if it gave Noah more time with his family, it was a win in his book. "What do you have in mind?"

Evangeline finished her tea before opening her seashell clutch purse, pulling out a golden lipstick, applying it slowly to her lips. Popping her lips once, she re-pocketed the tube before walking toward the door.

With a double flourish of her hands, it swung open, revealing a hallway Lewis had never seen before.

"Come," she said, not turning around, knowing he would follow. "We don't want to be late."

As they crossed over the threshold, Lewis instantly realized this long hallway, with its brown and gold colors, didn't feel like any location he'd been to before. And yet, something about it felt almost familiar.

When he realized half a trek down the hallway that every single person who'd passed them, more than half a dozen, had the same skin color as him and Evangeline, he realized why.

"We're in Africa, aren't we?" he asked.

Evangeline didn't speak at first, rounding the hallway and leading him to an expansive atrium. She took stairs that spiraled upward. The sharp clicking of her heels echoed in the mostly empty space.

"Did you know I'm not completely British?" she asked. "In fact, I'm not British at all. It took me a while to learn this accent, to be one of them."

At the top of the stairs, she made her way forward, pausing as they stood at the doorway of a rounded room, with a ceiling that reminded him of a chapel's. Inside sat more than a hundred people, each with paddles in their hands, raising and lowering them like a choreographed routine as a woman with a purple-and-gold outfit that hugged her body manipulated their offerings from behind a podium.

"Do I have one hundred? One hundred and ten? One hundred and thirty?" the auctioneer asked, her eyes darting from one side of the room to the next.

"I left Nigeria around the same age as when you started college in Georgia," Evangeline said, locking her eyes on the woman. "There weren't many opportunities for people like me, magicians who wanted more, to reach above their station." She leaned her right shoulder against the doorframe, her voice low in respect to the auctioneer.

"Nigeria isn't very fond of magicians working in the international field," she explained. "Especially women. We've seen what outside influence has done to our continent. And folding in on ourselves is considered more important than reaching out."

"I wouldn't say that's a bad thing," Lewis muttered.

Evangeline smiled faintly. "I don't disagree either, but it wasn't what I wanted." She nodded her head to the auctioneer. "That," she said, "is Adeze Madueke, owner of the Omagbemi Auction House, the largest and most connected in Lagos, in Nigeria—perhaps on the continent. We do some business with them."

They help funnel magical artifacts to England, you mean, he speculated. "There's a painting here?" he asked. "Is it being sold? You said that you knew her."

Evangeline shook her head. "No, the painting's not for sale. I'm just waiting until this is done to talk to her. Adeze and I grew up together, not far from here. We were quite close, once. But we fell apart when I left to go to London. And she stayed here."

For a moment, Lewis noticed something on Evangeline's face he hadn't seen before: regret. Evangeline wasn't stupid, she knew what it meant to be in the proximity of a Macabre painting, and she knew, better than others, what happened to those in contact with them.

"It's in her office," Evangeline finally said. "I talked to her about it earlier. She's more than willing to give it to us . . ."

The way that her voice trailed off told Lewis that wasn't all. "What aren't you telling me? This is all too easy. And if you could just get it by asking, why didn't you do it months ago?"

Evangeline pursed her lips, crossing her arms over her chest. "I'm afraid this isn't going to be as cut-and-dried as we want it to be," she said, her voice low. "Adeze lost her husband some years ago."

Lewis understood with no more explanation. These paintings latched onto individuals in their weakest moments; that death was linked to this painting just like the one in Mumbai was linked to Noah's family. "Is she a caster?"

Evangeline shook her head. "Not a drop of magical blood—which is what concerns me. She's smart, though, which could be more dangerous." A flicker of a grin passed over her face. "She understands magic in its fundamental elements—the scientific principles of it, the idea of how to use push-and-pull resonance. But as a general rule, magical families, especially old ones, don't function like that in Africa. Our magic is linked to the Orishas. Many people still call upon them."

"But not you?"

"Doesn't get you as far in England, as I'm sure you can imagine, when your magic comes from your homeland."

"And you wanted to succeed," Lewis continued for her. "That's capitalism for you."

Evangeline gave a tiny smile. "In countries where the triumph of capitalism is not so all-encompassing, many people still follow God-magic. You might have seen some even in Japan. As forward-looking as the country is, there is still a deep reverence for the past, for tradition." She looked at him. "Magic used to be defined by your place of origin. And there is power still in that. Connecting to your roots can allow you to perform better, stronger spells with less of a toll."

"So why abandon that?"

"The new breed of magician—we are transients," she said. "We move throughout the world. We give up the power of our origins, but in exchange, we gain access to a common, universally applicable language of magic. And that has tangible benefits in the broader world."

"Professional success," Lewis said. "Rising above your station."

"I don't regret the bargain I made," she said, as if Lewis had asked. "I don't regret leaving Nigeria. I am one of the highest-ranking members of any magical organization in the world, a Black woman in charge of England's magical front line. I wouldn't give that up for the world." She hesitated. "But perhaps I did lose something along the way. That's what these Dumonts do, isn't it? They prey upon your doubts. And they know I've been looking for them. Perhaps that's why this one has chosen Adeze. It's teasing me—taunting me with what might have been."

As Adeze finished her auction and the crowd lightly cheered the sale, Evangeline caught her eye; Adeze nodded, then handed off her gavel to another auctioneer—a handsome gentleman with a stark white beard and bald head—and exited through a side door.

After a few more lots, the bearded auctioneer called a break and the room began to clear. Lewis and Evangeline approached the side door through which Adeze had gone. Beyond it, Adeze was seated at a large desk, writing in a ledger. The office was as elegant as the rest of the auction house, except in here the color scheme was red, black, and green.

"Colors of the Pan-African flag," Lewis murmured.

Adeze glanced up from her writing, her hand frozen in mid-pen stroke. "You're well-versed," she said with a small smile. "Is that because you're an artist or because you're Black?"

She was playing with him. "Both," he said.

She chuckled low, pressing her hands to the desk to stand. She gazed fondly at Evangeline. Her eyes were honey brown, almost golden. But there was sadness behind those eyes. Looking at her again, he saw suddenly how weary she seemed.

"Is he the one who's going to help us?" Adeze asked.

Evangeline nodded.

Adeze sighed. "I knew this day would come eventually. I just didn't know who it would be. The British Museum, the Americans, someone else—it wouldn't be my own people, I bought them off long ago—but eventually someone would come. The balance always reasserts itself."

Lewis said nothing, letting her words wash over him as he took in the appointments of the office. There were sculptures, busts of people he didn't recognize but assumed were African figureheads.

He didn't notice the painting at first, but after a moment he registered a shape against the far left wall, draped in a quilt—something rectangular and flat. He felt a prickle in the back of his head, almost like a headache, that shifted into something else, something familiar, like the whispers of a voice speaking to him. Someone's lips right against his ear.

"You hear it, don't you?" Adeze said.

With some difficulty, Lewis pulled his gaze away and looked at her.

"It speaks to you," she said.

He was surprised how cavalier she seemed. Evangeline had said Adeze didn't have magic. Perhaps she didn't truly know what she had gotten herself into. "What does it do?" he said. "Whatever it's promising you, it's not real."

She chuckled. "I might not be like you and Evangeline, boy."

"Lewis," he corrected.

"I might not understand the intricacies of magic as you do, Lewis, but I do know the difference between a fake and a real thing. And what this painting gives me is real." She walked around from behind the desk. "Because what I pay is the ultimate price."

She poured three cups of tea from a steel kettle, silently offering one to each of them. Lewis was impressed with her almost despite himself. It was clear that Adeze was a woman of stature and respect. At least, Evangeline was treating her as such, not as a criminal.

"What do you know about these paintings?" Lewis asked. "About the Dumonts?"

"I can tell you that most people in the world have no idea of their value," Adeze said. She sipped her tea. "The market values scarcity, but also notoriety. Names are forgotten. Whole bodies of work are lost to history, assumed to be worth nothing. There are some curators who understand their value, but not enough to actually change the market price. Having more than one helps, because it attracts attention. They are financially valuable on their own. But together, in a set of two or three? When they tell a story? That's where the value is."

"But you're smart enough to know that their value isn't in their market price," he said. "If you didn't, we wouldn't be here talking. You're a curator—art is more than just paintbrush strokes and images. These more than others."

Adeze smiled, her glance moving over to Evangeline. "He's good. Is he your protégé?"

Lewis felt a pang in his heart; it was Noah, not he, who was Evangeline's chosen acolyte and apprentice—Noah, whom he had abandoned in Mumbai. He briefly wondered what was happening in India—if Noah was okay. But he couldn't worry about that now. He had a mission.

If Evangeline was perturbed, she didn't show it. "I'm considering it," she said dryly. "Please, do go on. I'll let you and Lewis hash this out. I'm just an observer."

"More like backup." Adeze smiled. Her tone was playful, but Lewis and Evangeline both knew she was telling the truth. If things turned ugly, there was no doubt Evangeline would put the success of the mission even above the life of her friend.

Adeze turned her attention fully to Lewis. "The painting that I have—this artifact, which is the reason you are here—allows the owner to talk to the dead."

Lewis blinked. "You're joking."

Adeze shook her head. "I'm being entirely honest. You pay a toll—a sacrifice, if you will—and the artifact allows you to speak to the dead."

"And the toll?"

Adeze smiled and said nothing.

"You said before that you paid the ultimate price," he said. "Unless I'm mistaken, that means life. And you appear very much alive."

"*I* am," said Adeze.

At that moment, Lewis's mind, for some reason, thought back to one of his college sociology classes. The topic was the way that the costs of prosperity fall upon the backs of the poor. When a company needs a bailout, the taxpayers foot the bill. When someone in power makes a mistake, the blame gets pinned on someone more junior. When a corporation builds a power plant that spews out toxic fumes, there's no consideration for the people who have to pay the cost in the ruination of their health ten or fifteen years down the line.

And if the wealthy are called to account, what then? They pay a fine. And if a crime is dismissable by paying a fine, well, it's not *really* illegal, is it? Not if you can pay. Some pleasures are more expensive than others, to be sure; but given sufficient wealth, nothing is truly forbidden.

And here was Adeze, with skin like his, and very wealthy even by Western standards, with all the impunity that came with it.

"You're having other people pay the price for you," he said with dawning horror. He looked to Evangeline. "She's killing people."

Adeze raised her hand. "Do you know what the poverty rate is in Nigeria, Lewis? Forty percent. Roughly 260 percent higher than America—and with even less mobility and opportunity for people to reach above their station. I am *helping* people. I am changing lives."

"By murder?"

She made a noise of disgust. "Such a backward way of looking at it," she murmured. "People come to me willingly. One member of a household. They understand what is required, and they understand the rewards. Their sacrifice buys me time with my husband and secures a future for their families. College educations paid in full, debts cleared, new homes, unlimited food. I have the money to do that, and I provide."

"It's not that easy, though, is it?" Evangeline interjected. "It never lasts, does it? If it did, you wouldn't have to keep doing it." She leaned forward. "How long, Adeze?"

Just for an instant, Lewis saw something like grief flicker across Adeze's face. Then she composed herself. "Twenty-four hours at most," she said. "But my husband always perishes again. It's a different way each time. Heart attack, slipping on the steps—one time, we were out in public and a bird flew straight into his skull through his eye. No matter what happens, no matter how many times I pay, he always dies. And so, I keep making the deal. Another life, more time. Always hoping this time it will last. Wouldn't you do the same?"

Lewis wanted to say no, to take out the full depths of his disgust on her. But already the thought had crept in that this was the painting he could use to bring his mother back; but he rejected the notion before it had time to take root in the soil of his mind. He wasn't going to hurt other people to do it. He wasn't going to let other people suffer because of him. He wasn't.

I can help you.

The painting's voice was an amalgamation of Akana's, of Noah's, of Evangeline's, even Adeze's, of hundreds of others. It was so soothing, so enticing.

I can help you if you're willing to pay the price, I can give you whatever you want. You can see her. You can talk to her. All you have to do is say the word.

It would be so easy to make the pact. Deep within his chest, he felt as if a lock had been sprung, and a strongbox down inside him, a safe that had been closed for as long as he could remember, was swinging open.

Adeze and Evangeline were still talking, debating the merits of her actions, just two friends chatting over tea. All very pleasant. There was no moral urgency to it. But Adeze wasn't really looking at Evangeline. She was staring at him, as if she, too, heard the voice.

"Be careful," she said to him. "You might not like what the price is. Trust me, the first time I did it, I was sick. I couldn't get out of bed for three days."

Evangeline looked confused. "What are you talking about? Lewis, do you hear something?"

Lewis didn't answer. He felt like he was here but not here, like there was an in-between space between the folds of magic and non-magic into which he had somehow stumbled.

And perhaps that presented an opportunity. An opportunity to get a step ahead of Evangeline. Maybe even to end this. After all, if Evangeline could hide the truth from him, why couldn't he do the same?

He raised his voice. "I'm not here as a descendant of Edgar Dumont, I'm here as a patron seeking a contract," he said. "I request an agreement. Show me the truth and I'll give you whatever of equal value you want."

Evangeline's eyes grew wide; but before she could speak, the room disappeared, expanding outward and out of sight in the blink of an eye.

Lewis was alone in transit, his body snared as by an invisible hook and yanked halfway across the world. No: not this world, not the one he knew.

He was somewhere dark and lonely. Someplace magical. There was no floor, no ceiling, no walls—a void without direction or dimension.

And a single voice that spoke all around him, as if it came from everywhere and nowhere.

And so it is done.

Twenty-Nine

LIKE MELTING BLACK WAX, THE INK THAT ENCOMPASSED HIM DRIPPED down the walls, revealing a blurry world.

Lewis had gotten used to this shifted reality. It was much like the first Dumont painting he had fallen into in the British Museum. As the blackness disappeared and the hazy fuzziness of the new world appeared, Lewis tried to guess where he would end up and what the painting would show him. Slowly, everything became sharper. His senses tickled with the feeling of a cold draft.

It was winter, he reasoned, and nighttime, judging by the faint orbs of light that peppered the cobblestone street. In front of him was a building, much like the hospital in the present time, derelict and broken down, shutters half falling off, each only holding on by a single hinge. The wood was splintered and warped, the glass shattered in some of the windows. But on the top floor, four stories up, a singular bright hue attracted his attention.

Lewis couldn't be sure where he was, but judging from the design and style, it looked somewhere European. At first, he resigned himself to the fact that where he was and when he was didn't matter. But stacked against the stoop of the abandoned building were piles of yellowed papers. Newspapers, he quickly realized.

He picked one up and noted the date and place: *1888, London, England*. A quick calculation told him that Edgar would most likely be in his mid-thirties by now.

Had Edgar stayed in London after *The Stain,* or did he return after a hasty departure? Though perhaps it didn't matter. Using his shoulder to push open the door, Lewis winced as the weakly framed wood collapsed under his force. It wasn't the most inconspicuous of entrances, but he supposed it made no difference. There was no place for Edgar to go. Their paths would cross eventually.

Lewis took a moment to survey the ground floor. The room barely contained anything of value, a few chairs here and there.

A rat scurried away as soon as he entered its domain. The staircase to the left didn't look safe. As he took the steps one at a time, each one creaked to announce his presence. He paused, steadied himself, and waited to see whether the wood would collapse under him. The painting in Lagos had brought him here as part of its agreement. He asked for the truth, and in some way, shape, or form, that existed in London in 1888, he assumed, tied to Edgar Dumont.

What he had sacrificed to get here, he wasn't sure, and Lewis was confident he wouldn't know until it was too late. The whole conundrum reminded him of the stories his grandmother used to tell him when he was a young teen, spending time with her in Atlanta for the summer. Stories and parables about the harrowing consequences of making a deal with the devil. Exactly what Lewis had done.

Except unlike the characters in those stories, he had no choice. If he had to give up whatever, even his own life, to end this, perhaps it would be worth it, especially if it kept the painting out of Evangeline's hands.

Once Lewis reached the top step, he saw there was only one door in the hallway. Faint light flickered under the doorframe. Lewis reasoned it was a single oil lamp.

He stood in front of the door, pressing the palm of his hand against the wood, feeling its grain, its uneven jaggedness. He braced himself for what might be on the other side, or rather who might be on the other side.

He assumed it was Edgar, but he had to be prepared for anything. Noah wasn't here to help him, and he worried he couldn't rely on the Contract House to whisk him away if trouble reared its ugly head. He pulled his hand back and balled his fist.

"Here we go," he whispered, pushing open the door, letting the creaks echo and bounce off the wall.

Sitting in the center of the room was a man, or some version of one. His body was thin, ravaged from a lack of food. Loose-fitting clothes with holes and dirt-stained patches covered his frail body.

But that wasn't what was most important to Lewis. The room was filled with buckets, at least a dozen of them, each one with a different shade of paint, black and gray, maroon and brown: muted tones. In color theory, this would signify sorrow or pain, maybe even disgust.

Adorning the walls like wallpaper were more than a hundred pieces of paper, abstract art, swatches of paint in unusual designs: meaningless, at least to him. At first glance, Lewis thought they were drafts, initial sketches used to help the painter in question find the art within the art. But some of the symbols spoke out to him, maybe ten out of a hundred. He had seen them before inside the books the Contract House had nudged him toward.

"Runes," he whispered, looking over at the man, who hadn't registered his presence yet. "You're a magician now."

A weak, raspy chuckle left the man's throat. As Lewis inched closer, he saw what he was hunching over—a larger canvas, three, maybe four times the size of a standard sheet of paper. Black and gray ripples started out from the corners, darkening as the rings closed in on the center, where the painter was working. There in the brightest of reds was the shape of a woman.

No defining characteristics had been applied to her yet, but the figure was clearly a person, an object of worship, one that gave Lewis pause, causing a chill of warning to run down his spine.

"I knew you'd come again."

The man's voice confirmed what Lewis had thought: It *was* Edgar. Even fifteen years later, the man's voice hadn't changed from that of the man in his twenties whom he had seen in London, nor from that of the boy he had first seen. "I knew I didn't make you up."

Lewis frowned. Though Edgar acknowledged him, he didn't stop painting.

And it was then that Lewis's nose crinkled. He raised his thumb to it, rubbing away at the itch, realizing that the smell was strong, salty, and coppery. It lingered in the air. Each inhalation forced more of it down his lungs. It smelled like blood, just like the room in Perth when all those bodies had turned into indistinguishable muck.

It was a smell he would never forget.

It was a scent that told him to run.

"What did you do?" Lewis whispered. "Edgar, what did you do?"

Still, Edgar Dumont didn't stop painting, but he did speak.

"I've spent the past fifteen years looking for you," he said slowly, "wondering if I was going mad. But then I realized something I had always known, tickling in the back of my head.

"That the world is bigger than any of us can imagine."

He kept painting, Lewis watching him with fascination . . . and not a small touch of fear. "There was something weird about you," Edgar continued. "The way that you dressed when you first came to me."

Edgar's gaze shifted away like that of a rat checking its surroundings for a threat.

Panicked eyes, blown-out pupils darted around the room, landing on Lewis for a fraction of a second before going back to the painting, as he hunched his back as if to keep it from Lewis's view.

"And I started to wonder, where were you from, or maybe even, *when* were you from?"

Every fiber in Lewis's body told him he should leave. Neither Evangeline nor Noah had considered that Edgar might have figured their mission out. While they were looking for him, Edgar was looking for Lewis. And something told Lewis he had fallen right into his trap.

"I wondered," Edgar kept going, "if I was right, if you had come from a different time, and how that was possible. I searched the world for evidence that I wasn't crazy, that it was conceivable that you were real. And do you know what I found?"

Edgar stood slowly, fingertips stained black and red from his ministrations over the canvas. He grabbed it on the left and right sides. And as he stood, he turned the piece, showing it in its completion to Lewis. The piece was exactly as Lewis had assumed, a figure surrounded by pulses of black and gray.

But as Edgar tilted the image slightly to the left and then to the right, it changed, like one of those holographic playing cards one could get in a Happy Meal, or like a consolation prize that held two images, one on top of the other.

And the second image was a pair of golden scales.

The scales were a stark background, with one side, which leaned down, holding a heart, half rotten, and the other side, a skull, with a snake coiling through its eyeholes and mouth. From behind the golden scales, if you looked closely, it appeared as though someone with a black, bony hand was grabbing and holding the scales, but the figure wasn't fully visible.

Balance. *The Balance.*

Lewis's eyes slowly trailed upward to Edgar's face, expression no longer wild, as an overly bright and contagious smile spread across his lips, showing a mouth only half full of rotting teeth.

"I found *magic*," he concluded. "I found that the world is filled with it. Plants, the air, the waterways, bricks, all of it; magic exists in varying degrees inside of everything. And there are people in the world who know how to pull that resonance out of items and manipulate it. But there's no greater source of magic than a person. And there are far too many people in London. Always have been, always would be. And so, I thought, why not fix that?"

It took Lewis a moment to understand what Edgar was saying. But as each building block clicked into place like a machine coming to life, Lewis remembered why that date had stood out to him. Why 1888?

Plenty of things stood out, especially from his art history classes. But it was the location that really drove him to a conclusion.

London.

1888.

Fear...

The reign of Jack the Ripper.

Lewis reacted a fraction of a second before Edgar did, and perhaps that saved his life.

The man threw the painting to the side, lunging at Lewis, brandishing a flash of silver from his pocket. Lewis raised his hand, blocking the blade. He winced as the razor cut his flesh. Surging magic and will through his right wrist, he pointed it toward one of the buckets and flung it toward Edgar.

The bucket hit Edgar's head with a sickening thump. The contents spilled over his face and chest.

Edgar roared. But it didn't stop him. He lunged forward again, blindly swinging the blade.

"If you have so much resonance that you can make your way back here," Edgar roared even as he was blinded, "then you can bring her back! You can bring my sister back. I just need to bleed it out of you."

Lewis barely kept a step ahead. Their dance put him farther

and farther from the door. He was closing in on the opposite wall. No exit in sight.

"Edgar—"

"I need you to shut up," Edgar bellowed, stabbing forward.

Lewis turned his body, the blade catching his shirt, cutting a slice of it, but missing his skin.

"I don't want to hurt you," he told Edgar.

"I want you dead," Edgar replied.

As Edgar lunged forward again, Lewis knew he would have no other choice. Willing the magic into the rune on his right arm, he forced a single command.

"Get away!"

Edgar's body froze as if it was bound, the blade an inch or so from slashing ribbons across Lewis's chest.

For a flicker of a moment, it looked like he was glowing. And with a right-to-left movement of Lewis's right wrist, Edgar's body was thrown like trash out the window, glass and wood shattering and splintering. The time before the loud, crunching thump below felt endless.

Lewis didn't dare to look out the window. A four-story fall would mean death for anyone. *There is no need for me to look out the window*, he told himself. But if Edgar was dead, Lewis could reasonably assume what would happen next.

The world, the illusion, whatever it was, would begin to collapse, and he didn't have much time to find what he was looking for. The runes on the wall meant nothing to him besides the fact that they were magic, a protective circle perhaps to fend off prying eyes or shake a police tail. Jack the Ripper was never found, after all, and perhaps this was why. Lewis filed that away for later, scanning each piece of art on the wall.

Individually, they were nothing, just half-completed pieces with no rhyme or reason or direction toward a result. But as Lewis took a step back to look at the room and the door he had entered, he tilted his head to the right and noticed something. Each piece of art on the wall was connected. And as he squinted, the gaps between each piece of paper seemed to disappear, and the haphazard, meaningless symbols formed words written in French.

LA RÉPONSE EST INVERSE.

Lewis didn't know French well, but he committed the expression to memory, not sure of its importance even if the words were easy to translate from French to English. And as he did, the tingling sensation of a presence behind him prickled his thoughts.

As he turned quickly to meet it, the world blurred. No longer was he in the dilapidated house, but back in Lagos, with Evangeline staring at him with a mixture of confusion and anger.

"What did you pay?" Her words were cold and direct. No compassion for what he might have seen. No care for what piece of information he'd pulled from the painting. Lewis stared at her, his own gaze stone. He had been Evangeline's pawn long enough, but he was curious too, because although the piece of information he'd come back with seemed worthless, the rules were clear: He had to pay for what he had received. At first, he had no idea what the painting had taken from him. But as he thought back to Adeze and considered a price of equivalence, a life for a life, he considered what was at the center of the memory he'd just visited—art and magic.

It was then that Lewis noticed the minute changes in the world. It was less bright, the colors muted, quieter. The Pan-African flag and Nigerian flag in Adeze's office? He was no longer interested in the richness of their history. He didn't question how the fabric was made or care about the work that had gone into sculpting the pieces that adorned the office.

His love for art was gone, his ability to see art as more than just objects in front of him vanished and, Lewis had to assume at this point, also his ability to create. The world for Lewis Dixon had never, not even when he was younger, seemed so . . . cold. So barren.

So lifeless.

And now it did.

Hot tears fell from Lewis's face as he combed frantically through his mind to find any morsel the painting might have forgotten or missed in its clean sweep. But there was nothing. All of it sacrificed for a stupid sentence in French, and he had no idea what it meant.

Curious, but confident he knew what would happen, Lewis brought his hand up again to touch the painting. There was nothing; no hum of magic, no pulse of life. Just . . . the feel of rough brushstrokes and cold paint against his fingers.

The painting was nothing more than a painting to him now. And through his hot tears, he spat out words of venom at Evangeline, his voice breaking and wet.

"I'm done."

Evangeline didn't respond at first. She didn't even stop him as he began to walk toward the door of Adeze's office, intending to call upon Abernathy to send him back to the one place he wanted to be: Mumbai with Noah.

He managed only ten paces before his body betrayed him. His knees buckled, sending him to the floor. Pressure fell on his shoulders, his head, his joints.

Indescribable hot pain spread throughout his body, as he felt hairline fractures begin to spread like a poison. His vision turned blurry and white. Pain became the only thing he registered. He couldn't even scream through the pressure. But he heard her voice.

Evangeline's crisp, British voice.

"You're done when I say you're done."

And then everything turned black.

Thirty

CASSANDRA WAS A WOMAN WHO KNEW THE VALUE OF BEING PREPARED for anything.

She was also a woman who liked to be on the offensive, to be in control of her situations, to be the one who made the first move. She was the white queen who brought the king down in a checkmate. She was the bullet in the back of the head before you could whisper your apologies. She was the sudden hostile takeover of a family business moving swiftly in the middle of the night.

But this time, she was off-kilter.

She had no one to blame but herself. There wasn't enough time between trips to recuperate and rejuvenate. Yes, she might be immortal, but that didn't mean that the stress of manipulating and spinning the threads of resonance didn't wear at her soul. It felt like a pinprick in the very beginning, as if someone was poking holes within her flesh and threading white-hot thread under her skin. At that point, she could usually push the feeling aside. But if she didn't, and she ignored it, this was the consequence.

The runes that she had set up in her different abodes across the globe flickered in and out like a dying battery. Her senses, naturally sharp but subconsciously re-enhanced by magic, were dulled and hazy. She barely noticed the feeling of resonance behind her. It took her longer than she would like to admit to realize that she knew that sensation. Much like a fingerprint, a favorite perfume, or a voice, every person's resonance had a signature. Learning that signature meant you could know who cast a spell, or who was in a room hours before, without needing any other clues.

And she knew the signature of the one who had been stalking her well.

It was ironic, really. The one time she decided to take a break, to divest herself from the cat and mouse game that had spanned the past hundred and thirty odd years, evil came knocking at her door.

Cassandra snorted, an unappealing action but an action, nonetheless. *Evil* wasn't the right word. Her stalker was nothing more than a woman scorned. She remembered that, remembered what it felt like to be betrayed, to have the most vulnerable parts of herself ripped out of her and displayed for everyone to see like an exhibit. One hundred thirty years ago, a man had done that to her. A man that she thought she could trust. Someone who she thought cared.

She would never make that mistake again.

And yet somewhere along the way, the power dynamic had shifted. She was no longer the hunted but the hunter. She was the reason that someone had left the safety of their home country behind and traveled across the world. Looking for her. Seeking revenge.

That dark-power core of energy had led the Japanese girl to Brazil. Roughly eight and a half hours southeast from São Paulo and seven hours southwest from Rio de Janeiro, Cassandra had found refuge in Café e Confeitaria Bistro Dona Belandira em Campos do Jordão. She wouldn't consider herself a regular, though she often found herself in South America, this specific spot, hidden away from most major cities, nestled within the small municipality of Capivari, that had become her home away from home when she needed to think. To recenter herself. To remind herself why she had stepped through the veil of darkness and forsaken her vows as a servant of God, all to get back to Him and beg for His forgiveness.

Because it wasn't just for His grace. Of course, that was the majority of the goal. Her reasoning for the bloodshed, the crime, the pain and suffering she caused others, when not too long ago, Cassandra used to be a forgiving angel of mercy. It was to feel the warmth of the sun against her skin. Feel the ache of heartbreak, and the joys of love all over again. She was immortal, yes, but only physically.

Cassandra still felt pain, she still felt longing, she still felt the ache of emotional anguish. Those sufferings were not taken from her along with her mortality. But they were no longer the same. When there was no end in sight, when time was not a limiting factor, and she could live many lives, as many lives as she wanted, those things, once so precious and fleeting, were stale.

She missed the fleeting nature of life the most. That is what she came back here to remember. And this girl was ruining it.

She had considered, at first, ignoring her. Letting her strike first from the shadows. Cassandra didn't make the same mistake as she did last time, scanning for other signatures that didn't match and were sharpened by refined magical skill. There was no one else with her.

Around the rim of her espresso cup, she smiled, tendrils of her mind extending outward to connect with Akana's.

"You came alone."

At first, silence. And then, a crackle. Cassandra had no doubt that magic would come lashing out at her. The question was from where. She had scanned the café before she entered, a habit that she had developed many years ago, and she repeated it again. There were about a dozen people within the small shop. More than half of them patrons, two servers, and a handful in the back and around the facility. But Akana was nowhere to be seen.

At first Cassandra assumed it was a masking spell, Akana using resonance to change her appearance to blend in with the café goers. She did hail from a powerful family, Cassandra reasoned. If she wanted to, hiding her appearance even from Cassandra's scanning eyes and mind wouldn't be too hard. Japanese agents, the kages being a prime example, were more than talented and skilled in the field of espionage and camouflage. Striking from the shadows and manipulating the geopolitical landscape with sleight of hand and minor adjustments. In fact, she would reason Akana was an outlier. Her family bloodline trait was more of a sledgehammer than a scalpel.

That made her smile. She tossed a few coins onto the table—more than enough, considering she had already paid—before standing.

"Outside."

Cassandra moved like a whisper, gliding through the café. She'd grown to love this place, yearned for it and itched for it when life was too tough, even when she was in the most glamorous cities across the world, such as San Francisco and Singapore and London. There would be an ache in her heart that she would not be able to easily fill if this place was destroyed because of her magical duel.

In Cassandra's mind, she was doing the shop a favor. The family that owned the café didn't deserve to suffer because of her crimes. But when she stepped outside, the overbearing heat of a Brazilian summer pushing against her skin oppressively, Cassandra realized she had made a mistake.

It was right in front of her. And she could only assume Akana did that on purpose. Hanging from a tree was a mass of twisted wood, string, and bones spinning lazily counterclockwise in the air. It aligned only for a moment, a brief second where the sticks and twine and the paint on each individual piece of wood lined up just perfectly for the symbol to be clear as day. Cassandra let out a sharp hiss before turning left and then right quickly to look behind her, only to see the same symbol in three other locations. A sigil leaning against a car. Another one sunk deep into the earth in an alleyway. And the final one, poised precariously on the top of the café.

If she hadn't stepped out of the café, Cassandra realized, she wouldn't have been within the field of the four sigils. But now she stood roughly in the center of the diamond. And Cassandra didn't have to guess what would happen next. Akana was a brilliant magician, maybe even the best she had ever met. So the sharp sting of pain as a glint of silver passed through the air thinly slicing her forearm wasn't a surprise.

"Go on," Akana's voice said from everywhere. "Try and heal."

Cassandra didn't need to try. She knew, in the pit of her soul, that for now her immortality was gone. It had been like a sticky shadow she couldn't shake. The moment she had discovered her gift it clung to her, weighing her mortal soul down. But for the first time in one hundred thirty years, she felt lighter. She felt human. Any other time, she might have praised the accomplished magician who had found a way to undo what had been done to her. But as Akana came into view, her body rippling as she stepped over the threshold to where magic was no longer allowed to exist, Cassandra for the first time felt fear.

"You know, Japan had a whole file on you. The immortal nun going back more than one hundred years, killing agents across the world, slinking in the shadows like vermin. You're famous. Not only to us but to other government entities too."

Akana stepped into the arena, allowing Cassandra to get a good look at her. Magic had aided in Akana's healing, her wounds completely gone, leaving only an aura of anger swirling around her. Cassandra knew it well. She felt the same thing toward Edgar. The same burning vengeance, the desire to do anything in her power, explore any profane act of magic to assist her in getting her revenge.

Akana just did it faster.

"You're playing with magic that you can't possibly understand," Cassandra quietly whispered. "I understand that you probably hate me for what happened to your father, but it wasn't my fault."

"That's the thing about you Caucasian magicians," Akana replied. "You always want to warn others when they step out of line. It was like that American and Noah. Well. I told them the same thing: Japan has dealt with magic far longer than either of you. We know the consequences of it. We know how to use it in moderation. Hell, we know things about resonance and the arcana that would unfurl every single law of magic that you swear by."

"Did your higher-ups support this?" Cassandra asked. "Those sigils—"

"Keii no hashira," Akana interjected. "Pillars of reverence. Individuals willingly sacrifice their souls, and they're imbued inside of them. Spiritual resonance is the strongest, purest form of raw magic. You know this, I'm sure. Containing it, especially in massive quantities, and using it as a conduit through an item, can allow you to make a field that overpowers most all other forms of magic. Even whatever makes you immortal."

To test her theory again, Akana got close. Cassandra didn't dare move, knowing when she was at a disadvantage. Though Cassandra's magic was vast, and deeply impressive, Japanese agents weren't just magicians. They were warriors. Always had been and always would be. Akana was incredibly skilled with her magic, but she was equally skilled in hand-to-hand combat. Which is why, as a sliver of a blade slashed her cheek, Cassandra only noticed it when she felt the blood trickle down her face.

"Magic like this is forbidden in Japan. You wouldn't believe the strings I had to pull, and the sins I had to commit against my family name, in order to get my organization even to consider authorizing the use of this."

"You did all that for little ol' me? I'm flattered."

"It wasn't that hard, when we really looked at you. Followed your trail of bloodshed through the years. The problem before was we just never looked at you that closely. I don't think anyone wanted to admit it. That someone had truly found a way to beat death and achieve immortality."

Cassandra's porcelain facade crumbled, just for a moment, a flicker of disbelief passing over her face. In return, Akana smiled.

"There, right there. I think we would call that emotion . . . fear.

"There is no way that immortality of yours came through good deeds. Messing with death doesn't come without sacrifices, doesn't come without ripping the fabric of magic apart. It's why we decided to use the pillars. Something like you, something so profane that wants even more magic from those paintings? Cannot be allowed to live."

"So, you're going to kill me? How boring. You said so yourself. The Japanese have a file on me. I could be of use to you. Perhaps even help you figure out how to bring your father back. There is a way, you know. A painting that—"

"I said that you cannot be allowed to live, I didn't say I was going to be the one to kill you," Akana clarified. "And if you think that my father, that his *soul*, would allow me to use whatever profane dark magic *you* know to bring him back, then you know nothing about my family, let alone my people.

"I *should* kill you. Japan would want me to. I was given the orders and have full jurisdiction to do so. But those boys from Britain? They were one step ahead of you, one step ahead of me. So, I'm thinking they might have better use for you. But first," Akana whispered, dragging the tip of her blade from Cassandra's left wrist all the way up to the joint of her elbow. She sank the tip of the metal into her flesh, forcing Cassandra to grit her teeth, an embarrassing whimper of pain leaving her mouth as bloodred, thick liquid dripped down her arm, her eyes locked with Akana's.

"I'm going to ask you some questions about the Macabre, see what you know. You are a woman of faith, yes, Cassandra. Consider this your flagellation. I'll be the one to decide when your penance is done. Right now, in this arena, I am your god, and you will bleed until I say otherwise."

PART V

I never paint dreams or nightmares. I paint my own reality.
—Frida Kahlo

Thirty-One

WHEN LEWIS RETURNED TO CONSCIOUSNESS, HE KNEW SOMETHING WAS wrong.

He sat in an uncomfortable wooden chair in the center of a room, just like the room he had found *The Drowning* in. The white, antiseptic walls burned his vision, bouncing back a light with no obvious source, and making him close his eyes and wince.

He struggled to stand and remove himself from the chair. But each time he attempted to rise, his body was pulled back down by a force that only grew stronger the more he struggled.

"You know, I really tried," Evangeline said.

As Lewis slowly opened his eyes, letting the light enter his vision, Evangeline's visage took form. She stood maybe five feet away, hands on her hips, looking down upon him.

"I gave you a chance. The Crown didn't believe you could be swayed. Their reasoning was that your country would be more important to you than anything else. You aren't the first American that we've had to—"

"Abuse?" Lewis said slowly.

"I wouldn't consider that the right word, but sure, if that's what you want to use."

"It's no different than what you did to my mother, is it?"

A flicker of annoyance passed over Evangeline's face. And

even if he didn't make it out of here alive, that bit of satisfaction was all he needed.

"Your mother was an exceptional agent."

"While she worked for you, or should I say, while you manipulated her and lied to her."

Evangeline's nostrils flared. "I have no time for this. What you know or might not know is a fraction of the truth. But I can tell you, Lewis, what is fully true is that you are going to help us find those last paintings so that we can rewrite history."

"That's your goal, right? Using these paintings to change it so that England is the only superpower. You believe the world would be better off like that? And you've been promised what? Right hand to the Crown? Some other fancy title?" He remembered what she had told him when he'd first pressed about what she got out of it. *Head of the Royal Arcane Intelligence Agency.* But he also knew it would piss her off for him to get it wrong.

"You sound just like your mother," she said. "That's not a compliment."

"It's the highest compliment, because she bested you."

"Something that you have failed to do," she reminded him.

Evangeline circled him like a shark, standing behind him, running her soft hand over the side of his face and his shoulders.

"I was willing to take a risk on you, make you something great. Extend to you the same offer I extended to your mother. But insolence runs in your family, a poisonous gene that I will ensure is plucked out when we redraw the world."

Lewis's body tensed for a moment. And the moment he did, he regretted it. His hesitation had provided a bit of information to Evangeline.

"No, you thought that you were—what? Going to go scot-free? That I would just forget about you? No, Lewis, you have all the makings of a very talented magician. You will do well under my services," she said after a moment's pause. "You *will* suit the Crown well."

"There's no fucking way I'm going to help you."

"No, not you. You never would," she replied. "But, and perhaps this is more a philosophical question, I'm almost certain the *you* that is you now will be the same *you* when the world is rewritten."

"To do that," he said slowly, "you have to get the last painting, and I'm not going to help you with that. You can cut off my other hand. You can do whatever magic you want."

"Such posturing," she said, almost wearily. "No, you're not going to help me—you've made that very clear. And in doing so, subconsciously, perhaps, you've showed me your true nature every step of the way. Challenging my authority. Going against Noah's best interests when he truly did have your safety at heart. But here's something you don't get:

"I don't need you to get the paintings."

She leaned down to whisper in his ear. "I only need your power. You might not be able to access it because you gave up your painting ability, but it's still there, Lewis. Just inaccessible to you."

As she stood, Evangeline's hands clashed against the back of his head, the heels of her hands touching, her long fingers like claws wrapping around the sides of his face and knitting over the front like a clasp.

"I would tell you that not resisting would make this hurt less, but your bloodline trait is tied directly to every part of you. Every part of your being is knitted with it. And forcing it to activate will hurt no matter how willing you are.

"So, the best advice I can give you is to understand that your pain and your suffering will help a higher cause. And maybe that will give you some solace."

It didn't.

But he quickly forgot about anything but agony. Lewis didn't know whether he would describe it as pain. It was something worse, something dark and hollow, like she was reaching her fingers into the most secret and sacred parts of him and strangling them. It felt like what made him, him, his DNA, his soul, and every bit of flesh and bone, was being violated.

He wanted to cry, wanted to scream, wanted to plead, knowing that this feeling, this harrowing invasion, would now define him. When he closed his eyes, he would think about her rummaging around inside of him.

And when he tried to get close to someone, her face would be what he saw. Innocence in that moment was taken from him, a bit of him broken by an unspoken contract that was made null and void between two people. His sacred sanctity was taken, not physically, but emotionally and spiritually.

He was bleached of who he was, conquered, twisted, and played with, reduced to nothing more than a thing, not a person.

Whiteness filled his mind, not as before when she had exerted her magic to make him submit, but as a form of self-defense. He focused on it, on the nothingness that had once been filled with colors and shapes, with skilled techniques and his favorite art pieces.

But that had been sacrificed to the painting in exchange for that stupid, worthless French expression. Just hours before he had had a gift, something that he could shield himself within.

He was nothing more than a tool for her to use and discard when she was done. He had lost. Lewis didn't hear Evangeline speak, but he felt through their connection her frustration as he attempted to put up his walls. Each one he put up, she broke down, sending it bursting into an explosion of dust.

But he kept trying, kept shielding her from the richest part of him, the magic she was hunting to use for her own. The problem was, he was a novice. A dilettante at best. And he wouldn't be able to hold out for long.

Something told him his body was breaking down, the manifestation of magical consequence. Something else told him Evangeline wouldn't stop. Even if it killed him, she would bring him to the brink of death. A mindless husk of nothing but harvestable magic, or perhaps something worse. There was no limit to what she would do to secure her claim, of that he was sure.

Even knowing all that—knowing it was almost certainly pointless—Lewis wouldn't let her win. Because after he gave up, after he lost, who would stand between Evangeline and the Crown and their goal? Like his mother said, there was more at risk than just them.

Yet as quickly and suddenly as the blinding whiteness had set in, it slinked away, revealing a familiar space with familiar people.

The sun had now set in Mumbai, a hospital room filled with just two people. Noah's father was in his bed and Noah was slumped in the corner, his blazer thrown over his chest, arms crossed under the fabric. He was half asleep, dozing in and out, but his eyes snapped open and locked on Lewis.

"How did I get here?" Lewis brokenly asked.

Noah didn't attempt to move, just studied him, looking him slowly up and down.

"You're not," he said quietly. "You're projecting yourself here. Except you don't know how to do that, which means you're reaching out to me, which means something's wrong. Where are you?"

Lewis swallowed quickly, slowly standing. The chair in London hadn't transferred with him. He had collapsed on the floor. As he stood, he looked at his hand, held it up to his face, and could see through it faintly, the color going in and out as if the connection were weak.

"I'm with Evangeline," he said. "She's trying to use my power to find a painting."

"Forcing a bloodline trait to activate like that is against a multitude of laws," Noah whispered. "She would've had to obtain permission from the Crown to do it, which means she must be desperate."

Lewis knew he didn't have time to explain everything to Noah.

"I don't know if I can keep this up, don't know how long I can keep her out."

"Don't fight it," Noah quickly added, rounding the side of the bed to stand in front of Lewis.

"I can't let her find it. You saw what she wants to do when she finds the last one."

"And we can do nothing to fight her if you are dead," Noah gently but firmly said. "Combating evil is not the only way to defeat evil, Lewis. Keeping you alive, the last current descendant of Edgar Dumont, is more important. But if you let her win, if you let her strip away your consciousness, you're good to no one."

"I saw something in the painting, a phrase. I don't know what it means, but I know she shouldn't have it."

"Focus your energy on that. Imagine it draped in cloth, shrouded from the rest of your mind. Let her sift through all your mental drawers and cabinets. She is looking for something specific, she won't care about what you're hiding if what she wants is easy to access. Breaking into someone's mind and forcing their bloodline trait will affect her too—use that to your advantage."

Noah raised his arms, pulling Lewis into an embrace. He placed his right hand against the back of Lewis's head, holding him close with the other.

"I'll find you," he said. "I'll get you out of there, I promise, but you have to stay alive. And if that means giving her all the paintings she wants, do it. You're no good to me gone. And . . . I'm no good with you gone.

"Besides, I still have to take you out on that date, or my mother will kill me."

Giving in felt like giving up. It was like standing on the precipice of a cliff and telling yourself it was safe to jump with no guarantee that it actually was.

But he had to trust Noah. He had to trust someone.

And so, with a deep, shaky breath as he felt the heaviness of Noah's chest drift away, Lewis gave in and let Evangeline's magic take over his own.

Thirty-Two

THE PAIN OF HAVING HIS POWERS PULLED FROM HIS SOUL WEIGHED ON Lewis.

It felt like every inch of him had been methodically filleted from his bones with a sharp knife, as if the chef holding it found pleasure in not only creating the meal but in exacting as much pain as possible from his ingredients in the process.

When Evangeline was done with him, she deposited him in his room in the Contract House. No longer did it give him any sense of hims home in Baltimore, though. The bookshelf—and the familiar books—had been removed. The bed was still pressed against the wall, but the desk and his clothes, anything that made the home feel personal and welcoming, were gone. This was now truly his prison, and he was its prisoner.

She had said something to him along the lines of "Next time, perhaps you'll be more willing," but her voice was so distant, lost in the sea of pain as his body floated weightlessly, he wasn't sure what he heard.

The only thing that helped ground him was remembering the feeling of Noah's chest against his cheek. He held on to that feeling even as she combed through his magic, plucking and choosing what to use and what to throw away. That helped keep him here, helped keep him from shattering and breaking into a million pieces.

He trusted Noah. He had said he would come for him, and he would. He just had to hold on. Lewis wasn't sure how long he lay in that bed, but eventually Evangeline returned. No knock on the door. No question about whether he was decent or willing to meet with her.

She stood and cleared her throat, the two agents who flanked her walking over and grabbing Lewis under each of his arms, forcing him to stand.

"You'll rise when I enter," she said slowly. "Do you understand?"

Lewis nodded, his body feeling like a machine going through the motions, his eyes focused on her shoes, noticing scuffs on the tips of her Louboutins. She had worn them out of the office, he reasoned, in a hurry, and had been unable to replace them with something more practical.

As a third agent entered the room, his white gloves with black runes on the back of them glowing brightly as if the magical batteries that powered them were functioning over capacity, Lewis realized why and where those scuffs had most likely come from.

In the agent's hand was a painting, black, with a man kneeling in penance, bony arms longer than any human arms, much like he had seen in *The Drowning*. The man in the painting was reaching upward and pulling down the flesh of his face, revealing white, harrowing bone.

It reminded him of a painting he knew he held some personal connection to, although those memories were hazy and just out of reach. Whatever painting that morose image of a man pulling at his own skin in anguish reminded him of was important to him, and knowing he was missing that memory sent a pang through his chest.

"You helped us find this," she said. "It was in Brazil, of all places, in the basement of a café. We paid the owner handsomely for it, if you care," she muttered, walking around the room, tracing the windowsill with the tip of her finger.

She flicked the glass. It rippled and hummed with protective magic, and she gave a sign of approval before turning her gaze back to Lewis.

"So now we need you to neutralize it."

Part of him wanted to scream and spit in her face. To tell her "Fuck no." But the warning that came as an automatic response, a soreness that was so deep he knew no medication or sweet words would soothe it, reminded him what would happen if he refused.

So instead, he nodded.

"Good boy." She grinned, and he hated how she said that last word, as she gave a silent command to the two holding him up. They gently let him go, forcing Lewis to rely on his own weight, his body almost threatening to give out under him. The man holding the painting with the gloves that must have somehow protected him from the effects of it stood in front of him.

The agent was no older than him, perhaps a year or two younger, a junior agent, he assumed, who had been given the opportunity of a lifetime to be involved in something great, bringing glory back to England.

"We don't know what this painting does," Lewis said, surprised at how raspy and quiet his voice was. "These men shouldn't be here."

"They know what they've signed up for," she replied, a tinge of annoyance simmering in her voice. "We've all taken the necessary precautions."

As if to show what she meant, Evangeline's image flickered much like his had in Mumbai. She wasn't here. She was just a projection of herself, while these three men were paying the price that they didn't even know they had offered. Lewis wondered if that meant she couldn't hurt him, but he didn't dare risk finding out.

Sighing in defeat, he squeezed his hand tight before reaching forward and pressing his palm against the black ink.

He took a deep breath, riding the wave of weightlessness that crashed around him and the sickening turning of his stomach as he fell through it. The stark gray blandness of his prison cell changed only slightly as he entered the new world. It took Lewis several moments to gather his bearings.

This time, diving into the painting felt harder, like he was pushing through molasses and forcing his way against a current. His stomach churned, and bile threatened to leak out of his mouth, but he swallowed it back. Focusing on the room around him, he smelled something sour, something that threatened the contents of his stomach once more.

Soiled sheets mixed with urine and scat plagued his nostrils, and that familiar scent, once again, of blood. There was no confirmation of when or where he was. There were bars on the windows that looked out onto a courtyard.

It was night once again like it was in the previous painting. He was in a massive room. Stone walls aligned with mattresses on the stone floor on the left and the right.

All of them were occupied with sleeping occupants, at least that's what he thought at first, until his vision adjusted to the dim light of the room. Yes, there were people in the beds, but their sheets were soaked with liquid so dark it almost looked black.

Arterial blood, he concluded. The cuts were deep and intentional. Each one of them killed in their sleep. All but one man, who sat in the center of the room. Lewis stilled his breath.

He didn't feel as much fear and terror as he did before, perhaps because whatever Evangeline had done inside of him had turned that switch off. There was no question that Edgar had killed the men, and judging by his fingertips and the way the trails of blood all led back to him, he was using their blood for paint.

It was similar to before, the same smell in the derelict house, but stronger than when he was using the bodies of the women he killed in London to accomplish his goal, using blood as a conduit to try to activate some profane magic. But now the bodies were here—wherever *here* was—not just their blood, and there was a miasma that seeped beyond Lewis's nostrils into his consciousness.

"I didn't intend for this to happen," Lewis breathed, not sure if it was a prayer or an apology.

Edgar didn't even acknowledge his voice, continuing to use the blood that had pooled around him—though not pooled in a natural way, Lewis noticed. It was almost like a moat of viscous fluids separating them, neither flowing nor spreading. Lewis looked around and saw that the image on the floor wasn't simply painted on stone, but had first been sketched out using a bedsheet.

"I didn't mean to hurt you back then," he said, louder.

"I should be thanking you," Edgar said, voice distant and monotone. "It was getting harder and harder to find people to lure back to my place. Fear. But here—it's perfect. No one bats an eye when they hear a madman screaming in pain."

Lewis swallowed thickly, sealing off his nose to prevent the sickening smells from overpowering his senses. He couldn't stop what happened in the past, but at least he could perhaps learn from it. This was the only space where Evangeline had no control over him. She didn't need to know what he saw. And as long as he neutralized the painting, she wouldn't care.

Right now, the biggest strength he had against her was that she thought him to be worthless and broken.

"What happened after . . ." Lewis paused. "What happened after the last time I saw you?"

"I almost died," Edgar said matter-of-factly, as if he had been asked about the weather. "Landed on the cobblestones, broke my leg in six places. Doesn't work right anymore. I can't walk straight. They took me to a hospital, fixed me up, and that's where my luck ended.

"One of the men working there," Edgar continued, "I had met six years prior, when I started looking for you, finding a way to do what you could do."

His eyes flicked up for a moment. "You've barely changed since I saw you last. Well, minus your hand. How cruel the world is."

"What happened in the hospital, Edgar?"

"The man remembered me, remembered my interest in bodies. We had bonded over our love of alcohol, the hardness of a man's body, and, of all things, music." Edgar paused. "Men of the occult, ultimately, but where we differed was that he wanted to use his power for good, to make the world a better place. Saw that he could help fix those who ailed and stave off death."

"And you didn't care about that?"

"Not in the way he did. I didn't give a shit about others. I just wanted my sister back. I believed we could accomplish our goals together, a shared interest, a shared path until it deviated, but he would never go as far as we needed. He would never understand that the dead have no power, that the living are where all that energy exists and thrives and grows."

"You tried to convince him to kill people," Lewis concluded, "and he refused."

"I tried to convince him of the right course. He was weak. But now he worked at the hospital, and when he saw me in the bed, he reported me, claimed that I was insane. And so I ended up here, a place where no one would care what happened to those who went missing or were killed in the night. As I said: All of that was thanks to you."

Lewis kept his distance from Edgar, distance being the one thing that protected him.

Maybe . . .

"It's been five years," Edgar muttered, putting the final touches on the painting and using multiple coats of red blood to darken the background.

He flicked both hands in opposite directions, speckles of blood landing on the edges of the sheet and on the stone. Placing both hands on the ground and letting out a pained grunt, he stood, favoring his right leg over his left.

"Five years since you put me in here, five years to sift through every piece of magic I have read or seen, cobble it together, stitch it in some Frankenstein fashion to create something to prove that I can do anything, that I can defy the laws of physics and science and do what every man says they want to do."

"What's that?" Lewis asked, afraid to ask.

"Why, make their own destiny, of course. But you know what else I discovered along the way, in between the runes and the spells, the foreign languages, and the choices that damned my soul to hell? Every single one of us, magician or not, is mad down here. And up there and below? The Gods laugh at us, finding pleasure in our suffering.

"And to that, I say: No more."

Lewis took half a step back as Edgar finished, preparing himself for what might come, but what he didn't imagine was for the sheet to stir, and from beneath it for something to rise. As the fabric draped over its shoulders, it molded to the outline, taking the form of a human fusing with the shape of the fabric. It had no face, as if the sheet itself was a cloak, hiding its almost recognizable form. But it was a person, and it loomed eight feet tall. The black hollow where the face should be was pointed directly at Lewis.

And without warning, it lunged.

Lewis was quick to react, his body moving without thinking. He pointed his magical wrist toward the ground and pushed backward, launching himself to put distance between himself and the attacker.

His eyes flipped over to Edgar, seeing the manic hunger in his face, but Lewis had no time to linger on the man because the sheet creature struck again, moving faster than any person would be able to move. This time, it would have made contact, except in the pit of his stomach—much like when he was yanked out of *The Stain*—Lewis felt the same feeling suddenly take over.

The world went rushing by him, the madhouse cell replaced with his own prison once more. Evangeline had a grip on the back of his shirt, and there was a body's length of distance between him and the painting.

"If you care about those men," she said, her eyes focused on the painting, "say its name."

Lewis's gaze left her, glancing at what he had just been touching. And then he looked at the three men in the room, all clutching their heads, all screaming in agony. The young man who had held the painting had loosened his grip. He stumbled backward, crying out in broken English, his eyes rolling back, detaching with an audible *snap* before spinning in their sockets.

Round and round they went, blood and bile spilling from his mouth. And the painting just floated, its malevolent energy falling over Lewis's shoulders.

"Lewis," Evangeline warned, "it is only you, me, and these men in here. They do not deserve to die because you hate me."

She was right. Lewis knew it. Deep down, he couldn't let innocent souls pay the price for her evil. His vision focused back on the painting. Gritting his teeth, he saw no other out but to say the first words that came to mind.

"The Madness."

Thirty-Three

NEUTRALIZING *THE MADNESS* HAD NOT COME WITHOUT LOSS OF LIFE.
The young agent who had been carrying the painting had been the closest imitation of an illustration Lewis had ever seen. Before the painting had been silenced, the boy had dug his fingernails into his skin and, much like the image, pulled his flesh down, his face now only bone; flaps of skin hung lazily at his chin. His dead form slumped in a kneeling position, head bowed backward.

Evangeline had been nice enough to remove the body, but the bloodstain on the floor had been left.

"Do not clean it up," she ordered the house. "Allow him to see what his hesitation has wrought."

My hesitation? She had no idea what he'd endured. What he'd witnessed. And yet she thought it was that easy—go into the painting, decipher a code that only he had access to, and then provide a name that felt both true to the painting and to Lewis's soul . . .

What a goddamn bitch.

But he couldn't articulate that, just as he couldn't easily say the name of the painting when he was pulled out. So he was left with the horror of his memories and the example of what those memories pertained to always present. Lewis spent the rest of the day curled up on his bed, knees pulled to his chest, looking at the bloodstain. That man had had friends, lovers, a mother, a father who cared about him; and Evangeline had just tossed the agent aside, justifying his death as a service to the Crown.

Justifying his death as a lesson for Lewis to learn.

He wondered if the agent's parents would ever know. Would they be given something in solace to remember him or told some lie about his valiant service? Would their minds be wiped with some spell?

Would Evangeline even remember his name after a week?

The next morning when the door opened, Lewis had just dozed off but jolted awake. He half expected Evangeline to appear, but instead, two agents, different from before, walked into the room.

"Does she want me?" he asked, watching them carefully.

Neither of the agents said anything at first, the older of the two closing the door behind himself and locking it. Lewis's hackles rose, his muscles tightening. He hadn't eaten in almost three days. The little water that he had forced himself to consume barely held him over. He was weak and tired, the pain of the torture from before finally subsiding.

But even in his best condition, he wasn't sure he could hold his own against these two.

The taller of the two spoke. "We don't have much time."

At first, Lewis didn't understand, but he didn't relax his body. The agent cleared his throat, using his right hand to hit the side of his own face once, twice, then three times before shaking his head. When he spoke again, the voice was familiar.

"Sorry," Akana said through the man. "Your minds are heavily fortified, more than I thought, but no, we don't have much time."

Lewis still didn't understand. "What are you doing here? Or should I ask *how* are you here?"

"Technically we're not here, but I'll let that slide," Akana muttered.

"Who is 'we'?"

"Me." Another familiar voice, prim, proper, French, and smooth, spoke, in sharp distinction to the short, stout man with a wide-set beard that it emanated from.

A voice he had last heard in Osaka.

Lewis's body tensed up again as he took a step back. Yes, he was weak, and no, he couldn't imagine holding his own against an agent of the British Museum, let alone this powerful mage, but if he struck fast, using the bed and hurling it at the man who had been overridden by Cassandra's consciousness, maybe he could deliver a long-lasting blow . . .

Cassandra raised her hands, and Akana stepped forward.

"I know you have no reason to believe me, but I need you to trust me," Akana said.

"She almost *killed* you," Lewis growled. "She killed your father, and she will pay for that when this is over."

"To be fair, I almost killed *you*, remember? But right now, none of that is here nor there. Just know that our interests align, and neither of us is here to hurt you. Besides, Noah sent us to you."

Immediately, the burning hatred toward Cassandra was stifled, his gaze focused on Akana over Cassandra.

"Is he okay? Is he alive?"

Akana nodded. "He reached out to us. The moment he made contact with you."

"Is he still in India?"

Akana shook her head. "I don't think it's wise to say where he is, considering where you are right now," she muttered. "And like I said, time is not on our side, but he told us what happened, and we're here to get you out."

There was no doubt in his mind that Akana was telling the truth. But Cassandra, on the other hand . . .

"How do I know that she's not controlling you?" he asked. "You are a powerful magician, Akana, but—"

"No *but*. I'm a powerful magician, and that should be the end of that sentence," she firmly stated.

"Trust me," Cassandra said, and paused. "I know how ironic that sounds, but I am here of my own volition, and Akana has allowed me to live, as long as I follow *her* rules. Right now, the rules state that we are putting aside our differences and stopping Evangeline. I told her everything."

Lewis kept his gaze on Cassandra. "Everything?" he asked.

At first, Cassandra didn't speak, letting out a soft sigh. "So, you know?"

"That you knew my mother, yes."

Akana chimed in, "She told me that. She told me about Evangeline's goal, about the Crown's mission, about your mother, Lewis, and about the time she met you."

Lewis hesitated, confusion passing over his face.

"The first time we met was in Japan. You were there."

Cassandra shook her head. "I was there in the hospital when your mother died, when you were waiting. We had multiple conversations, multiple opportunities for me to pry and see what your mother had told you about me, about the paintings. Perhaps find out if you even knew their origins.

"And each time the conversation ended, I started it again and again and again, wiping your memory over and over. You knew nothing." She quickly added, "And I regret the role I played in manipulating you. But for now . . ."

"For now?" Akana cut her off. "We don't have time for this. The Contract House that you're in is tied to Evangeline, no longer to Noah. According to him, that's basic protocol. She probably has already gotten an alert that we're here. The only thing keeping her from coming to us is Cassandra's magic."

"I overrode some of the rooms that exist here," the French woman explained. "The agents are probably right outside the door right now, struggling with the runes, but they won't last forever."

"If what you say is true," Lewis said slowly, working his way through his decision, "then you understand Evangeline will stop at nothing to get that last painting."

"Which is why we're here for you," Akana said, annoyance prickling at the edge of her voice.

"That's *not* what I'm saying," Lewis corrected. "I need you to get me to Baltimore."

The agent's face was masked by confusion.

"My father lives there," he said. "Evangeline will come for him if she cannot get to me, and he's all that I have left."

"Lewis, we cannot risk..."

He raised his hand, cutting Akana off. "I'm not letting him suffer any more because of Evangeline. My mother, me—all of this goes back to that woman and her singular focus on power."

Akana sighed, glancing over at Cassandra. Cassandra's eyes stayed on Lewis, unblinking, and he matched her gaze.

"You owe me."

Eventually, Cassandra agreed. "I can create a portal that will take him to Baltimore. This house is old. Its magic is grounded but flawed."

"We'll meet you there," Akana said, "make sure your father is protected, and then go and deal with these paintings."

Lewis nodded. It was good enough.

Cassandra walked forward, pressing her hands against the wall of the house. She took a deep breath and pushed the rippling stone. As her hands passed through it, the Contract House groaned and shuddered, cracks appearing in the wood and stone that instantly healed. But each time one healed, two more appeared.

"Interesting," Cassandra said, her voice distant, her eyes closed. "There are systems set up to prevent someone from tampering with the house. But," she continued after a pause, "there's a clear path forward, as if the house is telling me how to override its defenses."

Which was exactly what it was doing, Lewis thought. He looked upward toward the ceiling, smiling softly, mouthing *thank you*.

A moment later, the bathroom door swung open, and Lewis saw a very familiar sight: his family living room, a place he hadn't been in for over five months.

"Go," Cassandra muttered. "I won't be able to hold this forever. I also need to remove the memory of where we went from the house's ledger. It'll save us some time, but I can't do all this while you both linger."

"But to do that, you have to stay here," Akana said.

"I'm aware." Cassandra nodded, her eyes still closed. "Evangeline will come in. She'll try to pull my mind out of the agent's. She won't succeed." She smiled.

"It's going to hurt like a bitch," Akana informed her.

Cassandra opened one eye, glancing over at them. "When you've lived as long as I have, you don't mind a little pain," she said.

Akana's eyes locked with Lewis's. "I'll meet you there. You might want to turn away, though."

Lewis didn't have time to ask why before Akana turned to face the opposite wall. She walked forward putting only four or so inches between her and the wall, brought her head back, and slammed the agent's forehead against it, causing his body to slump forward.

Lewis winced, and he wanted to go and check to see whether the man was still alive, but Cassandra chimed in.

"Go," she said firmly, her voice a hiss. Sure enough, the image of Lewis's living room began to ripple, fading in and out.

With a deep breath, Lewis lunged forward and dove into the image, Alice diving down the rabbit hole once more.

Thirty-Four

IT FELT WEIRD TO BE BACK HOME, CONSIDERING EVERYTHING THAT WAS happening.

After his mother's death, Lewis took refuge in his art. It didn't give him the solace that he thought it would. But he distanced himself from mostly everybody, including his father. It had been almost half a year since he had been home. An unheard-of occurrence before his mother's passing. Weekend dinners were common, and sometimes his visits were even more frequent, to do laundry or to just be around those who knew who he truly was. Stepping into the living room, a weight was lifted off his shoulders.

Even if his father wasn't here, currently at work at the nonprofit he ran, Lewis felt him in the air. The half-finished grocery list pinned to the refrigerator, the lukewarm cup of coffee on the counter, even the lunch pail his father always forgot to take sat by the door untouched. This was where Lewis belonged, not in London or Paris or Perth or Lagos. He should be *here*. And in any other reality, in any other circumstance, he would be still processing and mourning his mother's passing, figuring out how to move forward.

Regret and longing were left at the door as Akana pushed it open. No longer was she in the body of one of the British agents, but her own, including the short-cut black hair with strands of silvery gray peeking from the roots. Lewis's eyes drifted to them before he quickly focused back on her face, but not before she noticed.

"The price of magic," she said. "I'm sure I've shaved three or four years off my life."

Lewis arched an eyebrow, and she waved it off.

"I'll explain later," she said. "Your father's not here. He's at work." Akana nodded, seemingly to herself. "That will make this easier." She paced through the house, dragging her fingers over the walls and countertops.

"Hmm," she said in the back of her throat. "There's magic here."

"My mother was a magician—"

Akana raised her right hand, cutting him off. "Not that. Not the lingering magic of someone who lived here in your walls." She tapped her nails against the drywall. "It's stitched into the foundation, threaded into the wood. There are runes and spells here. Deactivated now, but the last pulse they gave off was only about five months ago."

He said after a moment, "That's when my mom died."

Akana turned to look at him. "If your mother enchanted this house, then they would have stopped working when she passed."

"I saw a vision of her," Lewis explained. "In it she was talking to Evangeline, and she said she would make sure the British Museum would never find her or me."

"And I'm guessing it worked. There are layers upon layers of runes here. It's impressive how they sync. This is very accomplished magic. There are runes here that I wouldn't think would work together, and yet they do. Balancing each other's weaknesses to become stronger."

Akana was looking past him, and Lewis imagined even past the physical into the metaphysical. She had that look of someone who was experiencing something very few could.

"This will make reinforcing your home easier," she promised. "I can activate the old runes, maybe even strengthen them, and put new ones in. It'll take me about fifteen minutes."

Lewis had nowhere else to be, so, leaving Akana to her work, he made his way down the hall and up the stairs.

The first door on his left was his bedroom, exactly like he left it when he moved out. Half-drawn sketches with different mediums of charcoal, watercolor, paint, pencil, even ballpoint pen when he went through a phase.

Posters of Paramore and Taylor Swift, of Josh Groban and other men he had been infatuated with in his younger years. His father had wanted to turn the room into a study to work on his model trains, but his mother was very firm.

"In case he ever needs to come back," she said one Thanksgiving.

The idea of returning home had been sickening then, but he let her have it. As he sat on the bed now looking around, he couldn't have been happier. Sitting on the counter next to his now-obsolete desktop computer was a photo of him and his family.

Lewis walked over and ran his fingers over the glass, the memory washing over him of them at Disney World right after high school graduation, a reward for getting into SCAD, his top pick. They were all happy then. There was no magic, no paintings—none of this—just a normal family with normal hopes and normal dreams.

Even if that was never true, he believed it to be true and that was enough for him. Lewis paused when he heard a new voice from downstairs. At first, his body tensed, worried that it was Evangeline who had found them, but the highly aristocratic, almost lyrical way the person spoke confirmed it was Cassandra. His attention drifted back to his room as something at his desk caught his eye.

Curiously, he pulled a piece of paper from under the keyboard. Thicker than most, it was the type of paper that would be used for watercolor. On the back, in typical Lewis fashion, was a date roughly eleven years prior to today's. Frowning, he unfolded the paper, the creases dividing it into four quadrants. It was a rudimentary piece of art, a by-product of him just dabbling into not only art as a whole, but watercolor in particular.

It took him a moment to decipher what the image was supposed to be.

The view passed through two cast-iron gates in an archway into the graveyard about a mile or so from his home, the same graveyard where his mother was buried. But that wasn't what interested him about the drawing. On the lower half of the watercolor, spanning the two bottom quadrants, three people stood looking into the graveyard. Their backs were fairly nondescript.

He gritted his teeth as he thought of how much better the image would be if he had painted it now, if he still had that skill. But as he studied it closer, familiar traits of the three became clear, and a gasp left his mouth. Folding the paper up and shoving it into his pocket, Lewis ran out, taking the stairs two at a time, almost tripping and falling.

Cassandra frowned, looking over at him. "Can you please not kill yourself before Evangeline has a chance at attempting it?" she said, bored.

"How'd you get away?" he asked.

"Magic," was her infuriating response. "When you and Akana left, Evangeline wasn't far behind you. I scrubbed our location as best I could."

"That doesn't sound like you succeeded," Akana noted.

"You try and do that while a high-ranked magician is pulling your veins out of your body through your pores. Pity about that boy I hijacked, though. Well, I suppose not much pity. He had a girl he wanted to propose to, did you know that?"

Lewis ignored her, instead unfolding the paper and showing it to the two of them. Akana's and Cassandra's faces were puzzled.

"I gave up my ability to paint and everything connected with it," he said in one breath, before Akana or Cassandra could complain, bark at him at how stupid the decision was. He shook his head. "I gave up my ability to try and end this all. Because even if I go into a fugue state, I can't actually draw where we need to go . . . a contract I made with one of the Macabre."

"Great deal," Akana growled. "You gave up the one advantage that we had in finding them. Such a stupid—"

"Be quiet," Lewis hissed.

Akana's face screwed into anger, and her shadow flickered like a serpent ready to strike.

"I *do* have a way to get it back. This isn't far from here," he said, placing the paper on the counter.

"What is that?"

"It's where my mother is buried."

"They look like us," Cassandra chimed in, standing in the same position as they were in the painting, with herself on his left and Akana on his right.

"Exactly. I painted it a little more than a decade ago. It must've been one of my first fugue states, before I knew what they were. But I can *feel* the truth of this painting. And that means there's something there for us."

"We have nothing to lose," Cassandra explained. "This is a dead end here, and we need to get moving anyway."

"I have my father," Lewis reminded her. "I know you don't have an idea of what it means to care for someone, but that's why we're here."

Cassandra shot Lewis a look he couldn't exactly place. Was it anger? Had he touched a nerve? He didn't know much about Cassandra, not really. If she had someone to care for, she hid it well.

"Of course I know that," she hissed. "But the best way to protect him, and everyone we care about, is to end this. And we can't do that by standing here and being caught."

"I have an idea about how to do that," Lewis said, folding the paper and slipping it into his back pocket. "I read it when I first got to the Contract House."

Akana crossed her arms over her chest, not convinced, and the knitting of her brow told him she was still angry at him for before. Perhaps for speaking out of turn or for making such a stupid decision that she would never make, but she rolled her eyes and stepped back.

"Let's go."

Walking between houses through alleyways and walkways cut the walk to the graveyard down to less than five minutes. When they arrived, Lewis paused, Cassandra and Akana making it a few steps forward before noticing he wasn't following them.

"I haven't been here since the funeral," he whispered, not sure if they heard him.

Cassandra sighed, the first of the two to move back to him, putting her hand on his shoulder. "One way or another," she said gently, "this will be over soon. And no matter what happens, I know this much: Your mother would be proud of you."

"I never lived up to my mother's expectations," he muttered in disbelief.

"Maybe not, but few people do," Akana said. "My father was never proud of me. I could never do enough for him. Live up to our name."

"And that's not who your mother was," Cassandra countered. "I admit I only knew her in the confines of her working for Evangeline, and I'm sure in some way that clouds my opinion of her. There was only a part of herself that she showed to me, but when she figured out what Evangeline was doing, the only thing she cared about was you. You are fighting back against Evangeline. Win or lose, your mother would be proud, and I see her in you.

She was a problem solver, Lewis, and that's what you're doing right now."

Her kind words didn't absolve her of what she had done to him, to Akana, and to how many other countless people Lewis didn't know about. But they were enough to make him walk through the archway to the graveyard.

As they walked, weaving their way through tombstones, with Lewis leading the way, he explained his plan.

"I read in a book about magic how it can't be created or destroyed, like every other form of energy."

"That's correct," Akana said, sounding almost bored by this rudimentary mansplaining. And yet she also built off it, as if she herself couldn't help but show off the depth of her knowledge. "It's how magicians work. We siphon magic, push it into things, pull it out, but we don't ever get rid of it. It just occupies a different space than before. It takes a different shape. The magic that you lost when you made the agreement with the painting didn't disappear. It was just placed inside the painting."

"Exactly," Lewis said. "So, when my mother died, the magic didn't leave her."

As they stopped in front of a gravestone on a hill with lilacs and lilies freshly placed on the cold stone, Lewis fell silent. *Jessica Dixon*, it read. *Loving mother, accomplished wife, stellar human being.*

Both Akana and Cassandra gave him a moment before Cassandra spoke up.

"Repeat what you just said," she said slowly. Lewis's gaze focused on the tombstone, unable to look at either of them.

"My mother might have died physically, but her magic is still inside her body. And if her magic is connected to Edgar Dumont just like mine was, we can pull it from her and use it."

He glanced at the two of them.

"You said it yourself. Magic cannot be created or destroyed. It just changes vessels."

"You can't put one person's magic into another person, though. Not easily, at least. It's like different types of blood. And even then, there are major complications," Akana informed them both.

"That's true," Cassandra said, slowly processing what Lewis was thinking. "For most people. You have a bloodline trait. Consistency is being a blood relative. All a bloodline trait is, is a genetic marker triggering a magical ability. So maybe it will recognize his mother's magic inside of him, and he can then use it."

"Say that's the case. Even if you do take in her magic, it only has a temporary window," Akana warned. "It's not yours. There's only so much magic within her body, and she's not going to be able to draw more in. Once you use it, it will go into the ether and continue its cycle. You'll have maybe one chance to get it right. One more time to use it on a painting."

"And I'll use it on the final one," he said. "All we need is one chance to turn the tide in our favor."

"It's dangerous," Akana muttered, disapproval on her face. "It's also borderline necromancy."

"That's rich coming from you," Cassandra said, arching a brow. Her eyes drifted over to Lewis. "When she found me in Brazil, our little agent here used some very profane magic on me. I doubt Japan approved that."

Akana fell silent, not willing to argue with her. Instead, Cassandra continued.

"It *would* mean defiling your mother's grave, Lewis. There would be nothing left of her. Pulling magic out of her bones would turn her to dust."

"There's no difference between that and time and the earth taking her."

"No," Cassandra said, agreeing. "But those are passive actions. You are willingly doing this. Are you sure that's what you want?"

"We don't have another choice," he said.

Cassandra shrugged. Glancing over at Akana again, she said,

"You are the most accomplished of the three of us. Do you think you can pull the magic out?"

Akana hesitated for a moment before conceding. "In theory, yes."

"Then it's settled," Cassandra said. "We do this, we get the magic, and we cut Evangeline off before she can finish what she is aiming to accomplish. How many paintings have you purified for her?"

Lewis did a quick calculation. "Four or five," he said. "I have reason to believe she might have found another one or two."

"Shimen-soka," Akana uttered, squatting in front of the grave. She whispered another word in Japanese, bowing her head and clasping her hands together in reverence. "It means we're surrounded on all sides. At a disadvantage. You all might say, 'behind the eight ball.'"

"We're further behind than that." Cassandra sighed. "Evangeline wasn't completely honest with you. She doesn't need all of them to find the last one. She just needs enough of them. Each painting contains a bit of magic that can be used to track the last one. Doing so will burn the magic out of them. But how many she needs is the question."

That made Lewis start. *Burn the magic out . . .*

He remembered after *The Drowning*, the fire Evangeline had cast over the painting. To neutralize it, he had thought. But he realized that wasn't what she was doing.

She had been gathering the magic out of it, using it to point her toward the last one.

All this time . . .

"A onetime spell," Lewis concluded.

Cassandra nodded. "But with you in the equation as a conduit, as a grounding anchor, she can use you as a point of triangulation to find the last one. Funnel the dangerous magic through you. She just needs enough of them to do it."

"So we're too late," Akana said. "Which means it doesn't matter if we defile this grave."

"No, because the same thing can be said in reverse. You have come in contact with most of those paintings," Cassandra said to Lewis. "You are the descendant of a Dumont. The power doesn't come from the paintings like she believes."

"It comes from a descendant," Lewis whispered.

"Exactly. The paintings are what allow any person to find them. Your mother knew this. It's what she discovered." She paused. "Rather, it's what I told her. And when she added it up, figuring out what Evangeline was doing and how close she was without her knowing, she fled. But you, Lewis, you can find the tenth painting on your own. Without the others, because, in simple terms, the last painting is your birthright."

Lewis finished, "That's why my mother hid me and herself."

Cassandra nodded. "I believe Evangeline is hedging her bets, finding enough paintings so that if for some strange reason you refuse or can't accomplish the goal, she has a backup plan. Coincidentally, you are the threat to the paintings. Keeping you close until she was sure of your allegiances and then taking you out if she had to was her way of guaranteeing the plan."

"If you knew this for so long," Akana said, standing up, "why didn't you do anything about it?"

"I could have," Cassandra muttered. "In fact, I tried."

Her eyes drifted down to Lewis's arm. "I tried to kill you in Perth. Bringing the house down. That would've ended all of this."

"I thought the house collapsed because of *The Stain?*" Lewis said, angry.

Cassandra raised her hand and sighed. "It's in the past now."

"Attempting to *murder* me is not in the past." He held up the stump that used to be his right hand. "*This* is not in the past."

Cassandra fell silent. A pregnant pause among the three of them. "Not to interrupt this," Akana chimed in, "but also to totally interrupt this, your feelings are valid, Lewis—trust me, I get it—but we can deal with this *after* we deal with Evangeline. Add it to her ledger of crimes that she has to pay for. For now, we have something we need to do. I'll set up the perimeter. I'll pull the magic out of this, and we'll use it to find the last painting before Evangeline can."

"While you do that," Cassandra said, "Lewis, will you walk with me? I have something to tell you."

"I don't want to talk to you," Lewis said plainly.

"Fair," she replied. "But I think you should know what I have to say. If something happens to me, this information should not die with me."

"Go with her," Akana said. "It's going to take me at least ten minutes to do this, and you looming over my shoulder isn't going to help."

Lewis glared at Akana, but begrudgingly agreed, following Cassandra. She had already started walking down the hill they had come up. He didn't like the idea of being alone with her, but the way Cassandra showed her back to him reminded him if she really wanted to, she could snap his body in half right here and now. So perhaps he should at least hear what she had to say.

Because Cassandra was right. Who knew what could happen in the next hour to all three of them?

───◆───

LEWIS FOLLOWED CASSANDRA down to the bottom of the hill, where she found shade under a tree that loomed over a dozen or so graves.

"What did you . . ."

"Give me a moment," Cassandra whispered, her eyes closed as she tilted her head upward, letting the breeze graze her cheek. She let out a deep sigh, holding the air inside of her before opening her eyes and turning her gaze to Lewis.

Without a word, she extended her hand to him, palm upward.

Lewis hesitated, noticing the lines on Cassandra's palm. He knew people believed you could tell a person's future by the lines etched within their skin: their financial success, how many kids they would have, their love life—all of it, divination based on biology. It was a fun thing to play when he was a kid, like a game of MASH. But he didn't believe in it, not until now. He wondered what the lines on her hand said.

The moment they touched, Lewis felt different. The lingering smell of mildew and death in the damp air disappeared almost instantly. The world around them melted away into something familiar, the reverse of how the color had drained before, becoming bright once more. For a moment, Lewis thought that Cassandra had done something to him, cast a spell. And in a sense, she had. They were no longer at the grave site. They were in a convent—bells chiming, the sound of women exchanging quiet words in French, hymns and the intonations of scripture being read in the distance.

"Where did you take me?" Lewis said.

There was no accusation in his voice. Part of him knew they hadn't left.

"My memories. I want to show you something before I ask you for a favor. Come. It won't take long."

Cassandra led Lewis along the cobblestones and through the archways with familiarity, her hands behind her back. She was still dressed like she was in modern times, in the same pantsuit that fit her so well. Women in habits and a few priests moved by them, completely ignorant of their presence.

"I'm not like you and Akana, Lewis."

"No, you're a murderer."

Cassandra chuckled lowly, not at all disturbed by the moniker, which made Lewis shudder. "Yes. But that's not what I mean. I have been around far longer than you, or Noah, Akana, or even Evangeline. And like most things of age, I hold knowledge you would be wise to know before moving forward."

Cassandra pushed open a door, leading to a room with more than three dozen cots. People laid strewn out on them, the smell of sickness palpable in the air.

Lewis covered his nose. Even as a guest within her memories, he could still sense death, its lingering presence, its hunger. He frowned, glancing at Cassandra as they walked.

"What's the point of this?"

"Back roughly a century and a half ago," she said, "I wanted to serve God. I found my calling at this convent. In English, it would translate to the Church of the Holy New Martyr, Cassandra of Trebizond."

"Where you took your name from."

"My father was not a man who saw much in women, their only value being what they could provide for a man. And I didn't want that. I couldn't save my older or younger sister, but I could save myself. And the best way back then for a woman to have agency was to devote herself to another man, to God.

"I found a calling here," she said, stopping in front of the cot of a wheezing boy. There was a nurse, a nun, tending to the sweat on his brow. She didn't look like Cassandra, but from the way Cassandra smiled at her, he assumed she remembered her fondly.

"I was good at what I did. So good that when they found a man after midnight leaning against our church doors bleeding out, they called to me and asked me to soothe him through the night and be the last happy face he saw."

"Edgar," Lewis whispered.

With a flick of her finger, the images in front of them changed. It was late now, only a few candles lighting the room, but he saw

Cassandra sitting at the edge of the bed where an older version of Edgar than Lewis had seen before was covered in blood.

"Did you ever figure out what happened to him?"

Cassandra nodded. "It took some time. First of all, we were all surprised that he lived through the night, but yes, he confided in me, found comfort in me, and he explained his fantastical tales. How he had escaped from an asylum in London. Found passage across the ocean to France as a stowaway."

Cassandra continued, but for Lewis, her voice drifted off. He remembered the asylum well, remembered what magic Edgar displayed there. The only way he could have gotten out was by using *The Madness*. And if it did to the residents what it had done to the people in the Contract House . . .

Lewis forced his attention back to Cassandra. "If you knew what he was, knew he was a criminal, you should have turned him in."

"I very well should have," she agreed. "But you see, Lewis, I was a woman of God, a woman who feared the afterlife, and the tales of magic and woes didn't interest me. I thought they would corrupt me, but I listened because I knew that's what he needed. He was never far from death's door. Wounds he had ignored for far too long had turned septic. He could have gone at any night, any day, really, and I thought it would be nice to be there with him. And if listening to his stories made him happy, then so be it.

"He told me of a choice that he made, a dark choice. Edgar's life, as I'm sure you have seen now, was often filled with strife and pain. When we were in Japan, I mentioned to you a woman that he loved, the inspiration for *The Lingering*."

"That woman that he killed?"

"That woman who was killed was his wife. But was no fault of Edgar's, I would soon learn," she hastily added. "It was poor fate, pure unluckiness, but Edgar didn't see it like that. He saw it as another person in his life taken from him. So he turned to dark magic, searched the corners of the earth to find it, using blood and souls in the hopes to bring her back. I believe you have seen the painting that inspired this."

"*The Madness*," Lewis explained. "It wasn't just his wife, though. It was . . ."

Cassandra's hand rose, squeezing his shoulder. "I know."

Lewis frowned, looking up at her.

"Time is a fickle thing at best, Lewis. You going back, dealing with *The Drowning*, set Edgar's life in motion. He latched onto you. The idea of you. The power that you, blinking in out of time, showed existed. As such, he would do anything to have that power."

"To save his sister."

"Exactly. Love is a powerful thing, Lewis. But so is guilt."

"Are you saying," Lewis said slowly, "because I helped Evangeline with *The Drowning*, I set Edgar on his course?" He mulled it over, just speaking his thoughts aloud. "I am the one who made him create the painting back in London that caused him to kill all those people. Sent him to the asylum."

"Nothing is that finite and absolute when it comes to magic. Did you play a role? Yes. But so did I. So did Akana. So did Noah. Every person who you have come across has played a role. Even those you didn't. Time and magic are two of the most unpredictable forces. They move backward and forward, up and down, through and in between. You shouldn't dwell on your role in this. It will only lead to the same fate as Edgar's."

Cassandra shrugged, waving her hand again. Time unfurled around them as if it was played on twice the speed. He saw Edgar slowly get better and then wax and wane in sickness and health. It was at least a month, maybe two, that he was here, with Cassandra always by his side.

The memory accelerated again, this time stopping at a moment with Edgar out of bed walking, barely, and wheezing heavily, but he was getting better.

The look on Cassandra's face didn't reflect joy, though. There was something dark in her eyes.

"What happened between you and Edgar?"

Cassandra was silent for a moment before letting out a small sigh.

"Men happened, Lewis. They always do. I viewed my kindness as a strength. I viewed the ability to help others as my calling. I saw God in the work I did, and I was happy with it until Edgar wanted more. As he was starting to get better, we were discussing sending him out of the convent. He didn't need our sanctuary, and we needed the beds for others—others who were closer to death, who needed absolution, but he didn't want to go."

"And it wasn't that he didn't want to go but that he didn't want to leave *you*," Lewis finished.

"I had known that Edgar was a painter. When he was in a lucid state, he would ask for charcoal or ink, anything to take his mind off the pain. So we provided it. His drawings and sketches were beautiful, usually of his vista outside the window or things from his memories. I have them in my home if you would like to see them one day. It might help you understand."

Lewis wasn't sure he wanted to understand Edgar. All of the pain and strife that man had caused him, he just wanted to put it behind him, but he let Cassandra continue.

"One day it was decided that Edgar would be sent to a neighboring city to recover. I was to deliver the news to Edgar. He did not take it well. He showed me paintings of me that he had done. Not just one, not just two, but dozens. They were beautiful, elegant paintings, but there was something twisted about them.

"There was a sense of possession in his drawings, inferences about my body, the curve of my hips, the arch of my back. It was as if he thought I was his to manipulate in every single way. And in this way, I suppose he was right. I had no other patients, only him. There was a rumor that Edgar came from money, and the one thing Catholics love more than power is money. So, when I rebuked his advances, when I refused to see him, when he was forced to go, Edgar cursed me. Not just literally. He screamed my name and demanded I be with him. I remember huddling out of view from the window, some of my sisters holding me.

"I thought I was rid of him as the carriage left. I thought I would never see him again, until a year later. Carrying a pitcher of water for a patient, I tripped. It was dark. The hallway was barely lit. The steps were steep. More than two dozen other sisters and priests had fallen and broken bones. We were always told to be careful."

Cassandra raised her right hand, running it through her short hair.

"I felt my head hit a corner. I heard the crack, and I knew what it was. I knew what was about to happen. I lay there at the foot of the stairs waiting to die, saying my prayers, accepting my peace, but it never came. I sat up and felt where my head had been hit, but there was no wound. There was blood on the steps. My clothes were ripped, but there was no sign that I had fallen, not physically at least. Death had not claimed me as it should have.

"It took me a few more years. I hid it, of course, thinking I had somehow been touched by the devil, one of my sins from another life, a younger life coming back to bite me. But eventually curiosity got the best of me, and I left the convent searching for answers. No wound could affect me, Lewis. I couldn't retain any scars. My skin is exactly how it was when I met Edgar."

"Because Edgar had immortalized you in one of his cursed paintings."

Cassandra nodded. "Eventually I learned how to steel myself from pain. That was helpful in touring the world trying to find the source of this curse. It took me to some dark places. You'd be surprised by the type of people who are yearning for immortality, but at its core, it all led back to one person. His love, his obsession to always have me gave me this, and I became another one of his paintings. I'm sure you know this by now, but I've been looking to break this."

"Why didn't you just find your paintings and destroy them? Break the curse?"

"I tried," she said. "But you saw what happened in Japan. I can't destroy them. I thought perhaps if I could pull the magic from the paintings, like Akana is doing with your mother's remains, I could overpower them. But it's not that easy."

"Love is a powerful thing," he surmised. "So is guilt."

"And so is obsession," she added. "Its own twisted form of enchantment that lives on even after his death, because his descendants live on."

Cassandra snapped her fingers, the illusion of her memories melting away, returning them to present-day Baltimore.

"We're ready," Akana said, speaking within their minds.

Lewis hesitated with a confused look. A sea of torrid emotions crashed inside of him. One part pity. One part confusion. Cassandra was just as much a victim of Edgar Dumont as Lewis was, as the men and women he killed. Someone who was a piece of fodder for him to accomplish his goal. To hell with whoever stood in his way.

How different would Cassandra's life have been if Edgar had never met her? If Lewis hadn't thrown him out that window, sending him to the asylum, forcing him to flee? Those thoughts bounced around in his head as he and Cassandra walked up to Akana.

The grave hadn't been defiled, not in the way he expected. A single rune was drawn on the dirt, glowing a vibrant purple like the hottest of flames, a tendril of white mist shooting out like a geyser. From the grave, Akana's shadow pooled outward.

"That's pure magic," Akana said. "It's isolated for now, unable to dissipate into the air."

She glanced over at Lewis, beckoning him forward. Lewis stepped into the ring of darkness. Much like before, the space in the dark circle was cold, colder than before. Lewis also noticed in that moment his heart had stopped beating.

"Don't worry, you're fine," Akana said. "I just made a pocket separate from reality to house it. I need you to take this, and breathe it in like smoke. Remember, we'll only have a day, maybe two. Are you ready?"

Lewis was ready, but he didn't say anything. Not yet. He was still hung up on what Cassandra had said about the paintings, and she had never asked that favor of him. Explaining the reason she had shown the memories had been cut short.

"Lewis?"

Glancing back at Akana, he nodded.

"Take a deep breath," she said. "Hold it until you can't breathe anymore. Exhale. And right before you inhale, I'll give it to you."

Lewis followed, taking the deepest breath he possibly could. Then he held and released it. He nodded just before the urge to inhale automatically took over, and with a flick of her hand, she threw the magic at him. It clashed against his face, feeling warm. It was as if his body had been missing this heat, and it was the exact thing he needed.

Every vein and every neuron tingled with excitement. His vision became sharper and the world brighter. It was as if he had never felt such joy or completion before. It was a high like no other.

Akana smiled as she stood, her shadow retreating behind her.

"How do you feel?"

Lewis didn't speak but nodded, silently telling the two to follow him. Walking away a few feet from them, he looked at the sky. The clouds were no longer just clouds, their shapes shifting and turning in front of him.

"Dragons," he said. "I also see a three-headed elephant over there," pointing to what he assumed they would just see as a mountain of white, puffy clouds.

Akana sighed. "Good, because that could have gone horribly wrong," she said. "I wasn't sure that you weren't just going to explode right in front of me. That's actually part of the reason I had the void set up. Magic like that can act temperamentally and basically turn you into a nuclear bomb."

"I'm sorry," Lewis said, snapping his gaze to her. "You were going to just let that happen without telling me?"

"If I had told you, would you have gone through with it?"

Of course he wouldn't have. And he had full intention of telling her that, but the thought left his mind and was replaced with another.

Those memories of Cassandra came rushing back to him, but they weren't just replayed. He saw them through a different lens now, saw the subtext of what she was showing him, and why. In midsentence, he turned to her and saw a soft smile, almost a sad one.

And he knew.

"Are you sure?" he asked.

Cassandra nodded. "It's your choice. You can only do it once."

"I'm sorry, what are we talking about here?" Akana said. "Need I remind you, that amount of magic we just used is probably going to attract attention, especially if the museum is looking for us."

Lewis nodded, not fully listening. "You can't take it back. If we do this, if I do this . . ."

"I know," Cassandra said. "But you also know it's a onetime thing. You have to make the choice for yourself. You had to see everything to make an informed decision."

It was a Faustian choice. No one would be happy, but he understood all of this was about saving one person, making someone's life a little bit better. There was no guarantee they would beat the British Museum or whoever came for them, but he could help Cassandra.

His eyes focused on Akana. "You're going to hate me."

Akana frowned in confusion. "Why would I hate you? What are you—"

Lewis turned to Cassandra before Akana could finish. "Where is it?"

Reaching into her pocket, Cassandra pulled out a single tarot-size card. She tossed it into the air, the card spinning once and growing in size as it landed in the dirt, the size of all the other paintings and with a wooden trim. The image was of Cassandra but personified differently. Like an angel, she draped her arms over a man's shoulders, a halo illuminating her crown, white wings spread outward across the canvas.

"Do you know your name?" he asked Cassandra. She nodded.

"The Mother."

Akana stepped forward, clearly understanding what was about to happen.

"Don't you dare," she said. "We did not do this for you to—"

"Akana," Cassandra said softly. "There's a role for you to play in this too. Please let him do it."

"We don't get another shot," Akana hissed. "I'm sorry. I don't know what happened to you, and I don't know what you did to twist his mind to make him think this was a good idea, but we are all sacrificing things to be here. We're not doing it for—"

There was no debate that could change his mind and none that could change Akana's. It was just a leap of faith. So in the middle of her tirade, Lewis threw out his hand like he had when he first met The Drowning and whispered Cassandra's name.

Cassandra let out a gasp, stumbling backward. Lewis braced himself, expecting a scream like all the other paintings, but there wasn't one. There was a sigh of contented relief. If the other paintings feared death, feared their release, Cassandra didn't. Joy and elation poured from her as tears streamed down her face.

"I can feel," she said. "I can feel everything. I can feel my heartbeat. I can feel the air."

Her right hand rose to her face, shaking, and without hesitation she slapped herself. A whimper left her as she pressed her hand against the blooming red mark. "I felt that."

Akana, on the other hand, was not as joyous. "What the fuck did you two just do?" she said.

"I made a choice," Lewis replied. "I . . ."

Lewis cut off, unable to speak. There was a brief moment in which he saw it all, her whole life, the memories that Cassandra had just shown him through her eyes. He saw the gaps she had left out, felt the pain as she fell down the steps, and saw the journey across the world twice over she had done. Every single memory over the past one hundred thirty years flooded into his mind, making him want to split his head open and scoop out the extra that threatened to spill. But there was nothing, no more magic.

As quickly as it had come to him, as quickly as he had it, it was gone like a spark that didn't catch. Before, when he had lost his magic, he felt like he was missing something. Now he felt complete.

"You just screwed us," Akana said. "Both of you. What the hell did I sacrifice all this for? What the hell did I even just do if you were going to throw it all away for her? And if you were going to bring us here just to suit your little mission?"

Cassandra raised her hand, but Akana cut her off.

"No, I don't fucking want to hear it," she snarled. "I should turn both of you in. Return to Japan and batten down the hatches."

"Akana," Lewis said.

"I risked it all. My name. Everything. For *what*? For you to help *her*?"

"Akana," Cassandra said, her eyes following Lewis.

"You know you both screwed us. I want that to be perfectly clear. We had one shot. One chance to beat Evangeline and put this to rest, and you—"

"Akana," they both said firmly.

"*What?*"

Lewis pointed to Cassandra's painting. In front of their eyes, the paint burned, starting from the center and working its way outward. As it did, a new image appeared. No longer a woman with her arms draped over the shoulders of a man, but truly Cassandra, bowing and reverent, a nun's attire on her body, her eyes looking upward, presumably at God.

But that wasn't all that had changed. At the bottom of the painting, words written in Lewis's handwriting appeared.

"*The Stolen*," Lewis read.

"What the hell just happened?" Akana asked.

At first Lewis didn't speak, frowning as he attempted to reason it through.

And then it all clicked. La résponse est inverse. The answer is in the inverse.

"Oh my God," Lewis whispered. "Oh my God. We've been going about it all wrong."

Pacing around the painting he turned to look at Cassandra and Akana. "Each painting we've been treating like a weapon. Something that needs to be stopped. Tamed. Killed. But the paintings, like Cassandra, are victims. And when we look at them like that, see them as those who have also suffered at the hands of Edgar . . ."

"They change," Akana said. "The inverse of their origins."

"The answer is in the inverse," Lewis repeated. "Edgar believed he could get his sister back by stealing the magic from the living, no matter the consequences. When all that's done is bring him further and further away from her. He's trying to beat death. To undo one of the most fundamental principles of existence. You can't do that, not without consequences. And each painting suffers more and more than the last as he tries more and more perverse things to get to her."

"What happens," Lewis continued, "if we don't treat the paintings as evil? Evangeline said the paintings react the way they do to me because they view me as a threat. They view me as Edgar Dumont. What if I used my gift to put them to rest?"

"In theory," Akana said slowly, "you could end it all."

Cassandra looked over at her painting. "There's no magic coming off of it," she said. "It's just paint and canvas now. Not even a fragment of magic lingering."

Akana confirmed that with a nod. "So how do we do it?"

"You said I'm a conduit that can find the last painting because of my bloodline," Lewis said. "We need a painting, then. Something to provide the connection."

"Evangeline isn't going to just give you one."

"We don't need her to," Cassandra whispered. "I have the one from your father's home in my apartment, Akana. We can end it there."

Akana's face—for the first time since Lewis knew her—was painted with something that looked almost . . . uncomfortable on her features: hope. But her sharp, attentive gaze returned as she looked past the gravestones.

"Something's coming," she said.

"*Someone's* coming," Cassandra corrected.

The air rippled in front of them. Akana and Cassandra moved to protect Lewis. Magic crackled and filled the air with the scent of cinnamon. An image flickered, once, twice, three times, and before it even took form, Lewis pushed past the two women.

"Noah."

Lewis bridged the space between them just in time. As Noah appeared, his footing gave way, Lewis bending his knees to cushion his fall and catch him. He took a moment to look at Noah, really look at him. The sharp angles of his face, the thinness of his skin. He looked like his father in the hospital bed.

Noah smiled, his eyes slightly lidded. "Hello, Mr. Dixon," he breathed out, as if speaking was hard. Swallowing through the pain, he grabbed Lewis's shoulders, forcing himself to stand on his own.

"She's coming," he breathed out heavily. "For you all."

"We were just about to move," Cassandra replied. "Let's go," she ordered, leading the pack. Walking briskly down the hill, she began flourishing symbols with her fingers.

Akana flanked Noah on his other side, helping Lewis walk him down the hill toward the cast-iron gates they had entered. The arched alcove separating the sidewalk from the graveyard rippled, revealing a well-designed French apartment.

"I still don't trust you," Akana told Cassandra.

"You don't have to," she said, putting her hand on Akana's back. "But think about it like this: If we die, or Evangeline gets her hands on us, you'll never get to ensure I pay for my crimes against humanity."

Akana paused and nodded. "Fair." And with that, she stepped in through the alcove first. Cassandra gestured to Lewis and Noah.

"Allons-y," she said. "We have a world to save."

Thirty-Five

LEWIS DIDN'T HAVE TIME TO APPRECIATE THE BEAUTY OF CASSANDRA'S home when they entered it.

The moment they stepped through the archway, the world of Maryland dissolved out of view. Cassandra made a beeline toward her study.

"We don't have much time," she said firmly.

"I'll start fortifying the defenses," Akana chimed in. "Evangeline is going to come with the full force of the British Museum."

Noah gasped, pressing his hand against the wall as he slid down into a nearby chair with Lewis's help. "I should help you."

"You can barely stand up," Akana said as softly as she could. "I'll be fine. Besides, we don't need to hold her off indefinitely, just long enough for Lewis to do what he needs to do."

Lewis frowned at that declaration. Akana didn't let him speak, instead answering the question he was about to ask.

"This is not about making it out alive, Lewis. This is about stopping Evangeline so that you can finish this."

"That wasn't part of the plan," Lewis countered.

"That was always part of the plan," Cassandra said loudly enough that she could be heard from the study. Her back was turned to them, and her hands were flitting wildly as drawers opened and papers fluttered out on her command. She was searching for something specific. "The only thing that matters is you stopping Edgar and putting these paintings to rest. If that means that we have to be sacrifices along the way—"

"I'm not letting anybody else die for these paintings." Lewis was firm about that.

But Noah took a deep, shaky breath and squeezed Lewis's wrist. "Magic requires sacrifice," he said. "Stopping it requires sacrifice. There's nothing in this world that can be accomplished of import without it."

"There has to be another way," Lewis muttered in disbelief.

"There isn't," Akana finished. "And the longer we spend here debating, the less time I have to prepare."

"You're going to need every second you can get," Noah said through pained breath.

Lewis paused and saw how Akana swallowed thickly as if even she was processing what this meant.

"We all have something to atone for," she muttered. "Perhaps this is the way we do it, ensuring that the next generation doesn't fall down the same rabbit hole we did. We can put an end to a curse that has been around for more than a century and a half. What better way to change the world than that?"

Akana glanced behind her toward the hallway that led to the front of the apartment.

"Someone's here," she muttered. "In the building, ground floor. Many someones."

"I feel it too," Noah hissed, forcing himself to stand. He wobbled and almost fell over but kept his balance. "I know those signatures. I know those agents."

He took a half step forward, then another, then another, each step seeming more painful than the last. "You're going to need my help."

Akana chewed on her bottom lip but didn't wait long to decide on her answer.

"Fine, but don't be a liability."

Akana turned, disappearing down the hallway to set up incantations that would fortify the building. Noah half turned and tilted his head toward Lewis, a soft, almost sad smile on his handsome features.

"You're not going to make it back, are you?" Lewis whispered.

Noah didn't answer. Instead, he reached forward with his right hand and cupped the side of Lewis's face. His thumb stroked his cheek, and through the connection, Lewis felt small tremors rippling through his forearm and into his palm. He couldn't tell if it was fear or muscle spasms. The pain that passed over Noah's face was apparent, no matter how hard he tried to fight it and hide it.

The painting Noah was bound to was stripping every bit of life force he had, and he had used his last few moments to come and help Lewis. Lewis would never be able to repay that.

"You can," Noah whispered, leaning forward and pressing his forehead against Lewis's and closing his eyes. Lewis imitated him. "You can pay me back by ending this."

"Lewis," Cassandra said loudly, "I need you. And you too, Noah."

Puzzled, the two looked at each other before glancing at Cassandra's back.

"Now would be preferable," she said with a tinge of annoyance.

Without another word, Lewis draped Noah's right arm over his shoulder and helped him walk into the study. The moment they crossed the threshold, a cool feeling passed over them as though they had passed through a sheet of water. Magic rippled outward, cascading around the walls. It shimmered for a fraction of a second like glass beads catching the light.

"It's a barrier," Noah said. "Nothing can enter that isn't allowed."

"It will be the last line of defense against Evangeline," Cassandra muttered, turning to face them with a grimoire in hand. Lewis intended to ask what it was, but before he could, Noah spoke.

"Where did you get that?"

Cassandra's eyes looked up at him, and the solemn nature of her gaze said everything the two of them needed to know.

"Ah," Noah concluded. And that was that.

"I think you're the one who can help me unlock this," she said. "Your sister was very good at protective charms, but what we need to help Lewis is in this book."

Noah nodded, reaching out with his right hand, palm facing downward over the cover of the book.

He took a deep, shaky breath, muttering a sentence under his breath in Hindi before twisting his pointer finger and middle finger over each other, spinning his palm counterclockwise and then clockwise, and slamming his hand over the cover. A puff of magic burst out of the book like an exhalation, filling the air with a sharp, strong smell of vanilla for just a fraction of a second.

"It was one of the first spells my sister taught me," Noah said. "She found it in an old Sanskrit book and adapted it for our family. It keeps things hidden from prying eyes."

Cassandra nodded, opening the book. And with a flick of her hand, the pages spun through to the end. Her eyes darted over each one, and she nodded before looking up at Noah.

"You should go and help Akana."

Noah agreed, glancing over at Lewis and flashing him a soft smile.

"Remember," he whispered, "I stand by what I said before. You are marvelous. Show Edgar how marvelous you are."

With that, Noah hobbled away, his gait becoming stronger and stronger with each step—not because he was getting his strength back, Lewis assumed, but because the last gift Noah could give

Lewis was seeing him put on a brave face as he went to face the inevitable.

"Come on," Cassandra said the moment Noah was out of view. "I'm going to need your help."

Guiding him over to the counter, Cassandra opened the grimoire containing Ishita's spells. She placed her palm against one of the pages, swiping slowly from right to left. The illegible letters morphed into English.

"Noah's sister was onto something," Cassandra muttered. "She was only a few steps away from figuring out how you were indirectly responsible for Edgar's creation of the Macabre. I believe she probably brought this information to Evangeline. Maybe she was even able to put the pieces together about Evangeline's end goal."

"Are you saying Evangeline killed Noah's sister?"

Cassandra shook her head. "No, I don't think that's it. I think Evangeline didn't know what conclusion Ishita was drawing, but the information she passed on to her did change the trajectory of her conclusions."

With a flip of the page, Cassandra revealed a makeshift map of the world, not much different from the ones Lewis would see in a geography or history class. There were red dots here and there, and it took Lewis only a moment to connect them.

"Each one of these is where a painting was found," he whispered. "Baltimore, London, Perth, Brazil, Osaka, Russia . . ."

From the corner of his eye, he saw Cassandra step away toward a chest. He paid little attention to the incantation she used to open it but did notice that it opened slowly without pulleys or contact. A painting rose from the depths. The chest was clearly bigger on the inside than the outside.

It was the same painting that had been in Akana's family home.

"Ishita was close," Cassandra repeated, bringing the painting over. "Closer than perhaps any non-Dumont had ever been."

Holding the painting at chest height, Cassandra locked eyes with Lewis.

"What you proposed is untested. There is no science or magical data that can support your claim. But if you're right, all of this could end today."

What Cassandra was really saying was that there was no way she could help him in this process. This hope, this Hail Mary of his, had to be tested alone.

The walls shuddered before Lewis could speak. A distant boom from the outside pulled his focus away from Cassandra. A fight had begun in the hallway, no more than twenty or so feet away from them.

Cassandra sighed and cursed in French under her breath. She gently placed the painting down and leaned it against the counter.

"I need to go help them," she said. "Three is better than two."

"You're going to die," Lewis said. It was a matter-of-fact and blunt statement, but he didn't retract it. "Without your immortality . . ."

"It'll be nice to feel something again," Cassandra glibly replied. But there was a hollowness in her voice that Lewis didn't like. "And besides, this is my home. There are magical secrets here that can help, that neither Akana nor Noah know about. Someone needs to be there to activate them."

Cassandra walked toward the threshold and stopped.

"No matter what happens, Lewis," she said, seemingly unwilling to turn around and show him her face, "you did your best, and your mother would be proud."

Cassandra stepped over the threshold and then turned to face him. She gave him a soft smile and mouthed a word Lewis didn't hear. The barrier shimmered once more, distorting her image like he was looking at her through frosted glass.

Cassandra raised her hand and pressed it against the barrier, showing him what she had done. She had revoked access to the room for herself and, most likely, everyone else but him. This room was now the true last line of defense. Cassandra turned, her blurred image now impossible for Lewis to make out clearly, and headed down the hallway to join Akana and Noah.

Lewis was left alone with the painting. He forced his gaze back to it, taking a shaky breath as he grabbed its edges and lifted it to place it on the counter, leaning it against the wall. He didn't need to know its name. He wasn't trying to enter it, not this time. What he needed was to find a way for it to see him not as a threat but as an ally.

"I'm not going to hurt you," he whispered, with a level of desperation in his voice he wasn't proud of. "But I need you to show me the truth."

The painting didn't respond, but it didn't threaten him either. Another shudder followed, rippling through the walls this time. It was loud and heavy enough for books to drop from the shelves. Lewis frowned and turned back to the painting.

"I'm trying to help you. I know what Edgar did to you. I can fix it. If you just give me—"

Lewis jumped. A thumping sound against the barrier had pulled his attention away again. He turned and saw a body slumped against the wall. Slowly, it slid down, leaving a trail of blood in its wake.

Lewis couldn't make out whose body it was, but he could see an agent standing in front of him and looking into the room. The only thing separating them was Cassandra's last spell. He couldn't make out the man's face.

The man raised his hand and punched the barrier. It rippled outward, the pulse of kinetic energy manifesting in a bright white light. The light spread out and then back in again at the spot where the agent had struck the barrier. Instantly, the agent was sent flying back in a surge of power that was threefold as intense as what he had mustered to hit the barrier. Lewis gulped and concentrated on the painting again.

"We don't have much time. If I die, this whole thing will start over again. She will find another descendant, presuming there is one, and the pain that you're experiencing, it won't end. At least I'm trying to end it."

And for Lewis, that's when everything clicked.

"Pain," he said slowly. "Even if you're a happy painting, you were still made from pain. A moment of sorrow and anger that Edgar Dumont forced inside of you. That's the only thing you can feel. It's all you know. The creation of it, the existence of it, the channeling of it."

He spoke to himself as if working through a math problem.

"But what if someone showed you that they're willing to share the pain with you?"

Lewis looked around the study. It was beautiful: bookshelves much like the ones inside the Contract House, scribbled-on papers that he could only assume were magical hypotheses or theories, a coffee table off to the side, a chaise longue that rested against the window, which was also frosted from the spell Cassandra had cast. It was a peaceful place that he could imagine Cassandra lounging in, studying and conjecturing how to find the next painting or maybe even how to kill Lewis.

His eyes landed on one thing, a letter opener that was glinting in the sunlight. Using his magic hand, he willed the knife upward. It floated lazily, its tip facing up. As it hovered in front of him, spinning slowly on its axis, Lewis's eyes studied it. His gaze flickered past it to the painting.

Lewis swallowed thickly and glanced over his shoulder at the barrier once more. The sound that came from it was different now. It was not a heavy thump, but a crack. His eyes focused on a single spiderweb of splinters that started from the center and expanded slowly outward with each passing moment.

He looked up. Lewis couldn't make out the person; their body was only a distorted blob, but the height and the rough shape told him exactly who had replaced the man from before and was breaking Cassandra's spell. He knew he didn't have much time. Evangeline would ensure that. A simple barrier wouldn't keep her from the future she believed she was owed.

Lewis squared his shoulders, dug his heels into the floor, and took a deep breath.

"We are connected through pain," he said to the painting. "I have lost many people I love, and you were never given a chance to experience anything but sorrow. Let me change that."

Lewis didn't hesitate. He knew if he thought about it too much, he would falter. He took a deep breath and ordered the blade to slash.

The pain was sharp, much like a pinprick or a paper cut. As the blade slid across his throat, he coughed. It fell to the ground as his hand clutched his throat. Warm blood began seeping through his fingers.

Lewis could feel his body threatening to fall over, but he didn't let it. Holding himself up as best he could, he let the blood coat his fingers. The throbbing and burning of the clean cut felt like every nerve of his body was on fire. His mind screamed. It was a single note blocking out everything and almost making the sound of the barrier shattering behind him inaudible. Lewis thrust his bloodstained hand forward and pressed his palm against the canvas.

His words a wet gurgle, he spoke in perfect French:

"La réponse est inverse."

Thirty-Six

LEWIS DIDN'T TUMBLE THROUGH THE PAINTING LIKE HE DID THE OTHERS.
Instead, the ground under him opened up, color rushing upward in reverse as if a vacuum in the sky was sucking the canvas blank. The feeling of weightlessness lasted only a moment before the pressure of gravity yanked him down.

When Lewis finally found his senses again, he was no longer standing but lying on his back. Slowly sitting up, eyes closed, he ran fingers over his throat. There was no cut, no wound. In fact, his missing hand had returned. Using both his palms to stand up shakily, he noticed something else. Pressing his forefinger and middle finger against his throat, he could feel no pulse.

It was as if he wasn't alive. He existed somewhere between the outside and inside worlds. He wondered what was happening in the former.

Was his body still anchored to the painting, easy prey for whatever Evangeline wanted to do to him? Was she setting up a perimeter to catch him when he exited the painting? Or had she sawed his body away, leaving only his hand attached and making good on her promise to keep him on the edge of death to be her plaything?

But he couldn't worry about that now. There were more important things—like who else was in the room with him.

His eyes opened. He could see nothing but endless white at

first, but slowly, like a painting being drawn on a canvas, the surroundings came into view. It was a study much like Cassandra's, or even like Evangeline's. But this one existed within a home, or an atrium.

Curved glass separated the inside from the outside. Plants loomed tall and bowed their heads as they touched the ceiling, populating the room as if it was their own. There was faint classical music playing in the background. Lewis discerned that it was coming from a room or two away. A door must have been left open so that it could be heard by whoever was in this atrium. As he looked around, Lewis realized where he was.

He was back in the home he had noticed in the distance when he first met Edgar Dumont.

"I'm over here," a voice said in the atrium. Lewis paused, debating if he should follow it. He knew who he would probably see.

"There's no point in hiding," Edgar said. "We're both here now."

"To that, we can both agree," Lewis muttered.

Lewis took a deep breath and used his hands to clear a way through the plants. He pushed his way forward to where the voice was. Soon, he stepped into a clearing. Lewis frowned. Edgar Dumont's back was to him, and he was standing in front of a large canvas. It was in landscape style—longer than it was tall—and set up on an easel. It was so large that four people could have worked on it, each with their own section.

But that wasn't what interested Lewis. Rather, his attention was drawn to the unevenly spaced paintings arranged around the two of them in a semicircle. There were nine familiar paintings, each with a chain extending from their center that was attached to shackles on Edgar Dumont. There were two on each ankle, two on each wrist, and one on his neck.

"What do you think this needs?" Edgar asked without turning to Lewis. "I think it needs more blue."

Lewis didn't answer, not because he couldn't think of anything but because the canvas was blank. There was no color, no outline, no sketch. It looked as if Edgar was painting with air.

"Or perhaps some green," he whispered. "Green is always nice."

Edgar tilted his head toward Lewis. He was older than when Lewis had seen him in *The Stain*, but younger than when he saw him in The Balance that he had made a contract with. Early thirties, maybe, Lewis thought. The same age that Lewis was. As if, in some way, Edgar or the Macabre were trying to put them on equal footing.

Or it was a warning that this was a crossroads in Edgar's life, one that Lewis was about to face himself.

"Well," Edgar said, "you're like me, a painter. You have no thoughts?"

Slowly and apprehensively, Lewis approached until he was standing next to Edgar. He was done playing games, done being on the defensive and trying to understand the rules of whichever domain he was in. From Cassandra to Evangeline and even to Noah's initial manipulations and Akana's threats, he'd always been on the defensive. He wouldn't do the same with Edgar. Not this time.

"Where are we?" he asked. It took Edgar a moment to answer.

"I suppose this is the afterlife. I remember dying in some disgusting home in the New World. It was a place that I called my own once I left France. Took a boat over to America, tried to make a life for myself for a few years, but consumption got the best of me and I died alone. I woke up here."

He raised his hands, the shackles clinking. The paintings attached to the chains bound around his wrists shuddered and groaned, not in pain but in annoyance. It was as though they were threatening him to stop moving.

"And I've been here ever since, finishing this painting." Edgar glanced back at Lewis. "How long?"

"Long enough for you to have lived a full life."

"And yet I accomplished nothing." Edgar sighed.

"I wouldn't say that," Lewis muttered, turning to face him. "You hurt a lot of people. Killed a lot of people."

"But I couldn't save her."

Lewis didn't need to ask who Edgar was talking about. As if on cue, he heard from behind them a child's laughter. It was bright and warm and squealed with joy. A soft, feminine voice spoke next.

"Edgar," the voice gently scolded. "Come on, you have to get dressed. I need you to meet my husband to be. You're going to love him." It was Edgar's sister, Amelia. Pain and sadness flooded Lewis and, for a moment, he almost felt sorry for Edgar.

"You know what the cruelest punishment is?" Edgar asked. "These chains. I hear her, hear my family. Memories of my life playing themselves over and over, just out of view, just out of full earshot, in the room over there. And I can't get to them because of these blasted chains."

"You did this to yourself, Edgar," Lewis said carefully.

"Did I?" Edgar asked. "Did I deserve this punishment? The world took from me over and over again—my sister, my wife, my lovers. What did I do to deserve that, Lewis?"

"The world deals everyone a shitty hand. You don't get to go out and hurt people who have nothing to do with your sorrow. You don't get to extinguish others' lives in hopes of having a second chance at your own."

"And why not?" Edgar snapped. "Why don't I get a happy ending?"

Lewis didn't flinch. He felt like he should have, but what could Edgar do to hurt him now?

"These paintings," Lewis said quietly. "What these paintings that have you trapped here with their chains have done is no different than what you did to them. Each time you made one to process your grief or your anger, you created a moment of darkness. The painting had no hope of experiencing anything else but that same horrific emotion you felt. You somehow found out how to take the sorrow and anger you were feeling, compartmentalize it, and pull it out of your body and put it into these paintings, giving yourself a moment of reprieve but damning them to feeling that sorrow for the rest of their existence."

Edgar didn't challenge Lewis's words, so Lewis continued speaking.

"Just like you yearned for belonging and comfort, so did they. They latched on to people throughout the centuries who sang the same song of sorrow they did, and they hurt people like you hurt people.

"And so, when you died, they reached out and put you here. That last bit of your soul that still existed, connecting all of these paintings because they were a part of you, prevented you from experiencing the one thing you ever wanted—peace—because you did not give it to them. This is your afterlife, yes, Edgar, but it's not one that's brought about by the Gods; it's brought about by you."

A new voice filled Lewis's ears from the distance. It was deeper, heartier. A man's voice. There was an undertone of chaos. Lewis could hear a group of people laughing and the clinking of glasses. It was the sound of a party.

"Do you know how much I love you?" Edgar said. An older version of himself was speaking to the man whose voice Lewis had heard.

"More than Galileo loves his theories?"

The voice wasn't familiar to Lewis, but it reminded him of the grief-stricken man he saw in the hospital in *The Stain*. Lewis could only assume that the person Edgar was talking to was the father of his lover who had been killed in the explosion.

Lewis turned back to Edgar. "This painting you're working on, you didn't finish it in your real life, did you?"

Edgar didn't answer, but Lewis didn't need him to.

"That's where the rumor came from. An unfinished painting. In the real world, people believe this painting can give them power over time and reality itself.

"And maybe they're right. I can feel it in the air. I can taste it on my tongue and my teeth. Pure magic exists here, locked in this pocket reality that's your prison and that was brought about by these paintings that you damned to hell."

"You're lost too, Lewis," Edgar said. "You were looking at me, and I found a way to look back at you. They were only glimpses, fractions of moments through your eyes, feelings that snuck through time and found their way to me. You understand what it means to lose and to suffer. And as my descendant, this painting and its magic could be yours. You could change history. You and I could bring back the ones we lost."

"They're gone, Edgar. All of them. We don't mess with the afterlife. We don't change the course of time like that."

"Because you're afraid," Edgar concluded.

"No. Because other people are affected by the choices we make. Individuals who have nothing to do with our sorrow and don't deserve to suffer. Bringing back your sister or my mother could mean that other people aren't born, that wars that never happened do happen. We have no idea. But damning them to a sentence for a crime they didn't commit, to bring back someone they don't know, is no different than what you did in London."

"So why are you here, then?" Edgar asked.

"To bring peace," Lewis said without hesitation. "To you, to these paintings, to me. It's what I promised."

Lewis turned his gaze away from Edgar. He scanned the

room, his eyes lingering over each individual painting. Much like with the drawings from the Jack the Ripper room, if he tilted his head just slightly to the left or right, each piece looked different.

On the one hand, there was *The Drowning*, a morose image of a woman in a bloodstained lake. But there was also *The Stolen*, a woman at peace who had finally escaped a life of oppression.

Each one followed the same pattern: a version of sadness and darkness and a version of peace and light. The before, and the after. The pain, and the healing. Lewis had made a promise to the paintings, to help them heal, and he intended to keep it.

As he closed his eyes, and placed the palm of his left hand on the canvas Edgar hadn't finished, Lewis felt nine different sensations, each slightly different but familiar at the same time. All Lewis could picture was Noah. Lewis could see his smiling face. He hoped that whatever happened in Cassandra's apartment, he wasn't too late to bring Noah, Cassandra, and Akana the one thing the Dumont family always wanted: peace.

Thirty-Seven

"LEWIS, YOU'RE STARING AGAIN."

Lewis snapped out of his reverie. His blurred vision came back into focus. Sure enough, he had been staring. His eyes had been focused on a painting hanging above the fireplace of the coffee shop where he and his mother sat. It was a beautiful piece. He didn't know the artist, but he liked how the strokes evoked a mixture of peace and sorrow all at once.

Lewis made a mental note as he pulled out his phone to take a picture so he could find the artist if they were still alive. Perhaps he could talk to them, mentor under them. And if they were dead, perhaps he could buy a print himself.

"Sorry," he said, turning back to his mother.

She was sitting across from him. She narrowed her eyes playfully and crossed her arms over her chest. She glanced behind her at the piece and then back at Lewis.

"Always distracted," she teased.

Lewis grinned softly. It had been six months since he had put the paintings to rest, since he last saw Edgar Dumont.

As he had closed his eyes and thought about Noah, Akana, and the rest of them, the world faded away and he awoke in his family home in Baltimore. He could smell cinnamon rolls and hear the soft, sultry voice of Ella Fitzgerald downstairs. It was a normal Sunday morning. His mother had called him down. Sounding both annoyed and playful, she chastised him for sleeping in like he was a teenager all over again.

Springing up and noticing that he still had both of his hands, Lewis ran to his computer. He googled Noah, Akana, and the British Museum. There was no information on any Macabre paintings, magic, or anything of the sort.

Lewis surmised that when he gave the paintings peace, they gave him a gift in return, rewriting time so that the magic linked to his family never existed.

And if there was no magic, there was no reason for Evangeline or Cassandra or anyone to come for his mother.

He had the life he wanted. And the first thing he did was convince his mother that they needed to see the world.

For the past six months, they had been traveling. London, Osaka, Perth, Brazil, Russia. Their second-to-last stop was Chicago. They were in a coffee shop not far from The Bean, which his mother badly wanted to visit. That was their afternoon plan.

"You can't chastise me for having a vision," he said. "For seeing the world in a different way."

"Oh, no, I love it," his mother said. "It means you take after me instead of your father, which, between you and me, is every mother's dream."

Lewis rolled his eyes and barked out a laugh. He checked his phone and showed it to his mother. "We should get going soon," he said. "We want to see that show, and the last thing I want to do is be late."

"Can't reinforce the stereotype that Black people show up to things late," his mother confirmed.

Lewis nodded. "Exactly."

His mother smiled before also pulling out her phone and showing it to him.

"Your dad's calling, probably to ask if we're coming home at the end of the week."

"We've been gone for six months. I'm sure he misses his wife."

"I'm sure he misses me *and* you."

Lewis nodded. "I'll pay the bill. You go and talk to him."

His mother smiled, letting her gaze linger on him before standing up and walking out of the coffee shop with her phone at her ear. Lewis watched her retreating figure before flagging down the waitress with the universal symbol for the check.

He turned back to the seat his mother had just vacated. It was no longer vacant. Instead, Noah was sitting across from him, dressed in a perfectly tailored black suit. His hair was a little longer than Lewis remembered. Noah had pulled it back into a slick ponytail.

"What are you doing here?" Lewis said shakily.

Noah didn't speak at first, just looked Lewis up and down.

"Do you know who I am?" Lewis asked slowly.

If the painting had rewritten the past and given him his mother, it was reasonable to assume that, with no magic involved, there was no reason for Noah to reach out to him. Also, Lewis had never thought about it, but if there were no Macabre paintings for Evangeline to hunt, Ishita wouldn't have died.

And if she hadn't died, would Noah have followed in her footsteps and gone to work at the British Museum, or would he be in India?

With no information to confirm or deny any of his theories, Lewis had made the conscious choice after that first Google search to let sleeping dogs lie. And yet here was Noah, sitting across from him and looking directly into his eyes.

"I've been searching for you," Noah said. Lewis's hackles were raised, and he clenched his fists by his sides.

"I don't know what you're talking about," he said.

"Yes, you do, Lewis," Noah said softly. "You know this isn't real."

Lewis blinked. It was a normal reaction to an inexplicable

statement, but as he did, the world flickered like it had inside Akana's home.

The coffee shop, which had been bustling with people, which had soft music playing and warm light from the fireplace embracing everyone inside, which had such a welcoming atmosphere that provided the perfect respite from the cold Chicago winter, disappeared. It was hollow, empty, derelict, abandoned. Only Noah and Lewis remained sitting at the table. Lewis blinked once more, and the coffee shop flickered back into existence.

"I don't know what you're talking about," Lewis repeated.

Sighing, Noah reached his hand forward, palm upward. Lewis leaned back.

"You know that nothing has ever been this easy for you. Why would it start now?"

Lewis didn't say anything. Out of the corner of his eye, he could see the waitress approaching with the receipt. The quicker he could get out of here, the faster he could return to his mother. And the faster he returned to his mother, the sooner he could put Noah and whatever this was behind him.

He had won. He had done what they had asked, he had beaten Evangeline, and he had put the paintings to rest. There was nothing more Noah could or should ask of him. There was . . .

Lewis paused and looked up at the waitress. She had been a freckled girl with reddish-brown hair and a tattoo of a snake coming out of her shirt and rising up her clavicle. But now she had a familiar Japanese face and was dressed in the same outfit the freckled girl had been wearing.

"It wasn't easy to find you," Akana said. "But Noah's right. None of this is real."

The bell over the coffee shop door chimed cheerfully and Lewis quickly glanced over, hoping it was his mother.

Though his mother did open the door, the woman who flashed her a smile and slipped inside was the last of their little quartet.

Cassandra brushed snow off her shoulders and made a beeline for their table. She took the third unoccupied seat and sat down on Lewis's left.

"I'm sorry," she said quietly. "I'm sorry. We couldn't leave you here."

"It's a beautiful tapestry—you're an artist once again, that's for sure. But it's a forgery, Lewis," Noah said. "It's too perfect. You *know* this."

And now, of course, Lewis knew it. Everything had just been too easy. An upgrade to first class as they headed to London; an encounter with one of his favorite actors while leaving the West End; an offer from an artist in Berlin to come back sometime and talk shop with him; a handsome man that, according to his mother, was very clearly flirting with him. Every city, things had happened just a little bit too perfectly.

And yet . . .

"I *deserve* this," Lewis said. His voice was a whisper.

"You do," Akana allowed. "But when have we ever gotten what we deserve without fighting for it?"

"When has magic ever worked without a sacrifice?" Noah asked.

Sighing, Cassandra pulled off her leather gloves and placed her hand gently over his. "Let me show you."

Without asking for permission, Cassandra pushed her memories into Lewis's mind. The coffee shop spun counterclockwise as if their group was the center of its axis. Images flashed through his mind similar to when Cassandra had shown him her memories of France.

From an outsider's point of view, Lewis saw Evangeline shatter the barrier Cassandra had erected for him. He saw the magic pulse outward when he touched The Lingering and healed it. It was a blast of magic so pure, so raw that it should have killed Evangeline, Akana, Noah, and Cassandra. But it simply warped around those who had pledged to help him, whereas it made Evangeline scream.

"When you touched the painting," Cassandra's voice said in his mind, "you unleashed all their magic. It was like a thousand nuclear bombs of arcane energy. But your mind also protected us. We couldn't say the same for Evangeline."

As the effect of the magic subsided, the painting they had taken from Akana's home, *The Lingering*—also known as *The Kindness*—no longer was the portrait in front of them. Now Lewis was at the center of it, and flanking him were two people.

Edgar Dumont was on his left and his mother was on his right. There were others fanning outward behind Edgar and his mother in an angled pattern. They had faces he didn't recognize, but he assumed they were other relatives and descendants of the Dumont line.

Back at the coffee shop, Cassandra pulled her hand away from Lewis's. He could see his mother again, still leaning against the glass outside and talking to his father on the phone. Lewis felt hot tears streaming down his face. Without needing to be asked, Noah reached over and placed his hands in Lewis's palms.

"It's okay," he said. "It will be okay, but you can't stay here any longer."

"Where is here?" Lewis asked.

"You know," Akana finished for him. "You know."

Lewis looked past Noah at his mother. "She's so happy," he said quietly.

"She's not real, my love," Cassandra whispered. "Don't fall into the same trap your ancestor did. Magic cannot fix what hurts us. It cannot change what broke us. I know that better than anyone. Because when you try to play God, others suffer the consequences."

"The law of equivalent exchange, Lewis," Akana reminded him. "If you try to change what shouldn't be changed, other forces that should be immutable have to give. The world is worse off when people try to break the rules that hold our existence together."

Lewis knew this all to be true. Deep down, he knew they had only come to save him, somehow or another, but it would be up to him to decide if he wanted to leave. After all, he had told Edgar the same thing. They had no right to play God. They couldn't play God.

"Is everything to your liking?" a woman said, appearing suddenly at their side.

Lewis blinked and looked up. Cassandra, Noah, and Akana had disappeared. Everyone in the coffee shop, including his mother outside, had disappeared. Only he and the woman remained. There was no music; no warm, dripping cinnamon buns; no crackling fire; no art. Just a single table and the woman who Lewis had only ever seen from a distance. She took the seat opposite his. But even up close, her more distinguishable features were distorted, like a painting that had been smudged with the swipe of a hand.

Deep down, Lewis knew exactly who she was. He knew her soft features and warm smile.

"I was being honest," she said softly. "If there's something not to your liking, we can change it."

At first, Lewis didn't speak. He was processing her words.

"What do you mean by that, Amelia?"

Amelia Dumont shifted her weight. Lewis wasn't sure if it was the real her or something the paintings had created to communicate with him. He didn't think it mattered.

"We can change things. Make you president, make that cute boy of yours your boyfriend, or your husband. This is your world, Lewis."

"It's not real."

"Does it have to be?" she asked. "Can't it just be a kindness that was given to you? Something to make everything that you went through, your sacrifice, worth it? You chose us over power, over life, over everything. We want to help you."

"It has been a good six months," Lewis concluded. Given his whole life beforehand, he had to admit he had started to believe. To believe that such happiness was possible. That his happily ever after was within his grasp. That it was something he had earned. But, no, it wasn't earned. These memories, these joys, these highs, these successes were gifted to him. They lacked substance.

"I want to go, Amelia. I have to go."

Amelia studied Lewis. The soft smile on her face never left it. He noticed that her eyes didn't blink. They were frozen in time, exactly like a painting.

"You will never see her again," she said. It wasn't a threat, just a statement of fact. "You will go back to that cruel world and have to face whatever challenges come your way with no guarantee that you will succeed."

"Those are my choices to make. Failures or successes—they are what make a life. That's what your brother never understood. Life may deal me a bad hand, sometimes many bad hands, but it's still my life, and I will be the one who decides my fate."

Amelia nodded and let out a soft sigh. Lewis couldn't tell if it was a sign of resignation, acceptance, or annoyance. "My brother would have done well if he had someone like you in his life," she said. "And I hope you're happy with what comes next."

Amelia leaned forward and whispered, "You have brought us peace, Lewis, and I hope this choice brings you some too."

She rested her elbows on the table and brought her right hand up to the center of Lewis's face. "Take a deep breath, Lewis. This is going to hurt."

Before he could say anything, Amelia snapped her fingers. She was right: Pain erupted in the pit of his stomach and inside his lungs. He felt a burning sensation, like hot lava had been forced down his throat. He fell to his knees on the wooden floor, which shattered under him. Darkness, whiteness, and all the colors in between flashed in front of him. He choked and clawed at air. He was unable to see, to determine what was up, down, left, or right. He was falling, he was rising, he was being pulled apart. But there was something else. He felt a gripping sensation, an anchor grabbing on to him. Lewis reached for it, using both his hands. He blindly grabbed it and held on for dear life. He tugged and felt as if his entire being was pulling apart.

He wanted to scream, wanted to give up, to tell Amelia to pull him back. Every bit of pain, every physical agony, every emotional suffering he had felt in his whole life—he was experiencing them in every cell of his body at once. He held on to that familiar feeling, knowing that it would save him because he had promised he would always be there. As the shifting colors solidified into something real and tangible, Lewis let out a gasp. He panted heavily and turned over onto his chest. A violent cough escaped him. "I've got you," Noah said, holding him close. "You need to fix him," Akana's voice said. Lewis continued to cough, but he couldn't breathe. The sharp burning feeling returned to his throat. The gash he had given himself in Cassandra's home had returned. Noah manhandled him, flipping him onto his back and using his right hand to cradle Lewis's neck as his left hand moved upward and slid against the cut.

"Hold on," Noah said. Warmth pooled outward from his fingers as the gash healed. Lewis's whole body burned with pain, but slowly, surely, he could feel the wound closing. His vision cleared: Noah looking down at him. Akana and Cassandra standing over Noah's shoulder. The painting behind them with Lewis in the center and his ancestors and descendants seeming to look down on him in judgment. Two words were written at the bottom of the painting. Four letters were in his handwriting, three were in his mother's, and three were in Edgar's. The words gave up the title of the last painting of the set:

The Macabre.

Epilogue

FIVE MONTHS LATER

"THIS IS THE PLACE."

Cassandra studied the little red book she'd been carrying around with her for as long as she and Lewis had been traveling. He hadn't gotten even a glance inside the book. Cassandra and the book were never separated. The few glimpses he'd had showed Bible verses, a few illustrations she'd done over the years, and notes—notes that had always seemed to help them over the past few months.

After dispelling the Macabre in Paris, Lewis had spent about two weeks recovering before jumping back into the action. There were logistics for them to work through, international questions about why a Parisian apartment complex's top floor had been completely blown off and how no other floor was affected by the blast.

Of course, the magical organizations who were in the know across the world understood, and they'd done their best to keep the explosion under wraps. America, England, France, even Japan in some way, shape, or form had a hand in what had happened.

Noah had agreed to keep what happened under wraps, but, with his new title, he couldn't act in the same way he had before. "The Crown will not pursue you," he said as acting director of curation for the British Museum. "And with your offer from France and the Direction Générale des Arts Occultes, we won't interfere with your choices either."

That had been the last time they'd talked.

Lewis wondered how Noah was doing, whether he was settling into his new responsibilities as director, or if he felt the echoes of Evangeline's presence in the same office she'd claimed as her own just months ago. But if Cassandra was right, and they did their job well here, he'd see him soon enough.

"Would you like to do the honors?" Cassandra asked.

Lewis nodded, approaching the door of the home. It was nondescript, much like his own in Baltimore, a simple two-story house that had a hum of love and community pulsing out of it. He wondered how the resident inside would handle what he was about to say, whether they knew their life was about to change. And so, he took a deep breath and rapped his knuckles against the wooden door.

"Just a minute," a clear voice spoke.

There came shuffling noises of something falling, the laughter of a baby, and the sound of a TV upstairs, muffled but clear. Lewis smiled as he stepped back, the door opening a moment later. A woman with tight brown coils that were a shade lighter in some spots than others—either victims of a poor dye job or bleaching from the sun—opened the door. She was only a few years older than Lewis, something he wouldn't have been able to tell from her features, but the file Cassandra had on their target gave them as much information as they needed to complete their task.

"Nalini?" he asked.

The woman frowned, her brown eyes twisting in confusion. "Yes," she said slowly, stepping out, halfway closing the door. "Can I help you?"

Lewis looked over his shoulder at Cassandra. They'd grown close over the past five months, ever since France and the DGAO had made its apology offer, even providing him citizenship in exchange for helping them understand magic that focused on reality altering. They'd spent more time together than not. Cassandra's magic and knowledge had been essential to tracking down the other Macabre paintings and, ultimately, finding this woman.

"You have no idea who I am," he said, "but I'm going to ask that you trust me."

Nalini closed the door behind her, a mix of confusion and a tinge of anger on her face. "Look," she said, "I don't know if you're selling me something or trying to get me to join a church, but—"

Lewis shook his head, interrupting her. "I promise you, neither of those things. But from what I know about you, you're a woman who's spent her whole life in Argentina. You had to stay here in Rosario, though you wanted to go and get an engineering degree at the National University of San Luis. You fell in love with a boy because he was there, and he gave you two beautiful children.

"You have a good life. I'm not questioning that, but I'm offering you the chance for something great, something extraordinary. You wanted to become an engineer to make the impossible possible. And if you give me your hand, I think we can make that happen."

Lewis extended his good hand palm up. Quietly, Cassandra bridged the space between them, resting her own hand on Lewis's shoulder. Nalini studied the palm and looked back up at him.

"Is this some sort of sex thing?" she asked slowly.

Cassandra chuckled. "Trust me, child, even if it was, this boy here is not my type, and you and I are certainly not his," she said. "But maybe you'll meet the one who *is* his type if you're curious. Trust me, I'd be curious enough to take a leap of faith if I were you."

Lewis glared at her, but Cassandra just shrugged. "We were going to need his help anyway."

"He's busy," Lewis argued.

"Not too busy to help his lover," she teased.

Both their gazes turned back to Nalini. A voice from inside, an older woman's, raspy, and speaking Spanish, called her name.

"We'll have you right back," he promised.

"My children—"

"You won't be gone more than a few minutes."

Nalini chewed on her bottom lip, and Lewis could tell she was juggling the two thoughts in her head, staying or going, the possibility of something great or the comfort of something convenient.

"I have to be back in time for dinner," she said.

Lewis nodded. "Promise."

Slowly, Nalini put her right hand into the palm of Lewis's left. The pads of her fingertips were rough, but her overall touch was soft and warm. Lewis smiled but didn't have enough time to warn her before the world around them folded in, as if the space where they stood was a drain, and all the color and mass around them was being pulled down.

A moment later, that feeling of gravity pulling them down polarized and reversed. But instead of being in Argentina, they stood inside a Parisian apartment overlooking the Seine. Nalini stumbled backward, tripping and almost falling onto her rear end, but Lewis extended his right arm, catching her with his magic, gently stepping backward, and pulling her upright like a rope was wrapped around her.

She settled back on her feet. Cassandra grinned proudly. "You've gotten better at that."

Lewis didn't say anything, but smiled, turning his attention to Nalini. "I know that was terrifying."

Nalini took a step back, pulling out a silver cross that dangled from a chain that caught light from the window. She whispered a prayer, her backside bumping into the nearby wall, lined with about a hundred books of magic he and Cassandra had gathered not only from her collection or lent from the French government, but also from their travels around the world. Lewis hadn't even scratched the surface of the information hidden inside them, but he would.

"If you want to go home, darling, we can make that happen. And you won't even remember what you just saw," Cassandra promised, raising her right hand and wiggling her fingers at her. "It will only take a second, and you won't feel a thing."

"Cassandra," a voice to the right warned, a familiar, masculine, smooth voice.

Lewis turned his gaze as a form rippled into appearance—Noah, dressed in a crisp, black suit, his hair slightly longer than it was before, now shoulder-length. He smiled at Lewis before turning his gaze back to her. "Don't make me call Akana. You know she has feelings about you hiding out in France. She's still mad you decided to side with the DGAO instead of the Naikaku Jōhō Chōsashitsu."

"You don't need to call me." Akana's voice rang out through the room as her own form appeared. She touched down as if she'd stepped from the second ledge of a landing and spiraled herself into thin air to land on the ground floor of the apartment. Akana was wearing overalls, a bandanna wrapped around her short hair, and smudges of dirt on her arms.

Lewis arched his brow, his gaze focused on the marks. Akana's eyes followed his own. Seeing what he saw, she cursed in Japanese, licking her thumb and rubbing the dirt away.

"I'm trying this whole new thing," she said, bored, as if she'd given the explanation a hundred times. "Cleaning my father's house without magic is supposed to be therapeutic, but honestly, it's just a pain. I don't understand how humans do it."

"*You're* human," Lewis said.

"Barely," she muttered. Then, louder, "By the way, the offer still stands if you get tired of Parisians."

"Who are you people?" Nalini gasped, pressing herself more

firmly against the wall, as if she might blend in with it. "I don't have any money. I don't have whatever you want."

Noah turned his gaze to Lewis. It was soft, warm, longing, and all Lewis wanted to do was walk over and talk to him, but they all knew why they were here.

"Would you like to do the honors?" Noah asked. "This was your idea, after all."

"And I don't have forever," Akana added. "I'm waiting for a delivery."

Lewis rolled his eyes. "Nice to see you both too," he said, before turning his gaze back to Nalini.

He walked over to her and noted how she stood on her tippy toes as if trying to get farther away from him.

"I promise you, nothing I said is a lie," he said softly. "And I'm not going to hurt you. No one here is going to hurt you. You don't know this, but you have an ancestor, a man who was much like us, much like you, about two hundred fifty years ago. This man was a magician. And I know, before you call us crazy or the devil or anything, it sounds far-fetched. It sounds insane, really. But it's true. And I only need you to do one thing for us. If it doesn't work, or if it's too much for you to handle, or if you just completely don't want to ever see us again, you won't have to. But I think you might be curious, just like I was, about the world around you that you can't see with your naked eye."

Lewis extended his hand to her, beckoning her once more to take it.

"If I do what you say, you'll send me back?" she asked.

Lewis nodded. "And if you want, Cassandra will wipe your memories of all this, as promised."

"That's exactly what I want," Nalini grumbled, taking his hand and pulling herself away from the wall.

Lewis smiled as he led her into the main room of the apartment. France had been nice to him, offering him a beautiful place to live and as many resources as France could offer. It was a surprising gift from his ancestral home, considering his descent from Edgar. Citizenship would've been more than enough. Ignoring what had happened and giving him a pass back to America was all he'd hoped for. But here he was, working for France, helping them understand magic. He had found his purpose, and maybe he could do the same for Nalini.

Noah had contributed too. As its new director, the resources of the British Museum were at his disposal. That included allowing Lewis access to the Contract House as he saw fit. It had been a great help, especially when he wanted to travel without France knowing. And, Lewis could only assume, it helped Noah keep tabs on him in case he needed to intervene.

It was nice being able to see his friend Abernathy every once in a while too. Though he knew even that was about to change.

As he and Nalini walked into the living room, there was one door between two windows that, if anyone thought about it too closely, they'd realize didn't lead to anything. In fact, the windows overlooked the street. There was no second room attached to it, but the door was there. It was a door that didn't attract attention unless it was needed—and now it was.

"Put your hand on the door for me," Lewis asked.

Nalini frowned. "That's it?"

Lewis nodded. "Just put your hand on it. If nothing happens, then we're good."

Nalini hesitated, looking behind her, seeing the three other individuals in the room had joined them.

"They're not going to hurt you," Lewis promised.

She was skeptical—for good reason, Lewis thought—but, hesitantly, with a shaking limb, she raised her hand and pressed the palm of it against the door. And just as Lewis expected, she gasped, her head thrown back like electricity had jolted through her body. Her warm eyes glazed over white, no pupils, no irises. Her mouth hung slightly agape.

Lewis took a step back, glancing over at Noah. "Is this what I looked like when I touched the painting?"

Noah nodded. "Except your eyes were black," he said, a beat passing. "How have you been?"

Lewis shrugged. "We haven't apprehended any of the other paintings, but they're out there. What about you?"

Noah also shrugged. "Cleaning up Evangeline's messes isn't easy."

"How're your mother and father?" Lewis asked.

"The moment you dispelled the painting, it released its hold on us. My father got better. He still walks with a limp, but he's alive. My mother asks about you," Noah said, without giving Lewis a chance to respond. "She asked when I'm going to take you out on that date."

Lewis smiled, tilting his gaze downward at the floor, licking his dry lips. "When are you?"

"How about after this?"

Lewis considered it. "Depending on what happens here . . . I might be a little busy."

"True," Noah said slowly. "But I think you can make time for me. Or maybe I could take a leave of absence from the museum."

"You do know that, if this succeeds, they're going to be very pissed at you."

Noah shrugged. "This was always just a temporary gig until they found somebody better to replace me. And besides—" He looked around at the apartment. "Looks a little big for one person. I think you could use a roommate."

They hadn't seen each other in months, and yet this felt so right, so familiar, that the implication of what Noah said didn't register at first. Eyes wide, Lewis nudged Noah with his shoulder, a shove that made his partner in crime lose his balance, but Noah didn't get a chance to respond as Nalini gasped and stumbled back. Her eyes wild, she panted, a sheen of sweat on her brow.

Lewis moved into her view, Akana and Cassandra close by.

"Is she okay?" Akana asked. "I told you this was a stupid idea."

Cassandra raised her hand. "Hush."

Akana snapped a sharp gaze over to her, but before she could respond, Lewis spoke. "Don't say anything yet," he said to Nalini. "I know that was crazy, but I need you to say the first word that comes to mind."

Nalini's eyes focused on Lewis before looking at Noah, Akana, and Cassandra, at the door in front of her and then back to him. She spoke one single word. The word Lewis was hoping she would speak.

"Abernathy."

The wood shuddered, the apartment groaned, as if it was in pain. The grain on the door, which Nalini had just touched, glowed white, as if something behind it was pushing its way through, an orb of energy, of blinding light.

The wood crackled and split as Noah and the rest of them took a few steps back. Akana muttered a single word under her breath, her shadows swirling around them, creating an area of protection for the five of them.

"Haven't had to do that in a while." Akana smirked, looking at the door.

Lewis watched carefully, cracks appearing like spiderwebs, expanding faster and faster, thousands of them, the door barely holding itself together.

"Three, two, one . . ." he whispered.

Before he could say, "zero," the wood exploded, shrapnel flying and stabbing itself into every single object within the room except for them.

Akana's ring of protection isolated them, phased them out of existence. Standing there in the spot where the door should have been was a man—tall, slender, dapper, dressed in a black suit. His eyes were wide, his face gaunt and skin ashen. He looked at his hands in surprise. He dragged his fingertips over his cheek and pinched his right arm before his gaze rose up and he looked at Lewis.

"Who the hell is that?" Nalini said, clutching Noah as if he was her savior.

Lewis glanced over. He knew that feeling well. Noah had that effect on people. Slowly, Lewis stepped out of Akana's protective circle, standing in front of the man.

"Hello," he said. At first the man didn't speak. He swallowed and opened his mouth, but nothing came out. "Take your time," Lewis said. "What's your name?"

The man swallowed again before a raspy voice, almost a whisper, spoke. "George Abernathy."

Lewis nodded, turning back to Nalini. "This is your ancestor. He was locked inside of a house, a house connected to hundreds of houses, if not thousands, across the world, a house that doesn't exist in time and space, but that threads itself through it. He was a prisoner, and you as his descendant were able to let him go by speaking his name. You did that. You changed someone's life. And I have a feeling there's so much more you can do if you're interested."

Nalini didn't speak at first. She stepped out of the ring carefully, as if the blackness would make it hard for her to find her footing. Once she was sure, she stepped slowly forward, looking at Lewis and then back at George.

"Thank you," George said to Lewis and then turned his gaze to Nalini. "Thank *you*."

Nalini didn't speak, her eyes wide with wonder. Her gaze moved over to Lewis. "I did this?"

He nodded.

"I can help people?"

"We all here, some of us more than others, have tried to help people. I think you can do incredible things, Nalini, with that gift of yours, if you want."

"Yes," Nalini said, after he barely finished. "Absolutely yes."

Cassandra, Akana, and Noah walked over, Akana checking her phone as it vibrated in her pocket. "Great. I missed my delivery."

Cassandra rolled her eyes. "Are you ever happy?"

"No," Akana said directly. "At most, I'm mildly amused."

Lewis chuckled a bit, looking over at Noah as he stood by his side.

"It worked. Which means every house connected to Abernathy has just become a normal home," Noah said. He sighed. "The British are no longer going to be able to use him to transfer and move between countries or continents. This is going to be a problem."

"We had a feeling it would."

"No—*you* had a feeling it would work. And seeing it now, I'm glad it did," he said warmly.

"Is it a problem you're going to have to deal with?" Lewis asked.

Noah shook his head. "As I said, I was only a temp. I turned in my resignation before I came here. Successful or not, I'm not leaving your side again."

Lewis smiled, a heady glow spreading through him. And as Nalini and George talked, Noah nodded his head toward Akana and Cassandra, slipping his hand into Lewis's and walking with him to the other side of the room.

"Before I left, I did get some intel, though. The Crown has been following a source that might interest us," Noah said, keeping his voice low. "Evangeline's presence has been detected in three different locations. Cairo, Mexico City, and Singapore. Only blips, but it's her."

"She was burned alive, Noah," Akana reminded him. "We all saw it."

"And I did it," Lewis added.

"If you think Evangeline Thompson was killed that easily then you underestimate my previous boss. I don't put it above her to have transported her mind outside of her body last minute. She was an agent like me. She was an even greater magician. She still has contacts, people at the museum—and beyond—who support her. Informants."

"She can't be left to her own devices," Cassandra firmly stated. They all stared at her. "I know—that's rich coming from me. But she has no country to call home now. She's a fugitive."

"She's a *mercenary*. And she has nothing to lose," Akana finished. "That makes her dangerous."

Lewis considered it. He had a life now. He had a purpose. Helping France wasn't just a fun pastime. The DGAO had taken a chance on him. Would he be considered a criminal if he abandoned them?

But wouldn't going after Evangeline be helping them?

Noah's eyes cut to Lewis. "What do you want to do?"

Lewis looked over at George and Nalini. Her shoulders had relaxed a bit, as she'd found refuge with her ancestor in a pair of chairs. From the way her hands moved she was describing something to him, and he watched with wonder.

"Perhaps," he said slowly, "she can be redeemed. We gave *you* a chance, Cassandra."

Cassandra shrugged. "I've been helping you as my penance and donating the money I've made over the years to the descendants of those I've killed, Lewis."

"And you're not nearly done yet," Akana reminded her. "Be that as it may. Cassandra's right. She *wanted* to atone. Can you say the same for Evangeline?"

"We won't know until we try."

"Is it *worth* trying?" Akana insisted.

"It's always worth it," Lewis said.

"So, it's settled," Noah said firmly. "We go after her. On our own. No countries to back us up."

"And then we're done," Akana said, even if the way she said it didn't sound confident.

"And then we're done," Noah finished. "Who knows—maybe I'll work for my parents' telecom business after this."

"Sounds boring." Lewis grinned teasingly.

"That's because you don't know what's coming after 5G. Seriously, though—it might give me time to figure out what I want to do in life without knowing . . ." Noah fell silent. He didn't need to finish for Lewis to know what he meant.

"'Who in the world am I?'" Lewis quoted. "Ah, that's the great puzzle."

Noah arched his brow at him as Lewis shook his head, squeezing his hand.

"Never mind, come on. We have a soul to save." He walked over to Nalini and George.

"For now, we're going to take you home," he said gently. "George, do you want to go with her?"

"I'd love that."

"Great," Lewis said. "And when we get back, Nalini, we will show you this new world that you're now a part of."

"You cannot just show me this"—she gestured wildly—"and then abandon me."

"I'm not doing that, I promise. We'll come back for you. But right now, there is something the four of us have to finish. You'll find, though, that George here is a fount of magical knowledge and history. Let him be a part of a home for a bit, rather than *be* a home. Learn from him, and share your family in return. That's magic too."

"Okay," she breathed. "But then . . ."

"Then we find you. And the next part of your journey starts."

Nalini nodded, and she and George stood up and walked over to where Cassandra had created a portal, through which Lewis could see the door to Nalini's house.

"See you soon," he promised.

They walked through and disappeared.

Noah came over to stand right behind him.

"You're a good man, Lewis Dixon," he whispered into Lewis's ear.

"So are you," Lewis said, and he could feel Noah stiffen. He turned around and looked into Noah's eyes.

"You *are*. It's why I want you to take me on that date. It's why I want, when this is all over, for you to find yourself here, in my apartment. With *me*."

"Together," Noah said quietly, hopefully, a question more than a confirmation.

"Together."

And then Lewis did something he'd wanted to do for a long time.

He kissed the beautiful young man standing before him.

"Gross," Akana said.

"It's love, Akana," Cassandra chastised her even as Lewis and Noah disengaged. Lewis's heart was beating fast, and Noah's eyes gleamed, and it was all Lewis could do to not kiss him again. He lingered on that word Cassandra had just said. *Love.*

Now, that was magic he wanted to explore.

Which he would. With Noah. He was as certain of that as anything.

"I'm aware," Akana replied. "I'm also aware we have a madwoman on the loose."

She was right. Yet, she also wasn't. Because Lewis wasn't sure *madwoman* was right. Evangeline was a woman, yes. And she was probably angry. But not crazy. No. Scared? Alone? Confused? He could believe that. He could also believe that, somewhere in Evangeline, there was a person who needed their help. And despite Akana's, Cassandra's, or Noah's opinions of Evangeline, if he could save her, Lewis would. It would have been what his mother wanted. But more importantly, it was what he wanted.

And that was all that mattered.

Acknowledgments

The Macabre was a book that I never thought would be a reality. Four-ish years ago, I came up with the idea of a cursed nun, thanks to a Florence + The Machine song. I knew it would have to be an adult book. And I didn't think I could do it.

My agent, Jim McCarthy, was the one who pushed me, never letting me turn my head away from the idea. For that, I'm super thankful. Thank you for always supporting me, for reeling me in, and for having my back every step of the way.

Thank you to my editor, David Pomerico, for not only seeing the heart and soul of *The Macabre* (when you told me, "This is a story about loneliness," my heart BROKE and my mind reset), but also for taking a risk on me. For buying this book on a proposal, and for buying two more books, sight unseen, this is the relationship an author dreams of.

Thank you, Isabella Ogbolumani, for being an amazing partner in this and helping steer me directly. Your directions have always been clear and your support palpable.

Thank you, Danielle Bartlett, for securing EW for the cover release and for all the support, leading the charge in getting this book into the hands of the right people. Marketing is what makes and breaks books, and your guidance has been amazing.

Thank you, Carol Burrell, for finding all my errors. I'll never be a clean author and you all are the lifeblood of this industry.

To everyone else at Harper Voyager, thank you for believing in me, championing this book, and making it the success it is. Books are not just one person, or two people. There are so many unsung heroes, and I appreciate each one of you.

And of course, thank you, as always, to my boyfriend, Jordan, who believes more in my books than me; and my friends Ryan, Caleb, Adam, and Kevin, for always keeping me sane. To my parents for always believing in me and my words, and to Wes and Shelly, for making my 2024 bright.

The Macabre, like David said, is, sure, a book about magic, and art, and power, but it's also about family, about how we treat one another, and how one act can change the world. Our world is . . . for lack of a better word . . . shit right now. But art, and how we treat each other, can, in fact, change the direction of our future.

Let's be kind to one another. After all, you don't want someone binding you to a cursed painting, do you?

About the Author

KOSOKO JACKSON is the author of YA novels championing holistic representation of Black queer youth across genres, including *Yesterday Is History* and *Survive the Dome*. He also writes adult romance and works as a digital media specialist focusing on digital storytelling and email, social, and SMS marketing. His work has been featured on Medium, Thought Catalog, and the Advocate and in several literary magazines. He lives in New York City, and you can visit his website at kosokojackson.com.